MYST

Bo Jenkins was
who had gone ov
tle girl hostage
crazy accusation:
could easily be b
in custody.

Mike Svenson was a dedicated police detective who proved himself an irresistible lover as well. He had so awakened and satisfied Nell Matthews's longing that she wanted to give him her trust—and anything else he wanted of her.

Svenson's father was the late, legendary police chief of the small Oklahoma city where people knew how to take care of their own. He was a model of rectitude in his job and a pillar of morality in his marriage until his tragic accidental death.

Nell Matthews had only one problem with these facts. She couldn't believe any of them....

PRAISE FOR EVE K. SANDSTROM

THE VIOLENCE BEAT

Eve K. Sandstrom

AN ONYX BOOK

ONYX
Published by the Penguin Group
Penguin Putnam Inc., 375 Hudson Street,
New York, New York 10014, U.S.A.
Penguin Books Ltd, 27 Wrights Lane,
London W8 5TZ, England
Penguin Books Australia Ltd, Ringwood,
Victoria, Australia
Penguin Books Canada Ltd, 10 Alcorn Avenue,
Toronto, Ontario, Canada M4V 3B2
Penguin Books (N.Z.) Ltd, 182–190 Wairau Road,
Auckland 10, New Zealand

Penguin Books Ltd, Registered Offices:
Harmondsworth, Middlesex, England

First published by Onyx, an imprint of Dutton Signet,
a member of Penguin Putnam Inc.

First Printing, November, 1997
10 9 8 7 6 5 4 3 2 1

 REGISTERED TRADEMARK—MARCA REGISTRADA

Printed in the United States of America

PUBLISHER'S NOTE
This is a work of fiction. Names, characters, places, and incidents either are
the product of the author's imagination or are used fictitiously, and any
resemblance to actual persons, living or dead, events, or locales is entirely
coincidental.

In memory of the late Louise B. Moore,
sponsor of the University of Oklahoma student paper,
who gave a generation of journalists
high standards and a love for their profession.

And to Paul McClung,
former executive editor of the *Lawton Constitution*,
who demostrated that good reporting and
good writing are the same thing.

ACKNOWLEDGMENTS

The *Grantham Gazette* is not based on any newspaper that ever existed—certainly no paper I ever worked for. From parking garage to personnel policies, it represents my own ideas on how a newspaper should operate, rather than picturing any news gathering institution which exists in the real world.

In committing fiction, however, I shamelessly exploited friends, acquaintances, and complete strangers to make sure my phony newspaper and fake police department had authentic backgrounds. Special thanks go to Inspector Jim Avance of the Oklahoma Bureau of Investigation; to Lieutenant Beverlee Hill of the Lawton, Oklahoma, Police Department; and to Commander Hugh Holton of the Chicago Police Department. Thanks also to Luci Zahray, who knows about poisons; to Joe Worley, executive editor of the *Tulsa World*; to the *World*'s editorial staffers, who are kind to visiting researchers even when their work is interrupted; and to Tom Jackson, designated hitter for the editorial staff of the *Lawton Constitution* and a good, true friend. I also owe much to a dozen or more police reporters I've worked with in a lot of years in the news business. Most of them showed me how crime reporting should be done. A few of them showed me how it shouldn't.

CHAPTER 1

Just after sunset, in the fourteenth hour of the hostage situation at Grantham Central Police Headquarters, Coy-the-Cop Blakely called me out of the knot of reporters and photographers.

Coy glared as he yelled my name. "Nell! Nell Matthews! We need you inside!"

Coy was the press spokesman for the Grantham PD, and I was the dayside reporter on the violence beat—police, sheriff, and fire departments—for the only local daily in our midsized city. I saw Coy five days a week—seven if we were working a big story. Our relationship was a delicate balance of trust and distrust. I didn't think he would actually lie to me, and I don't lie to anybody. But either of us was ready to omit a few facts in a New York minute.

Coy never did me any favors, and I wouldn't have accepted any. For one thing, it would have made every other reporter in town mad at us, and Coy and I both knew we needed to get along with those folks. So why was Coy calling to me, singling me out from the other reporters?

I ducked under the yellow tape the cops had strung up to keep the press in its place, squinting in the floodlights, and climbed over the bumpers of a

couple of the patrol cars that lined the street. Coy
stood waiting for me, breeze ruffling his well barbered
brown hair, hands on his skinny hips. He ignored
the catcalls from the dozen or so people behind the
tape—the three TV crews, the two radio types, the
housewife who worked part-time for the neighborhood weekly, our photographer, the hotshot from the
Associated Press, and the usual hanger-on, Guy Unitas, steward of the Grantham Amalgamated Police
Brotherhood.

Our photog, the cuddly looking Bear Bennington,
pushed the button which makes his camera whir.

Guy Unitas opened his wide, thin-lipped mouth—
I always thought he looked like a fish—and yelled
out, "Watch out, Nell! He'll have your eyeteeth out
before you get in the building!" Guy began as a police reporter, sold out to public relations—he held
Coy's job before Coy had it—then sold out even further by becoming steward of the local police union.
But he still likes to hang around with reporters, and
we tolerate him because he knows where every single
body in the Grantham PD is buried and doesn't mind
telling the locations.

The AP hotshot, Ace Anderson, put his little fingers in his mouth and whistled as if I were a taxicab.
His dark slacks were drooping over his flat fanny as
usual. "Wish I had your pull, Nell! But I guess I
don't have the build for it!"

I ignored him. All real reporters ignored Ace. His
nickname was as big a joke as he was.

Coy-the-Cop waited impatiently for me to run the
obstacle course.

"Come on." He put his hand under my elbow and
tried to push me in front of him, toward the stairs

that led to the terraced yard, toward the pillared portico of the big, old-fashioned brick building that had housed Grantham's first high school for a lot of years before it was remodeled into the central cop shop.

I yanked my arm away. Not that there was anything sexual in his touch. For several years Coy had been separated from his second wife, but apparently neither of them had made a move toward a divorce. The station house gossip was that he lived an angrily celibate life. He'd certainly never as much as flickered an eyelash in my direction.

No, there was no man-woman meaning in Coy's touch. I simply made it a rule that no cop ever touched me. We weren't buddies; we just worked together. The worst thing a reporter can do is get too close, too friendly with any news source. Unless it's not being friendly enough.

When it came to Coy specifically, I didn't like some public-relations type shoving me around. And I definitely didn't like the appearance of getting any special attention, being pulled out from the other reporters. If Coy had some tip for my ears only—it happens sometimes—he could call me at the office or take me aside privately.

So I stood there on the Central Police Station lawn, facing Coy. "Just what is going on? All day you've made us cool our heels out in the sun and the wind— me, along with all the other reporters in Grantham and surrounding parts. And now you're shoving me inside."

"Bo Jenkins wants to talk to you, Nell," Coy said. "Svenson said to bring you in."

"You've got to be kidding! Mike Svenson wants me to talk to Bo Jenkins?"

"I didn't say that." Coy tried to grab my arm again, and I dodged once more. I saw that five cameras were filming my little dance with Coy, and I felt a perverse pride as I avoided his grip.

"Mike wants to talk to you himself," Coy said.

"I'll be glad to talk to Officer Svenson. You don't need to shove me around over it."

Coy stepped back, held both his hands at shoulder height in an open-palmed "hands off" gesture, then used one of them to motion me ahead of him. I walked into headquarters with all the dignity I could gather on a Saturday when I'd been hauled out of bed at seven a.m. to cover a hostage situation. I was wearing jeans, tennis shoes, and a dirty sweatshirt which bagged halfway to my knees. My makeup had been applied in the back of the photographer's van, and my semi-red and totally straight hair had not had its morning wash and blow-dry. I was fueled by fast food and caffeine. So I might not have looked very classy on television, but at least I wasn't being hustled into the cop shop by some PR flack who thought he could manage the news.

Officer Mike Svenson had set up his command post in a downstairs waiting room. It was only a few feet from the central hall under the rotunda, the rotunda where Coy-the-Cop had told us Bo Jenkins was barricaded, along with a pistol, an eight-inch hunting knife, and his eighteen-month-old son.

Coy had already told the press that Bo had repeatedly dangled the kid over the railing, saying he'd better get what he wanted or he'd toss the baby down three stories onto the terrazzo floor, splat into the center of the city seal.

As we passed through the wide entrance hall, I

could hear the kid whimper. The sound made me gulp. When you're outside covering a story, joking to convince the other reporters you're tough, it's easy to forget that a real baby is in danger inside. In fact, you have to forget it. You can't do your job if you're crying.

All day long Coy's communiques had hinted that the negotiating team headed by Mike Svenson wasn't sure just how to deal with Bo. This was largely because Bo wasn't too clear about just what he wanted, or so I'd deduced.

The command post for the negotiations had been set up in what usually served as a public waiting room adjoining the main desk. When I came through the door, Mike Svenson was staring out the window at the crowd gathered in front of the cop shop. I realized he must have been watching my little go-round with Coy. He immediately turned toward me.

Mike Svenson was a big, rugged-looking guy, around six-two, with heavy muscles, a crooked nose, and remarkably red hair. I knew the nose came from a high school football injury, because I'd asked him. In appearance, he was the ideal "bad cop." But gossip had it that he starred at playing the "good cop" role. He was a smooth talker.

But when Mike Svenson turned around, he didn't waste time on smooth talk.

"What do you know about Bo Jenkins?" he said.

"I never heard of him until this morning," I said.

Mike Svenson and I stared warily at each other, just the way we had every other time we had met for the past eighteen months.

Then he sighed. He dropped into a vinyl-covered chair, the kind that masquerades as comfortable seating in a city office. A red telephone sat beside him on the seat of a straight metal office chair he seemed to be using as an end table. He rubbed the back of his neck with his left hand and pointed toward another easy chair with his right.

"Please sit down, Nell. I'm sorry if I sounded abrupt." He gave me the grin that had the hormones of every secretary at city hall in an uproar. "I can only handle one set of negotiations at a time, so I don't want to get crosswise with you, as well as Bo Jenkins. I'll try to level with you."

Which means you're about to tell me a lie, I thought. But I sat down on the edge of the chair.

"I'm listening," I said. "I know you've got a bad situation here, Mike. I'll help any way I can, of course. But I do not know one thing about Bo Jenkins. I never heard of him until this morning. Captain Blakely says he's asked to speak to me. I can't imagine why."

"He says it's because you're the only honest reporter in Grantham."

I thought Svenson was kidding me, but he looked perfectly serious. "That's a dumb thing to say," I said. "But I suppose Bo isn't making a lot of sense or he wouldn't be in this pickle."

Mike Svenson gave me long look. "I saw you talking to his wife out there. What did you find out?"

"She's too hysterical to make much of an interview. She's mainly mad at the judge who said Bo was entitled to visitation with the kid, even after she told him Bo was on the verge of something desperate. I'm sure she told your team the same thing. I wrote it up on the laptop and one of photogs ran the disk over to the office. It should be in print in a couple of hours, when the state edition rolls. Or I can ask the city editor to make you a printout if you need it more quickly."

"Did the other *Gazette* reporters find out anything?"

"With the interviews of Jenkins's neighbors? That'll be in the state edition, too. I think it was the usual stuff. Bo never had the reputation for being any too bright, but he was a good guy, a steady worker—you know that, since he was a mechanic for the city-county garage. About a year ago he went off the deep end. Beat the wife up. She left him. He began to drink heavily. Left town, then came back. No job. Had to stay at the Salvation Army shelter. He's been all messed up over the divorce.

"Maybe he was a secret boozer all along. Maybe he's on drugs, hooked. Could be a brain tumor. But a year ago he apparently underwent a complete personality change. Nobody understands what happened to him."

Svenson nodded. "You could be the one who finds out the secret."

"Because he wants to talk to me? I doubt it. He'll just want to tell me some crazy story he's going to claim will be a major exposé. That's what every nut claims. But they never really know anything important."

"Are you willing to listen to his crazy story?"

"You mean talk to him?"

Mike Svenson nodded.

"Sure," I said, "if you guys have the knife and the gun. You're the certified hero, Officer Svenson. The guy with the medals. I'm just a cowardly reporter."

"Sorry, Bo still has the weaponry. Plus the kid. But

we have rigged a phone line. You can sit in here and talk to him."

"That I could handle. But"—I stared at my notebook, formulating my question before I spoke—"you're the expert on negotiations, but this situation confuses me. I always thought one of the main points in negotiating was never to bring in any person that the hostage taker demanded to talk to."

"You're absolutely right. Nine times out of ten, the guy claims to want to talk to a family member or somebody else, but what he really has in mind is getting the right audience for his own suicide. Or else bringing some particular person into his rifle sights."

"So what's different about this time?"

"Bo asked for you, not for Channel Four."

I thought about that. "You mean, if he really wanted an audience, he'd want cameras?"

"Right."

"Okay. I see that. But I thought another part of the negotiating process was to limit the hostage taker to one or two contacts, to make him dependent on those people."

"That's right, too."

"You wouldn't ordinarily let any outsider—such as a reporter—speak to the guy."

"No, we wouldn't. But time seems to be getting short. We're convinced Bo doesn't really want to hurt his son. But Bo is alternately popping pills and stuffing down chocolate candy. Between the pills and the sugar rush and his nerves, he's losing control. We're afraid he'll drop the kid—simply by accident."

I started to speak, but he held up his hand in a traffic-stopping gesture.

"Since he says he won't tell anybody but you the

conditions for his surrender, we're pretty well out of options. Ordinarily, we'd just wait him out. But the kid makes that chancy. We're down to the sharpshooter, but we don't like that idea, either—because of the kid."

"Yeah. Getting splattered with his daddy might give the kid a bit of a trauma."

I use that tough stuff when I want to get a rise out of a cop. Every one of them thinks he's as hard as a petrified prostitute. And I've never known one yet who wasn't using that shell to hide something soft. Sometimes it's his brain.

But Mike Svenson didn't take the bait. He ignored the comment. "So you're right about this being a break with standard practice. We wouldn't ordinarily let a civilian in on the deal. This will only work if you understand the rules and agree to abide by them."

"The rules?"

"I'll be on the phone, too, though I may not talk. I'll be giving you instructions—either on a note pad or verbally. If this will infringe on the freedom of the press—" He shrugged. "Then the deal's off."

We studied each other. A floor lamp behind him was tilted in some strange way, and it hit his hair, close-cropped, but definitely red. His hair marked him to all the Grantham old-timers as the son of Carl "Irish" Svenson, chief of police for a dozen years. Irish Svenson had died three months before I moved to Grantham, but I'd heard the legends. Mike Svenson was apparently a lot like his dad in appearance. But not entirely like him in personality.

Irish Svenson had had a reputation for honesty in two senses of the word: integrity and truthfulness. In contrast, Mike Svenson had made his law-enforcement reputation on the basis of intelligence, in at least two senses of that word: He was smart, and he was subtle.

I'd always regarded Mike with caution. Honesty, even honesty that crossed the line to bluntness, was more to my taste than the kind of intelligence which verges on trickiness.

Mike smiled again. "Are you interested in talking to Bo?" he said.

"If you think it will help," I said. "But I'm no good at lying."

"I wouldn't ask you to lie. A good negotiator never breaks his word. You just listen and ask questions."

"What questions do you want me to ask?"

The grin grew broader. "You mean I really will get to tell a reporter what to ask?"

"Is that baby actually in danger?"

He nodded.

"I'll ask anything you want if it will help save the kid."

"Great." Mike Svenson reached over and squeezed my hand. "Now, there's nothing complicated about this. The main thing to remember is to just listen. Don't argue with him."

"Keep my opinion out of it?"

"Correct. You don't need to tell him he's a total jerk."

"You don't want me to mention he's costing the city thousands of dollars and causing his family lots of grief?"

"No, I wouldn't bring that up. Sympathy. That's the ticket. He's had a hard life, everybody has treated him like dog doo-doo, and you can understand why he's been driven—" Mike Svenson shrugged.

"Up the stairs?"

"That's right." He picked up the red phone beside him and gestured toward the black one.

I touched it. "This one's mine?"

Mike nodded. "Are you ready?"

What a question. My impulse was to yell. "No!" and run out the door. I had no business in delicate negotiations, with a kid's life at stake. But how could I refuse? I picked up my ballpoint and wrote down an opening question. "You've been a real hard-luck guy in the past year, Bo. Can you tell me about it?"

I showed it to Mike Svenson. "This is okay?"

"Sure. That ought to kick him into the talking mode." He punched at the phone. Through the open door of the waiting room, I could hear another phone ring. It rang a couple of times, echoing off the rotunda, then Mike Svenson spoke. "Hi, Bo. This is Mike."

A pause. "Yeah, we've got her here." Another pause. "Bo, I can't allow a civilian up there. You'll have to talk to her on the phone."

A loud bawling yell burst in the door of the room we were in. Mike winced and pulled the phone away from his ear, and I could hear the hollering coming through the receiver as well. The yell bounced against the terrazzo outside, ricocheted off the plaster walls and reverberated against the dome, circled around our room, then made the circuit again. It seemed to grow and grow until it filled the entire building.

I snatched my black phone off the hook. "Bo!" I held the receiver to my ear as the yelling gradually died away. "This is Nell Matthews. I thought you wanted to talk to me."

Nobody said anything for a long moment. Then I heard a sort of sniveling sob and a voice croaked, "You're my only hope."

"I want to talk to you, Bo," I said. "A reporter rarely gets a chance at a story like this one—an interview with a man in a position like yours. But you know how cops are. All those rules about civilians. They won't let me come in there."

"They're listening in."

I couldn't lie to him. Besides, I knew he wouldn't believe me if I denied it. "Does that matter?"

"Yes. They're out to get me. I know too much. My only hope is to tell someone."

I knew it. A big conspiracy.

"Tell me."

"No! Not on the phone."

And he hung up.

I felt as if I'd been slapped. Had I ruined the negotiations? I looked at Mike Svenson, almost panicky.

"Did I blow it that fast?" I said.

Mike Svenson shook his head. "You didn't blow it at all, except maybe you expected Bo to be rational. We'll give him a few minutes, then call back. Or maybe he'll call us. Do you want some coffee? A Coke?"

I shook my head, but I looked around the command post then, and I saw the coffeepot in the corner. I saw some other details, too. The chief was there, and so was the regional supervisor for the state police. So Mike Svenson wasn't entirely on his own. The top cop was overseeing his red-haired boy's first big negotiation.

Mike Svenson might be the son of a Grantham police chief, but he'd been away from his hometown nearly ten years, earning his spurs on a big city force and getting plenty of specialized training. He'd earned medals recognizing his courage as a TAC team member, and he'd been trained as a negotiator. He'd come back eighteen months before the day Bo Jenkins barricaded himself in the rotunda of the Central Police Station and six months after his dad had been killed in a car wreck. Among the station house gossip passed on by Guy Unitas was speculation that the chief, Wolf Jameson, wanted to groom him for the day ten or twelve years down the line when Jameson would hit retirement age and Mike Svenson might be in the right position to move into the top cop slot.

Now Mike Svenson turned to Jameson. "I thought I'd make another offer of food for the baby," he said. "As soon as we get him back."

The chief nodded. "Sounds good," he said.

Svenson faced me. "We're concentrating on the idea that Bo doesn't really want to hurt Billy," he said. "Apparently it was the threat of losing access to the boy that brought this situation to a head. We'll give him five minutes to cool down. Sure you won't have coffee?"

I stood up, shaking my head. "No, thanks. We have plenty of coffee and soft drinks outside. What we're short on is plumbing. Mind if I wander down the hall?"

"You'll have to go across to the chief's office," Svenson said. "Stay out of the rotunda area."

"I'll show you," Coy Blakely said.

"I know how to get to the chief's office," I said.

Svenson grinned. "I'm sure you know this building from one end to another, Nell. That's why I'm not going to let you loose in it."

"I have no desire to get between you all and Bo," I said. "But if you want me to have an escort, I won't argue."

I followed Coy out of the room, and he led me across the foyer, around the corner into the main hall, through the door of the chief's suite. He pointed the way to the chief's private potty. It wasn't anything fancy. I wiped the seat with toilet paper before I sat, and I took a look at Jameson's personal reading matter stuffed into a wastebasket beside the commode. A collection of *New York Times* Sunday crossword puzzles. Huh, I thought. Jameson put on such a good-ole-boy act. Who'd have thought he was a secret addict of the NYT crossword? The Sunday crossword, too, the one which takes me all week.

I was drying my hands on a paper towel when I heard the rumpus outside.

Yelling. And something else. A kid screaming. Pounding feet. A lot of people shouting. Something was happening.

I threw the paper towel in the direction of the wastebasket, slung my purse over my shoulder, grabbed my notebook, and flew out the bathroom door.

The chief's office was empty. Where was my keeper, Coy-the-Cop? I ran on through the private office, through the outer office, and out the door to the main hall. Then I took a sharp left and ran toward the noise.

And I ran headlong into Bo Jenkins.

At least I thought it must be Bo Jenkins. I'd never seen the guy—even a picture of him. But how many people were running around the Grantham PD with a baby in one hand and a pistol in the other?

Bo and I whanged together like football linemen. We were all tangled up for a minute. Then I jumped back, and he jumped back, and I became aware that a whole bunch of cops were circled around us. Most of them were standing in such grotesque positions that they seemed to be playing an absurd game of Swinging Statues. All of them were looking real cautious.

Bo and I were the center of attention. All the cops seemed to expect one of us to do something.

Do what? What could he do? What could I do?

"Bo!" I guess I yelled it. "Give me the kid! I know you don't want him to get hurt!"

Bo's stringy, colorless hair was standing in all directions, and his skinny chest puffed in and out with each panicky breath he took. His eyes rolled wildly. God knows what kind of chemicals were seething behind them. He made two frightened sounds, like a cornered chimpanzee. Then he suddenly thrust the baby at me. My notebook flew across the foyer, and I fell to my knees with both arms full of squalling kid.

"Stay back!" Bo's voice screeched in my ear.

For a minute I thought the kid was strangling me.

But it was Bo's arm around my throat, Bo's arm choking me, Bo's arm pressing against my collarbone, forcing me to my knees. Bo's voice yelling, "Stay back, or I'll kill her!"

All I could see in that moment was Mike Svenson's face. He was across the hall, and he looked like a thunderstorm.

Why shouldn't he be angry? His fourteen hours of negotiations were out the window.

Now Bo Jenkins had two hostages.

CHAPTER 2

Nobody said anything, but the kid kept squalling. I held him hard against my body, but he wriggled. And Bo still had me by the throat, and I began to feel something very hard pressing against the side of my head. It must have been the pistol. The barrel felt as though it were three or four inches across.

It was lucky that Bo had pushed me to my knees. I was so scared I would have fallen to them if he hadn't.

The little boy cried, and no one else did anything. Mike, Bo, and the assorted cops just stood around, still in their grotesque positions. Then Mike Svenson reassumed command of his operation.

"Okay, Bo," he said. "You've got the reporter you wanted to talk to. Now the rest of us are going to back off." He looked around the hall. "Everybody! Out!"

The assembled cops began to back up, moving by inches. Nobody made any sudden moves.

Except Bo. He yanked me to my feet, stretching my neck a couple of inches in the process, and we backed up, too. I realized he was trying to get his back to the wall. Luckily there was a bench along that wall, a long old-fashioned oak bench that matched the old-fashioned building that housed the police headquarters. Bo shoved me down onto one end of it, and he stood beside me. The pistol was still against my head.

I got a hand loose and tugged at the arm he had under my chin. I gasped pitifully, to indicate that I couldn't breathe. He moved his arm from beneath my chin and gripped my shoulder instead, but he didn't move the pistol.

I sat little Billy down in my lap, and his squalling died away to a gurgle. I took stock of the situation. The last TAC cop—bullet-proof vest and all—was moving out of sight. I knew they weren't going far, but I had mixed feelings about their disappearance. If they stayed, they might spook Bo into some action I wasn't going to enjoy. But if they were out of sight, and he took a notion to blow my brains out, there wouldn't be a lot they could do to stop him.

But Bo and Billy and I weren't alone. Mike Svenson was still there. He had backed up slowly, crossing the twenty feet of terrazzo floor until he got to the opposite wall. And there he reached a bench which matched the one I was perched on. As I watched, he sat down on it, threw one arm along the back and propped his right ankle on his left knee. He looked supremely casual.

"Okay, Bo," he said. "Maybe we can talk better face-to-face."

"You get out!" Bo said.

"I can't do that while Ms. Matthews is here," Svenson said. "She's my responsibility, just the way Billy is yours."

Bo took a deep breath, and I could feel the hand on my shoulder tense. I had to do something. Bo had eased the pressure of the pistol, and I could move my head a little. I looked at the baby.

"Kleenex!" I said. "Bo, Billy's nose needs attention. I have a pack of Kleenex in my purse. I can get it out and clean up his face. Then he'll feel better."

I tried to assume a matter-of-fact expression, as though I were just trying to help Bo out. Then I slowly turned my head to look up at him.

I was staring into the barrel of his pistol.

The barrel was within two inches of my right eye. A small-caliber, silver-colored automatic. I'll swear I could see the bullet in the chamber.

I believe my heart stopped. Then it began to pound like machine-gun fire. Luckily, I was frozen with fear. If I'd made a sudden move, Bo might have pulled the trigger.

Instead, he looked at me. Then at Mike Svenson. Then back at me.

"Dump the purse out on the bench," he said.

I slid the strap off my shoulder and dumped the contents out on the bench. I felt better as soon as I looked away from the barrel of that gun. Casual. I had to act casual. The way Mike Svenson was acting.

"This is an embarrassing thing for a woman to have to do," I said. "I never let anybody see all the junk in my purse."

I picked up the packet of tissues and began to work on Billy's face. He twisted, yelled, and fought, just the way my cousin's baby did when his nose was wiped. I was afraid to look at Bo, but the process didn't seem to worry him. When I finished, I stood Billy up in my lap. Once I'd stopped pawing at his face, he seemed almost cheerful. He was a cute little

fellow, with curly brown hair and big brown eyes. He was wearing a dirty blue blanket sleeper.

"Now, young man. See how much better you feel!" I looked up, past the pistol, into Bo's face. "He's a beautiful little boy, Bo. I know how proud you must be of him."

Bo's face contorted. "Julie's never gonna let me see him again." A tear ran down from the corner of his eye. "The judge is gonna be on her side."

Right, I thought. After today, everybody's going to be on her side. But there was no point in saying so. "The future stretches on forever," I said. "Sure, you need to get your life straightened out before you can take care of Billy, but that doesn't mean it won't ever happen."

I shot Mike Svenson a look. He was sitting absolutely still. He gave me a barely perceptible nod. I gathered that he wanted me to keep on along the same lines.

"I talked to Julie today," I said.

"She hates me."

"That's not what she told me. She told me she's heartsick because you two have split up." She's also told me Bo scared her spitless, but I left that part out. "Bo, she loves Billy just the way you do. She's frantic about him."

"I wouldn't hurt him."

"I know that! Julie knows you don't mean him any harm! It's all these cops. You've got them scared, Bo. On the defensive. She's afraid one of them will hurt Billy—just by accident."

Tears were running openly down Bo's face.

Mike Svenson moved then. He leaned forward, put his elbows on his knees, and spread his hands im-

ploringly. "Bo, let Nell take Billy out of here. Let her take him to his mother."

"No! No! I can't give up until I get what I want!"

"You won't be giving up!" Mike raised his voice slightly. "I'll still be here!"

I could feel Bo's hand tighten on my shoulder, and his shaking increased. The knot in my stomach tied itself into a double hitch. Bo was not going to let me leave. That was plain.

Bo shook like a flagpole in a windstorm. He moved the pistol slightly. Toward Mike. I couldn't just sit there.

"I'll be your hostage!" Mike said.

"No, Mike!" I said. "I'm not leaving until I get the interview Bo promised me." I looked up at Bo, doing my best not to look at the barrel of the pistol. "Bo, let Mike take Billy out to his mother. I'll stay here, and you can tell me what's on your mind."

Bo's eyes were pools of misery. Somewhere in the back of my conscience, I felt like a rat for leading him on. Whatever Bo had to tell me probably wouldn't be anything the public wanted to read. I tried to smile. "Come on, Bo. This may be the story of my life. It may make my career. I'm not leaving until you've told me the real reason behind all this. Mike can take Billy out."

Bo's fingers gripped my shoulder. "I can't let you hand Billy to him."

"I'll carry Billy to the middle of the hall and put him down. You can go with me. Then you and I can come back over here. Mike can pick Billy up and carry him out."

Bo thought about it. Then he nodded and gulped.

I scooped my car keys up off the bench and stood up slowly. "Okay, Mike?"

Mike hadn't changed position, but his body had grown tense. His hands, which had been open and imploring, had clinched into fists. "Okay," he said.

Bo and I moved halfway across the hall. I handed Billy the car keys, and I gave him a little kiss on the forehead as I sat him down on the floor. Then Bo pulled me back across to my bench.

The car keys barely caught Billy's attention. He held on to them, but he twisted around and looked after us, questioningly. Then Mike spoke, he looked toward the new voice.

"I'm going to get him now," Mike said.

He moved smoothly, but rapidly, and he scooped the baby up with a quick motion. He went to the door to the foyer, but he didn't go through it. Instead, uniformed arms reached around the corner and took Billy from him.

"Straight to his mother," Mike said. The phrase might not have had a subject or a predicate, but it was definitely an order.

Then he moved smoothly back to his bench and sat down again.

Bo gestured with his pistol. "You were supposed to leave!"

Mike looked pained. "I can't do that, Bo! I told you. I can't leave a civilian in here."

I felt so grateful I could have cried. I didn't have the slightest idea what Mike Svenson could do to help me, but it was great to have somebody around who was on my side. I could have kissed him. I suppose that right at that moment I would have

kissed the devil himself, if he hadn't left me alone
with Bo Jenkins.

"Bo, you've done what's best for Billy," I said.
"Now you've got to do what's best for yourself."

It was right then that we heard a bunch of yelling
outside. Bo looked up. "What's that?"

"There's a huge crowd outside," I said. "You've
drawn a lot of attention, Bo. I expect the police
spokesman just announced that you've released
Billy."

Bo let go of my shoulder and wiped his eyes with
the back of his hand. "I'll never see Billy again," he
said. "I'll never see him again."

Not if the kid is lucky, I thought. I scooted down
the bench and motioned to Bo. He sat beside me.
Funny how he could cry and stand up and sit down
and never stop pointing that pistol at me.

"Listen, Bo," I said, "if I'm going to interview you,
I need my notebook. It fell in the floor when we ran
into each other, and it got kicked way down the hall.
I'm going to walk over there and get it."

Bo nodded. I stood up slowly and slowly walked
down the hall, away from Mike Svenson, toward
the notebook.

This put Mike, Bo, and me in a triangle. Bo was
about twenty feet from me and twenty feet from
Mike, but Mike and I were around thirty-five feet
apart. Bo really couldn't keep an eye on me and on
Mike at the same time.

I glanced over my shoulder, and I saw that Mike
was tensing again. Bo was looking at me. He didn't
see Mike gathering his muscles into bunches, figura-
tively scraping his feet in the dirt, getting ready to
spring.

I knelt and fumbled for the notebook, knocking it away, crawling toward it, picking it up and dropping it. I was shaking, and it wasn't hard to put on a klutzy act. Maybe it wasn't an act. And maybe because I'm a reporter—a member of the most curious class of people in the universe—I managed to scramble around so that I was facing Bo. I could see Mike, slightly behind him and to his right.

Mike was obviously getting ready to do something. I expected to see his sports shirt turn into a cape and lift him through the air.

"Bo!" I said. "You had a high-pressure job—responsible for the maintenance of police and sheriff's vehicles. Lives depended on you. Was it work pressures that made you take these desperate measures? Or did something else happen? Something that made you feel—"

The questions were stupid, but they kept Bo's attention on me for the second it took Mike Svenson to take four long strides and reach him.

He was at Bo's elbow before Bo realized he had moved. Bo tried to turn the pistol toward him, but Mike was too close for Bo to stretch out his arm.

"Hit the dirt!" Mike yelled.

He didn't have to tell me twice. I dropped as flat as my billfold on the day before payday. I put my notebook over my head—fat lot of good that was going to do—and I peeked out from beneath it.

Mike had Bo's wrist, and he was shaking Bo's hand, and the pistol it held, like a dust rag.

"Drop it!" he said. "Drop it!"

Bo was whimpering. He didn't exactly drop the pistol, but it left his hand. It flew across the hall, hit the bench where Mike had been sitting and chipped a big chunk out of the oak.

I might have expected Bo to give up then, but he began to fight harder. He and Mike grappled, and suddenly Bo twisted loose.

By then the TAC team cops were pouring in from the foyer. Bo couldn't get out that way, so he ran toward me. I made it to my knees before Bo reached me. He fell on his own knees in front of me, and he grabbed my shoulders. His lips were moving, but there was so much noise I couldn't tell what he was saying.

Then, suddenly, he pulled me against his chest, and his lips were right beside my ear. His words became clear.

"They killed Eric," he said. "They killed him!"

Then the cops were on him, and they pulled him away from me.

Bo yelled one more time as they took him away. Cops were holding his hands and his feet. He was struggling like fury, kicking and wrestling. But he looked over at me, and he screamed out one more phrase.

"He made me help!"

CHAPTER 3

The foyer was crammed full of action then, but the crowd parted, and Mike Svenson plunged through.

He grabbed me and swung me to my feet. He had to yell to be heard. "Are you okay?"

"Weak with relief!"

He shook his head. Our faces were so close we were almost rubbing noses, Eskimo style.

"Woman, you are one class act! Cool and classy!"

"You're pretty cool yourself!"

Then Coy-the-Cop appeared beside us, and Mike put me down. He began to beat Coy on the back.

"Coy, we did it! Thanks to this lady keeping her head! Nobody hurt!"

Coy beat Mike's back with one arm and hugged me with the other. Chief Jameson appeared, and we all stood in a circle and jumped up and down in glee. The state cop joined the circle. For a minute I thought we were going to balance wine bottles on our heads and dance.

Then I realized that Coy was trying to calm everybody down.

"The media!" he said. "We've got to make a statement."

"Where's my notebook?" I said.

Coy laughed. "You're on the other side of the questions this time, Nell. Everybody will want to interview you."

"Hell's bells!" I said. "Let me comb my hair."

That remark sent Coy, Mike, the chief, everybody into hysterical laughter. We all knew it wasn't really funny, but we were so high it would have taken anti-aircraft fire to get us down. We were in the Alps. On trapezes at the top of the circus tent.

Then I looked at my watch. "Sorry, Coy," I said, "I can't hang around for any press conference. I've got a deadline."

Coy was going to object, but Mike Svenson beckoned to one of the older cops. "Get Ms. Matthews out of here, Joe," he said. "Take her out the back."

"Sure, Mike." Joe motioned. We can get a car at the jail exit." I scooped up my purse debris from the bench, and he led me out of the hall and hustled me down some stairs into the modern building which had been added to the back of the old school when it was remodeled for police use. We came out at the desk area that controlled entry and exit to the jail section of the Grantham PD headquarters.

Of course, I knew all the guys on the desk, since I check the blotter five mornings a week, and they'd heard what happened, so I had to stop and be hugged and pounded on the back and join in some more exultation. I completely ignored my no-touchy-the-reporter rule.

But I kept edging toward the back door. I was already writing my lead in my head, and I was getting antsy about the deadline for the state edition.

Joe, my escort, told the jailer to open up. "She's got to get to the *Gazette* office," he said. "Mike Svenson said to take her out the back. Avoid that crowd in front."

"Sure." The jailer started punching buttons. The door to the jail section opened, and Joe and I went in.

The jailer yelled after us. "I think they already got Bo Jenkins out of there."

Joe and I dashed down the hall, past the doors into the cell blocks, past the kitchen, past the exercise yard, toward the big garage used to load prisoners who needed transportation to courts or hospitals or other places prisoners need to go. We rushed out into a loading area, and we almost ran headlong into the side of an ambulance.

The jailer was wrong. Bo wasn't gone yet. He was wrapped up and securely strapped to a stretcher. Guys in white jackets that said GRANTHAM MENTAL HEALTH CENTER on the backs were loading him into the ambulance.

At our sudden arrival, the cops surrounding the ambulance whirled around. They left a gap, and as I tried to stop my headlong rush I found myself teetering over Bo. His eyes rolled wildly. He was still completely hopped up on the pills he'd been popping and the candy bars he'd been stuffing down.

He whimpered.

I felt sorry for him. Exasperated, but sorry for him. Even when I remembered looking down the barrel of that pistol, Bo was a truly pitiful person. He had lost everything—his family, his job, his home. He was down and out. Strapped down and going away to be locked up for a long time.

Everything was going great for me. I was alive, I was unharmed, I had a big story. And poor old Bo hadn't even been interviewed, in spite of all his trouble.

I felt so sorry for him that I leaned over his stretcher. "Bo! As soon as the doctors say it's okay, we'll have that interview!" I said.

Bo lifted his head off the pillow. "They killed him," he whispered. "They killed Eric."

The mental hospital attendants shoved him into the ambulance. His voice echoed from inside. "They made me cover it up! I had to do it! They lied to me!"

Then the door slammed, and almost immediately the ambulance pulled out, escorted by two patrol cars.

Joe was shaking his head. "That S.O.B. is plumb cuckoo," he said.

"Right," I said. "I'm sure looking forward to that interview. Which way's that car?"

Joe drove me into the *Gazette*'s parking garage, up to the back door, the door most employees use. There was a line of vans and pickup trucks at the loading dock, waiting for the presses to roll. A half dozen of the contractors who deliver out-of-town papers always come early and jockey around to be first in line for papers. Sometimes they sit beside their trucks in lawn chairs, watching portable television sets and arguing about sports and politics. They mostly stay inside the vans and sleep.

As I got out of the patrol car, I saw the contractor we call "Redneck Hal"—because he'll bend your ear for hours with a far-right brand of politics and outdated social theories if you let him—stand up and wave his Dallas Cowboys' cap at me.

"Hey, Nell! If you'd keep a pistol in your purse you wouldn't get in all this trouble!"

"If I packed heat I'd have shot you long ago!" Hal and I argue about guns all the time. He's pro. I'm not exactly con, but I think guns should be carried only by people who really know how to use them. And I don't.

I ran toward the back door. The lineup of circulation vans and trucks had told me I'd probably missed the state edition. I checked my watch and realized that the presses were due to roll in thirty minutes—at ten o'clock. Would the city editor want to hold the presses for me?

I used my electronic card to get in the back door, then ran two flights up the back stairs into the newsroom, a big, brightly lighted room dotted with pods of cluttered desks.

My greeting in the newsroom was different from what had gone on at the Grantham PD.

The few reporters on duty on a Saturday night gathered round, of course, but none of them yelled or pounded me on the back. That's not our style. Tom Quincy, the city hall reporter, had the most typical reaction. "My God, Nell," he said, "if I'd known you'd go to those lengths for a story, I'd have let you cover the planning commission." Chuck Ewing, the weekend cop reporter, barely looked up from his terminal.

The city editor, Ruth Borah, merely pointed at my video display terminal. Ruth's the mother of three teenagers, and she treats the reporters the way she does her high schoolers. We'd better be in by deadline or we're grounded. "Start hittin' those keys," she said.

"Can I still make the state?" I asked.

"State edition rolls at ten." Ruth looked at the big

clock on the back wall. She smoothed her sophisticated chignon, then ruined the effect by sticking a
pencil through it. "We'll save you a hole. See what
you can come up with in fifteen minutes."

A hand firmly grasped my elbow, and I whirled
around to face the managing editor, Jake Edwards.
Jake rarely talked to mere reporters. Now I realized
he was pushing me toward his office.

"In here," he said.

"Jake, I haven't got time to talk now," I said. "I'll
miss the state edition."

"Forget that," he said. "Chuck's on the straight
news story already. Ruth! Chuck's story will do for
the state."

He frog-marched me into his office and pushed me
into the chair behind his desk. "What we want from
you, Nell, is the real stuff."

"The real stuff?"

"Yeah. What does it feel like to be grabbed by a
guy with a gun? How did you keep your head? What
did you think when he shoved that baby at you?
How in God's name did you think of cleaning that
kid's dirty nose? Did Svenson give you some sort of
signal that made you hit the floor?"

Astonishment paralyzed me. I gaped and gasped
before I spoke. "How did you know all that happened?"

Now Jake stared back at me. "Didn't you know
you were on television?"

"Television?"

"Yeah, that whole last episode happened right in
front of the closed-circuit television that monitors the
entrance to the chief's office."

"You don't mean it got out live?"

"Hell, no! But Coy Blakely played it back for Jameson's news conference a few minutes ago."

"Did you tape it?"

"Yes, but I don't want you to see it until you've written that story."

He reached into his desk drawer and pulled out a box of Kleenex. "Come on, Nell. I've brought you in here where nobody's going to bother you. Don't worry about the deadline. We'll let the state go and aim for the final home. Just start spilling your guts."

I swung around to the VDT and stared at the screen. In Intro to Journalism they teach future reporters to leave their own opinions out of the stories they write. It's an early and important lesson. Jake and I both knew that.

"I've been carefully trained not to spill my guts in the newspaper," I said.

"Nell, any reporter can tell how long the standoff was, what the results were, what the cops say they did, where Bo Jenkins is now. That's the straight news story. The real story is what happened to you. Being held at gunpoint has got to be the scariest thing that the average person can imagine happening. Admit it! It scared you shitless!"

"God! Yes! I'd be a fool if I hadn't been absolutely terrified."

"Great!" Jake stabbed his finger at the VDT. "And you're a good enough writer to tell the tale. Get it down!"

He left the office, and I began to write.

"I could see the bullet with my name on it," I wrote. "I was staring down the barrel of the gun, and—I swear to God—I could see the bullet at the other end. It looked as if it were twitching, ready to rocket out right into my right eye."

I read it over. Then I moved the cursor back to the beginning and took out the first sentence. Yeah, that had more impact. And it got rid of a cliche. I took "right into" out of the second sentence and replaced it with "straight at." That was better.

"I was staring down the barrel of the gun, and—I swear to God—I could see the bullet at the other end. It seemed to twitch, ready to rocket out, straight at my right eye."

Not a bad lead. Or should it be "straight into" instead of "straight at"? I kept writing.

Jake was right about the Kleenex. After about ten minutes the excitement wore off, and I thought of Bo—pitiful, infuriating Bo—and of that snotty-nosed kid who'd have to grow up with the knowledge that his dad was a real nutcase—and I was bawling as hard as the kid had been. I mopped my eyes and blew my nose, but I kept writing. Thank God for almost-white eyelashes. Mine are so fair I dye them, so I didn't get mascara all over my face.

After thirty minutes, I saved my story to the main computer, then made a printout for Jake. He liked to edit hard copy. He made me stay in his chair while he read it.

"Great stuff," he said. "I knew you could do it. I remembered the job you did on the interview with the mother in the Coffee Cup killings." He tapped the printout. "You've got three typos. Fix those, then send it over to Ruth."

He came around the desk then, pointing at the three words he had ringed in red on the hard copy.

He gave me a fatherly pat. "Then go get drunk. If you don't want to drink alone, I'll buy."

It was a very generous offer, considering that the only time Jake ever hobnobbed with reporters was at the Christmas party, but I just smiled at him and started correcting my typos.

Actually, I didn't feel like getting drunk. I was still so pumped up with adrenaline that alcohol was not what I needed. I didn't want to go home either. When I looked at the clock, I was amazed to see it wasn't yet eleven.

I went over the straight news story Chuck had written. Although Chuck looks like a junior executive, complete with suspenders, slickly styled hair, and spiffy little mustache, he's our beginner, a part-timer who's still a student in the Grantham State University Department of Mass Communications. He works weekends, and it's up to Ruth Borah, J.B. Penn the nightside violence reporter, and me to teach him how real-life police reporting works.

Chuck accepted my changes after our usual discussion. These undergrads think they know everything. One of these days Chuck will leave his "E. Charles Ewing" byline behind, and he'll turn into a really good reporter.

After that I hung around the office. By then all the reporters but Chuck and the kid who writes the obits were gone. Chuck stays until one-thirty, when the last edition rolls.

It was stupid for me to stay, but I didn't want to leave. I phoned my roommates and assured them I was all right. My only living relative, my nutty Aunt Billie, had also called, so I used my credit card to call my hometown across the state and reassure the old bat. She never liked me when I was growing up, but since my grandmother died, she's assumed the burden of being my family. It's a burden for me, too, but I like my cousin, even if she is Billie's daughter.

Then the obit kid played back the video of the press conference for me.

There I was—wrestling the baby with the dirty nose again. Since the police department monitor was in black and white, the whole thing had an unreal look to it. But when I watched the video and relived that moment when I turned my head and looked down the gun barrel, my heart jumped back into my mouth. I had to go for my own box of Kleenex after seeing that.

It was nearly eleven o'clock, and I was trying to think of one more reason not to go home when the elevator opened, and two uniformed cops got off. Mike Svenson and Coy-the-Cop were behind them.

I walked over to meet them. "What are you all doing here?" I said. "Coy generally makes me come to the PD. I don't think he's ever seen our office before."

"Actually," Coy said, "it's a pretty serious situation, or we wouldn't have come."

All four of them looked grim, though Mike Svenson was holding his mouth oddly.

"What's the deal?" I looked from cop to cop. Now I realized that the other two guys were members of the TAC team which had been working at the Grantham PD Headquarters for the hostage crisis. They'd stayed out of the way of the negotiators, but they'd been in the bunch that rushed in and collared Bo.

As I stared, the guy on the left pulled out his Miranda card. "We represent the Grantham Police Department, and you stand accused of refusing to associate with police officers. We are here to place you under arrest." Then he lifted the card and began to Mirandize me. "You have the right . . ." he began.

"Huh?" I said.

The other cop pulled out his cuffs. "If you'll just put your hands behind your back, ma'am . . ."

"What?"

The other cop continued to read. "You have the right to remain sober. Should you give up the right to remain sober . . ."

"Sober?"

The TAC cop scowled and went on, "Should you give up the right to remain sober, nothing you say will be taken down and used against you in a court of law."

I began to laugh, and Coy and Mike joined in. The TAC cops grinned.

"Come on, Nell," Mike said. "We all know you make a point of not socializing with cops, but this is a special occasion. We're hauling you down to the Fifth Precinct for a drink—even if we have to take you in handcuffs."

"I'll go quietly, officer," I said. "If you're all so hard up for feminine companionship that you'll settle for a woman who put on her makeup in the back of a photographer's van and who didn't wash her hair when she got out of bed"—I glanced at my watch—"fifteen hours ago, I'll come."

"It's okay," the TAC cop on the right said. "My girl and I will give you a ride home."

So I broke my longtime rule and went out drinking with cops. I knew it was going to be a strange experience and the strangeness began in the *Gazette* elevator.

The *Gazette*'s night elevator was added to the front of the building mainly as a concession to the handicapped access law, or at least that's the theory around the office. It's just about big enough to hold one wheelchair. Three large-scale cops, one average-scale woman reporter, and one thin cop spokesman filled it up. To add to the muddle, you get in that elevator from the front and you get off it at the back. It has a front door and a back door, and you can walk straight through it. This confuses people.

It seemed to confuse Mike Svenson. Coy and I got on the elevator and faced the back, ready to exit that way. But Mike and the two TAC cops were facing the front. This left me standing with my nose almost against Mike's chest. As the elevator began to move, I had an unexpected sensation. Coy was talking, but I didn't understand a word he said. All I was aware of was a high volume of testosterone radiating from Mike Svenson.

Mike seemed to be broadcasting sex appeal, and my receiver was picking it up.

I was amazed. Talk about unexpected. Was I imagining it? I sneaked a glance at Mike's face, and I decided I was. He looked completely unconcerned. He was talking to one of the TAC cops. I was definitely imagining the whole thing.

Then he looked down at me. Direct eye contact.

Maybe I wasn't imagining it.

The elevator stopped, the door behind Mike opened, and we all got off. The odd sensation had been so disquieting that I nearly made a dash for my car, ready to head home and give the Fifth Precinct a miss.

But Mike touched my arm, very gently, and pointed at a car with a city seal on the side. "We're in Coy's car," he said.

The public relations director for the Grantham PD only rated a two-door, near-compact vehicle. Coy-the-Cop was opening the door on the passenger's side. I hesitated, but I climbed into the middle of the backseat, assigned seating for the shortest person in any group. A TAC cop and Mike got into the backseat with me. The second TAC cop climbed in front, and Coy drove.

The Fifth Precinct is a "club," which is the term we denizens of the southern plains use to mean a restaurant that serves liquor. Our part of the country rarely calls drinking establishments "bars" or "cocktail lounges"—too many Baptists. But people still have favorite hangouts, places they can be sure to run into friends and fellow workers.

Grantham PD uses the terminology of the Chicago police, not New York's, so its police force has "divisions," not precincts. And, since the city is only about 350,000 in population, it has only three divisions. Some years earlier an opportunistic club owner had given one of the favorite cop hangouts a name associated with the police, but one which was not in use in Grantham. The Fifth Precinct. I guess it's the equivalent of a golf club's Nineteenth Hole.

The Fifth, as it's usually known, is a block from police headquarters. Not all cops go there, of course. All around town there are coffee shops and drive-ins and fast food joints that draw cops. But the Fifth is known as the main watering hole for the headquarters crowd. Not the chief, of course. Jameson, like our managing editor, keeps his distance from the troops.

I spent the ride assuring myself that the sex appeal emanating from Mike Svenson was simply part of my overwrought imagination. Certainly Mike acted normal. He didn't pinch my fanny or nibble my ear. He was just there, looming up in my libido. If anything, he was a bit quiet. Coy and the TAC guys talked enough to make up for his silence.

The Fifth was really jumping when we walked in. Country-and-western music was playing loudly, and the rest of the party was way ahead of us in consumption of booze.

As soon as we got inside, I stopped to get my eyes accustomed to the dark. That was when the second interesting incident occurred. Because when I stopped, Mike Svenson didn't. He walked into my back and stood touching me for a moment, his chest against my shoulder blades, his thighs against my fanny.

Then he moved, and I discovered I had been holding my breath. The episode had only lasted a few seconds, but somehow it hadn't felt like an accidental touch in a crowded bar. I glanced over my shoulder, but Mike wasn't looking at me.

Then a path cleared, and I saw a couple of women waving from the back of the room. Coy passed me, pointing toward them and saying, "They've saved us a table."

I started back, weaving through the crowd. It was gratifying when people stopped me—Guy Unitas, slightly tight, gave my cheek a slobbery kiss with his fishy mouth—but I kept moving. And I was aware that Mike Svenson was close to me.

"Go on back," he said in my ear. "They've got a booth. What do you want to drink?"

"I don't need anything," I yelled back. "I'm still flying on excitement."

"Maybe you need something to bring you down."

"A beer, then. But I'm not sure I'm ready to come down."

Mike went over to the bar, going up to the spot that's usually reserved for the waitress. "Two Coronas, with lime," he yelled.

In spite of the crowd, he got quick service. It was easy to see he was the star of the evening. I took my beer, and he guided me through the crowd, to the very backmost booth in the place, a circular booth. The two TAC guys had already slid in beside the two women, and Coy-the-Cop was sitting down on the left side.

Mike and I slid in on the side opposite Coy. The booth was crowded. I saw that one of the women was a dispatcher, Mary Jane Dorsey. She was snuggled up to one of the TAC guys. I knew her, of course. I knew all the dispatchers. Mary Jane whacked me on the arm. "Way to go, Nell!" Then she introduced me to the other woman—or she tried. I never could understand her name. She was on the force herself and was apparently the wife of the other TAC cop. But I didn't know his name.

I turned back to Mike. "This is going to mean more medals for you," I said.

First he shrugged and looked into his beer. "I'm too egotistical to get much of a boost out of medals," he said. "I'm so stuck on myself that my own opinion is the only one that counts." Then he grinned, and he looked directly into my eyes.

There was no mistaking this. It was no accidental closeness in an elevator, no unintentional jostle in a crowd. It was deliberate eye contact at close range.

I looked back. No blinking. And, somewhere just above and behind my pelvis, an involuntary muscle squeezed so tight I couldn't breathe. The noisy crowd seemed simply to fade away.

I knew I wanted to get Mike Svenson in bed as quick as I could.

CHAPTER 4

The rush of lust caught me completely by surprise. I don't often blush—unlike many fair people, I don't find that a problem—but I could feel my face getting hot and my lips getting swollen.

Just then, one of the state cops came over, and Mike stood up to talk to him. I turned around and pretended to listen to the conversation in the booth. But my mind was racing. My reaction to Mike Svenson had me completely amazed.

Actually, I reassured myself, it wasn't as if Mike were a stranger. At least I knew him. I wasn't getting the hots for some guy I picked up in a skating rink. If Mike had been a doctor or a banker or a teacher or a lawyer—well, maybe not a lawyer—or a bricklayer or a catfish farmer, I suppose I would have simply thought Mother Nature was telling me to take a good look at this guy.

But Mike was a cop. And if I didn't drink with cops or hang around with cops or even let Coy-the-Cop touch my elbow—what was I doing fantasizing about going to bed with a cop?

It wasn't even as if Mike was the best-looking cop on the force. His beat-up nose was one of the first things I'd noticed about him. And I sure didn't like his hookups.

Among Grantham police, "hookups" means political connections. The term comes, I'm told by old-timers, from an early day mayor named Hooks who was notorious for his patronage system. Mayor Hooks has been dead for seventy-five years, but his name lives on in local slang.

And Mike Svenson had "hookups" dating clear back to his childhood status as the chief's son. He would probably never have been hired without those hookups, and the department gossips had it that Guy Unitas and the board of the Amalgamated Police Brotherhood had taken a close look at his selection as chief negotiator for the department.

He'd gotten all this attention because it's considered weird for an officer with eight years on a big city police force to resign and start over as a rookie in a smaller city, even one his father once served as chief. But, eighteen months earlier, at the age of thirty, after eight years on the fast track at the Chicago Police Department, Mike had started over in Grantham.

The law in our state—in all states, as far as I know—demands that every officer begin on the bottom rung in a new police department. I've been told that it's some quirk of the public employees' pension system, and that the variations in training requirements from state to state are also a factor. But for whatever reason, cops in nonsupervisory slots do not bounce from city to city, the way teachers or engineers or salesmen or newspaper reporters do, moving at the prospect of a better job. Cops can rise in rank only by staying in the same department.

So eighteen months earlier, when the word went around the Grantham PD that Irish Svenson's son wanted to join the force, there were hoots of disbelief. When Mike left Chicago to come back to his hometown, he lost pension benefits, he lost rank, he lost seniority. One day he was a sergeant of detectives in a city of several million. The next he was a rookie patrolman in a city of 350,000.

Why? The Grantham PD buzzed like a sewing circle.

The personnel office, speaking through Coy-the-Cop, assured me Mike Svenson's application had been handled routinely.

Sure, it had. I laughed derisively and demanded an interview with the chief, Wolf Jameson.

Face-to-face with Jameson, I went for the jugular with my usual penetrating style of interviewing. "What's the deal on Mike Svenson?"

Jameson put on his good ol' boy expression and rubbed his hair, as if he were feeling for wisps of hay. "Waal, young lady, it seems like a pretty good deal for our department. We get an experienced officer with high-falutin' education and training—not to mention an outstanding record—for the same price we'd pay for a rookie. Can't beat that."

"But does Mike Svenson really have an outstanding record?"

"He's jumped from grade to grade at the first moment he was eligible for promotion. He's been decorated for heroism. He's solved some important cases."

"But if he's doing so well in Chicago, why does he want to leave? Is he in any trouble?"

"His boss says not."

"Yeah, sure. I'll bet his boss says he's sorry to lose him."

"Yes, he does." Jameson frowned. "Nell—I'm not

saying 'off the record' because I know you won't take information from me that way—I had the same questions you have when I heard Mike wanted to come back. I didn't get directly involved in the application process, but I did call several Chicago cops I've met at conventions and short courses over the years, guys I know well enough to ask for the real horse manure. They all said Mike has a great record and has never been involved in anything questionable up there."

He spread his hands and shook his head. "I've checked foreground and background, and there's no indication Mike has any ulterior motive for leaving. I think he just wants to come home. His mother's still here."

I laughed. "Don't try to tell me Mike Svenson is coming back to Grantham to take care of his poor old mother. I saw the Widow Svenson at the APB dinner. She was beating guys off with a stick. She's also one of the hottest real estate agents in town. Having a grown son around may cramp her style."

Jameson grinned. "Like you say, Wilda Svenson is one fine lady. And she can certain sure take care of herself without the help of a grown son. No, I think Mike's just tired of the big city and wants to come back to God's country.

"And we're lucky to get him. For one thing, he's an experienced negotiator, and that's a field where we're a little short."

"But he'll be a rookie, a patrolman, for at least a year."

Jameson waved at his intercom. "I'll get Millie to give you a copy of our hostage situation policy. It says a negotiator is a 'qualified person, not necessarily a member of the department.' We've called in psychologists from Grantham Mental Health Center to handle negotiations before. We've called in people from Grantham State University. There's no reason we couldn't put Mike to work as a negotiator the day he goes on the force."

"What effect is his hiring going to have on department morale?"

"That depends on Mike. If he throws his weight around, acts like a big city cop helping out a backwoods department—well, heckfire! We'll let Chicago have him back."

So, for whatever reason, Mike Svenson had come back to his hometown. In one sense he was a conquering hero—a hometown boy who had made good in the big city. In another sense, he was an interloper. Before he even had his electricity turned on, I was getting calls about him.

He's a spy for Jameson, the patrol cops told me.

His job was to infiltrate the union, the detectives said.

The TAC team members, the people some cities call a SWAT team, were sure they were the target for Jameson's plan. Mike Svenson, they told me, was being brought in to feed Jameson information on what that division—a notoriously independent crew—was up to.

"And just what are you up to?" I asked.

"Not a thing!" they said. "We're innocent little lambs."

Heaven knows what other tales went around. I began to feel a certain sympathy for Mike Svenson. And I felt a certain curiosity. It wasn't only his news value which made me ask Coy-the-Cop to set up an

interview with him the first week he was on duty. I
wanted to meet the subject of all this gossip.

Mike did the interview during a break from rookie
school, so he was wearing his solid navy blue patrolman's uniform. A big, redheaded guy with a slightly
off-center nose and a wary look around the eyes.
Brown eyes, I noticed, very close in color to his ma-
hogany hair. No freckles.

Mike Svenson turned out to be the reporter's nightmare—a guy who answers all questions smoothly,
bland with a capital *B* but says nothing. He wouldn't
talk about his background. He just gave me a one-
page resumé. He shrugged off his decorations for
heroism. "Just lucky," he said.

Why was he back in Grantham? "I wanted to start
work on my masters in public administration, and
Grantham State has a good program. Besides, I got
tired of smog and snow. Until you've pulled mid-
night-to-eight surveillance in subzero temperatures,
you don't know how good the weather can look on
the southern plains."

He was Mr. Cautious. Dull, duller, dullest.

So finally I went outrageous. "Of course, everybody gossips about a thirty-year-old guy who's still
a bachelor," I said. "Do you have a girlfriend? A
fiancée? A special friend?"

I'd never met a cop I couldn't get a rise out of by
a slur on his masculinity, and for a minute I thought
Mike Svenson was going to say what he thought
without mapping it out first. His eyes widened, and
he took a deep breath.

Coy-the-Cop, who was sitting in on the interview
at Mike's request, cleared his throat. "Now, Nell, that
question is a little out of line. What relevance—"

But Mike silenced Coy with a gesture. "It's okay, Coy," he said. "She's just trying to get a rise out of me. That's her job."

Then he spoke seriously. "I'm sorry if I'm hard to interview, Ms. Matthews. I'm not as colorful as my dad was. If your readers are really interested in my personal life, you can put me down as a practicing heterosexual."

I left that out of the story, of course. Coy was right. It wasn't relevant. The word "single," inserted early in the story, was all that was needed. And I hadn't seriously suspected Mike Svenson was anything but a practicing heterosexual. In fact, something in his self-assured air hinted that he'd had quite a lot of practice being heterosexual.

But I was glad I'd asked. I didn't learn anything about Mike Svenson's sex life, but I found out that he could shut up Coy-the-Cop with a wave of his hand. Many's the time I'd wished I had that knack.

Mike and I had crossed paths fairly often during the eighteen months since that interview. Once the photog and I ran on a four-car smash-up on Plains Parkway, with two dead, and Mike was directing traffic around the scene. He handled a semi with the same aplomb he'd used on Coy-the-Cop.

The fall after Mike had returned, a year before Bo Jenkins holed up in the Grantham Central PD station, I'd decided it was time to drop the guy who talked me into moving to Grantham, the one I'd begun to call "Professor Tenure." I think he was tired of me, too. At any rate, we called off the rather vague plans we'd had for a wedding, and for the past year I had concentrated on the violence beat. I'd even begun to eat breakfast in Guy Unitas's booth at the Main Street Grill once a week or so.

Guy's big corner booth is the place to find out what rank-and-file cops really think about the world. No bosses ever join that group, so it gave me a new slant on the violence beat, different from the official word I got from Coy-the-Cop Blakely, the department spokesman.

Mike also turned up there sometimes. It was interesting to see him work the higher-ranking cops— some of them were younger than he was, of course. He could use a deferential tone without seeming servile. And he never mentioned Chicago, no matter how well it would fit into the conversation.

That's when I began to see how intelligent he was—intelligent as in crafty.

After a year Mike moved from probationary to full patrolman's status, and he was driving one of the first cars to reach the scene of the Coffee Cup killings. That turned into the most grisly crime story I've ever covered—a holdup gone wrong that left four waitresses dead and a cook in the hospital. As one of the first officers on the scene, Mike was the guy who secured the item which turned out to be the key evidence—a blue jeans jacket dropped in the gutter halfway down the block—and Jim Hammond, the senior detective in charge of the case, pulled him onto the investigative team as a uniformed gofer. He just happened to be the one sat down for coffee and chit-chat with one of the suspects after the guy had had a session with Hammond. I've listened to the tape, and it was an amazing performance. Mike kept begging the guy not to tell him anything, kept repeating that he should have his lawyer present. And the guy kept talking. Talked himself right onto death row.

That's when I really began to see how subtle Mike's intelligence could be. He played the guy like a harp. And all perfectly legal.

The Coffee Cup killings turned out to be a turning point for me, too. My interview with the mother of the waitress whose boyfriend had dropped the jacket made the national wire and won an award at the state Associated Press convention. It also gave me the nerve to write more personally, when the situation called for it. There's more to journalism than the five W's and an H—"who, what, where, why, and how."

After that case Mike had been pretty well accepted in the Grantham PD, and very few had griped when he had been named the chief negotiator for hostage situations just three months earlier. He'd handled only a few suicide threats until Bo Jenkins erupted into the news. The standoff at the Grantham Police Department had been his first big negotiation, and it had ended so well we were all celebrating at the Fifth Precinct.

Now I realized Mike was sliding into the booth beside me.

"Does this place have food?" I asked. "I never got any dinner."

"They have hamburgers," he said. He waved a hand, and a waitress appeared. Those gestures of his were magic. "Can you bring a menu?"

"Never mind," I said, yelling over the noise in the joint. "I'll have a hamburger and a side of fries."

The waitress nodded. "What do you want on the hamburger?"

"What comes on it?"

"Pickles, mustard, onion, lettuce, tomato, and mayonnaise."

"Pickles and mustard only, please."

"That's a Number two. Pickles, mustard, and onions."

"No! No onions! Hold the onions!"

I yelped the request out loudly. Then I felt like a fool. I gulped my beer and tried to assure myself that the crowd at that table had no way of knowing I normally ate onions on my hamburgers. They couldn't tell that sitting beside Mike Svenson made me want to avoid onion-breath at all costs.

You're a complete idiot, I told myself. You may be hot for Mike Svenson, but he hasn't indicated that he's all that interested in you. The elevator incident may have been your imagination, and that eye contact may have been meaningless. And that jostle in the crowd could well have been an accident.

Then Mike scooted over slightly. The length of his thigh pressed against mine. His leg moved slightly. He looked directly at me. "Sorry," he said, "I'm about to fall on the floor."

Well. That changed matters. We were sitting cheek to cheek. His meaning was hard to mistake.

I had to make a decision. Quick, Nell! Are you serious about going to bed with this guy? I looked directly into his eyes. He looked directly back. My pelvic muscles did their little exercise again. I took a deep breath and made up my mind.

"Here," I said, "I'll try to give you some more room." I wriggled in my seat.

My shoulders may have moved away from Mike. But I didn't move my leg. We were still sitting thigh to thigh.

He put his arm along the back of the booth, and he touched my shoulder as he did it. I moved infinitesimally closer to his rib cage. His thigh pressed harder.

Then I looked across at Coy-the-Cop. Was he noticing this? To my relief, he was standing with his back to us, talking to the state cop. He hadn't been looking at us.

Coy motioned to Mike then, and Mike got up again. I began to talk to the dispatcher. How long have you been on the force? Are you from Grantham? Why did you want to go into law enforcement? It's a poor reporter who can't make conversation.

Mike was up and down, and I was interrupted quite a bit while I wolfed my hamburger. He slid in and out of the booth, and we rubbed knees and thighs. As I was chomping on the final few fries, he sat down one more time, and we were once more sitting cheek to cheek. His face remained completely innocent.

"Still hungry?" he said.

"No," I said.

"Thirsty?"

I tapped the bottle on the table. "Somebody bought another round." I tried to look as innocent as he did. "If I need anything, it's quiet. This place is pretty noisy."

Mike's hand dropped casually onto my shoulder. "I've had about all the celebration I can stand."

"Me, too."

"Do you need a ride home?"

"My car's at the *Gazette*."

"I could give you a lift."

"Thanks. I accept."

We looked at each other, and Mike began to move out of the booth. He held his hand out toward me.

"Wait," I said. "I guess I should speak to Coy before I leave. You go ahead."

Mike frowned, then nodded. "Not a bad idea. I'll wait at the corner. A black pickup, with a camper shell."

He walked across to one of the detectives, and I busied myself with saying good-bye to the people in the booth. Both couples were involved in their own dialogues. None of them had seemed to notice Mike and me. I assured them I had a ride. I didn't say who was giving it to me.

Then I had to make my way across the room. I know a lot of cops, and they all seemed to be there. They all wanted me to stop and talk. Mike went on out the door, and I got more and more impatient, ready to get out of there.

By the time I tapped Coy on the shoulder, I was definitely in a hurry. Walking across the room had taken me so long that I was afraid Mike might lose interest. Or I might lose my nerve.

"Coy, thanks for arresting me and making me socialize with cops," I said. It was still loud in there. I was almost yelling.

"Hey, Nellie!" He'd gotten way ahead of me in the beer department, I deduced. "You're not leaving?"

"Yeah. It's been a long day."

"I'll take you."

I laughed. "No way. I've got a ride. You'd better not even drive yourself."

Coy giggled and pointed at a big cop named, believe it or not, Clancy. He was sitting near the door.

"Clancy's our designated driver," he said. "He's a teetotaler." He put his arm around me and gave me a big hug. "It's been a hellova day, Nell. Hey, Joe Simpson told me you spoke to Bo Jenkins as they were taking him away."

"We accidentally wound up nose to nose. I couldn't pretend we hadn't met." I pulled away from Coy. Funny, Mike put his arm around me, and it was terrific. Coy did it, and I had an impulse to stomp on his instep.

He gripped me more tightly. "What did Bo have to say?"

"Just muttered his usual gibberish," I said. Mike was waiting for me. Why wouldn't Coy let me go?"

"Joe said you told him you'd interview him."

All I could think of was Mike. I elbowed Coy in the ribs and pulled away. "Coy, once he's detoxed, he won't want to be interviewed."

"Would you really interview that kook?"

"I wouldn't want to break my word, Coy. Listen, I'm exhausted. I'll talk to you Monday."

I escaped his grasp and waved good-bye. I reached the door with only a few more greetings and a couple of beery kisses. I nodded to Clancy, the designated driver. He did not insist on running a Breath-a-lyzer on me.

I shoved the door open, went out, and looked left.

Lights flashed off and on, and I saw the black pickup, with camper shell, up the block. I conquered the impulse to run. I forced myself to walk toward it calmly.

Mike got out and came around to open the passenger's door. I could have told a cop owned the truck. The inside lights had been disconnected. Mike handed me in as politely as a teenager at his senior prom, then he leaned in after me, sliding his left hand around the back of my neck.

The kiss nearly melted my teeth. It went on for quite a while, involving creative tongue action and inspiring heavy breathing from both of us.

When Mike stood up again, he left his hand on the back of my neck.

He sighed deeply, and the sigh had a tremor to it. He looked directly at me. I wasn't ready for the question he asked.

"How much have you had to drink?"

I laughed. "One beer."

"You're sure you're not under the influence?"

"Not of beer. Euphoria, maybe. Why? Do you usually have to get girls drunk before they'll accept rides from you?"

He grinned then, and I remembered that his grin could be nearly as stimulating as the kiss.

"Okay," he said. "You're sober. So that's your last excuse for escaping the ultra-deluxe, A-number-one, wide-screen, supercolossal effort to get you in bed."

"Shut up and drive," I said.

CHAPTER 5

I guess suave is in the eye of the beholder, but Mike met my personal test. He got in the truck, then leaned against me, and pulled my seat belt over.

"Buckle up," he said. "I don't want anything to happen to you before we get to my house."

Buckling up, of course, involved a bit of touching. And another lengthy kiss.

He drove a couple of blocks, then he looked over at me. "Is my house okay? I'm flexible."

"Do you live alone?"

"Yes."

"It sounds better than my place. I share a house with three other people, and one of our rules is no boyfriends."

"No boyfriends?"

"Not overnight. Not after the time one refused to leave for a month. Two of us didn't like sharing a bathroom with him."

Mike laughed. He put his right hand on my knee. I turned sideways in the seat and ran my forefinger around his ear. He seemed to like that.

"On the other hand," I said, "how well-equipped is your house?"

"I've got plumbing. A coffeepot. A king-size bed.

Maybe some beer in the icebox. What do you want?"

"I'm not too particular about the size of the bed, but I quit taking the pill nearly a year ago."

"Oh. I'm not sure—" He swung into a convenience store at the next corner. "Just be a minute."

Like I say, suave is in the eye of the beholder. If he'd had condoms in his wallet, I might have gotten out and called a cab. A guy who's ready to get lucky at all times turns me off. I figure a guy like that isn't too particular about whom he gets lucky with. And what does that make me?

Mike was cool about buying condoms. He didn't sneak in or look around guiltily. In fact, he bought several other items—I could see him walking up and down the aisles. When he came out, he put a sack behind his seat. "I got some orange juice and a toothbrush," he said, "in case you decide to stay over."

Like I say, suave.

After that the party began to get exciting. Seat belts don't have to be too confining. Besides, Mike lived in an older neighborhood of Grantham, just ten minutes away from the Central Station. It's probably lucky that it wasn't any farther.

I discovered that he liked the hand on the knee business as well as I did, particularly when I let my fingers walk up his thigh, toward the groin. Then I'd back off, pull away, and fold my hands together.

"Sorry, I didn't mean to distract you from your driving."

He laughed. "I didn't know you'd turn out to be a tease."

"Do you mind?"

He stroked the inside of my thigh. "Nope."

All this fooling around had quite an effect on Mike, but I can't say it was because I'm particularly tantalizing. He was in the mood. I was in the mood. We'd shared an awful day, but it had ended right. Adrenaline was coursing through our bodies and leaving us both feeling euphoric. Teasing and exciting each other was the entertainment for the evening. By the time he punched the garage door opener on his sun visor, we were both in a state of high sexual excitement.

Once we were in the garage, I flipped my seat belt off and reached for him. But he pushed me away.

"No! I don't dare," he said.

"What! Have you brought me clear over here under false pretenses? I thought I was going to get sex."

"You can have it, but not in a truck. I may not be the coolest guy in the world, but I don't make out in vehicles. Especially vehicles that don't even have a backseat."

He slid out of the truck, then leaned over to pick up the sack behind his seat. I crawled across the seat and managed to have my face upturned, waiting, when he straightened up. I caught a handful of his shirt front and stopped him before he could stand—well, erect.

"You nut," he whispered. But he kissed me again. About three minutes later he pulled away, but I still had a fistful of his shirt.

"Don't you know that girls who tease get in a lot of trouble?" he asked.

"Is that a promise?" I let go of the shirt and reached for another part of his anatomy.

Mike laughed and shoved my hand away. "Nell,

I'm going to embarrass us both unless we get in the house. Now!" he said.

I stood demurely while he opened the door. We went through a utility room and into a pleasant kitchen with white-painted cabinets and a round table in one corner. There were two glasses and a plate in the sink, but they'd been rinsed.

"Very nice," I said.

"Glad you like it." Mike put his sack on the counter and dug the box of condoms out. Then he reached purposefully for my hand. "In here," he said, nodding toward the next room.

Somehow going from the kitchen to the living room required quite a bit of maneuvering. It's hard to walk and kiss and take a guy's shirt off all at the same time. Awkward. But we finally got through the door, and Mike shoved me onto a big overstuffed couch that sat in the middle of the room.

"Ooooo. Leather," I said. "I'm impressed."

He ignored the comment and sat down at the other end of the couch. "Let me have your feet," he said.

"Wait a minute! I didn't sign up for anything kinky! If you're into feet—"

"I can take feet or leave them alone," Mike said. He reached down and lifted my foot onto the couch. "I may not be a rocket scientist, but I know enough about physics to see that those tight-legged jeans of yours are not coming off over those tennis shoes."

As soon as he pulled the left shoe and sock off, I moved the foot over and buried it in his lap.

"You nut!" he said. "Who's got the thing about feet now?"

He fumbled with the right shoe and sock, and as

soon as they were off, I yanked my feet away. "Now, you," I said. "You've got shoes, too."

He bent to pull his loafers off, and I stood up and slipped out of the tight-legged jeans. This didn't leave me in too immodest a position, since my sweatshirt was enormous and hung well past my hips.

Mike looked up at me and shook his head. "Absolutely nuts," he said. "Nutty as a big hunk of pecan pie, and just as tempting." He pulled me over in front of him. "Maybe not as sweet," he said. "Luckily, I like spicy better than sweet."

We began to try to get the big baggy sweatshirt off, and the love scene quickly became slapstick. I got my arms out of the sleeves, but when I lifted the shirt over my head, Mike unhooked my bra and began to practice a technique usually used on ice cream cones. This made me so weak I dropped my arms and grabbed him around the neck. The shirt fell down, covering both of us like a tent. Mike's face was buried in my cleavage.

"I'm smothering." He gasped dramatically. "But I'm going to die happy."

We finally got the sweatshirt off. Mike stood up long enough for us to drop the rest of our clothes in a heap at our feet. He sat down and reached for the box of condoms. I ripped the box open and fumbled around with one—like I said, I'd been on the pill and in a long-term relationship.

Then Mike pulled me onto his lap. He began to gasp almost immediately. "You nut," he said. "You wonderful nut."

Mike held me tightly, pressing my head into his neck. He even murmured my name a couple of times.

Then we shifted around and wound up lying side by side on the couch. It was a tight fit, but I was on the inside.

"So you're a tease," he said. "Tease me until I have to hurry. Well, two can play at that game."

He began to kiss me, caress me and do generally terrific things to all the most sensitive parts of my body. But he didn't tease. He kept it up without stopping until I did my own moaning and gasping.

"Suave," I said, as soon as I could talk. "Suave. And if I ever find out her name, I'll write her a thank-you note."

Mike kissed me. "Are you implying you're not the first woman I've ever done this with?"

"Certainly not. I'm sure you got all those moves out of a book. I was referring to the librarian."

Mike laughed, maybe a little longer than the joke deserved. "I read a lot. It's surprising how much good a library card does a boy," he said. "And now, I'm moving before I fall off this couch."

I gave him a little body English then, and he did fall off. He lay on the floor, naked and laughing for a couple of minutes. Then he sat up.

"I've always been afraid to pick up girls in bars because I was sure I'd get a crazy," he said. "And I finally did it, and—by gollies!—I was right."

I started to sit up, too, but he kissed me again. "Don't move, you crazy, sexy coot."

Right at that moment, the phone rang.

I jumped all over, and Mike said, "Damn." But he didn't get up off the floor.

"Are you going to answer?"

"The machine will catch it. I'm off duty."

But we both sat listening until the answering machine picked up the call after the fourth ring. At the sound of the beep, Coy-the-Cop's voice came on.

"Okay, Mike. The national television and wire services tracked me down. They're demanding equal time with Nice Nellie. I've set a press conference for three o'clock tomorrow, Sunday, at headquarters. I hope you get this message in time to make it." Coy clicked off.

I wasn't too thrilled at being recalled to the real world.

Mike stood up, went to the phone, and fiddled with the answering machine

"I'm not ready to be interrupted," he said. "Let technology handle the world tonight." He shook a finger at me. "Don't move."

He went into another room. A light went on, and I could hear a door opening. Then he was back with a terry cloth robe. "One size fits none," he said. "If you're chilly, please try this. I don't think I can face that sweatshirt again."

The robe had apparently never been worn, because he ripped tags off its sleeves before he handed it to me. I put it on. It was one of those short, kimono styles. It swallowed me, but not entirely. Mike disappeared again, and the noises told me he'd gone into the bathroom. I picked up a few of my clothes, and he was back.

"Neatening up?" he asked.

"I hate to be too messy. You seem to be a pretty good housekeeper."

"No, I have a pretty good housekeeper."

Mike's house was in an area of Grantham which had been the "in" neighborhood back in the 1930s and 1940s, so the houses had plenty of character. His was no exception. It had a tiled fireplace, and an area rug centered on hardwood flooring. The living room really was pleasant—very much a bachelor's, with the overstuffed leather couch, a matching chair, a big-screen television, and bookshelves flanking the fireplace. They actually held books, along with some speakers and a CD player. A computer was on a desk in the corner, surrounded by textbooks and papers.

It wasn't messy. All the magazines were lined up on the coffee table. There were no spiderwebs on the lamps.

"I'm glad we didn't go to my place. It's Clutter City," I said.

Mike put his arms around me. "That's the advantage of having a mother in the real estate business. She can always dredge up a cleaning woman. Happens she came yesterday. The cleaning woman, not my mother." He nuzzled my neck. "Are you hungry? Thirsty? Want a shower?"

I gave a happy groan at his last suggestion.

Mike led me to the bedroom, which featured a king-size bed in which one person had slept the night before, judging by the way the covers were thrown back. Behind it was a very modern bathroom with no bathtub, but with a giant stall shower. We got in it and scrubbed each other's backs, among other activities. When we got out, Mike took clean towels from a cupboard, and we dried each other's backs. While I toweled my hair, he left, and when I went into the bedroom, the bed had been straightened and both sides were turned down.

Like I say. Suave. I felt like an honored guest.

I tossed the robe on a chair and got into the bed.

The pillows were fresh and the blanket was soft and the sheets were smooth. It felt great.

Way off, I heard Mike laugh. "I thought going to sleep was the guy's bad habit," his voice said. But the sound didn't disturb me at all.

When I came to, the room was dimly lighted, and Mike was asleep on the other side of the bed. I pulled my watch out of the pocket of the terry robe. Two A.M. I'd been sleeping like a rock for more than two hours.

I turned over and watched Mike. The house had grown chilly, but he had pulled the blanket only up to his waist. He was sort of good looking, I decided. The rugged features would never make it in the movies, but they suited me. His hair didn't look so bright in the dim light. It was thick and tried to curl—I wondered if that was why he clipped it so severely. He had great muscles in his shoulders and arms. His body wasn't particularly hairy. I find chest hair a turn-off, so that suited me, too.

What was wrong with the guy? Something had to be. Nobody's perfect. But right at that moment, I couldn't find a thing to complain about.

He's thirty-two years old and never been married, I told myself, closing my eyes again. Maybe he's got a problem with commitment. My eyes popped open. Why had I thought that? Professor Tenure had been my final try at commitment. I wasn't cut out for permanent relationships. Mike and I ought to get along fine. No strings for either of us. I closed my eyes.

I woke up again about three A.M., when the earthquake hit.

At least that's what it felt like in that wild moment between being asleep and being awake, that moment when I realized the bed was shaking and rocking. When I managed to wake up, I realized that Mike was doing the shaking and rocking. His legs were jerking, and he was twisting his head and shoulders from side to side.

"Mike, Mike!" I said. "Wake up! You're having a nightmare."

I touched him, and he lashed out with his arm. He grabbed my wrist, and his grip was like iron. He flipped over and pinned me. In the dim light, his face looked fierce and angry, like a gorilla who'd just seen me eat his last bamboo shoot.

"Mike!" I yelled. "It's me! Nell!"

He looked around wildly for a minute, then focused on my face. Gradually, he seemed to become aware of my identity. He threw my wrist down and rolled back onto his own side of the bed.

He began to mutter. "Shit! Shit! Shit!" He didn't say it loudly, but he said it as if he meant it. Then he jerked his head toward me. "Did I hurt you?"

"No."

He sat up and swung his legs out of the bed. "Go back to sleep." He made it a command.

Instead, I sat up. Mike went to the bureau, yanked a drawer open, plucked out a pair of boxer shorts and went into the bathroom. "Go back to sleep," he ordered again. Then he slammed the bathroom door and locked it.

Locked the bathroom door? Did he seriously think I would walk in on him?

Obviously, the nightmare had upset Mike a lot. He'd calm down in a minute. Come out and apologize. Maybe we'd make love again. I stretched and felt the smooth sheets along my bare body. It felt sensuous. I felt as voluptuous as a 34B can feel.

The feeling was still there when the bathroom door was unlocked. Mike stalked out. He didn't look at me, or even at the bed. He walked on through the bedroom and into the living room. He'd left a dim light on in there, too, and I heard the leather couch creak as he sat down. Then I heard a very low voice. It took me a minute to realize Mike had turned on the television set.

Well.

He obviously wasn't interested in coming back to bed. Maybe I should go home. Then I realized he'd have to take me, since my car was still at the *Gazette* office.

Stupid, I told myself. You knew it was dumb to socialize with cops. So here you are in some strange guy's house, and he's having a fit and actually threatened to hurt you. And you can't get up and go home because your car is clear across town. Stupid is not a strong enough word.

Another sound began to butt against my consciousness. A low sound, a sort of clicking. It was coming from the living room. I sat up and listened intently. Then I quietly got out of bed and put on the terry cloth robe. I walked to the door and looked into the living room.

Mike was sitting with his back to me, just four or five feet away. He had bent forward and was holding his head in his hands. I could still hear the low clicking sound.

Violent shudders were racking Mike's body. The strange sound, I realized, was the chattering of his teeth.

CHAPTER 6

I almost panicked. The guy was sick. Was he having a heart attack? A nervous breakdown? Should I call 911?

Then the small amount of common sense I had left kicked in. Mike was a grown man. He was fully conscious. If he needed a doctor, he was smart enough to instruct me to call one.

What he had told me to do—and he'd made it an order—was to butt out. Go back to sleep.

I stood there in the doorway, remembering his first reaction. When I roused him from his nightmare, Mike had been angry. Annoyed, but not frightened. And he hadn't been shuddering yet.

He must have known that this shaking and chattering of teeth were coming, I decided. So it must have happened before. It made him mad, but it didn't frighten him.

So I decided to not let it frighten me.

I walked the two or three steps to the couch and put my hand on Mike's shoulder. He yanked away.

"Nervous reaction?" I said. "Nice to know you're not made of stone."

"G-g-g-go b-b-back . . ." Mike chattered out the two syllables, then quit trying to talk.

"I won't bug you," I said. I touched his shoulder again, and this time he didn't yank away. "But you're cold. That's not going to help matters."

My bare feet were chilly already. I looked around the room. A thermostat was near the door leading into the kitchen. I went over and turned it up a couple of notches. I heard the furnace kick on. That wasn't going to help very quickly.

Mike needed to be wearing something besides a pair of red-white-and-blue-striped boxer shorts. Should I get dressed and give him his robe?

Or maybe he had another robe. I went back into the bedroom and opened the door that did not lead to the bathroom. It revealed a deep, walk-in closet. Grantham PD uniforms, summer and winter, were hung at the back. Khakis and jeans hung in plastic dry cleaner bags next to striped sports shirts and knit polos. There were few long garments, however—mainly the pants to four or five suits, hung full-length on pants hangers. No robes were visible.

It looked as if I'd have to offer Mike the robe I was wearing. I started to pull off the kimono wrap, then I looked up. A folded quilt was stored on the shelf above. I pulled it down. It was a gem. A well-worn gem, true, but a gem. Handmade and washed hundreds of times, until it was soft, pliable and a bit ragged. And it was large.

I carried it into the living room. "I hope this is all right," I said. I shook the quilt out. Mike let me tuck it around him, but he wasn't very gracious about it.

"G-g-g-o b-b-ack to b-b-ed," he said.

I gestured at the television. "And miss one of my favorite movies? No way."

Mike had turned on a videotape of *Big*, a silly

movie, but a good one. It's a fantasy about a thirteen-year-old boy who wishes he were "big" and wakes up the next morning a thirty-four-year-old man. I like it; its got some witty observations of adult antics, from a thirteen-year-old viewpoint. So I perched beside Mike, with my knees tucked under me, and looked at the television screen. I put my arm around his shoulder.

He leaned his head against my elbow. "S-s-s-tupid," he said.

"What? This reaction? It's not stupid. What would be stupid would be somebody who could go through a day like you had and not have any reaction."

"Y-y-you're not s-s-shaking. Y-y-you went through it."

"I wasn't responsible for the negotiations, the way you were. I didn't have to grab the guy with the gun, with a civilian present, the way you did.

"Besides, I did my shaking earlier. That's one of the advantages of being a writer. When I got back to the office, I had to sit down at the keyboard and go through that whole ghastly mess for the benefit of the readers of the *Grantham Gazette*. I used up half a box of Kleenex and a year's supply of adrenaline. By the time you all got there to take me to the Fifth, I'd been from the roof to the basement and back again—emotionally."

Mike's arm came out from under the quilt and reached around my waist. He pulled me close. I retucked the quilt, so that I was inside, too. He rested his head on my shoulder, and I put my arms around him. He kept shaking.

We sat there, staring at the comedic antics of a kid pretending to be a grownup, for fifteen or twenty minutes. Maybe half an hour. Just after the point in the movie when the kid-turned-into-a-grownup tells the pretty girl she can spend the night but that he gets to sleep in the top bunk, Mike's shuddering slowed to an occasional tremble. His teeth stopped chattering.

When he spoke again, his voice was soft, but it sounded normal. "Thanks for not fussing," he said.

"I'm not very fussy by nature," I said. "Not much of a compliment to you."

"Oh, you've got real good taste," he said.

He kissed my neck several times. When I arched my head back, so he could have a better angle, he gently turned me so that I was lying across his lap, cradled in his arms. He began kissing my face, my lips, my neck, and my collarbone.

"You have to tell me what's good for you," he said.

I sat up, moved my arm outside the nest of quilt which still swathed both of us, and reached for the VCR's remote control. "You're doing fine," I said, "but I want your full attention."

I punched the STOP button.

"Maybe we ought to move into the other room," Mike said. "We might feel acrobatic."

We moved, but we didn't get acrobatic. We simply looked into each other's eyes, and we moved very slowly. Nothing fancy. Classic. Absolutely perfect.

Later, with our bodies still demonstrating their impeccable fit, Mike rested on his elbows and put one hand on each side of my face. "Nell, this could turn into something—"

I put my hand over his mouth, gently.

He stopped talking, and we stared into each other's eyes some more. Then he blinked and kissed the fingers which were signaling for him to be quiet.

"Let's keep it just the way it's been," I said. "Suspended in time. Perfect."

He frowned and kissed the palm of my hand. "That's okay. As long as you understand I won't be satisfied with just tonight."

I could feel a tear forming in my right eye. I was filled with all sorts of tenderness, but the cynical, smart-ass core of me wanted to say, "Tell me more, sweetie. I'm not going to hold you to anything you say in the position you're in right now."

With Professor Tenure, I would have said it. But this time I kept my mouth shut. Was I getting soft?

This time Mike was the one who fell asleep right away, and I was the one with the shakes. At least I was able to keep my quivering emotions internal. The way he could make me feel was pretty scary. Would he have the same feelings for me when he wasn't in the grip of passion? Would I dare feel the same way about him outside of bed? He slept peacefully. I don't think he realized how frightened I was. He was upsetting my picture of myself as permanently uncommitted.

I dozed fitfully until around six A.M., when Mike woke again, too. After we experimented with yet another position, I fell deeply asleep. When I opened my eyes, the blinds were letting in strips of sunlight, and I could smell coffee. Nine-fifteen. The answering machine in the living room was making unintelligible clicks, and this time Mike picked up the phone.

He spoke in a low voice, but the house was quiet, and I could hear him. "This is Mike, Coy. I got your message. One-thirty at the PD. I'll be there.'

He paused. "I hope you find her. I don't want to face the national television alone."

I grinned. Coy had apparently told Mike he hadn't been able to find me, and Mike hadn't volunteered to tell him my whereabouts. I appreciated his discretion.

I sat up. Time to return to the world.

In the bathroom mirror I looked less haggard than I felt, though my hair was in tufts which pointed in several different directions.

"You look like you spent a mad, passionate night wallowing in some guy's bed," I told myself. "Or on his couch." I reached for the toothbrush Mike had bought me. "Time for Missy to go home."

Mike had put on jeans, but no shirt or shoes. He was sitting at the kitchen table reading the *Gazette*'s sports section.

"Glad to see you're a subscriber," I said.

He tapped his finger on A Section, which was lying on the table, facing the chair opposite his. "They have some good stuff. There's a great story this morning by that daring girl reporter, Nell Matthews." He hugged me around the waist. "That gal's got guts."

"Yeah, and they're empty," I said. "How about a bowl of cereal or something?"

"Sorry, no cereal. Happens I hate cereal. And I'm out of eggs. But I love toast."

"Toast is fine."

Mike got me a plate and put two slices of bread in a toaster on the counter. He poured coffee and juice. I looked at the front page of the *Gazette*. Ruth had spread my first-person account of the hostage situation across the top, above a four-column picture lifted from the police videotape. Chuck's straight news story was beside the picture, in the two right-hand columns. My story had the biggest, blackest headline the *Gazette* ever runs.

"Wow!" I said. "Seventy-two-point head in a condensed face. We're famous."

Mike handed me orange juice in an old-fashioned glass and lifted a similar glass in his other hand. "Here's to us celebrities. Alive and damn lucky to be so."

We clicked glasses and drank. Then the toaster popped. Mike buttered my toast and handed it to me. Then he put two more slices of bread in the toaster.

"When you interviewed me, when I was a rookie," he said, "nearly every question you asked boiled down to my reasons for coming back to Grantham."

"And you were darn clever in dodging those questions, too."

"Are you still interested?"

"On the record?"

Mike laughed. "I hid your notebook. But I guess at least one of the reasons is no secret anymore. In case you still want to know."

"Sure I do. Seems as if you denied practically every reason I could think to ask about. You didn't come for family reasons. Or for professional reasons. It wasn't money. It wasn't health."

"You didn't ask about the simplest reason."

"Which is?"

The toaster popped then, and he buttered two more pieces of toast, then sat down himself.

I cleared my throat. "You're not answering the reporter, sir. And just what is the simplest reason?"

"Romance. I broke up with my girlfriend."

"I see." I munched toast. Where was this leading us? I needed more coffee before I was ready for any major discussions on Mike's past.

"We were a steady item for three years—two of them at the same mailing address," Mike said. "Just as I was deciding it was time to get married, she was deciding she couldn't stand to live with a guy who got up in the night with his teeth chattering. So she moved on to a job at a Texas college."

"College?" Had Mike had an experience like mine with an intellectual snob? "What did she teach?"

"She's an academic librarian."

I remembered the joke I had made about writing "the librarian" a thank-you note. For a moment I felt like blushing. Then I got the giggles. Mike began to laugh, too.

"I thought my joke got a mighty big reaction," I said. "Sorry if I put my foot in it."

Mike shrugged. "It's been nearly two years since the breakup, so I've had time to get philosophical. In fact, you started me on the path up from the pits."

"Me?"

He nodded. "I moved back to Grantham with some idea I could slip down to Dallas and see her on my off days. But she wasn't all that eager for me to show up. Then, first week on the job, this reporter comes to interview me. And I'm thinking 'this is one sexy gal,' and having a terrible time keeping my mind off her legs and on the questions she's asking.

"So after the interview I give myself a lecture, along the lines of 'you're supposed to be in love with somebody else. What are you doing lusting after reporters?' "

"Sorry."

"Not your fault. Not anybody's fault. It was just some instinct telling me that it was time to move on. But it caught me by surprise. A few weeks later, when I thought about making a serious move in your direction, first there was this guy—"

"Professor Tenure. We broke up a year ago."

"—then everybody said you wouldn't date cops."

"There are several reasons—"

"Sure. I understand that." Mike reached across the table and took my hand. "I'm trying to tell you I've been nuts about you for a long time, and last night wasn't as sudden as it might seem."

I stared at my plate. What was Mike getting at? This sounded dangerously like a lead-in to a "commitment" speech. I didn't want to hear that.

Or was he being tactful? Was he trying to tell me he didn't consider me a mere bimbo because I'd gone to bed with him without much coaxing? I decided to work on that assumption.

"Mike," I said, "you don't have to soothe my ego just because I acted pretty slutty last night. Maybe I go home with guys all the time."

Mike stared at me. Then he laughed. "No, Nell. You don't go home with guys all the time."

"You have no way of knowing if I do."

"Sure I do. Deduction. I'm a detective, remember?" He tapped his forehead. "If you did, a girl as smart as you would figure out what to do with a condom. Besides, I told you I was egotistical. I'm special. You're special. And we're sure special together."

Well, that was true. I'd never been as attracted to anybody as I was to Mike, and we seemed to be extremely well suited to each other physically.

Besides, I liked the guy. That was the part that scared me.

"Therefore," he said, "as I said at one crucial moment last night, we've got to make arrangements to keep this going. How about if we start by going out to dinner tonight?"

I gasped. "Oh, I can't do that!"

Mike looked alarmed. "You aren't seeing somebody else?"

"Oh, no! It's just that—" I stopped in midsentence. My old excuse, "I don't date cops," hovered behind my teeth.

"It's my job," I said weakly. "Reporters shouldn't date sources. It's a rule I've always followed."

"You mean, if we go out to dinner, you get fired?"

"Of course not! I'd just be duty-bound to ask the *Gazette* to shift me to another beat." I leaned across my plate. "It's my own rule, not the *Gazette*'s. It's simply not a good idea to get personally involved with something or someone you cover."

Mike didn't say anything. He just looked at me, and a grin began to twitch at the corners of his mouth. In a minute we were both laughing.

I got up, walked around the table, sat down in his lap, and put my arms around his neck. "And that's about the stupidest speech I've ever made," I said. "If we're not personally involved at this point . . ."

Mike patted my fanny. "I think you're trying to tell me that if we start dating, you'll have to give up covering the PD."

"Yes."

He nuzzled me under the chin. "I hate to ask you to give up your career in exchange for dinner out."

I leaned back and drew a design on his shoulder

with my finger. "The violence beat isn't exactly a career. To tell the truth, it's considered an apprentice beat. Most reporters do it a couple of years, then move on to something else. The city editor's been wanting me to make a change."

"Then you could change to a different beat?"

I nodded, but I guess I frowned. "But—"

"But you're not sure you want to."

Silently, I buried my face in Mike's neck. The truth was too stupid to verbalize. I loved the violence beat. It had been a haven to me. It had used up my emotional energy at a time when I wanted to keep my personal life detached and unemotional. I couldn't lie about it, but I didn't want to explain.

So I nibbled Mike's ear.

"All those hostage negotiation courses you took," I said, letting the words puff out gently against his neck, "did they include mind reading?"

"No, but when you snuggle up like that, I hope it's because you're reading my mind." He pushed the robe open so that we were skin to skin. Then he nuzzled, beginning with the shoulder and dropping past the collarbone. He used the ice-cream-cone technique again. I arched my back.

And, somewhere, in the background, a motor began to purr.

Mike jumped all over. "Damn!" he said.

"What's that?" I asked.

"The garage door," he said. "Crap!"

He began to readjust the robe, tucking it into the belt. I tried to stand up, but before I could get to my feet, the back door opened.

Over Mike's shoulder, I saw a tall, blond woman framed in the doorway. She wore khaki slacks, a plaid shirt, and a flannel blazer. She wasn't young, but she was attractive and well-kept.

She and I stared at each other.

Mike finished adjusting the robe into a more modest arrangement, but he didn't look around. "Hi, Mom," he said. "Come on in."

I did manage to get to my feet then, and I made a move toward the door to the living room, but Mike caught my hand and kept me there. He stood up, too, and turned around.

Wilda Svenson hadn't moved. "I, uh, I tried to call," she said, "but you didn't answer."

"We turned the phone off," Mike said. "I left a message on your machine last night."

I made another move toward leaving the kitchen, and at the same time Mrs. Svenson moved back a step, as if she were leaving. But Mike kept his firm grip on my hand, and he gestured to his mother.

"Come on in, Mom. And it's okay, Nell. My mom knows that we're adults, and adults have needs, and sometimes one of those needs is not to be alone."

I was picking up a rather cold tone to Mike's voice. His mother looked at him with narrowed eyes, but she stepped into the kitchen. Then I saw that she had someone with her.

A tall, handsome, older man was behind her. He had a gorgeous head of thick white hair, a deeply tanned face, and heavy black eyebrows. Like Mrs. Svenson, he was dressed in expensive sportswear, including a beautifully cut camel-hair jacket. The two of them came into the kitchen.

"Mickey and I had gone down to the lake," Mrs. Svenson said. "We just heard about all the excitement this morning. I tried to call—"

The white-haired man's voice rumbled. "Your mom was worried, Mike."

"No need," Mike said. "Thanks to Nell keeping her head, we came out fine." He turned slightly toward me. "Nell, this is my mother. And this is Mickey O'Sullivan, an old family friend." I caught the coldness in his tone again when he referred to O'Sullivan.

I wasn't quite sure what was going on here, but it seemed to me that I ought to be out of it.

"Mrs. Svenson and I were introduced at the Amalgamated Police Brotherhood dinner," I said. "Mr. O'Sullivan, nice to meet you. If you'll excuse me, I'll go get dressed."

This time Mike let me leave. I forced myself to walk sedately toward the bedroom, picking up the quilt from the couch as I passed. I closed the bedroom door gently, then leaned against it weakly. That's why I was able to hear what Mike said next.

"Mom, I admit that I acted like a horse's rear end on Labor Day," he said. "I will apologize to both you and Mickey freely and sincerely—later. And you can say anything you want to me, later. But if you make one snotty remark to Nell—then it's gonna be a cold day in Hell before we settle our differences."

So Mike hadn't accepted his mother catching him half naked with a half-naked girl quite as calmly as he'd tried to make me believe. And he didn't expect his mother to be calm about it either.

But when Wilda Svenson answered him, her voice sounded calm. It also sounded syrupy. "I'm just glad to see you're getting some good out of the robe I gave you for Christmas," she said.

After that I quit eavesdropping and got dressed in a hurry. Then I made the bed. A heavy quilted bedspread was tossed in the corner of the room, and I started trying to get it onto the kingsize bed—an activity much like trying to raise a circus tent without elephants. Mike came in, and we worked together on the bedspread, silently, not looking at one another. But when I did glance quickly at him, I discovered he was glancing quickly at me. Then we both cracked up. We stood at the foot of the bed, holding each other and laughing and saying, "Shhh!" and laughing again.

We were still snickering when the phone rang.

Mike picked up the extension beside the bed, but the machine in the living room had already answered the call. By some electronic fluke, the caller's voice was broadcast throughout the house.

"Mike, this is Jim Hammond."

That got my attention. Jim Hammond is the senior detective who handled the Coffee Cup killings.

"Yes, Captain." Mike had gone into his patrolman persona. His voice stood at attention.

"Mike, we just got a call from the mental health center. I want you to get out there, in case we need your help."

"Not another hostage situation?"

"Not this time. But Bo Jenkins is still causing problems."

"What's he done now?"

"He up and died on 'em."

CHAPTER 7

"What!" Mike's voice was furious. "Didn't they have the guy under a suicide watch?"

"It may not be suicide. See you there. Pronto." Hammond hung up.

I was stunned. Bo Jenkins dead? After all he'd put the Grantham PD through? After all the humiliation he'd inflicted on his family? After the way he'd scared me? And it might not be suicide. This was going to make the wire. Heck'uva story. I had to get out there. Did I need a photog? Who did I know at the Grantham Mental Health Center?

Thoughts went racing through my head, but I didn't move. Then my attention focused on Mike.

While I'd been standing stock-still, he was rampaging around the room. Right at that moment, I took back all my beliefs that redheads were no more hot tempered than people with less vivid coloring. Mike's face had turned the color of his hair.

"Did you hear that?" His voice was a dull roar. "Shit! Shit!" He started to kick the bedside table, but seemed to remember he was barefoot, and stomped the foot instead. He headed toward the closet.

"You've got to get out there," I said. "And so do

I." I picked up my purse and opened the door to the living room. "I'll call a cab."

"No!" Mike was still roaring. He turned away from the closet and rushed past me, out into the living room. "Mom! Mick! Did you hear what Hammond said? Can you give Nell a ride home?"

Wilda Svenson was in the living room. "Of course, Mike," she said soothingly. "We'll take her."

"Don't bother," I said. "I don't mind calling a cab."

Mike started unbuttoning his jeans. "That bunch of jerks! We spent fourteen, fifteen hours saving that creep's life yesterday and today—they let—" Words seemed to fail him. He glared at me. "No, I don't want you to go home in a cab."

"We'll take her, Mike," Wilda said again.

"I'd better put on a uniform," Mike said. He went back into the bedroom, taking off his jeans as he went.

Mickey O'Sullivan came in from the kitchen carrying a coffee mug. "I'll take Nell," he said. "Wilda, you can stay here and—make your phone calls."

Wilda blinked, then gave O'Sullivan a long look. "Phone calls? Oh. Yes."

"Look," I said. "I don't want to put anybody out."

"Where do you live?" O'Sullivan asked.

"College Hills. Oh, but my car's at the *Gazette* building."

"No problem. We're less than a mile from the *Gazette* and less than two miles from College Hills. I'll take you."

I apologized for not doing the dishes, and Wilda Svenson and I gave each other a polite good-bye. Lord knows what I said to her. "Nice seeing you again," didn't quite fit the situation. But within a minute or so I followed Mickey O'Sullivan through the garage, out to a gorgeous caramel-colored Lincoln parked in the driveway. He politely opened the door, and I hitched my fanny across the tan suede seat covers and fastened my seat belt. I certainly didn't want to bash my head on Mr. O'Sullivan's tinted windshield and get blood all over his deluxe dashboard.

It promised to be a gorgeous fall day, the kind October and early November can provide in our part of the world. At midmorning on a Sunday, the neighborhood was mostly deserted. Three teenagers—one each black, white, and brown—were tossing baskets in a driveway across the street, their ball making loud thumps as it hit the backboard and the concrete, and an elderly woman was sweeping her porch.

O'Sullivan's car had barely moved when the kitchen door opened, and Mike came running out. He was still barefoot, but he had put on a white T-shirt and some dark blue uniform pants. He was shoving his right arm into the sleeve of his uniform shirt as he came. O'Sullivan stopped the car, and Mike ran up to my side. I found the button which lowered the window, and Mike leaned down to talk to me.

"I'll call you tonight. Or as soon as I get loose," he said. Then he leaned in the window.

Hell's bells, he's going to kiss me, I thought. I was acutely aware that Mickey O'Sullivan was watching all this with a sardonic expression, and I could hear the *thump, thump, thump* of the neighbor kids' basketball. What could I do? Push Mike away? Get my notebook out of my purse and use it to shield my face? If he gave me one of those wonderful, lengthy, wet kisses I'd loved so much the night before, I'd die of embarrassment. I sat frozen.

But the kiss was gentle, sweet, almost chaste. Then Mike looked beyond me. "Thanks for taking her, Mick."

O'Sullivan shrugged. "You get going," he said. "Better not keep Hammond waiting."

"Yes, sir," Mike answered. But he watched until we were headed down the street, standing in the drive buttoning his shirt. The kids gave a couple of catcalls, and Mike waved at them.

O'Sullivan and I rode silently for a couple of blocks. He adjusted the car's temperature, which already seemed perfect to me, and I tried to get my brain into gear. At least I could act as if I appreciated the ride he was giving a stranger. In fact, I didn't understand who this guy was. The car was gorgeous, and he had a prosperous look. Probably one of Wilda Svenson's real estate buddies.

I didn't really want to think about it. All I could think about was Bo Jenkins. Dead. It seemed impossible. I was burning to get out to the mental health center and find out what had happened. So I was nearly caught off guard when Mickey O'Sullivan spoke.

"Have you and Mike been going together long?"

"No, we just—" I bit my tongue. I'd nearly blown it. Mike and I hadn't dated at all. We'd just gone to bed together.

I wasn't ashamed because I'd gone home with Mike. We were both consenting adults, after all. But it wasn't the way I usually behaved. And I wasn't sure that Mike wanted a family friend to know he picked me up at a party and took me home for the night. I don't lie, but discretion might be a good plan.

"Mike and I haven't been dating long," I said. No, you couldn't call twelve hours long. "But we've known each other around eighteen months. I interviewed him when he joined the Grantham PD." I decided to turn my reporter's skills on Mickey O'Sullivan. Or turn the tables on him. I turned to face him. "How long have you been seeing Mrs. Svenson?"

He looked at me, and I thought I detected a twinkle under the bushy eyebrows. "Oh, we've been dating about six months," he said. "But we've known each other around thirty-five years."

I laughed. He'd mimicked my answer exactly. "Touché," I said. "Are you in real estate?"

"No, I'm in the security business."

My feeble brain clicked over. "Oh! You're M.P. O'Sullivan!"

"That's me."

M.P. O'Sullivan was a former Grantham cop. He'd been high up in the department when he retired, maybe ten years earlier, and bought a security company.

"We did a phone interview. Last year," I said.

"That's right. Story you wrote on jobs for off-duty cops. You did a nice job."

"Thanks. But I'm feeling like an idiot, since I didn't realize who you were." I tapped my head. "This has not been one of my better mornings. Mentally."

"Nobody can blame you. But you acted completely calm back there at the house. Just like you did with Bo Jenkins yesterday."

"I took my cue from Mike. Both times. You saw the tape?"

"Yeah. This morning. I nearly had Wilda to bury when she saw Mike moving in on the guy with the pistol."

"You shoulda been there."

"No, thanks. I've had all of that kind of excitement I want."

A vague memory stirred, M.P. O'Sullivan had been a division head for the Grantham PD. Traffic? TAC? I couldn't remember. Then there had been some sort of shooting incident. Had he shot someone? Or someone shot him? Or someone he shot shot someone? I'd have to look it up in the *Gazette* library. Anyway, he'd left the police department and developed a highly successful security firm, specializing in jobs for off-duty cops. He provided bouncers for bars, antishoplifting crews for discount stores, crowd control for rock concerts, bodyguards for jewelry salesmen.

"Gee," I said, "I sure feel safe riding with you, Mr. O'Sullivan."

"I'm not armed. And please call me Mickey."

"Well, thanks for the ride, Mickey. I've got to get out to the mental health center quick."

"To cover the story?"

"That's my job."

Mickey nodded. "You're pretty good at it, too."

"Thanks."

"Just talking as a reader, of course. Your stories are always clear. No dangling details."

"Thanks again. Of course, you're a former law officer. You may understand crime stories better than the typical reader."

He shrugged. "Maybe. But the cops I know think you write good stuff, too. Fair."

"That probably means I'm not doing a good job. Leaning toward the cops' point of view."

He shook his head seriously. "No. When they goof, the citizens have a right to know. Professionals understand that they're answerable to the public. A real pro doesn't expect favors, just fairness."

"That's nice to hear." My mind was leaping ahead to the mental health center. "And, by the way, thanks for thinking up an excuse to leave Mrs. Svenson behind. I'm sure she's a lovely person—at least that's what I hear from everybody who knows her. But this wasn't a good time for chit-chat."

O'Sullivan grinned. "Wilda's a professional talker. It would have gone all right. She can talk to anybody. But I thought this would get you and me out of the way, in case she and Mike want to go at it."

"They don't get along."

"Usually they do. Wilda's the let-it-all-out type. Yells and screams and then it's over. Mike's more like Irish was. Tends to take things harder. But they usually live and let live."

He stopped at a light. "Wilda doesn't drop in unannounced every Sunday morning. Mike lives his own life. And she lives hers."

I realized we were at the turn two blocks from the *Gazette* office, and I opened my purse. I felt in the pocket where I always stow my keys. They weren't there. "Oh, no!" I dug deeper.

"What's the matter?" O'Sullivan said.

"I don't have my keys." I tried to think of when I last had them. "I gave them to Bo Jenkins' kid yesterday, to keep him amused when Bo and I handed him over to Mike. Afterwards, I ran straight out the back of the PD, to write my story. I got a ride in a patrol car. I don't know what happened to the keys. House keys, car keys. The whole batch."

"I can take you home, instead of to the *Gazette*. But can you get in?"

"On Sunday morning, probably all three of my roommates will be there. And I have an extra set of keys."

"I can wait while you get the extra keys and bring you back to the office. Where do you live?"

I gave him the address. College Hills is an older part of town, near Grantham State. It runs to apartments, some in modern complexes and some in old houses. The streets are narrow and lined with cars, since parking is always a problem near the campus. The businesses are mostly college-related. It's a great neighborhood for copy shops, cheap and off-beat restaurants, book stores, T-shirt vendors, and faddish clothes. It's not so great for supermarkets and malls.

I share one of the old houses—I think it must have been built in the 1920s as a student rooming house—with three other people. Martha is a grad student, Brenda is a nursery school teacher, and Rocky—well, Rocky is Rocky. Rocky works as a waiter in a lunch-type restaurant and also owns a piece of a bar. And he owns the house we live in. He calls himself our landlady.

I directed Mickey O'Sullivan to my parking spot in the backyard and jumped out of the car. I was a bit dismayed when I saw that Brenda's car wasn't there. She was our early riser. Up with the blankety-blank birds, even on Sundays. I might have to pound on the door until somebody heard me.

"Come on in while I find the keys," I said. "I'll get you some coffee."

Rocky usually sleeps until noon on Sundays. But not this time. I could see him through the kitchen window. Damn. I didn't really want to have to explain Rocky to Mickey O'Sullivan. A former cop the age of Mickey O'Sullivan was practically guaranteed to be homophobic. But I didn't want to act ashamed of Rocky either. He was a friend.

I knocked, and Rocky shot the dead bolts and opened the door. He was wearing a sweat shirt and shorts, a sign that he was on another of his periodic exercise kicks. He stood in the doorway with his arms folded—six feet, four inches of pudge, topped by a young face and a balding head.

"Well, well, I hope little missy finally took my advice and got laid," he said. "I've been telling you for a year that it would help your disposition."

"Shut up, Rocky," I said.

Then Rocky saw Mickey O'Sullivan behind me.

"Oops!" he said. He grimaced and stepped back to let us in.

O'Sullivan's eyebrows were scowling so hard they were almost tangled together.

"This is Rocky Rutledge," I told him. "He's my landlord. And our resident busybody. But he makes great coffee. Rocky, this is Mickey O'Sullivan. A family friend." I didn't stop to explain whose family. "Please give Mr. O'Sullivan a cup of your best coffee while I go find my extra keys."

"Certainly. Mr. O'Sullivan, this way please." Rocky led O'Sullivan to the kitchen table and cleared newspapers from one side. "Cream and sugar?"

I ran upstairs. Rocky does his weird act around Brenda, Martha and me, but I thought he'd be all right with O'Sullivan. He's a professional restaurateur, after all. He understands hospitality. And he doesn't swish. I decided to take ten minutes to blow-dry my hair and change clothes. By the time I went back down, Rocky would have O'Sullivan wrapped around his pinkie, ready to leave him a big tip.

Five minutes later, when I turned off the blow-dryer, I ran to the top of the stairs and listened. I heard Mickey O'Sullivan laugh. So I took three extra minutes for makeup. Then I ripped off my athletic shoes, jeans, sweatshirt, and dirty underwear and put on clean underwear and my black-and-tan plaid slacks with a black shirt and loafers. I've tried more formal clothes for the job, but somehow I always wind up tramping through high grass at a crime scene. Casual is best for the violence beat.

I grabbed the black cardigan and raced back downstairs.

O'Sullivan was handing his card to Rocky. "Call me if you decide you need some psychological muscle," he said. "I have plenty of guys who could handle the job."

"I don't know. Having cops on the premises might inhibit a lot of my customers," Rocky said.

"The guys wouldn't have to wear uniforms," O'Sullivan said. "And I have plenty who could be polite to the clientele." He opened the door and stood back for me to go out first. "Nice meeting you, Rocky. Thanks for the coffee."

We got back in the Lincoln before I spoke. "Would you really provide security for a gay bar?"

"I have some very tactful guys on my list. They could handle a gay bar. I'll send security guards anywhere the client wants them. We guarded the gifts at the Schultz-Waldheim wedding last year."

Grantham, like any city, has its crime families—its mob. While Sicilians have a corner on organized crime in many parts of the country—or so I hear— the two major operations in Grantham are both headed by guys with German names.

"I got Schultz to pay me up front," Mickey said.

"You were one of Irish Svenson's best friends, weren't you?" I said.

"Right. I gave him his nickname."

"I didn't know that."

"We were rookies together. Grantham had an old-time, Irish cop-type police chief in those days. Francis X. Donavan. He'd come from the East Coast, where they pay a lot more attention to nationality than we do out here."

I nodded. One of the things I like about the Southern plains is that nobody gives a darn what nationality anybody else is.

"Donavan comes in to greet the rookie class on our first day, before we even get our name tags. He looks the list of names over, and he says, 'Well, sure and we've got one real Irishman in this group.' And he stops in front of Irish. Or Carl, that was the name he went by then. Of course, Irish really did look like a son of Erin—red hair, freckles. And I looked like some kind of a southern European. My hair was coal black then. And I've always had a dark complexion.

"So Donavan looks Irish in the eye and goes on, 'Young man, the map of Ireland's all over your face.' Well, Irish turns as red as a streetlight, and he says, 'Maybe so, sir. But there's a black Irishman in the class, too.' Then he nodded toward me. And he says, 'His name is Michael Patrick O'Sullivan.' And Donavan looks surprised. He checks his list again, and says, 'And what might your name be?' and Irish says, "Carl Svenson, sir. I'm not Irish, but nine hundred years ago my Viking ancestors hung out around that part of the world a lot.'"

We both laughed. Then Mickey went on. "Donavan laughed and laughed. Later, I thought it was a sign of how well Irish's career was going to go. He managed to see that the chief was about to make a fool of himself and to turn it into a joke. Donavan never forgot Irish. Or me either.

"After that I started calling Carl 'Irish,' and pretty soon the rest of the class did."

"So you go way back with the Svensons."

"I introduced Wilda and Irish. Wilda worked with my wife in a real estate office. Marie was receptionist, and Wilda was a bookkeeper in those days. Marie and I were Mike's sponsors in baptism." He looked at me. "Presbyterians don't call 'em godparents."

"Neither do Methodists," I said.

"Marie kept Mike the night Wilda went to the hospital to have little Alicia, the baby who died. Wilda and Irish were at the hospital with me when Marie died."

"That's real friendship."

"Best friends I ever had." He grinned at me. "I guess it was inevitable that Wilda and I would take up together. We were used to each other. Of course, my girls love Wilda. Mike thought it was fine, too. At first."

I wasn't sure how to respond to that. "I noticed a little coolness between Mike and his mother," I said finally.

Mickey pulled the Lincoln into the two-story parking garage the *Gazette* built for its employees. On a

Sunday morning, there were only two cars, both on the lower level—my little Dodge and the giant and ancient Olds that one of the security guards drove. Mickey parked where I pointed, beside the Dodge, then turned toward me.

"Mike thought old farts like Wilda and me were looking for 'companionship.' " Mickey said. "Somebody to go to the community concerts and the country club buffet with. On Labor Day, he showed up a few hours early for the picnic down at the lake. That was the first time he realized old farts still like companionship in the bedroom, too."

Mickey grinned, and I did, too.

"Don't let Wilda jack you around," he said. "Her executive nature will come out if you let it. You're okay, Nell."

"Thanks, Mickey. You're okay, too." I got out of the Lincoln, and Mickey sat and watched until I opened the door to my car. Then the window on the passenger's side of his car went gliding down, and Mickey leaned across the car and spoke to me.

"I wish I could be a mouse in your pocket when Hammond asks how you found out Bo Jenkins was dead," he said. "I know you're going to come up with a very creative yarn."

CHAPTER 8

Mickey O'Sullivan waved and drove away. I sat in my car and tried to get my thoughts in order.

What had Mickey meant? Why should Hammond wonder how I heard about Bo Jerkins's death? I shrugged. All I had to tell him was that I heard it on the scanner.

Unless it hadn't been on the scanner. Cops are often sneaky enough to keep all references to some touchy subject off the radio. After all, scanner traffic is pretty public. Lots of housewives keep a scanner in the corner of the kitchen. Most cities had even taken steps to encode their scanner traffic, to keep the public, and more particularly the press, from knowing everything that was going on. I knew the Grantham PD had channels we couldn't get on our radios.

I decided I'd better check before I went rushing out to the mental health center. In fact, I decided I'd better check a couple of things.

The *Gazette* doesn't have a reporter on duty on Sunday mornings. One of the photographers was supposed to be listening to the scanner, in case there was a ten-car smashup or a multiple ax murder, but no one works the violence beat. Hardly anything ever happens on a Sunday morning that can't be picked up after the nightside guy comes in at three P.M. The photog is authorized to call a reporter if something big breaks.

So, if I knew about an investigation in progress, I could run on it. I didn't need to tell some other reporter I was horning in on his beat.

But Mickey had raised a key point. Hammond might not have realized that he had been broadcasting via the answering machine when he called Mike. He probably didn't know there were others present when he called. He certainly didn't know I was present. And I didn't want him to know. So how else could I find out?

Covering up sources is one of the main tricks to the reporter's trade. Sometimes, for example, one of the secretaries in the assistant chief's office waggles her eyebrows and tells me, "Hey, did you find the Sunday night traffic reports interesting?" That means somebody prominent got picked up for DUI or had a fender bender with a pretty passenger in the car who wasn't his wife. If Coy-the-Cop asks me how I got onto the story, I'd never quote the secretary. I'd tell him I caught it when I checked the accident reports.. It's not really lying.

But this situation was touchy. I couldn't simply call the Grantham Mental Health Center's public information officer and say casually, "Oh, by the way. Have you had any suspicious deaths out there this morning? Anybody who might have held me hostage yesterday?"

Heck, I didn't even know the name of the public information officer at the Grantham Mental Health Center. And who was the director out there? It wasn't on my beat. I'd only been in the place a few times, when I was doing a story on the use of insanity as a defense in murder trials. I'd talked to some psychiatrist in the administrative section.

A little time spent finding out a few things now might save time later.

I jumped out of the car, searching my purse for the electronic card that opened the *Gazette*'s back door. The security guard is on duty only at the front door. He'd see me come in on the closed-circuit TV.

I'd better call the health reporter, Mitzi Johns, and get some names. And I'd better check out whether there had been any scanner traffic on Bo's death.

Flipping lights on as I went, I headed upstairs to my desk and looked up the employee phone list on the computer. Luckily, Mitzi was home.

"Mitzi, who's PIO out at Grantham Mental Health Center?"

"Rayette Lund. Her title's 'Public Information Specialist.' Why?"

"They've had an unexplained death out there. Who's the director?"

"Dr. Randall Wade. But he's 'president.' Do I need to come in?"

"I think it's purely police. But thanks."

"Call me if it needs a health angle."

Then I checked the list to see which photographer was on call that morning. Bear Bennington. Good. He answered on the second ring. No, he said, he'd heard nothing on the scanner about a suspicious death anywhere in town. And he'd heard no traffic involving the mental health center.

"Only odd thing this morning was a report that somebody stole a Salvation Army uniform," he said.

"Of course, I might have missed something." Scanners pick up all kinds of emergency agencies—sheriff's office, ambulances, civil defense, as well as police. There's continuous talk on them, and most of all it's along the line of "I'm 10-45 at Denny's," which means taking a coffee break, or, "There's a flat cat in the 900 block of Main" which means the dispatcher should call the animal control officers. It's easy to lose something important in the scanner trivia.

"Should I get out there?" Bear asked.

"Not yet. I'll call if there's a chance of a shot."

With my ducks in a somewhat ragged row, I headed for the Grantham Mental Health Center.

The center has gorgeous grounds, with oaks, pines, and rolling meadows. Actually, the grounds are not that big, but the center got a grant for landscaping. The main building itself, about ten years old, sprawls like an octopus. Each of the center's different functions—child counseling, outpatient drug treatment, alcoholism treatment—seems to have its own wing.

Only one section of the center has a second floor. The ward set aside for potentially violent patients—those who might do harm to themselves or others—is on top of one of the back sections. The approaches to it are not exactly guarded—they're just not convenient for the general public.

The administrative section was locked, so I went around to the high-security wing. The PD's mobile lab was parked outside. I flashed my press card at a uniformed guard inside a heavy glass door. He punched a button, then opened the door a crack.

"Nell Matthews. *Grantham Gazette*," I told him.

"Your front door is locked up tight. Is Rayette Lund around here?"

The guard turned and looked behind him, and I took the opportunity to push the door a little farther open and to slip inside. I looked in the direction the guard was looking.

"Miss Lund!" he called.

A woman and four men stood in a clump at the other end of a reception area. Three of them—the woman and two of the men—wore business suits. The third man looked as if the emergency had pulled him off the golf course. The fourth guy wore a navy blue uniform. That was Mike.

The woman turned, frowning, and one of the suits, Detective Captain Jim Hammond, rolled his eyes in annoyance. "Nell! How did the press get hold of this?"

"Well, hi, there, Captain Hammond." I tried to sound innocent. "I got a tip that there was some excitement out here. I'd say your presence confirms it."

Hammond shook his head. Mike looked like thunder. The woman—a very attractive black woman wearing a red power suit—looked stricken, and the other two men glared. One was a detective, young and so short he would have barely passed the PD physical. I try to know all the detectives, but I hadn't worked with this guy, and I couldn't remember his name.

The fellow in his golf togs was one of those who had gotten bald on top, so he shaved the sides off, too. His face looked as sour as a green persimmon. He turned to Hammond. "Captain, surely you won't allow publicity about this!"

Hammond's eyes narrowed. "Sorry, Dr. Wade. This is a free country, and I have very little control over what Miss Matthews's paper, or any other news media, puts out. And, considering the person involved, I think you can get set for some major attention. Like it or not."

"But—but—" Wade sputtered. "We need to make our own inquiry. We don't know what happened yet."

"Then don't say anything," Hammond said. He continued to glare at me.

I tried to look serious. "I gather it's true, Captain. Bo Jenkins is dead?"

Hammond punched a finger in my direction. "Nell, how did you hear about this?"

This was the key moment. I could see Mike opening his mouth. He still looked like thunder—and the bolts were aimed in my direction. I had to say something quick.

"Aw, com'on, Captain," I said. "You know I've got to protect my sources." I held my hands out in front of me, wrists side-by-side. "So lock me up."

I was looking at Hammond, but Mike was right behind him, and, of course, I was more interested in Mike's reaction.

Mike laughed. That seemed to ease the tension, at least for Hammond. The detective gestured at a plastic chair in the small waiting area. "Nell, it's going to be a couple of hours before I have anything for you."

"Sure," I said. I parked my fanny in the chair he'd indicated, clutched my notebook, and tried to look bright-eyed. "Have you told the family yet?"

"No! And you're not going to tell 'em, either!"

"No way! That's your job, Captain. I wouldn't go

near them. Until after they've been informed. I may not be perfect, but I'm not Channel Four." Channel Four is Grantham's sleaze channel, the one that specializes in dead bodies and gory scenes and relatives in hysterics.

Hammond turned to Dr. Wade and jerked his head toward a locked door at the back of the reception area. Wade looked at Rayette Lund and jerked his head in my direction. The guard pushed the proper buttons, and the four men went into the high-security unit. Rayette Lund obeyed her boss's pantomimed instructions and came over to me. She straightened her red jacket and stood erect, but I could see she was upset.

I smiled brightly at her. It's important to have the public information officer as an ally. That's one reason I try to be nice to Coy-the-Cop. I extended my hand. "I'm Nell Matthews, Rayette. Mitzi Johns says you're terrific to work with. Very professional."

"Well, I try. But this situation—" She shook my hand, and I could feel her hand trembling. I decided she was younger than I am. I'm twenty-eight. I guessed her at twenty-four. This was probably her first job out of college. Her duties, if this was a typical public-information slot, would involve putting out a newsletter for the employees and sending out news releases when Wade and the other top staffers gave speeches. Wade had probably hired her because she was inexperienced, and therefore cheap. I felt sure Rayette had never been forced to deal with a suspicious death before.

She definitely hadn't handled one that was going to get regional, maybe national, attention.

Public agencies like the Grantham Mental Health

Center are answerable to the press, because we represent the public. But they often want us to tell the good stuff, to support their fund drives or expansion plans or special events. They don't want mishaps and mistakes and misuse of public funds mentioned.

Rayette was trying to act her part. "I don't know what's going on with the police investigation, but at least I can offer you some coffee. In the break room, down the hall."

"Thanks, but I'd rather stay here, just in case Captain Hammond decides to make a statement." I tried to give her a reassuring smile. "I know this is really hard for you. I mean, things happen! And the bosses in agencies like this one rarely understand how important it is to deal frankly with the public."

"Oh, Dr. Wade is wonderful with the public. It's just that—well, they discovered Mr. Jenkins' body only a short time ago. Nobody understands just what did happen."

"I know you had him under a suicide watch. Just what does that entail?"

She relaxed slightly. A factual question. One she could answer. "Under a suicide watch, the attendant is in constant visual contact with the client. The client is not allowed anything potentially harmful, of course. His belt, shoelaces, and other things are taken away."

"No knives, guns, or explosives. Was Bo restrained?"

"Oh, no. They would be very hesitant to use a straitjacket or anything like that. But he was in an actual padded room. No sharp corners. The room has a big window, so the client is visible from a central area."

"How about access to the client? Who can talk to him?"

"Oh, that's limited, too. Normally, no one would be allowed in." Rayette tensed up again, and her hand began to tremble once more.

Ah, ha! She had put just enough extra emphasis on the word "normally" for me to figure it out. Someone had gotten in to Bo from outside.

"That's interesting," I said. "I'd expect that there would be people—family, friends—who could soothe a potentially violent patient."

"Possibly." Rayette stirred in her seat and looked at the door to the secure section. "But the doctors have to evaluate just who would be helpful and who would not. Of course, they hadn't had time to decide that in the case of Bo Jenkins."

I nodded. "So it's not like the movies, where they call in the patient's mother or the family priest."

Rayette winced and jumped to her feet. "I'd better check on some things," she said. "You're sure you don't want some coffee?"

"No, thanks. But I appreciate your giving me this background."

Rayette looked more panicky than ever. "Please don't quote me! I'd much rather your information came from Dr. Wade."

I smiled my reassuring smile. "Oh, yes. I'll talk to him. But this background will help me ask the right questions."

She went away, down a hall I thought must lead to the main administration wing. I thought about what she had said and how she had acted. She'd been doing pretty well. Then she'd panicked when I mentioned the family of the patient. Did that mean someone from Bo's family had gotten in to see him?

But our interviews yesterday had established that Bo had no family in the Grantham area. Except Julie, his ex-wife. And little Billy, whom he had held hostage. I couldn't believe Julie had come to see him. Or that the dumbest attendant would have let her in.

Just exactly what had I said to Rayette? Something about "his mother or the family priest." Well, Bo hadn't belonged to a church, either. Of course, J.B. had done that interview with the director of the Salvation Army Shelter, the shelter where Bo had been staying.

Wahoo! The lightbulb in my brain lit up. The Salvation Army is a social service agency, but it's also a church. And it's a church with clergy who wear distinctive garb. And Bear had heard on the scanner that a Salvation Army officer's uniform had been stolen that very morning. Bingo!

I stood up and walked over to the guard on duty, trying to keep from jumping up and down in excitement. "Is there a pay phone around here?"

"Down the hall." He pointed in the direction Rayette had taken. "But you can call out on this one."

"Thanks, but a pay phone's fine." And, I hoped, more private.

The phone was nearly to the main lobby. I could see both ways, so nobody could sneak up on me. I looked Bear Bennington's number up and dialed it.

"Bear here."

I cupped my hand around the receiver. "Bear, this is Nell. Did you tell me that the director of the Salvation Army shelter reported his uniform stolen?"

"Yeah. But it wasn't the director. Just one of the

officers. But it's weird. Who would want a Salvation Army uniform?"

"Maybe a murderer," I said. I thought about what to do next.

"Do you need me?" Bear's voice was curious.

"Get hold of Chuck." I said. Our Grantham State part-timer would be covering nightside police on a Sunday afternoon. "I'm at a pay phone, and I don't have a phone list."

"Sure. What do you want him to do?"

"Tell him to get out here to the Grantham Mental Health Center. In about an hour they should have a statement."

"What happened?"

"Bo Jenkins is dead. In the high-security unit. And as near as I can tell, the cops don't think it was suicide."

Bear whistled. "Wow! And where are you going to be?"

"I'm heading for the Salvation Army. Bear, maybe you'd better meet me there. There could be a photo in it. But get Chuck out here first."

I smiled at the security guard as I asked him to let me out the door. "Gotta check on something," I said. "Another reporter will fill in for me in a few minutes."

Something was tickling at the back of my mind, and I swung by the *Gazette* office. I hurried in through the electronic door and up the back stairway, turning on lights again. I went to the computer and made a quick access to the *Gazette* library—when it computerized, it lost its old-time nickname. Our newspaper no longer has a "morgue."

I pulled up stories on the Salvation Army shelter

for the current year. Ha. I found it. Mitzi had written a story. She handled nonprofit organizations, as well as health.

The shelter had had a mini-scandal six months earlier. A young guy had complained that an older man had made improper advances to him. In the end, the police had concluded that the young guy's story wasn't very credible. Coy-the-Cop was quoted as saying no charges would be recommended to the DA.

But the Grantham Salvation Army commander, Major Harold Smith, had announced a new policy. From that time on, not only would there be a professional shelter director, who was a social worker, on duty, but also the male Salvation Army officers assigned to Grantham would take turns spending the night at the shelter.

"We not only want to avoid evil, we want to avoid the appearance of evil," the major was quoted as saying. He was prepared to take his turn sleeping at the shelter, alternating with his three junior officers, he said.

So, I deduced as I closed out the library files, any reader of the *Grantham Gazette* could have known that a Salvation Army officer routinely slept in the shelter and might logically assume that he took his uniform off when he climbed into bed. I turned out the lights and left the *Gazette* building.

The Salvation Army shelter was near Grantham's downtown, in a down-and-out area where the people who need such a shelter would find it handy. It had a section for families, but the largest building was set aside for single men. Bear Bennington was pacing up and down on the sidewalk in front. He looked as cuddly as usual, plump and cheerful. His nickname refers to "Pooh Bear." Or maybe Teddy.

Inside, a shaky looking older man was sitting at a desk. I knew the Salvation Army, bless 'em, hires its own clients for simple jobs. This man was perfectly sober, but he had the look of a person who's spent a long time drunk.

"Hi," I said. "Sure is a beautiful day. We're from the *Gazette*. Is the director around? Mr. Cunningham?" I had made a note of the shelter director's name while I was in the files.

"Naw, he's off this weekend."

"Hmmm. Are you in charge?"

"Naw. Captain Eisner is. Want to speak to 'im?"

I nodded, and he paged the officer.

"Is Captain Eisner the one whose uniform disappeared?" I asked.

The receptionist nodded and grinned. "He was pretty hot about it. Especially when they found the open window."

I widened my eyes. "They think somebody broke in?"

"Naw. Out."

A door opened, and a young man poked his head around the edge. "Did you page me?"

The old guy on the desk pointed at Bear and me. "Newspaper."

"Captain Eisner?" I walked over and stuck out a hand in a shaking position. "Nell Matthews, from the *Gazette*. We never ever heard of anybody stealing a Salvation Army uniform before! This may make the national wire. This is Bear Bennington, our photographer. Can we talk to you about it?"

Eisner was a big man, maybe thirty. He had a

block-shaped, German head and extremely blue eyes. He looked as if he could toss out an unruly shelter resident without breaking into a sweat. But his handshake was gentle, as if he'd learned to control his strength.

He was wearing khaki slacks and a light blue shirt. He smiled ruefully. "I talked to the police. The whole thing is ridiculous. I feel like a complete fool. I hate the thought of publicity about it."

I nodded sympathetically. "I understand, but you all do such wonderful work here. Maybe this is an opportunity to let the public know a little more about it." God, I can be sickeningly sweet when I try. And I'd just committed myself to writing something about the Salvation Army shelter. Which wasn't even on my beat.

Oh, well. Anything for a story.

Eisner thawed a bit more and opened the door so that Bear and I could go inside.

I grinned at him. "I take it you weren't wearing the uniform when it was stolen."

He laughed. "No, but it's nearly that embarrassing. It was hung across a chair by my bed. Somebody came by and took it."

"Was your door locked?"

"There wasn't any door. I was sleeping out in the dorm with the men."

"You mean that the commander is requiring that you officers take turns spending the night here, and you don't even get a private room?"

Eisner looked embarrassed. "That's part of the deal. We're supposed to be in with the people we serve. Of course, Elwood Cunningham, the shelter director, has a private apartment. He lives here. But the rest of us—well, we're supposed to mix with the men. Eat dinner with them. Shoot a little pool or play Ping-Pong. Watch a movie or catch a TV show. Lights out at midnight."

"That's wonderful!" I had no trouble sounding enthusiastic. The social worker who feels superior to the people he's trying to help gives me a large pain.

"Actually, what we do here is nothing special. That informal contact—well, lots of times the men respond to that when they won't go near a worship service or a counseling session." Eisner stared at the floor, looking almost ashamed, and shrugged. "That's the reason we signed up with the Salvation Army."

"Can we see the dorm?"

"Oh, yes. It's empty now. Everybody has to get up at seven. The men can stay here free, but they have to help with the chores the next morning. They have to leave by ten."

"Then people don't stay here during the day?"

"No, we can't allow that. They can't just camp here. We're open on a first-come, first-serve basis beginning at five P.M. every day."

Eisner led us through a large dining room, with maybe a dozen tables seating eight each, and down a hall. Large dorm rooms opened off each side. Each held fifteen or twenty narrow beds, lined up like an old-fashioned military barracks. He showed us the bed he had occupied, and Bear took his picture pointing to the empty spot where his uniform had been.

"My wife had to bring me some clothes this morning," he said. "My other uniform is at the cleaners, so I'll have to wear civvies until tomorrow."

"I understand that a window was open this morning."

Eisner nodded. "Yes. A window off the dining room. The guy apparently got out that way."

"So you had a missing occupant this morning."

He nodded again.

"So the police have a definite suspect?"

Another nod. Eisner was looking at the floor again. "I shouldn't have let him in in the first place. I'll probably hear about it from Major." He looked up. "Major Smith, our commander."

I nodded encouragingly, and he went on.

"See, the shelter director was off last night. I was in charge. We usually don't let anybody in after eight p.m. But this guy pounded on the door just before midnight. Said he'd just gotten in town, didn't have money for a motel. He was hitchhiking. Needed a place where he could take a shower, because he'd been promised a job today, and he wanted to show up looking nice."

"A good story."

"I bought it. And we had the room. So I let him in. But he was the one missing this morning."

"Who was he? I'm sure he gave you a name."

Eisner stared at the floor again. "I didn't pay much attention to it last night, you know. There were more than sixty men here."

"But the name would be a real lead. What was it?"

"The police laughed," he said. "Maybe someday I'll be able to. The final name on the register is 'Jesse James.'"

CHAPTER 9

I didn't laugh. The "Jesse James" might have been funny if the interloper had been a college kid playing a prank. But someone who took a Salvation Army uniform to use as an entree to a secure mental health facility so he could commit murder—it didn't strike me as too amusing.

I asked a few more questions. "Jesse James" had been male, caucasian, maybe around forty or fifty, Captain Eisner said. A thin sort, fairly tall, his brown or black hair combed back slickly. Dirty shirt, wrinkled pants that drooped. Grimy nails. Smelled a little beery, but not drunk. Looked as if he'd hitchhiked clear across the country looking for a job, which was the story he'd told Eisner.

Would Eisner recognize him again? The Salvation Army officer grimaced. "Maybe," he said. "Maybe. If I saw the tattoo."

"Tattoo? Where? What did it look like."

"It was on his arm. Right arm. No, on the left. A dragon. And he had the initials 'J.J.' on the two middle fingers of his left hand."

That seemed to be the end of Captain Eisner's knowledge of the affair of the missing uniform. The police hadn't talked to him about the link with Bo

Jenkins's death, and I didn't enlighten him. They hadn't yet checked for fingerprints either, but I had a feeling they wouldn't find any.

Bear and I were driving off in our respective vehicles when Captain Hammond pulled in. I waved. He shook his fist at me. I stopped, and we each rolled down a window.

Hammond glared. "Did that dumb PIO girl tell you to come here?"

"Absolutely not, Captain. And she didn't strike me as dumb. Inexperienced, maybe."

"Then how did you—"

"Hey! Give me a little credit for deductive ability! I knew Bo had been staying at the Salvation Army shelter. And I knew—because it was on the scanner—that a uniform had been stolen here. You were all so antsy I figured it was a possibility that somebody got into that closed unit. The only person I could imagine doing that was a family member—not a strong possibility with Bo—or a minister. And who'd suspect the Salvation Army? Don't worry, I didn't tell the guy here about Bo's death."

Hammond rolled his eyes. "We're gonna issue a statement at three P.M. at Central Station, and you're not getting any information until then," he said. He gestured with his thumb. "Hit the road."

I grinned at him. "Yes, sir, Captain Hammond. Sir."

He shook his head, but he grinned back. Hammond and I spar around, but we respect each other.

I drove on, suddenly aware that a glass of orange juice, half a piece of toast, an interrupted necking session, and a dose of adrenaline don't make a very big breakfast. I was starving. But there was plenty of time for lunch before the briefing. I wondered if Mike was getting any. Lunch.

I pulled into a handy MacDonald's, bought a quarter-pounder with cheese and organized my notes while I ate it. I wanted to be prepared for the press briefing. The session on Bo's death obviously was going to cancel the meeting Mike and I were supposed to have with the national television. I decided to go back to the office and write up what I'd found out from Captain Eisner. Then I'd be set for the briefing at three.

The infrequent press briefings of the Grantham Police Department are held in a room designed for departmental meetings. It has an overhead projector, a videotape player, and a fairly sophisticated hookup for sound recording. Compared to the layouts in Washington, New York or L.A.—the stuff you see on national television—it's pretty informal.

Coy-the-Cop set up the room after Guy Unitas had left the job as public information officer and Coy stepped in. As one of Irish Svenson's protegés, Coy had held a variety of jobs in his law enforcement career—patrolman, of course, and then detective. He'd been in traffic control for a while. At one time he had worked vice, and he was supposed to have been the best undercover cop the Grantham PD had ever had, according to Guy. He had been a captain and supposedly in line to become one of the three division commanders when Guy suddenly left and Irish Svenson plunked Coy into the PIO slot, with an office right nextdoor to his own. After Wolf Jameson took over as chief, he reappointed Coy PIO, and the new chief relied on him even more than Irish had—

or so I heard. This put Coy in a unique position to influence not only the news that came out of the GPD, but also the policies which made the news.

Coy and I bumped heads on a regular basis, but I respected him. He had a very good grasp of just what a PIO's function should be, at least from a reporter's viewpoint. He answered phone calls promptly, he provided the facts, and he didn't play favorites among the reporters and the news media.

And he kept himself in the background.

If there's anybody a reporter hates, it's a guy who's not in authority, but who acts as if he is. Coy never fell into this trap. He rarely appeared on camera. Instead, he trotted out a department head or detective to speak. Of course, Coy coached the spokesman thoroughly. But at least we could speak to the real source, which pleased the press. This also kept Coy's fellow police officers happy, since they're human and like seeing their names in the paper as much as any society matron likes seeing her's there.

Chuck had come in to work, and he and I both went over the press briefing. Bear took a spot along the sidelines, where he could shoot some pictures. Ace Anderson, the Associated Press jerk, sat down beside me. There was going to be plenty of copy to go around on this one. We wouldn't be fighting over who got to write it up. And this briefing was bound to be an odd deal.

In journalism school they tell about the young reporter who was sent to cover a wedding, but came back and told his editor there was no story. "The groom didn't show up," he said.

The people at the press briefing essentially were in that position. They'd come to cover one story, but wound up covering another. As I looked around the briefing I saw a bunch of strange faces among the familiar Grantham news crews. These faces belonged to out-of-town reporters, mostly television, who had come to attend the press conference Coy had called Mike about the previous evening. They had come prepared to get sound bites on the hostage situation of the day before. "Just how does it feel to have a loaded gun pointed at your right eye by a madman, Ms. Matthews?" "What emotions swept over you, Officer Svenson, when you realized Ms. Matthews had blundered onto the scene and become Mr. Jenkins's second hostage?"

But the death of Bo Jenkins had relegated that story to page 2D, to the bottom of the telecast. The new news was Bo's death. Rumors of his death had already reached the press—not through me. TV guys know cops, too.

Behind us, Chuck and I could hear fluffy-haired women and men wearing pancake makeup rapidly reformulating questions. To my delight, all the questions I could overhear were coming from the angle that Bo's death was suicide.

Chuck and I exchanged deadpan glances. Our scoop on "Jesse James" and the possibility of murder was intact, so far. Of course, it wouldn't stay that way. I can pat my own back without dislocating my elbow, so I told myself that I had accomplished a slick piece of reporting by linking up the Salvation Army with Bo's death. But Hammond was bound to reveal enough information at the briefing to allow the TV crews to understand the situation in time for their evening newscasts. My "scoop" wasn't going to gain me a beat on the television. They'd be on the air at six P.M. that night, and we wouldn't have a paper out until the state edition at ten P.M.

Hammond came in then and went to the mike. Coy, Mike, and several others stood to one side of the platform. Mike looked the room over, scanning the twenty-five or so reporters and photographers who were there. His eyes stopped moving when he got to me, and he gave me a long look. Several of my internal organs went into spasms.

"What are you grinning about?" Ace asked.

I ducked my head and got my ballpoint out of my purse. "Quiet. Hammond's going to start."

Hammond confirmed the rumor that Bo had been found dead in Grantham Mental Health Center, then gave a very general sketch of the death scene. Bo had been in a high-security cell, he had been under a suicide watch, and the cause of death was as yet unknown. Commander Coy Blakely, the Grantham Police Department's public information officer, was handing out copies of the Grantham Mental Health Center's guidelines on staff procedures for a suicide watch. The department would investigate the death thoroughly, as would the center, but right now they had no cause of death and refused to speculate on just what had happened. Then the questions began.

"Was there any sign of injury?"

No. No bleeding. No bruising. No broken bones.

"Do you think Jenkins committed suicide?"

Considering that he was publicly threatening suicide yesterday, it would seem to be a possibility.

"How?"

We don't know.

"Do you think it could have been natural causes? A heart attack, maybe?"

That's possible, of course. We don't know.

It went on and on. Chuck and I sat silently. I listened with half an ear, glancing over the suicide-watch guidelines. Finally, I held up my hand, and Hammond looked in my direction. "Nell."

I might not be able to get my story into print before the TV could get it on the air, but I couldn't resist showing off. "Are you going to release an artist's rendering of your suspect?"

Hammond sighed deeply. "Yes, Nell, we'll have it in about an hour. But suspect is too strong a word."

"Witness?"

"Witness is better."

The assembled crowd murmured a little, and I admit Ace-the-Ass was the fastest on the uptake. He even jumped to his feet.

"Witness? What witness? Captain Hammond, are you saying someone saw Bo die?"

"No, we know that this person was not present at that time. Bo died after he left."

"After he left?" Ace thought ponderously. "Is this witness a member of the mental health center's staff?"

Hammond shook his head. By now the room was buzzing. "Nell jumped way ahead of me, Ace. Let's back up." He waited until the noise level dropped.

"Around six A.M. this morning, a person—the witness we're looking for—brought a toothbrush, underwear, and several other personal items to Bo Jenkins. The items were examined by the mental health center staff member on duty, and they appeared to be perfectly harmless. The person was allowed to speak to Bo—but only with the staff member present. One or two of the items were given to Bo.

"We have no evidence that this person did anything which contributed to Jenkins's death. But we don't know who he was, and we'd like to talk to him." He gestured toward Coy. "Commander Blakely will hand out a description, and I'd appreciate all of you helping to publicize it. As I said, the artist's version will be ready in about an hour. The sketch artist is talking to the people who saw this witness now."

The room buzzed some more, and again Ace stood up. "Are you saying someone may have murdered Bo?"

"I'm saying we haven't ruled out any possibility," Hammond said. "We don't know a cause of death yet. We don't know all the circumstances, so it could be homicide, suicide, or natural causes."

He gave a description of the missing "witness." It was almost word-for-word what the Salvation Army captain had told me, so I figured he hadn't gotten a very clear report from the mental health center staff member. It boiled down to a thin man, fiftyish, sort of tall, with dark hair. There are plenty around like that. Looking around the room I spotted a half dozen. Even Ace looked like that, though I'd never noticed that he had tattoos. Of course, every junior high kid knows about temporary tattoos. And writing initials on your fingers with ink.

Hammond did mention the Salvation Army uniform, and that caused some more excitement among the press.

"We have definitely—I repeat, definitely—established that no officer assigned to the Grantham Salvation Army unit is concerned in this matter," Hammond said. "That's firm. No Salvation Army officer is a susp—a witness."

And that ended the briefing. J.B. hung around to get the artist's drawing. Mike was surrounded by fellow officers. We exchanged a long look, but there was no way we could talk there. I headed for the office.

Ace Anderson followed me down the terraced front steps of the Central Station. "Nell, who told you that somebody got in to see Bo?"

I kept walking. "Nobody, Ace."

"Then how'd you know?"

"I figured it out, Ace. I'm sure the city ed will send my story to the AP as soon our state edition is off the press. Then you can read it." I walked on.

It makes me feel good to score that jerk off. He is the lamest excuse for a newsman who ever sat down at a VDT.

The AP generally has pretty good reporters, though they're handicapped by the general assignment way they're often forced to work. Or at least I think it works better if a reporter is assigned to a beat—city hall, education, health, or even violence. Then we can really get to know the background, the personalities, the ins and outs of our subject. But a local AP bureau, like Grantham's, doesn't have enough staff to do that. They only have four or five full-time reporters. So each reporter covers what's happening day by day—weather one day, a bank robbery the next, a strike the day after. It means they're always walking in on the middle of the story. The big, national AP offices have reporters assigned to specific beats. But a city the size of Grantham is barely big enough to have a bureau. A few reporters have to do it all, covering a third of the state.

Most AP reporters are highly professional. But the system allows a few showoffs like Ace-the-Ass to keep their jobs by snowing the bosses. They cover one story for a few days, and before they've written enough to reveal their complete ignorance of the whole topic, they're off to a new assignment. It may be years before anybody in authority notices they can't report a darn thing.

I put Ace out of my mind and went back to the *Gazette* office to turn out my own story. I was home in time to watch the six o'clock news on Channel Four, cursing them for stealing my scoop and for embellishing it with a pious little moral at the end. "Until the truth about Bo Jenkins's death is known, the Grantham Mental Health Center and the Grantham Police Department will be under the eye of public opinion."

That's the kind of thing my grandmother always called "cornball." And it's also an editorial comment. And it's unprofessional. The facts ought to speak for themselves in a hard news story. "As long as television personalities sum up every report with a little editorial, they will be considered the news equivalent of an emetic," I said aloud.

After I'd tortured myself with the television news, I ate a handful of cheese crackers and walked around the house, feeling uneasy. I didn't understand just what was worrying me. About seven o'clock, the phone rang, and I nearly jumped out of my skin.

It's Mike, I thought.

It wasn't Mike. Just Martha's mother, and Martha

wasn't home. But my reaction told me why I was uneasy. I had been waiting for Mike to call.

And now I realized something so important I said it out loud. "Hell's bells," I said, "he didn't even ask for my phone number."

And my phone number was unlisted. He wasn't going to call.

I stalked into the living room, where Rocky was watching a movie, and angrily fell into an easy chair. It's hard to kick yourself when you're all sprawled out, but I managed it.

Idiot, I told myself. You're just another pickup to Mike Svenson.

Well, that's what you wanted, myself answered. No strings. I remember you thinking that.

Yes, I snarled. But I wanted to suggest it myself. Idiot. I should have guessed Mike's modus operandi by how good he is at sex.

Calm down, dear, myself answered. Men who pick women up and drop them may get a lot of practice at sex, but they're exploitive. They don't offer quality performances—the kind that satisfy both parties. Mike makes love as if he cares about his partner. He said he didn't pick girls up in bars. I believe him.

Then you're a fool, I answered. He may not pick girls up in bars, but how about at parties, at swimming pools, in blankety-blank libraries? He's probably spending the evening calling his friends to brag that the *Gazette* reporter, the one who won't date cops, practically dragged him into bed.

Well, dearie, if you're so eager to talk, why don't you call him?

No, I pouted. I want him to call me.

But, sugarbabe, you just pointed out that he doesn't have your number.

I rolled that around in my imagination for a while, then went into the kitchen and got out the phone book. Grantham does not have a large Scandinavian population. There were only a half dozen Svensons in the residential section, and two of the listings were Mike's mom. She'd somehow gotten her real estate office in the residential listings. I eliminated the other listings pretty quick, too. None of them were on Mike's street, or even in his neighborhood.

Mike had an unlisted number, too.

If he were simply a news source, I'd call the central police dispatcher and ask him or her to have Mike call me. I thought about it. I could do that—I could pretend I was working on a story. No. I stuffed the phone book back on the kitchen shelf angrily. If word got around the PD that I was ga-ga over Mike, so be it. But I didn't want to let the word out myself.

I would not call him! I practically pounded my fist on the kitchen cabinet. Then I went back into the living room and threw myself down in the easy chair again. I would not chase him, I told myself. If it was a one-night stand, it was a one-night stand. I can accept the fact that I've been a slut. The night before I had been high on euphoria—and maybe gratitude. The guy had saved my life. He took advantage of a case of temporary insanity. If I killed him, it'd be justifiable homi—

A bowl of crackers was suddenly thrust under my nose. "Here," Rocky said. "If you're going to gnash your teeth, put something between them. And don't panic, sweetie. He'll call."

I was not amused. Sometimes I don't want to be

understood. I glared at Rocky. "I'm going to take a shower," I said. I would wash any trace of Mike's soap off my body, wash any lint from his robe out of my navel.

I was halfway up the stairs when the doorbell rang. I turned around, but Rocky already had his hand on the knob.

"Jamie said he might drop by," he told me.

I started back up the stairs as Rocky clicked the dead bolt back. "Oh, hello," he said. I knew that voice. It meant a good-looking guy was at the door. Must be Jamie.

"Sorry," a voice answered, "I must have the wrong address."

"Mike!" I whirled around and yelped his name out like a high schooler who was desperate for a date to the homecoming dance. Then I took a deep breath and tried to walk calmly down the stairs.

"Hi," I said. "Come on in."

Mike came in, but he looked dubiously at Rocky, who was beaming at us. I introduced them.

Rocky went into his host mode. "Have you kiddos had dinner?"

"Well, no," Mike said. "I'd said something to Nell about going out—"

I shook my head. "I can't do that—"

"Don't want to be seen in public with me, huh?"

"Mike—!"

Rocky gestured. "Children, don't quarrel! Go in the living room, and I'll call you when supper is ready."

Mike still looked dubious, but I laughed. "That's the best offer we're going to get, Mike." I led him into the living room and turned off the television set.

Mike leaned over and muttered in my ear, "Who's this guy?"

"Mickey didn't report on him?"

"I don't talk to Mickey all that much."

"Rocky is my landlord," I answered. "He has the downstairs bedroom and bath, and three of us have an all-girl upstairs. All four of us share the living room and kitchen."

"Oh." Mike was still frowning.

"It was an all-girl house originally. Then one got married, and we were looking for a fourth. Rocky was a waiter in a restaurant where we ate a lot. We knew him pretty well, and I guess we felt a little sorry for him. He wanted a place in this neighborhood, because his longtime housemate had entered the AIDS hostel two streets over."

Mike hissed at me. "This guy has AIDS?"

I could hear Rocky's Cuizinart begin to buzz. "Actually, Rocky's been tested and he's not HIV-positive. But it wouldn't matter much. None of us uses his toothbrush. Or anything."

Mike frowned.

"When Rocky's housemate died, he left his estate to Rocky. His family threatened to sue, so Rocky immediately put everything into heavily mortgaged real estate, figuring that would keep them from pushing too hard. He bought this house, and he bought into the Blue Flamingo on Parker Street."

"The Flamingo? Oh."

The Blue Flamingo, of course, is a gay bar. It's the most respectable gay bar Grantham has, or so I'm told by the vice cops. No loud music, no naked dancers, no sex at the tables. I'd checked Rocky out before

Martha, Brenda, and I let him move in, and I checked the Flamingo out when he bought into it.

Mike was still frowning slightly as Rocky came in with two glasses of white wine. "I'm fixing carbonara," he said. "I had to open a bottle of wine for the fourth of a cup that goes in it. You two might as well drink up the rest."

"We get this treatment from our landlord only on Sunday and Monday nights," I told Mike. "He tends bar at the Flamingo every other evening."

"Spaghetti à la carbonara in fifteen minutes," Rocky said. He went back into the kitchen.

Mike and I sipped wine, and a long silence fell.

"I had a hard time finding you," Mike said.

"It occurred to me tonight that you didn't have my number, and you didn't know how it was listed."

"I ran out to the car to ask for it, but I lost my nerve, in front of Mickey."

"That would have been a little embarrassing. I mean, I'm a liberated woman and all. I don't care much what people think of me." I couldn't believe I was saying that, after the teeth-gnashing that had been going on ten minutes earlier. "But I don't much like people knowing my business, either." I sipped again. "I did try to call you, but you're not in the book either. How'd you find me?"

"I went by the station and ran a records check on your driver's license. You don't make things easy. Did you know this state believes your first name is Mary?"

"Mary Nell. That's the name my mother picked out for me."

"And when you got that license, you had a different street address."

"Shelter Hills Apartments. Martha and I lived there three months. Before we found this place. But how'd you find out where I'd moved? The post office—"

"I wouldn't be able to get anything from the post office. I checked the city directory from last year and found Martha Henry and you listed at the same apartment in Shelter Hills. In the new book she's listed at this address. And luckily, you're still roommates."

I laughed. "Why didn't you call the *Gazette* office? They won't give our numbers, but they'd call me and tell me to call you."

"I wasn't sure you wanted me to do that."

I sipped my wine and looked away. Time to change the subject. "How's the case going?" I asked.

"Don't you know? You got way ahead there for a while."

"Just a fluke. Who killed Bo?"

"Maybe nobody. We won't know a cause of death until noon tomorrow. Maybe not for a couple of weeks."

"Lashing Jack Sheridan refused to give up his weekend to do the autopsy, huh?"

Mike laughed. "That's about it. I guess all doctors are arrogant, and pathologists take it to the nth degree. Of course, I don't really know anything. I was called in this morning only because I'd talked to Bo a long time yesterday. I'm not part of the investigation."

"Officially."

"At all." His voice sounded firm. "Hammond got enough heat when I worked on the Coffee Cup case. I'm not doing that again while I'm a patrolman."

"So you're not going to tell me anything about the case."

"I don't know anything to tell."

"Did the guy in the Salvation Army uniform give Bo anything to eat? It sounds as if he might have been poisoned."

Mike looked at his wineglass very casually. "I really couldn't say."

Ha. He'd evaded my question. The Salvation Army imposter really had given Bo something to eat.

Mike spoke again. "Or it could be Bo just keeled over with a heart attack. Or a stroke. But it's my turn to ask you something. How did your interview with the detectives go?"

"You were there for it. All I got out of Hammond was the press briefing."

"I don't mean your interview of him. I mean his interview of you."

I must have looked completely blank, because Mike spoke again.

"You're a witness, too, besides being a reporter. Didn't Hammond ask you about Bo?"

"About Bo?"

"Yeah. About what Bo said to you Saturday. You know, at the end. When he grabbed you as all the guys ran in."

"Oh. No, Hammond didn't ask about that. I'd forgotten it completely. I guess Hammond has, too."

Mike sipped his wine. "Well, he shouldn't forget. I'll remind him. Tactfully. What did Bo say, anyway?"

"Oh, just some sort of drivel. It didn't make sense. He claimed somebody was covering something up."

"Do you remember it exactly? Hammond will want to know."

I thought about it. "Well, at first I couldn't understand just what Bo was trying to tell me. Then he got real close to my ear, and he said, 'They killed'—somebody. Oh, I remember. He said, 'They killed Eric. They made me cover it up.' "

The effect of this on Mike was electrifying. He sat on the couch, completely immobile, with his wineglass halfway to his mouth. He looked as if he'd been turned into a redheaded fence post.

His reaction frightened me. I put my hand on his knee. "Mike! What's wrong?"

He put the wineglass down, then grabbed me by both arms and whispered urgently.

"Don't tell Hammond that! Don't tell anybody that! Whatever you do, don't tell anybody what Bo said!"

CHAPTER 10

I was amazed beyond words. One minute Mike had been urging me to tell Hammond all. The next he was ordering me, pleading with me not to tell Hammond something that I now saw could be important.

My face must have betrayed my shock, because Mike spoke again, more quietly, and eased his grip on my arms. "Please," he said, "don't say anything."

"Why not?"

"Don't you don't know who Eric was? I thought you knew everything about everything about the Grantham Police Department."

"Well, I don't know that. I figured it was a prisoner who died in custody or something. There are always questions about cases like that, but the department has strict rules for investigating the causes of death, and I didn't see anything suspicious about either of the deaths that I covered during the past eighteen months. I thought Bo simply had something crosswise in that drugged-up mind of his. So, who was Eric?"

Instead of answering, Mike got up, walked across the room and tapped his toe against the unlit gas logs in our phony fireplace.

"Who was Eric?"

"It's too crazy," he said.

"Who was Eric?"

He shook his head. "Bo definitely had it wrong."

"Who was Eric?"

"It doesn't make sense."

"Mike! Who was Eric?"

He finally looked at me. "You really don't know."

"No! Who was he?"

" 'Eric' was a code name the TAC team used."

"A code name? Who for?"

He looked down and kicked the gas logs again. "It was a kind of a joke. 'Eric the Red.' "

"A joke?"

"Yes. It was their code name for my dad."

Mike's dad, Carl "Irish" Svenson, Grantham chief of police.

"Eric the Red" would have been a better nickname than "Irish" for the man whose picture was on display in the entrance hall of the Central Station. Sure, he'd looked Irish if you saw only the open face and red hair. But those racial characteristics apply to Scandinavians as much as they do to the Irish. Once you knew his name, Carl Svenson looked as if he should be standing at the prow of a longboat, wearing a horned helmet. He'd been an Americanized version of a big Swede.

Bo had said, "They killed Eric. They made me cover it up." What did that mean?

Irish Svenson had been killed in a car wreck. Of course, it's possible to sabotage a car and cause a wreck. But I couldn't believe Irish's accident hadn't been thoroughly investigated. He'd had a very high profile in law enforcement circles, after all.

But Bo had been a mechanic. A mechanic for the

Grantham City-County Maintenance System. He had worked on police and sheriff's vehicles. The implication finally hit me.

"Hell's bells!" I yelped it out. "Mike, if somebody actually sabotaged your dad's car—caused his car wreck—and made Bo help cover it up—it would almost have to be somebody in the Grantham Police Department!"

Mike didn't react to my words, and I realized that he'd been way ahead of me. He continued to lean on our flimsy mantelpiece, looking down, staring at something several miles beyond the fake logs. His mind was obviously working overtime.

If I felt shocked by my new understanding of Bo's words, how must Mike feel? Bo had been talking about his father. A person he must have loved and probably missed every day, just as I missed my grandmother. It must be awful for him.

I got to my feet and moved toward him. "Mike—"

Before I could formulate a sentence, Rocky's sunny voice called from the kitchen. "Supper's ready! Bring your wineglasses, please!"

Mike didn't seem to hear him. Whatever he was thinking, he didn't seem to be ready to talk about it.

I took his hand. "Come on. If I've thrown your appetite into neutral, Rocky will be crushed."

Mike refocused his eyes, moving them from some hidden place to my face. "What did you say?"

"Dinner," I said. "Eat now. Talk later."

A strange expression played over Mike's face. I couldn't read it, but it made me feel as if he liked me.

He squeezed the hand I had thrust into his. "Don't you ever fuss?" he asked. "Don't you ever dither around?"

"I'm too heartless and calculating. Dithering doesn't get information. And that's my goal." I tugged. "Come on and eat."

Rocky's a real romantic at heart. With one candle and a colorful kitchen towel, he'd turned the round table in our old-fashioned breakfast nook into an intimate setting for dinner *tête-à-tête*. And dinner, since Rocky had prepared it, was superb. Smooth and tangy Spaghetti à la carbonara, which Rocky makes with skinny fideo pasta tossed with eggs, bacon, onions, parsley, white wine, and Parmesan cheese. He gave me the recipe, and I can make it—if I have an hour for chopping up the ingredients. It takes a pro with a kitchenful of appliances to make it in twenty minutes, the way Rocky had. And he had mixed a salad and grabbed some hard rolls from the freezer in the same time frame. No wonder the microwave and food processor had been going like mad.

Rocky watched nervously while Mike tried the spaghetti. Now and then you still run into these meat-and-potatoes guys. One of that type might balk at eating raw eggs scrambled up and semi-cooked by tossing them with hot pasta.

"Delicious!" Mike said. "Rocky, you're wasted behind the bar. You should be serving this up to the paying public."

Rocky beamed. "I'm glad it's okay. I didn't take time to grate the Parmesan fresh," he said. "Nell, I'm heading for my own TV set. You're stuck with the dishes."

He left, and I heard the door to his rooms close. Mike and I concentrated on food. Mike ate two helpings of carbonara, two rolls, and a big helping of salad before he began to speak intelligibly again.

As I was splitting the last of the wine between our glasses, he laid his fork down. "I just realized that I never stopped for lunch," he said.

"I was afraid you hadn't eaten." I picked my wineglass up.

Mike touched his glass to mine. "Here's to Rocky!"

"I'll drink to that." Somehow this exchange caused us to lean toward each other and exchange a kiss. It was a companionable kiss, rather than the ultra-sexy variety. Flavored with Parmesan and onion, but pleasurable.

We sat with our noses a few inches apart for several seconds after. "You handle your lips differently when Mickey O'Sullivan's not around," I said. "Are you ready to use them to talk?"

Mike laughed. "I think I feel an interview coming on."

"We can keep it off the record."

"I've been told you never accept information that way."

"I try not to, but I also don't print everything I know."

"I'd sure hate to see you print what Bo said."

I sat back in my chair and repeated Bo's words. " 'They killed Eric. They made me cover it up.' Mike, I feel sure Bo was just blowing smoke. Did you have any suspicion that there was anything wrong with your dad's accident?"

"No!"

Was his voice a little too vehement? I wondered. "In a mystery novel, you would have come back from Chicago to avenge his death."

"My life seems to be a soap opera rather than a mystery novel, and I had no idea anyone could have harmed my dad. I still don't. What motive could any-one have had?"

"Search me. I didn't know your dad, of course—he died three months before I moved to Grantham. But in two years of gossip around the PD, I've never heard anybody say anything bad about him—except that he was tough. Which is not a criticism when you're talking about a chief of police."

Mike stared at his wineglass. "My dad wasn't per-fect," he said.

"A human being, huh? I'm glad to hear it. But he certainly had the respect of both the community and the police."

"That was his character flaw. His reputation."

"That's a flaw?"

"Not the reputation itself, but the pride he took in it. He earned the reputation of being an honest cop very early in his career. You've heard the story about his picking up the state legislator for DUI?"

I nodded, and Mike went on. "My dad was twenty-three when that happened, and it set the pat-tern for the rest of his career. He always had that reputation for absolute honesty. He was jealous of that reputation. Maybe too concerned with what peo-ple thought of him."

"I see." Yes, I could see the problem. Irish Sven-son's high principles could have made him a bit ho-lier than thou. I did know they had led him to make some hard choices, and he had stepped on a lot of toes. He had battled with the police union over salary hikes he didn't feel were justified. He'd probably fired cops who felt he'd acted unjustly, and faced down city councilmen he felt were trying to influence the way he ran the department. From what I'd heard about him, he had been willing to be thought tough, blunt, and maybe even mean—as long as he was given credit for honesty.

Mike had drained his wineglass and was speaking again. "Besides, there's the practicality of it."

"Practicality?"

"The practicality of killing someone by rigging a car wreck. Dad's accident was thoroughly investigated by professionals who had a personal interest in the matter. Guys who knew him. A complete forensic report was made, and I got Jameson to give me a copy. And that report was from the state crime lab. Bo Jenkins had nothing to do with it. There was no mechanical failure to my dad's car. It was dark, it was raining, and he simply missed a curve."

"I suppose he could have been drugged. But I don't see how that could have involved a mechanic."

Mike shook his head. "Mom and I asked for a complete autopsy, too. There were no signs of drugs in his body, and he hadn't had anything to drink."

"Exactly when and where did the accident happen?"

Mike held his wineglass by the stem and swiveled it back and forth. "It happened at ten P.M. November first—in two weeks it will have been two years. He missed the hairpin curve coming out of the main parking lot at the Hotel Panorama."

"The Hotel Panorama? At Davisville?"

Mike nodded, and I took a minute to assimilate that information. It was surprising.

Our part of the Great Plains is remarkably flat, but a miniature range of mountains rises out of the prairie about twenty miles south of Grantham, just inside the county line. Seventy-five or eighty years earlier, some entrepreneur—that may have been a Prohibition Era word for bootlegger—had damned a creek running through the little town of Davisville, built a big swimming pool and declared the town a resort. He built a winding road up the tallest hill and topped it with a stone hotel and a fancy ballroom. The hotel did have a wide and spectacular view of the plains, so he dubbed it "Hotel Panorama." Over the years, the Panorama had been open, then shut, in fashion, out of fashion, respectable and disreputable. Currently, it was what my grandmother would have called a tourist trap.

The current owner made intermittent efforts to get the building on the National Register of Historic Sites, so the *Gazette* had run some articles about it, and Professor Tenure and I had driven out there one Saturday afternoon to take a look. We hadn't bothered to go back.

The Panorama didn't have a lot of ambiance, after you'd looked at the view. The few food items served in the restaurant were not worth the drive. It was heavily advertised along the interstate with gaudy billboards, although to get there you had to travel five miles off the main highway, passing three hamburger chain outlets and a Quick Chick on the way. The goods for sale included authentic Indian artifacts made in Hong Kong and plaster replicas of Panorama Peak, complete with a little plastic hotel on top. It was Junk City.

It was an odd place for an important city official to make a casual stop. It was an even odder place for one to go to deliberately.

"What was your dad doing at the Panorama?" I asked.

"That's the only funny thing about the accident," Mike said. "Nobody ever figured out why he was there. None of the employees could even remember seeing him in the restaurant, so he apparently didn't stop to eat."

I mulled it over. "I suppose he could have been meeting someone. An informant?"

Mike dismissed that with a gesture. "Chiefs of police don't go around meeting informants. That's what they hire detectives for. My dad had been an administrator—chief of detectives and then police chief—for more than fifteen years. He wouldn't have known an informant if he fell over one in the parking lot. Besides, he seems to have been out of town all that day."

"How did you know that?"

"His secretary, Shelly Marcum. He'd called in that morning, told her to cancel his appointments. Didn't say where he was going, just that he'd be out of touch."

"Isn't that sort of unusual?"

"Yes. He'd never done it before. He always carried a pager."

"So there were two odd things."

Mike nodded and stared at his empty wineglass.

I was more confused than ever. Mike had said there was nothing suspicious about his father's death. Then he'd immediately named two peculiar circumstances.

"What's going on here?" I asked. "You've named two rather odd things about your father's death—where it happened, and his prior movements. Yet you don't want me to tell Hammond what Bo said. I don't get it."

Mike took a deep breath. "I don't want you to tell Hammond because if—and that's 'if' with a capital I—there was anything funny about my dad's death, it pretty obviously involves somebody in the department. I doubt it's Hammond. But the word might get back to the very person we wouldn't want to know about it.

"But I was wrong when I said you shouldn't tell anybody. I wasn't thinking straight. You've got to get what Bo said on record. Though I don't think you're in any danger."

"Danger?"

"No. Even though somebody killed Bo Jenkins."

"Excuse me? Why should Bo's death put me in danger?"

"Maybe I'm leaping too far, but this is how it seems to me. First, we'll assume Bo really did help somebody cover up what happened to my dad. I'm not sure I accept that, but for the sake of argument. Okay?"

"Okay. But how would that affect me?"

"I'll get to that. Second, Bo goes along a year or so after Dad's death, and then everything falls apart for him."

"Right. That's actually what happened. And nobody knew why."

"Say it was because his conscience got the best of him. He began to feel guilty. Or worry about getting caught. He begins to drink, loses his job, leaves town, wife divorces him, and so forth."

"That's what happened."

"Then, Bo's faced with the final blow. His wife intends to get custody of the kid and tells him he's in such bad shape she won't let him see the little boy again."

"Right. That's what pushed Bo over the edge."

Mike nodded. "So, Bo decides to take drastic action. He's going to prove that he can get his life back on track. He'll reveal what he's been hiding all this time."

"But he doesn't dare tell the Grantham police!" I was getting into the swing of the story.

"Correct. Bo knows for a fact that someone in the department is involved. So instead of going to the police, he decides to go to the press. To the reporter who seems to have the best handle on the Grantham PD. Nell Matthews."

"Heck! He didn't have to barricade himself in the Grantham PD. All he had to do was call me up."

"We're not talking about a person who was thinking normally, Nell. He could have felt that he'd have to make a dramatic gesture to get your attention."

I drew a design in the remains of my spaghetti à la carbonara. "Mike, wouldn't it be awful if he tried to call, and I brushed him off?"

"Do you remember any such call?"

"No. Of course, I get messages. Sometimes they're incomprehensible. I get nut calls—we all get those. But I don't remember anything along this line. I know nobody left a name like 'Bo.' I'd remember that."

"If Bo tried to tell you, he obviously didn't get through. And that may be the reason you're alive."

I stared at Mike. "You lost me."

"Let's not forget that Bo was murdered—or that's how it looks. And he was murdered while he was in a high-security facility. It was not a simple matter to kill Bo. You would have been a lot easier to kill. The reason you're still alive at this moment—if our killer really exists—is probably because the killer didn't see any need to bump you off."

I took that in, then chuckled. "Gee, that makes me feel important."

"You are important—to me, to the Gazette's readers, to the world in general. That's why you've got to keep this killer in the dark about what Bo said to you."

"So you don't think I should tell Hammond, even though it may be vital evidence?"

"Not until I can give it some thought." He leaned back, giving me a level look. "I realize that I'm asking you to trust me, trust my judgment. You don't have any particular assurance that I'm right. I could be putting you in danger."

"You mean I might be safer if I publish what Bo said?"

Mike nodded. "It would probably be a good idea to write it out and put it in your safety deposit box."

I took that in. Then I laughed. "Do I mark it, 'To be opened only in the event of my death by violent means'?"

Mike scowled. I giggled. He glared.

"Mike, a reporter is a bystander! We stand on the sidelines and watch other people, then blab about it. I'm not involved in all this."

"Yes, you are! And I can't tell you the safest thing to do. If you tell Hammond, it could keep us from finding out more. If you don't tell Hammond, it might be worse, but like I say, I don't think so. But, at least you should get on record what Bo said."

"Oh, okay! It makes me feel as if I'm over-dramatizing the situation, but what do you want me to do?"

"Write out a statement about what Bo said to you. Put it in your safety deposit box."

"I don't have a safety deposit box."

"Then I'll put it in mine."

"I could give a copy to the managing editor."

"That's a good idea. If he won't read it."

"He's pretty trustworthy."

"Do you have a pencil and paper?"

"Better than that. I have a computer." I wriggled my eyebrows suggestively. "Upstairs. Wanna help me write it out?"

"I thought I wasn't allowed upstairs."

"Upstairs is allowed, if discretion is included. Just don't move in without paying rent."

Mike cleared the table, and I stuck the dishes in the dishwasher according to Rocky's method. Then we went up to my room, unmade bed and all. After all, I hadn't been in that room more than five minutes since I had left it at seven a.m. a day earlier. My room never looks like much anyway. It's lined with assemble-them-yourself bookshelves, except for the wall with the double bed and a cubbyhole by the window for the one comfortable chair. The TV set sits on top of one of the bookshelves, and the computer table does duty as a nightstand.

Mike looked over a couple of bookshelves while I opened up the computer and composed a succinct version of what Bo had said. Mike did not look over my shoulder or suggest improvements in my wording. I like that in a man.

I gave the statement Monday's date, turned on the

printer and ordered up four copies. I ripped the first hard copy off the printer and handed it to Mike.

"Better get it notarized," he said. "They've got a notary at your office, don't they?"

"The publisher's secretary. Shall I get your copy notarized, too?"

"Why don't you get it notarized and mail it to me. And give a copy to your editor."

I turned sideways in the director's chair I use at the computer and rested my chin on one of the knobs on the back. "You're really serious about this."

"I just don't know what to make of it. Yet." Mike sat on the edge of my bed and read the statement. He continued to stare at the page long after he'd had time to commit it to memory.

I almost wished that I hadn't told him what Bo said, that I hadn't remembered it. Bo's wild-eyed and probably baseless statement had turned Mike's mood upside down. He'd had two years to deal with his father's death, and I'd seen no sign that he hadn't coped with his grief in a healthy manner. But now his emotions seemed to have been kicked in a heap.

I plucked the statement out of his grip and took his hand. He clutched mine tightly.

"I think the violent death of someone you love is the hardest thing in the world to accept," I said. "It's so awfully sudden. My mother was killed in an accident when I was eight. I was sixteen before I really believed she was gone."

"You were eight? It's rough to lose your mother that young."

"Worse for her. She was only twenty-six. I was lucky. My grandparents took me in. I had a careful and loving upbringing. Financially secure. Emphasis on education. Camp Fire Girls and church camp. All that middle-class stuff. But it was still hard to grasp that my mother was gone. She was there one night when I went to bed and gone the next morning when I got up. I used to dream that it was all a mistake. That she'd been looking for me, and I wasn't where she'd left me, so she couldn't find me.

"Of course, because of the accident—my grandparents didn't want me to see her body."

Mike nodded. "Mom insisted on seeing my dad, for just that reason, even though we weren't going to open the coffin. I went with her. It—it wasn't easy. But I know it was a smart thing to do." He massaged my hand silently, then went on. "They were a really happy couple. His death was hard on her."

"Hard enough on you. You don't have any brothers or sisters, do you?"

"A spoiled only child. That's why I'm so irresistibly egotistical. I always think I should get what I want."

Mike gently pulled me out of my chair and into his lap. He kissed me thoroughly. As soon as he worked around to my right ear, he murmured into it. "Can I talk you into coming over to my place?"

"That's too far away." I got up and went into Brenda's room and found the right items in her top dresser drawer. She went on the pill after she and her boyfriend had made their engagement official, but I'd thought they were still there. I took them back to my room and closed the door behind me.

I dangled the box in front of Mike. "Take your shoes off," I ordered.

"Those things will not fit on my feet," he said.

"Then we'll have to use them on some other part of your body."

A half hour later, we were resting happily, with our arms around each other, when Martha and Brenda came upstairs. Mike and I had turned out the lights, and they shushed when they saw my closed door.

"Guess Nell made it an early night," Brenda said. "Have you got my *Vogue*?" They went into Martha's room.

"Should I leave?" Mike murmured.

"Not unless you want to."

"Nope." He snuggled closer. "I feel like I sneaked into the sorority house. That was my dream when I was nineteen. I wanted to be the sex slave of the Kappa house."

"Gee, can one reporter take the place of a whole houseful of Kappas?"

"Even more exciting. Especially since I'm not nineteen anymore. Massed Kappas no longer have the appeal they once did."

We snickered as silently as possible, and Mike began to slide his hand back and forth along my rib cage.

"I wanted to ask something," I whispered. "What did your mother have to say after Mickey and I left this morning? I've been wondering, in between the other exciting events of the day. I hope you didn't quarrel with her because of me."

"Not because of you." Mike laughed softly. "She told me that I was thirty-two-years old and that knowing I had a girl stay overnight made her a lot less worried about me than she would be if she thought I never did that." He kissed me. "She was especially pleased because I'd invited such a nice, wholesome girl over."

"I'll bet."

"Mom and I parted in better shape than we did the last time we got together."

"Glad to hear it. Mickey said you'd had a fight earlier."

"Did he tell you what it was about?"

I decided it was time to fudge a little. "He said you'd objected to their relationship."

"I acted pretty much like an asshole." Mike's arms tensed. "It's none of my business."

I couldn't think of a safe reply, so I didn't make one. Mike began to stroke my breast. I began to stroke his. Knowing that Martha and Brenda were within earshot seemed to excite us both, to give us a sense of intimacy even greater than we'd had alone in Mike's house. We fondled and titillated each other, taking care to giggle, gasp, and pant silently. Luckily, we discovered, my bed doesn't creak.

I could still hear Brenda and Martha's voices faintly when Mike's arms gradually relaxed, and his breathing grew deep and regular. I wondered if he ever snored, and the thought gave me an attack of giggles. We'd been so quiet. Snoring would give us away for sure.

My giggling passed away and was replaced by that internal shivering and shaking which had hit me the night before, after I had realized just how tender Mike could make me feel. Oh, admit it, I told myself. He made me feel loving. I wanted to hold him and protect him and be a haven for him. Which was absolutely stupid. Here was a guy who could grab guns from armed madmen, could stop a giant semi with a single gesture, and even had an excellent cleaning woman, and I wanted to take care of him? He was doing very well on his own, thanks.

But he did make me feel that way. I liked the feeling. But if I kept seeing him, I'd have to change my life around—long before either Mike or I was ready to make any sort of a commitment. I'd have to give up the violence beat, switch to some other job at the *Gazette.*

The violence beat had been my financial, professional and emotional security for a year. I'd even broken up with Professor Tenure because of the violence beat. He thought it was lowbrow, and I objected to his opinion.

At least, that was one of the excuses I gave him.

My internal organs quivered harder. This was all happening too fast, I told myself. When you fell for a guy, you were supposed to go to dinner a few times, catch a movie, watch a football game. Take a long walk and talk about your ambitions and goals. Then, if you decide it's serious, you both think about making changes in your lives to accommodate the relationship. You don't go out once, leap into bed, then rush to the office to quit your job.

But why did I even care about the cop beat? It was a beginner's beat, an apprenticeship, not a career. But I'd been covering cops and firefighters for six years in two cities. Most reporters did it a couple of years and then left rejoicing, ready to cover schools, health, courts, or government. The only reporter I ever heard of who made crime reporting into a real career was Edna Buchanan, and she finally quit to write fiction.

If I really cared about Mike—about anyone—I ought to be willing to drop the cop beat like a dead story.

Was I turning into one of those cop junkies? Those reporters who get so close to their subject that it takes over their lives? Who sell out their principles and become PD public information officers, or who join the force themselves? Had I already lost all objectivity about my beat?

Should I quit, even if Mike wasn't the reason?

The thought terrified me. The cop beat had been my security. Giving it up meant stepping off into the unknown.

Mike probably won't work out anyway. After all, how long could an affair this hot last? How long would it be before I deliberately set out to run him off?

When I got to that point, my internal shaking became so marked that I was afraid Mike would feel it. I slid my arm out from under his neck, lay on my side, and stared at his sleeping face in the dim light.

The men in my life never seemed to work out. My father had left my mother and me. My grandfather died. The guys I'd dated in college and afterward, even Professor Tenure—I'd never felt secure with them. When it got to the point when I was afraid they'd go, I dropped them. I was aware that I did this—I looked for an excuse and dropped them before they could drop me.

I could quit the crime beat and cover another one. But how long would it be before I got nervous and shoved Mike out of my life? Would I be stuck covering something I didn't like as well as crime? And would I be alone again, spending my Sunday evenings with Rocky? Could I take a chance on a different outcome this time? I dropped off to sleep without solving the problem.

Around two a.m., Mike had a shaking fit and woke us both up. After the shaking subsided, he whispered, "This doesn't really happen every night. I saw a counselor. He says it's not that serious. Just a nervous reaction to excitement."

I kissed his forehead. "Better than booze."

"Yeah." We both knew alcohol was a major problem for cops. It's a destructive way of dealing with stress.

Mike went back to sleep, and I worried some more about giving up the crime beat. Should I take a chance on Mike? On me? I dozed off with the question still oppressing me.

Sometime around five A.M., Mike nudged me awake and asked me to check and make sure the bathroom was clear.

"I don't want to run into a strange roommate in the hall," he whispered.

"My other roommates aren't as strange as Rocky," I said. Mike laughed quietly.

When he came back, he began putting on his clothes. "I guess I'd better go," he murmured. "I go on duty at seven."

I got up, put on a wooly robe that had been my grandmother's, then led him down the stairs.

"Want some coffee? Toast?" I asked.

"No, thanks. I'll stop at the Main Street on my way in."

I undid the dead bolts on the door. "I'm sorry you have to go."

"So am I."

We wrestled that situation through another couple of minutes of hard breathing. Then Mike actually opened the door and stepped out onto the porch.

"Good night," he said. "Good morning."

I watched him cross the porch. Damn! He was so sexy. So nice. So grown-up. So brave, clean, and reverent. Dammit. I wished I knew what he wanted out of this relationship. Would I even see him again?

Abruptly, Mike turned around. "Nell!" he whispered. "I still don't have your phone number!"

My purse was on the hall table. I got out a *Gazette* card and wrote the number for the direct line to my desk on the front and my home number on the back. He wrote his number on the back of a second card, and I tucked it under a paper clip on the inside of my notebook.

"I get off at three p.m.," Mike murmured. "I'll call you." He touched my shoulder. "Maybe I'll have figured out what to do about what Bo said. And I hope you'll let me take you out someplace tonight. I want to show you off."

Decision time was there. My innards quivered. I gulped and decided to go for it. "Okay," I said.

He put his hands on each side of my face and kissed me. "Let's give ourselves a chance, Nell."

A terrible weight lifted off my shoulders, and my internal Jell-O set as solidly as concrete.

Mike left, and I tiptoed back up the stairs. I went into my room and closed the door. Then I stepped up onto the bed and jumped up and down as if my mattress were a trampoline.

"Whee! Whee!" I whispered. I did a swan dive

down among the sheets, still warm from Mike's body, and lay there giggling. He was a wonderful guy, and he wanted me to be his girl. I wallowed back and forth, sniffing the scent of Mike Svenson.

I was happy. I didn't care how I was going to feel when I told Jake Edwards I wanted to drop the cop beat.

CHAPTER 11

By nine A.M., when I got to the *Gazette* office, I was still ecstatic, although I'd stopped jumping up and down. I intended to drop the violence beat, but I had decided to postpone action until the afternoon. Rather than going to the ME, I told myself, I should talk to the city ed, Ruth Borah. Ruth and I were pretty good friends. I should tell her, let her think about how she wanted the reporters shifted around, before I went over her head. Besides, I could level with Ruth, and Jake Edwards scared me. Maybe she'd talk to him for me.

However, Ruth didn't come in until two P.M., so I couldn't do anything until then. Besides, somebody had to run the violence beat that morning. It obviously was going to be me. I wasn't irreplaceable, but they'd have to assign somebody to take over before I could simply stop doing my job.

I guess I was nervous. For emotional support I put on my favorite outfit—the tan pants for comfort, the rust, tan, and blue shirt to make my hair look golden-red, and the sapphire jacket to make my eyes look blue. As I came into the building, I stopped down-stairs and asked the publisher's secretary to notarize my statement on Bo Jenkins. She didn't read it, of course. Just attested my signature.

"Have you recovered from the big weekend?" she asked.

I looked at her suspiciously. The *Gazette* is a seething hotbed of gossip, but surely she hadn't already heard about Mike. I decided she was referring to Bo Jenkins and the criminal things that had gone on—being held hostage and all.

"I'm nearly recovered," I said.

As soon as I got to my desk, I put the statements in two *Gazette* envelopes and sealed them. Jake Edwards wasn't in his office yet. I wrote his name on one envelope and put it on the corner of my desk. The scanner was on, but nothing much seemed to be happening on the violence scene.

Then I called Coy-the-Cop. "When will Hammond have a statement on the investigation into Bo Jenkin's death?" I asked.

"It'll be at least three P.M., Nell. Let's say four P.M. for a briefing. I'll call back if Hammond can't make it then. The ME won't have even a preliminary cause of death before noon."

Language is funny. Coy used "ME" to mean "medical examiner," and I used it to mean "managing editor," but we understood each other.

"Speaking of Bo Jenkins, what happened to my keys?" I asked.

"Keys? Oh, yeah. The kid carried them out. I'll track them down. They're probably in the evidence room by now."

"Anything else happening today?" I asked Coy. "Any new cases? Policy changes? Personnel matters? Rapes? Murders? Bank robberies? Interesting drunk drivers? Assaults with deadly weapons?"

This is a joke between Coy and me. He's pretty

cooperative, but some law enforcement spokesmen won't tell you anything unless you ask specifically. You call the dispatcher and say, "What's going on?" He answers, "Not a thing." Two days later you discover that particular outfit is working a double murder. When you complain, the dispatcher acts all innocent. "You didn't ask me if we'd had any double murders." Sometimes they'll tell you an assault was simply a fistfight. Later you find out it was a pitched battle between off-duty cops and the meanest gang on the north side. A reporter has to watch her sources every minute. So I ask Coy about everything I can think of.

"All routine," Coy said.

Jake Edwards came in just as I hung up, and I was in his office before he had time to sling his briefcase onto the desk. "Morning, Nell. Have you recovered?"

"Pretty much. Jake, could I give you something?"

"A present?"

"Nope." I explained what I wanted and handed him the sealed envelope.

Jake frowned. "This is like something from an overwrought novel. I expect it to be marked, 'To be opened in the event of my death.' What are you up to?"

"I'm not sure yet, Jake. I just want to have this on record a couple of places. But I don't really want to discuss it."

Jake tossed the envelope in the top left drawer of his desk and sat down. "Okay, Nell. Now I've got a new assignment for you. And I'm afraid you're not going to like it."

I sat on the edge of one of his chairs and looked at my watch. "Okay. But I haven't made my morning run yet." Reporters have to keep the editors in line all the time, too. Keep reminding them that the first step in putting out a newspaper is going out there on the beat—to the city offices, courthouse, and schools—and gathering information. We can't just hang around the office doing their little chores. "I usually try to head for the cop shop by ten or so," I said.

"We may call in the nightside guy—J.B.? I want you to work on a special project."

"What is it?"

"Ace Anderson—"

"Ace-the-Ass?"

"That's the one." Jake sighed. "I said you weren't going to like this assignment. Ace has some sort of a tip around a scandal in the Grantham Police Department. The AP bureau chief wants him to work on it. And we want you to work with him."

"Oh, no! You can't expect me to work with that idiot!"

"Yell all you want, Nell. But it's got to be done."

"Why me? Let Ace do his own dirty work."

"What kind of a job do you think he'll do?"

"Lousy. Just like he does everything. But that's his lookout. And maybe the AP will get wise to what a jerk he is."

"Yes, but what will happen to the Grantham PD?" Jake pulled a pica pole—a metal ruler—out of his center drawer and turned it over and over, the way an Arab handles his worry beads. "Ace claims we're looking at a major scandal."

"The Grantham PD is made up of tough guys and gals," I said. "If they've been up to no good, they deserve to get caught."

"By Ace?"

"Just because no self-respecting journalist likes Ace—"

"Liking Ace is not the point. Incompetence is."

"That's why we don't like him. He's a sorry excuse for a reporter."

"So? What do you think he'll do with a major scandal?"

I leaned back in my chair. "He'll mess it up."

"Right. He'll gather half the facts and understand only a quarter of those. He'll go off half-cocked, print stuff he can't prove. Hint at things to come—which will never develop."

"We don't have to print it."

"No, and we won't print his version. But if the story breaks all over the state, we won't be able to ignore it. We'll have to straighten it out. And just who is going to get that assignment? You're our expert on the Grantham PD, Nell, so it's going to be you. You can help Ace to begin with, or you can clean up after him."

"Hell's bells!" I said.

Jake didn't say anything. He knew he had me.

I glared at my tan loafers and decided to haul in my personal reasons. "Actually, Jake, I came to work today determined to ask for a major favor."

"What's that?"

"I was going to talk to Ruth first. But since she's not here, I'd better level with you. I've got to stop covering the Grantham Police Department."

Jake squinted at me. "Quit covering the PD? I thought you liked that beat."

"I do. But I've got to take a break from it."

"Why?"

I lifted my chin. "I've become too personally involved with it, Jake. I realized that this weekend."

"It's not showing up in your stories."

"Maybe not yet. But I need to take a break."

Jake and I stared at each other, and he twirled his pica pole a few times.

"Okay," he said. "Okay. I can understand that. The violence beat tends to take over a reporter's whole life, and that's not good. We'll put J.B. on the coverage dayside. We'll get that Grantham State kid—Chuck—to take the nightside for a few weeks. And as soon as you finish overseeing Ace and his project—"

"No!" I jumped up. "Jake, I can not work on the Grantham PD anymore! I could do the routine stuff better than I can do a major investigative piece."

"And just why?"

"I'm too personally involved!"

"Well, get uninvolved for a couple of weeks."

"I can't!" To my horror, I realized it was true. I was so crazy about Mike Svenson that I really couldn't see any way to live without him, even for a couple of weeks.

Jake was glaring. "What is going on? You're a highly competent reporter, Nell. But you're acting like a Journalism I student."

I decided I had to level with him.

"I know I'm being unprofessional, Jake. But I've fallen—into a strange situation. Believe me, I didn't plan to!"

"What's going on?"

I kicked the leg of the chair I'd been sitting in. "I'm sleeping—"

I must have paused there, finding it difficult to

choke out the words *with a cop*. This turned out to be lucky, because Jake's face changed, and he held his pica pole up to his mouth. Did he realize he was using it to make a gesture that shushed me? I didn't know, but I shut up.

Jake was staring over my shoulder, and I turned to see what was there. It was Ace. He was leaning against the door frame, leering his stupid leer. I'd nearly spilled my guts in front of my worst enemy.

"Hi, Ace. Come on in," Jake said.

But Ace was grinning at me. "Sleeping? Sounds sexy. What were you about to say, Nell?"

If I hadn't despised the guy so much, I might have blown it. But the anger and contempt that filled me at the sight of him kept me from making a complete fool of myself.

"I've been sleeping very poorly, Ace," I said. That was certainly true. Having sex three or four times a night and worrying about your job in between orgasms didn't leave a lot of time for rest. "I was just telling Jake I want to take a break from the police beat."

Jake came in the office and sat down. "Aw, Nell. Don't quit on me. I know you'll love this story."

"I doubt it."

"But it could be the Grantham scandal of the century. The story of how the community's idol had feet of clay."

"All idols have feet of clay," I said. "Even an Intro to Journalism student knows that. What are you talking about?"

"I'm talking about the most believed-in man in the city's history—Honest Irish Svenson. And how he took a payoff."

Aces's words hung there, and Jake's office seemed to turn into a carnival ride—that centrifugal force thing that pins you up against a wall.

Ace had definitely gotten my attention.

And he had acquired my reporting skills, too. I was whipped. Ace was going to go ahead with this project, whether I helped or not. But he was a grandstander, a showoff who was more interested in a sensational story than in an accurate report. For personal and professional reasons, I couldn't allow him to skewer Irish Svenson without making sure he had his facts straight. I owed that much to my profession. And to Mike.

I realized that the professional-personal conflict I'd foreseen when I fell for Mike Svenson had already developed. I was letting my feelings for him affect a professional decision.

I sat down again. "Hell's bells!"

Ace rubbed his hands together. "We're gonna have a great time, Nell! There's plenty of glory in this story. Enough for both of us."

"You can have it all. Just what is the story?"

He looked around, checked the newsroom through Jake's glass wall, then closed the door. He lowered his voice when he spoke. "It's the construction contract for rebuilding the Central Station."

"What about it?"

"I have a source that says Irish Svenson took a kickback in exchange for a recommendation on which builder got the contract."

"That's junk, Ace. The city council awarded that contract, not the police department."

"There's a city councilman who may be involved, too."

"But Irish Svenson was noted for not getting along with the city council. Why would they vote the way he wanted?"

"That's what we're gonna find out."

Jake cleared his throat. "I thought Ace could take that desk at the back, Nell. The one the sporties use on football nights. I'll tell Ruth when she comes in."

Jake obviously wanted his office cleared. Ace and I left. I took him to the empty desk and showed him how to open the computer file the three police reporters shared, but I'm afraid I wasn't very gracious about it.

"I'll lay you a bet, Ace," I said. "This is going to turn out to be a mare's nest."

He smirked. "I have a very good source."

"Who?"

"Someone who knows someone in the contractor's office."

"Who?"

He shook his head. "I'm not going to tell you everything I know, Nell."

"Then how are we going to work together?"

We both knew the answer to that one. We weren't going to work together. Ace would go one way, and I'd go the other. It was going to be a mess.

"You're going to have to give me an hour to do the Monday cop-shop routine," I said. "And I'm not getting muscled out of the coverage of Bo Jenkins's death. That briefing's at four p.m."

"I'll start by reviewing the stories on the contract for the substation," Ace said.

I led him to the library and found a librarian to help him print out stories. Then I put the police reporters' pager in my purse and left the building. Still furious.

I had to call Mike, but I didn't want to take a chance that Ace would overhear. I stopped across the street at a pay phone and called his house. The answering machine picked up on the fourth ring.

"Mike? Nell. Something's come up. A new assignment I can't duck. I won't be in the office late this afternoon, because Coy's called a briefing. I might not be able to talk there anyway. I hope I'll be home shortly after six, and I'll call you then."

I paused. "I'm very angry about this," I said. I couldn't tell if the answering machine got that comment or not.

It's only three blocks from the *Gazette* to the Central Station, and I usually walk. But today I was going on to the fire department and other spots on my beat, so I drove the Dodge. I was lucky I didn't get a ticket. I was still so mad I drove like a demon, speeding up and throwing on the brakes and cursing other drivers. After I got to the station, I tried to act a little more professional, making sure I smiled at the desk sergeant and spoke to the secretary. Those are key people when you're gathering news. I went back to the little interior room marked MEDIA.

A copy of every incident report made by the Grantham PD is supposed to turn up in a box in that room. That's another one of Coy's policies. The desk sergeant at the Headquarters Division is supposed to see that copies of all their incident reports are deposited there by eight A.M. each morning, and the division messengers bring them by from the other two substations after the seven A.M. shift starts. Another batch shows up at six in the evening for the nightside reports to pick up. They're numbered consecutively, so we can tell if any are missing.

The department uses a report form set by national standards. It lists time, date, place, name of victim, type of offense, suspects, vehicles involved, witnesses, and other details. After a little practice, a reporter can glance at a form and tell very quickly that a cab company is complaining about harassing phone calls made between midnight and three A.M. Then the reporter yawns and goes on to the next report.

Obviously, harassing phone calls to a cab company are not worth a story. Ninety-nine-point-nine percent of the stuff that's reported to the police isn't worth a story, at least in a city the size of Grantham. So you learn to check the forms quickly for serious crimes or prominent names or unusual events.

Some reports are stamped PLEASE DO NOT PUBLISH. I understand this is another of Coy's innovations. They used to be stamped DO NOT PUBLISH. Coy made it more polite.

Most of these cases involve juveniles. The law in our state is quirky on juvies. The police aren't supposed to release their names to the press, but if we get the name from another source, they can't do anything if we print it. We don't usually print names in juvenile cases, as a matter of policy. But we like to remind the cops that we can if we want to.

We don't print the names of persons who've been arrested until they've been officially booked. We want their names to appear in some sort of paperwork. There are lots of other names we leave out—rape victims, for example, and persons who are wanted, but who haven't yet been arrested. Again, we leave them out as a matter of courtesy and policy, not because we couldn't print them if we wanted to.

I guess all the crooks in Grantham had stayed home Sunday evening, because there were only about forty forms in the box. I riffled through them as quickly as possible and pulled a half dozen for possible stories.

A shooting in the parking lot at the Lone Wolf Club on the north side. That was getting to be a real trouble spot since the drug dealers began to hang out there. Victim treated at St. Luke's Hospital and released. Worth three or four graphs.

An armed robbery of a stop-and-rob convenience store at two A.M. Clerk had been bound and gagged, but she'd ID'd a semiregular customer and a warrant had been issued. I'd downplay it until they arrested the guy. I vaguely remembered that he was already a suspect in two similar robberies. If they cleared all three, it would be a pretty good story. A little pang of envy hit as I realized J.B. would probably be writing it up based on my legwork.

A case of domestic violence had put a woman in the hospital, her husband in jail and her children in the county shelter. I'd talk to the detectives about that one. Our DA ran for office on a promise of getting tough on domestic violence, and so far he was sticking with it, filing charges even if the victim didn't cooperate, even if he had to drop the charges later.

I photocopied the reports I was interested in, put all of them back in the box, left messages with Coy for the detectives I needed to talk to, then checked the city court records. No filings on anything but traffic so far that morning. City court is usually only misdemeanors, so we don't cover many things there. I don't worry about the DA's office because we have a separate set of reporters to cover that. They also cover felony trials and other happenings at the county courthouse.

I drove over to the Grantham Fire Department then and picked up three more stories from their reports. A trailer fire around midnight. With luck the night photographer had gotten a shot. A gas leak at a school and a house fire in a snazzy neighborhood. I went by the fire marshal's office to get a damage estimate on the house fire.

As I was leaving his office, my pager beeped, and I called in and talked to the switchboard operator. Bear Bennington was the photog on scanner duty. There had been a three-car collision in the downtown area. Ambulances en route. Bear was on his way. "I'll have to pick it up later," I told the operator. "Busy morning."

She promised to pass the word on to Bear on the radio. That story J.B. or I could get from the traffic division after they'd had time to fill out their reports. I wondered if Mike would be involved in it. He was on routine patrol out of the central PD, and routine patrol includes first call on everything—shoplifters, fender benders, missing kids, little old ladies with cats in trees, speeders.

It hadn't been such a bad run, for a Monday. I was headed back to the office by eleven. I went in the *Gazette*'s main door and headed for the stairs. Now to get this little dab of stuff written up, so I could think about Ace and his asinine rumor about Irish Svenson. Which I didn't believe.

I tried to dash by the switchboard, but Ellen caught me.

"Nell!"

I screeched to a stop. "Oh, Ellen, please don't tell me I have messages. I don't have time to be calling people today."

Our phone system has voice mail at each extension, but if people call in through the central switchboard—which means it's somebody who doesn't have the number of the reporter's personal extension—sometimes they leave a message with Ellen or her cohorts. The business manager hires Grantham State part-timers for that slot, so they come and go. Ellen's the only one whose name I know.

Ellen simpered. She's able to do this because she's nineteen and sweet-faced. "No messages, Nell. I just wanted to tell you you had three calls, all from the same person."

"Must be mighty eager to talk," I said. "I've only been gone an hour and a half."

"She won't leave a message, but she keeps calling back."

"No name? No number?"

"She wouldn't leave either."

"Then I guess she's not that eager to talk to me."

I had two messages on my voice mail, from the detectives I'd asked to call, and for the next twenty minutes I was tied up talking to them. Ace was still in the library, I was glad to see. I didn't need him in my hair right at that minute. I concentrated on getting the routine part of my job done.

I was writing the second story, the armed robbery, when the phone rang.

"Hell's bells!" I said. I seemed to be swearing a

lot that morning. But I picked up the phone and spoke into it. "Nell Matthews."

"Ms. Matthews?" The voice on the other end was breathy, timid. I could hear street noises in the background.

"Yes. This is Nell Matthews." I stopped typing. "Can I help you?"

"I hope so." The breathy voice grew fainter.

"What can I do?"

"If I have some information—"

"Yes?" I tried to sound encouraging, but I glanced at my watch. I didn't really have time to fool with this. "What sort of information?"

"About a murder."

"Which murder was this?"

"Well, the police don't know it was a murder."

I had a nut call.

As soon as a reporter gets his or her first byline, he or she is fair game for the crazies of the world. Every newspaper, radio station, and television newsroom has regulars who call. Maybe they listen to the scanner, and they call to find out about some house fire. Maybe they're sports fans who can't wait until the morning edition for the latest scores. We have one who calls every night for the numbers in the Texas lottery. We could kill 'em all dead. Why can't they simply buy a paper?

But the police reporter draws a special kind of news nut. This is the one who's going to give us the inside scoop on some crime and how the proper authorities are covering up. So I tried to sound brisk when my breathy caller said she knew the lowdown on a murder.

"If you have any information about a crime which

occurred in Grantham, you should call the Grantham Police Department," I said.

"Oh, I can't call them!"

"Well, despite what you see on television, reporters don't chase around solving murders," I said. "Basically, I cover the investigations of the Grantham Police Department. If they don't think a case is murder, we probably won't print a word on it."

"I've tried to convince myself I was wrong for two years," the breathy voice said. "But now they've killed Bo Jenkins, and . . ."

I must have gasped, because she broke off.

"Sorry," I said. "You touched a live nerve. I knew Bo Jenkins, of course. But I assure you, the Grantham police are well aware that he was probably murdered."

"I'm positive he was," the voice said, "but that's not the case I called about. I'm calling about the murder of Irish Svenson."

then went on. "Just happened to run off the road on the only steep hill within a hundred miles of Grantham."

"That doesn't make a lot of sense," I said. "Trish Svenson was chief of police. Police chiefs aren't usually out solving cases. Someone else in the department should have known about anything he was working on. So why hasn't that someone else dropped the bomb?"

"Because it was an internal investigation—inside the Grantham PD. He'd kept it secret from everybody in the department."

"Except you."

This time the breathy voice was silent. So I went on. "How do you know all this?"

"I can't answer that."

"I'd have to have some sort of proof," I said. "Some facts. For beginners, who is this?"

"Oh! I don't have to tell you that, do I?" The voice sounded panicked.

"Eventually I'd have to know," I said. "Knowing your connection helps me judge how credible your information is."

Silence again. Should I hang up? I decided to try a different tack. "Just what kind of a problem was Chief Svenson investigating?"

"What kind?"

"Yes. Was it bribery? Sexual assault? Tip-offs to drug dealers? Cops have lots of opportunities to go bad. What was going on?"

"Oh." The voice sounded younger than ever. "I guess we—I guess it would be fraud."

"Theft from the department?"

"No." Now she sounded uncertain. "Not really."

CHAPTER 12

I'd had a lot of surprises in the past few days. Some of them—like Ace's announcement that morning—had made my world spin crazily. But that one made it stand still.

"I'm calling about the murder of Irish Svenson."

I stared at the top of my desk, taking in those words. I was quiet so long the whispy voice at the other end of the telephone sounded anxious when it spoke again.

"Hello? Are you there?"

Was this one of the nuttier nut calls? Or could this caller know something? How should I react? I decided not to give anything away. I'd better act as if I'd never before heard a hint that Irish Svenson had been killed.

"Yes, I'm here," I said. "Irish Svenson's death happened a few months before I moved to Grantham, so I didn't cover it. I was trying to remember whether or not there was anything suspicious about his accident."

"The timing. That was what convinced me."

"The timing? What do you mean?"

"Irish was just about to drop a bomb on a major case. Then he just happened—" The voice broke off,

"Well, then—" Hell's bells. Across the room I saw Ace coming out of the library, aiming his jackass grin in my direction.

"Listen," I said, "I really can't talk here. Not now. Can I go to a private phone and call you back?"

"No!" For a minute I thought she was going to cry. Her breath sounded ragged. Then she took a deep breath and went on. "I can't let you call me. I could call tomorrow afternoon. Maybe. I could call tonight, but you won't be at the office, I guess."

She probably didn't know a darn thing. But I'd better try. I gave her my home number. "I'll be there after six," I said. "But I'd sure like to understand what your connection with this is. Do you work for the Grantham PD?"

Silence.

She hadn't said no. "Are you a police officer?"

"Oh, no!"

"Secretary? Clerk? Just what was your connection to Irish Svenson."

She breathed an answer so quietly I almost missed it.

"Friend," she said. "Good friend. He was the best friend I ever had."

The connection was broken.

When I looked up, Ace was standing at the end of my desk. He held a sheaf of printouts. "You got a lotta stuff in that library," he said.

"Have you read it all?"

"About half."

"Let me have the half you're through with. I'm going to take a long lunch and hide out from the scanner. I'll read it."

"Good! We can go to Goldman's. Talk about it."

Goldman's is a downtown sandwich joint, popular with the city hall and courthouse crowd. A reporter can pick up a lot of gossip there. But I shook my head. "Not today. Let me read up on this before we talk."

Ace wasn't too happy, but he didn't have a lot of choice. I told the switchboard I wouldn't be back until two, took half of Ace's printouts and drove home. I parked in my regular slot behind the house, opened both the locks on the kitchen door, then wandered into the front hall and picked up the packet of mail on the floor under the mail slot. I sorted it at the hall table and took my three ads and two bills upstairs. When I reached the door of my room, I tossed the mail at the bed and went back two steps to the bathroom.

As I turned the water off after I'd washed my hands, I thought I heard a noise downstairs. I was surprised to discover how much it annoyed me. I'd been looking forward to having a couple of hours alone, and the noise probably meant Martha was home. It had to be Martha, because Rocky worked all through the lunch hour every weekday, and Brenda taught preschoolers all day. But Martha was researching her thesis, so she didn't have formal classes, and she worked strange hours in a big department store. She always wanted to chatter, and I wasn't in the mood.

I called down the stairs, and to my pleasure, Martha didn't answer. When I went down, I discovered the mail I'd sorted had slid onto the floor. Hurrah, I thought. That must have been the sound I heard. It wasn't Martha. I fixed a sandwich, turkey and sprouts on cracked wheat. I was a little ashamed of being so pleased that Martha wasn't there. But I had a lot of thinking to do, and I needed solitude to do it.

The city editor on the first paper I worked on—in a town of under 30,000—taught me a bunch. And one of the first pieces of advice he gave me was never to accept information off the record.

"First off," he said, "most news sources won't offer to tell you until they really want to talk. So, nine times out of ten, they'll tell you on the record. Usually they'll insist on it. They'll force the information on you. The more you say you don't want to hear something off the record, the more they'll insist on telling you on the record.

"Second, if you're like most of us, you won't be able to remember what's on the record and what's off. Say you learn something in December—off the record—and you leave it out of the story you write for Christmas. Then the same topic arises around Labor Day. Can you remember what you knew on the record, and what you knew off the record after nine months? After a couple of years? Nobody's notes are that good."

Of course, that advice doesn't always work around the cop shop. I know lots of stuff I don't print. I knew which drug dealer the cops think shot Bull Williams in the scuffle behind the Choo-Choo Lounge. And our copy editor says getting shot in the scuffle is real painful. I know which bank refused to prosecute which assistant vice president when they found out just why the First Baptist Church's average weekly collections dropped after he took over the chore of counting the money. I know which prominent Grantham surgeon is going to go to jail if he drops out of counseling for battering spouses one more

time. The charges are sitting on the DA's desk, ready
to be filed if either his ex-wife or his ex-girlfriend
reports one more harassing phone call.

But this stuff is not that hard to remember. Lots of
people around Grantham know about the banker and
the surgeon, for example. As long as neither one of
them has actually been arrested, I can't put it in the
paper. But if I make a slip of the tongue in Goldman's, it's no big deal.

But I hate knowing things I can't talk about with
the city editor. And I was realizing I also hated
knowing things I couldn't mention to Mike.

But I was definitely not going to tell Mike I'd had
a call from a woman who claimed to be his father's
"good friend." Should I even tell him that such a
person had called? She probably didn't know anything. And I wasn't going to tell him Ace Anderson
thought his dad had taken kickbacks on the contract
for the Central Station. The whole thing was completely unproven, but it wouldn't be fair to Ace—the
ass—to tip off anyone who could sabotage the story
before he had time to get the facts. Should the facts
turn out to exist.

But I was in a bad position with the newspaper,
too. Once I'd deciphered Bo Jenkins's message, I had
realized he'd given me a hot tip. A serious crime
might have been committed, and I had promised
Mike I wouldn't tell anybody, wouldn't investigate.
I obviously hadn't been thinking with my head when
I did that. But, supposing I told the city ed or the
ME, what then? All we could do would be to go to
the Grantham cops—Chief Jameson or the chief of
detectives, Hammond, or maybe the DA. We really
had no way to launch an investigation on our own.

We could look at the PD records, but if Irish Svenson had kept private files, they probably wouldn't be there.

Actually, I decided, Mike had a better chance of finding out something than the newspaper did. Maybe it was best to leave it with him—for the moment. Maybe it was linked with Ace's investigation. Maybe Irish Svenson had been killed because he threatened to expose some kickback scheme, rather than because he was involved in one. Maybe the "friend" knew something. Maybe she really would call tonight.

I couldn't do anything about it. And I couldn't talk to Mike until that evening. So the next thing to do was read all those printouts on the contract for the Central Station.

Yuk. Dull. Dull. Dull. I put my dishes in the dishwasher, spread the printouts out on the kitchen table and started reading.

The librarian had done a complete job for Ace. The earliest story dealt with Irish Svenson's first proposal for a new police headquarters, a proposal he made six years before a contract was finally awarded.

At the time, the Grantham Board of Education had just declared the old Central High School building as surplus property. It hadn't been used for classes in years, but thousands of Grantham people had gone to school there, and there was an immediate outcry against demolishing the building. To add to the problem, the school building sat in a run-down area on the edge of the downtown. To the east and south, it adjoined substandard housing. To the west and north, it adjoined substandard business property.

Irish Svenson was the first person to say publicly

that it should be reconstructed and become a new central police headquarters.

Irish had envisioned a facility devoted to community-based policing. It would include meeting rooms for clubs and committees, a youth club, offices for social service agencies, and a park area on the old baseball diamond, as well as the police department's administrative offices. A new wing, much of it built underground, would hold standard police facilities—desk for complaints, detectives' offices and interrogation rooms, central evidence storage, squad room, even a garage for the combined city-county vehicle maintenance operation. A section of the underground area would house a thirty-cell holding area, easing traffic at the main city-county jail several blocks away. This would adjoin a city court area, so that misdemeanors could be handled there. The reconstructed building would replace an outgrown police headquarters built during the 1930s.

The chief had proposed this at a workshop session on city goals. No one could deny his idea was a good one. Still, the city council took a year before it okayed hiring a consultant. The consultant took nine months to come up with two proposals.

The first one was pretty close to what Irish had originally wanted. Under it, the city would build all these wonderful things and save the architectural elements of the historic school, with portions of the original building still open for general community use. It would cost a bundle.

The second plan was for a completely new building, using land the city already owned, adjoining a drainage canal on the northern edge of downtown. It abandoned the neighborhood concept almost en-

tirely, since it was a mile from the commercial center
and across the canal from any residential neighborhoods. It would cost two-thirds of a bundle.

So Irish Svenson had his work cut out for him.
Even his worst enemy on the city council, Harley
Duke, admitted Irish's idea was best, but it was also
the most expensive. Irish argued that it would be
cost effective, because it would reduce crime by putting the cops right in the center of where they needed
to be, not off in an area which would be extremely
inconvenient for the Central District residents and
businessmen to visit.

This argument raged for two years. During that
time Irish Svenson became a fixture at Grantham
civic and political meetings, lobbying the city's mov-
ers and shakers and its voters to promote his idea.
At the end of that time, the city council put the proposal on the ballot for a bond election. And Irish
redoubled his campaigning. He gave interviews, took
the press on tours, helped with voter registration
campaigns in the Central District, talked the project
up anytime he could get as many as three people
together.

I could see why Mike said that the idea of his
father meeting with an informant was unlikely. Irish
Svenson hadn't had time to do anything but hustle
for the Central Station project for years. Looked at
from another angle, his preoccupation with this
might have made it awfully easy for him to overlook
problems in the department.

That was the point where the printouts ended, but
I knew the end of the story. Grantham voters had
okayed the bond issue funding the renovation, and
the Central Station had opened for business two years

after their vote. After Irish's death, the community-service wing of the building had been renamed in his honor—the Carl Svenson Community Center of the Central Station of the Grantham Police Department. I'd had to write that lengthy title often enough.

Councilman Harley Duke had proposed calling the substation "Svenson's Palace." He was the most obnoxious loudmouth on the city council, and the *Gazette's* city hall reporter, Tom Quincy, made a point of quoting his most obnoxious loudmouth remarks.

But if it was a kickback scheme, which city councilman might be involved? Harley Duke seemed unlikely, since he'd opposed the project. Darn. It would be fun to nail Ol' Harley with something besides being an S.O.B.

James Montgomery had been the substation's biggest backer, at least in the early stages of the project. But he was a multimillionaire, a member of the current generation of Grantham's most prominent family. Why would he get involved with a kickback scheme?

Oh, well. There were six other councilmen. I assumed Ace's source would finger one of them. And speaking of Ace, it was nearly two P.M.

I ran back upstairs before I left for the office, and for the first time I noticed the flashing light on the answering machine in the hall. The message was from Mike.

"I forgot I have a seminar from six to eight-thirty tonight," he said. "I'll come by about eight-forty-five, if that's okay. I want you to go with me to talk to somebody who might know something about . . . the puzzle we were discussing last night." He hesitated, and I thought the answering machine had cut off. "Eight-forty-five," he repeated. "Take care."

A seminar. In spite of the pile of books and the computer in his living room, I'd forgotten that Mike was doing graduate work. And he'd thought of someone to question about his dad. Who? Who? I was wild to know.

There was no way to find out. Mike was on duty, and I wasn't going to call the dispatcher and tell her to have Mike call me. She probably wouldn't do it anyway. I just had to wait.

I drove to the office, steeling myself to face Ace-the-Ass. I did not want to fool with his big exposé on the kickback scene over the Central PD. I did not believe Irish Svenson had been involved in such a scheme. I wanted to investigate Irish Svenson's death. And between my pledge to Mike and my job responsibilities, I couldn't do it.

I resolved to make Coy's briefing on Bo's death at four P.M., whether I was still on the Bo Jenkins story or not.

As soon as I came into the newsroom, I knew I was off the Bo Jenkins story. J.B. was there. That meant he'd been called in early to take over the routine coverage on the violence run. My heart sank.

J.B., looking as boyish as ever, was sitting at his desk. He's actually two years older than I am, but J.B. manages to look as if he's about sixteen. He uses this youthful quality to good advantage. Sources want to help him out, so they pour information on him.

Ace was doing his star reporter act, lecturing J.B. on how things should be done. Ace could strut sitting down. I don't know where I heard that expression, but it sure described him.

"Hi, Nell," J.B. said. "We were just speculating on the cause of death for Bo Jenkins. Ace is betting on heart failure, brought on by the drugs he'd been taking. What do you think?"

"Cyanide." My answer seemed to surprise the two of them, and I realized it surprised me, too. Why had I answered so definitely? I hadn't said, "Poison." I'd said, "Cyanide."

Ace squinted suspiciously. "You've been talking to somebody in the department," he said.

"No." I could hear the hesitation in my voice. Why had I thought cyanide was the cause of death? "That was a purely off-the-top answer, but I guess I based it on two things. The first one I learned from a story I covered."

"What story?" Ace sounded angry.

"A year ago, I covered the Boucher case. Remember? She poisoned her husband with cyanide. They nearly passed it off as suicide, but she teetered over the mental brink and confessed. The charges are still officially pending, in case she ever gets out of the state hospital. And second, the PIO out at Grantham State Mental Health Center told me a few details about suicide watches."

"And?" J.B. sounded skeptical.

"Well, during a suicide watch, they keep the patient in a room with a big glass window. The attendant stays either in the room with the patient, or just outside the window. So that means Bo didn't vomit or pass out or go into lengthy convulsions. He died real fast. The attendant couldn't get medical help there soon enough to do anything. That points to cyanide."

"It's always that quick?" J.B. was still having trouble believing me.

I nodded. "I talked to a poison expert in Michigan and she said that cyanide antidote kits are almost never used. By the time they figure out they need one, it's too late to use it. And we know that this guy disguised in a Salvation Army uniform got in to see Bo. That's too big a coincidence for it to be anything but poison."

"But where would he get cyanide? Myself, I don't keep any under the bathroom sink."

"Actually, J.B., you may. As I recall from visiting your apartment for the party you threw after the Notre Dame game, you have a beautiful fish tank."

"Yeah. My whole family is into tropical fish."

"Check the label on your purification tablets."

"Cyanide?" He sounded terrified.

"There are lots of other places to get it, as I recall. Rat poison, for example. In the past, some types of photographic supplies contained cyanide. I don't know if they still do or not."

Ace sneered. "You make a pretty good case, Nell. Wanna back it up with money?"

"I'm not a gambler, Ace."

"If you're right, I'll buy lunch at Goldman's tomorrow."

"Sure. I'll order the shrimp supreme." *Gazette* staffers are in Goldman's so often that I knew the most expensive item on the menu.

"You're on!" Ace said. "I'm still betting on a heart attack."

"You're forgetting the fake Salvation Army officer."

He shook his head. "No. If I were going to poison somebody who'd been taking drugs, I'd use digitalin. Make it look like a heart attack. They'd never figure it out."

I looked at J.B. and raised my eyebrows. "If I drop over of a coronary, make sure Ace wasn't in the vicinity," I said. "He could be right."

Ace held a sheaf of computer printouts, and I tapped the similar batch I held. "Ready to trade?"

I glanced through the remaining stories on the Central Station. There was one surprise. Harley Duke had led the opposition to the bond issue it required, but once the voters had okayed it in spite of him, he became a major backer. He volunteered to serve on the oversight committee, which recommended a contractor and made regular reports on the construction. He had even backed the five cost overruns which were approved during construction. Irish Svenson had opposed three of them.

And the contractor for the project had been Balew Brothers.

Very interesting.

Balew Brothers had a checkered history in Grantham. I thought we should get all the background we had on them from our library. I put the request in, then Ace and I walked over to the Central Station to make Coy's briefing on Bo's death. My library stop had nearly made us late, and we had to dash up the stairs. It was worth the run, however, to see Ace's face when Coy read off the medical examiner's preliminary report.

"Okay," the Ass muttered into my ear. "What time do you want to go to lunch tomorrow?"

The probable cause of death was cyanide, Coy said. And the probable method of introducing it was in a candy bar with almonds. That was logical. Any murder mystery reader knows cyanide smells like almonds. No special knowledge needed there. An almond candy bar would be perfect for the poison, and the way Bo had been stuffing down candy during the hostage situation would have told anyone that he would grab a candy bar and inhale it. I'd included his chocolate binge in my story, and I thought it had been on Channel Four, too.

Hammond reluctantly admitted that a Grantham Mental Health Center employee—former employee would probably be more accurate at this point—had allowed Bo to have a candy bar brought in by the phony Salvation Army officer.

He didn't have anything to say about the source of the poison, but pointed out—as I had—that cyanide is readily available.

I'd come in late and concentrated on what Coy and Hammond had to say. So when I stood up at the end of the briefing, I was surprised to see Mike standing at the back of the room. He'd changed from his uniform and looked terrific in khakis and a rust polo shirt. I went over to talk to him.

"I got your message," he said quietly.

"I got yours," I answered.

"Unfortunately, I've already booked us for this evening, so you may have to appear in public with me. I need a chaperone."

"A chaperone? Where are you going?"

"I finally thought of someone who's very likely to

know what my dad was up to shortly before his death. However—'' He stopped and cleared his throat. "Well, it's a girl I used to date in high school. When I called her, she was a bit cool to the idea of meeting me. Said her husband wouldn't like it.''

I laughed. "Your past is catching up with you.''

"It's the remote past. Anyway, I finally suggested that I drop by their house—and said I'd like to introduce my girl to both of them. Think you can make it?''

I thought about it. "I guess I can. Just who is this old girlfriend?''

"Shelly Marcum Smith. I had a big crush on her when I was sixteen. After high school, she went to work for the city. She was my dad's secretary for three years.''

CHAPTER 13

Mike's idea was so elementary that I kicked myself for not thinking of it first.

Who knows more about a man than his wife? Than his mother? Than his best friend? Than his therapist or his barber?

His secretary, that's who.

I could recall telling Chuck this, when I was breaking him in on the violence beat just a couple of months earlier. I took him around the run, introduced him to Chief Jameson's secretary, to the head clerk at the sheriff's office, to Guy Unitas and his bookkeeper at the Amalgamated Police Brotherhood office, to the administrative assistant to the director of the Grantham area of the state police. Whatever their titles, these are the people who make those agencies function. With them on your side, the reporter's job is a lot easier.

"Check out the pictures on their desks," I told Chuck. "Ask about their kids. Find out where their husbands or wives work. Know what their hobbies are, what organizations they belong to. The day will come when the television scoops you completely, and the only thing that saves your fanny is the secretary who calls to say the Channel Four news crew came by to interview her boss."

Of course, the Channel Four news crew is working those secretaries just as hard as the newspaper reporters are. All's fair in love, war, and news gathering.

But your interest in the secretaries—or in their bosses, for that matter—has to be sincere. If you don't enjoy meeting all sorts of people, ordinary as well as powerful, the glibbest chitchat in the world won't put news sources on your side. If you have to fake an interest in them, their jobs, and their lives, then you're in the wrong business.

So I was ashamed of myself for not thinking of Irish Svenson's secretary. I knew Jameson had brought his own secretary along when he moved into the chief's office, and I hadn't had any idea who Irish's secretary had been or where she worked now. However, it seemed she and Mike were old friends. Or maybe enemies. I wondered who had dropped whom—back in high school. I decided I wouldn't get jealous of a former girlfriend from fifteen years earlier who was now married.

What would she have to tell?

I almost gnashed my teeth with impatience as Ace and I drove back to the *Gazette* office. In a few hours Mike and I might talk to someone who could really know something about the possibility that Irish Svenson had been killed. And I might get a phone call from my anonymous source. But at the moment I was stuck with Ace-the-Ass and an investigative story I felt sure wasn't going to amount to anything.

Another of Ace's annoying characteristics was laziness, but that day I was delighted when he knocked off as soon as we were back at the *Gazette* office.

The library had the information on Balew Brothers

ready for me, and I looked it over. Around ten years earlier, Balew Brothers had been involved in a major scandal involving a state project. A couple of executives—one of them an actual Balew brother—had gone to jail. As a result, an outside investor had bought a major interest in the company. One Balew was still around, but apparently the new group had kept their noses clean. They'd even dodged a threatened bankruptcy and tried to pay off the debts left behind by the old crew. I could see that their newfound honesty would have made them appealing to Honest Irish Svenson. I put the file aside to show Ace.

I wrote a followup on Bo's death, then took a half hour to go over current cases and working stories with J.B. and Chuck, who was to learn the nuances of the nightside cup beat. And I waited until Ruth Borah got off the phone with her son, then apologized to her for going to Jake with my request for a change in assignment. She told me I had caught her by surprise.

"But it's probably a good idea," she said.

"Thanks a lot!"

Ruth laughed and tucked a hairpin into her slicked-back black hair. "Yeah, it's not good form for an editor to tell a reporter she's working too hard. But for the past year you've seemed to concentrate on the job almost exclusively."

"I guess I have. It was semideliberate."

"You're too nice a person to turn into one of these tough old reporters who don't have any personal life, Nell. It's not good for you—and it's also not good for the paper, in the long run. Reporters who get that involved in their beats lose objectivity, and they don't do their jobs right."

She poked a pencil into the bun, giving herself the air of a businesslike geisha girl. Then she leaned toward me and lowered her voice. "One Felicia on the staff is enough."

Felicia Hess is the *Gazette* music and dance critic. She rides herd on the openings of the Grantham Symphony Orchestra, the Southwest Ballet Company, and a bunch of other arts groups. She drives Ruth crazy because she wants the presses held for her reviews. Are her reviews popular enough to be worth paying overtime to the press room? Ruth says no. She's not convinced that our readers are waiting with bated breath to learn just what Felicia thought of the second movement of Beethoven's *Fifth*. Felicia says yes, but she thinks Grantham's arts crowd is the paper's most important group of subscribers. We hold for sports scores, she whines, and arts events are as important as sports events. True, Ruth answers, but their fans aren't as fanatic.

It's a controversy that will never be settled.

By six-fifteen I was home, eating Chinese takeout, and waiting for the phone to ring. By the time Mike came by, I hoped, I would have talked to the mysterious woman who claimed to know about Irish Svenson's "murder."

I waited for her call nervously—fearful that she didn't know anything and fearful that she did. I paced the floor and wished that I had my own phone line, one with Caller ID. Martha, Brenda, and I had agreed that we'd have a minimal service for a minimal charge, so we had refused to install Call Waiting, Caller ID, and other extras. Right then, I'd have given anything to have that simple little gadget which would tell me what number the mystery woman was calling from.

I did have one piece of luck. Brenda and Martha were both out for the evening, so I didn't have to plead or threaten to keep them off the phone, and Rocky has his own line. Martha's mom called again, but I brushed her off quickly.

I did set up my tape recorder with the little microphone I stick onto the receiver if I want to tape a phone interview. I usually tell the subject I'm taping, but this time I didn't feel that I would be required to offer that information. If—if the mystery woman called, that is, and I actually did get an interview. And if she knew something worth taping.

So I waited. I sat in my room and tried to read, and my shrimp-fried rice grew heavier and heavier in my stomach. Then, at 7:35 p.m., the phone rang.

"Hello?" It was the same breathy little voice, this time with a steady, dull, roar in the background. "Is this Nell Matthews?"

"Yes." I must have sounded as timid as she did. I didn't want to scare her.

"I called this afternoon . . ." Her voice trailed off.

"Yes. You said you had information about the death of Irish Svenson. That you had reason to believe the car wreck that killed him wasn't an accident."

"Yes. That's right."

"Just what is this information?"

She sighed deeply. "I called back because I'd said I would, but it's really hard for me to tell you anything. I mean, I simply can't appear in this."

"Why not? If you know something about a crime, isn't it your responsibility to report it?"

She gave a nervous giggle. "Sure! But it's also my responsibility to stay alive! And if these people would kill Irish and Bo Jenkins, believe me, they wouldn't hesitate a minute to kill me. And maybe kill someone else, too. Someone whose life really matters."

"Who's that?"

Long silence. I tried again. "Look, I can tell that you're really frightened. I certainly don't want to put your life at risk. Let me go over what I've deduced. First, you say Irish was doing some sort of internal investigation at the time he died—looking into some problem inside the Grantham Police Department."

"That's near enough."

"Near enough? Was the problem outside the PD?"

"Inside and outside."

"Oh." I thought about it. Could she be referring to the kickback scheme Ace had dredged up? I decided to go on.

"Second, you say no one inside the department knew about what Irish was investigating. That's the reason nothing has come out about it since Jameson took over."

"That's right." Her voice became urgent. "Wait a minute!"

I could hear faint knocks, and I realized that she had dropped the receiver. It must be hanging by its cord and bumping against the wall. I pictured a wall phone, maybe a pay phone with a metal-covered cord. Well, that was no surprise. She would be afraid I would try to trace the call. So having Caller ID wouldn't have helped me.

Her voice sounded in the background, faintly. I couldn't understand most of the words, but I caught,

"No! No!" I could still hear the roar. Then she was back.

"I'm sorry. I can't talk much longer," she said.

"No! Don't hang up," I said. "I still don't even know your connection with the case. I'm guessing you work for the department."

"No."

"Then you worked for the 'outside' agency involved."

"Yes, that's right."

"Was it a construction firm?"

"No." She sighed. "Look, after I talked to you this afternoon, I realized I'll have to tell you the whole story. I'll just have to trust you not to let anybody at the GPD know about me. Who I am, or where I am."

"I obviously can't tell anybody what I don't know. You've got me completely mystified. I don't even know your name."

She gave a fruity laugh. "Call me Lee," she said. "But if you let anybody over at the PD know about my calls, I might as well cash in my burial policy. And I mean anybody. Believe me, the people involved in this would surprise even you."

"I always do my best to protect my sources," I said.

"I'm trusting you to do that." She sighed again. "Anyway, I've got the afternoon off tomorrow. I can meet you."

I almost gasped. She was being so mysterious, and now she was offering to meet me. "Sure. When and where?"

"It'll be late afternoon before I can get there. Say, four o'clock, in the Memorial Rose Garden?"

"Great!" It was great, as a matter of fact. The

Grantham Memorial Rose Garden is just on the other
side of the Grantham State campus, not a half mile
from my house. It would be thronged with college
students at four o'clock. "But that's a pretty big park.
How will I know you?"

"I saw you on television this weekend. Just sit near
the fountain."

She hung up.

Now where was I? I rewound the tape in my two-
bit tape recorder and played it back. Lee had mentioned the "PD." Did that mark her as a person who
had hung around the cop shop for a while?

I listened to the tape again. Had I promised not to
tell anybody in the Grantham PD about her call? And
did that include Mike?

I thought about that question and played the tape
a third time. Well, I hadn't quite promised. "Lee,"
or whatever her real name was, definitely would say
I shouldn't tell Mike. But I couldn't imagine Mike
being involved in a scheme which led to his father's death.

I wasn't being naive, even though I knew that the
most likely killer is a member of the victim's family.
So if Irish had been murdered, Mike and his mom
would be at the top of the suspect list. But I couldn't
bring myself to suspect Mike. His feelings for his
father were too open, too natural. Besides, he hadn't
been in Grantham when the car wreck happened.
He hadn't been connected with the Grantham PD at
that time.

What had I learned from Lee that Mike might be
interested in? Nothing, to be honest. Lee's information was extremely nebulous.

I decided not to mention Lee to Mike until I'd

talked to her. If she showed up for our appointment Tuesday. Which she very likely wouldn't.

At eight-forty-three-and-a-half the doorbell buzzed, and when I peeped through the peephole, I saw Mike. I was almost ashamed of the way my internal organs jumped around. I was as infatuated as a fourteen-year-old.

Mike came in, looking serious. We put our arms around each other and stood in the hall, holding tight for a few seconds. When I backed off far enough to see his face, he looked a little more cheerful.

"Boring seminar?" I asked.

"Problems in Supervision," he said. "Tonight was 'The Employee with Drug or Alcohol-Related Problems.' "

"Doesn't sound too scintillating."

"Some of these guys! If they're already supervisors, and you have to tell them that an alcoholic isn't going to get better until he gets treatment, and it's up to the supervisor to push the guy into treatment—if it's affecting his job. God! If they don't already know that—" He shook his head, then grinned. "I guess I was eager to get out of there. You ready?"

I checked my purse to make sure I had a notebook and pencil, and double-locked the front door behind us while Mike opened the door of the pickup for me. As soon as he was inside, I began quizzing him.

"Just what is the background of this interview, Officer Svenson?"

Mike started the motor. "Well, Shelly and I dated for six months or so when we were in high school. We broke up just after Christmas our junior year. By our senior year she was dating this guy she married, Rowdy Smith."

"Rowdy?"

"I think his name is actually Rowell, or something like that. I knew him fairly well, because he was a right guard. We played football together all through junior high and high school. We weren't really friends. Rowdy went on to college ball, played at Grantham State."

"You didn't play college ball?"

"No. I was sick of it by then. I wasn't good enough for the really top programs—OU, Notre Dame, Nebraska, Texas. I didn't see any point in playing for a smaller school." He grinned at me. "I'd already had surgery on my knee once. I wasn't willing to be a cripple for anything less than the Orange Bowl. And as a spoiled only child whose mom is a big-time real estate operator, I didn't need the scholarship."

"But Rowdy played?"

"A couple of years. I don't think he ever finished college. Anyway, he's an electrician now. Works with his dad. He and Shelly got married young. I think they've got good-sized kids."

Shelly and Rowdy and their good-sized kids lived in a brick home in a newish neighborhood. The trees in the yard were still scrawny, but some chrysanthemums flowered in a tub on the porch, and the flower bed had been planted with kale for the winter. A stub-nosed kid answered the door. When he saw us, he turned around and yelled, "They're here!"

He shoved the door open and motioned us inside ungraciously. "You're supposed to go in the living room."

We followed him through a tiny entrance hall and into a living room furnished with a deep sectional in medium blue and two tub chairs covered in a mauve-

and-blue floral. A plant stand was loaded with African violets of different colors, and a print of a dreamy garden scene was centered over the couch. I could hear the television set, but it was in a room behind the kitchen. Thank God. It's really hard to interview someone with the television on.

Mike and I sat on the sectional, and the kid sat on a hassock facing us. He had light brown hair and a pudgy, little boy body, but he was nearly as tall as I was.

He looked at Mike suspiciously. "You a cop?"

"Right," Mike answered. "You a student?"

The kid ignored Mike's question. "Are cops crookeder than crooks, or crooks crookeder than cops?"

I could feel my eyes widen, but Mike didn't seem to get upset. "What does your mom say?" he asked. "She's worked with a lot of cops."

The kid shrugged. Mom's opinion apparently didn't count for much. "What's the worst thing you ever did."

"Let me think about that." Mike's jaw twitched, and I could see that the kid amused him. "I guess the worst thing I ever did was tell a lie."

He had obviously disappointed our young host. A lie was nothing in pug nose's world. Then his eyes grew more hopeful. "What was the lie about?"

"Well, back when I was a stupid teenager, I told the rest of the football players a story that wasn't true about a girl I really liked. I've always been sorry."

A rumbling voice filled the room. "You didn't think anybody believed you, did you?"

"Rowdy!" Mike stood up, and he and a larger version of the stub-nosed kid performed some male bonding rituals. Shaking hands. Whacking each other on the shoulder. "You son-of-a-gun!" "You old buzzard!" I was a bit surprised at their enthusiasm. I'd had the idea Mike wasn't looking forward to seeing Rowdy.

By the time Rowdy had proudly admitted he had quite a paunch on him these days, Shelly came in. She ignored the guys and greeted me. I knew her immediately.

"You work up in records," I said.

She nodded. "Yes, when Chief Jameson came in, I transferred up there. And you're Nell Matthews. Mike said he was bringing his girlfriend, but he didn't say who she was."

"We haven't been dating long." I knew I sounded awkward.

Shelly was an attractive woman with dark hair and dark, expressive eyes. She was dressed in rose-colored pants and a loose, flowered shirt that almost matched the floral print of the chair she sat down in. She had a full-figured look, and Rowdy definitely looked like a lineman gone to seed.

It took us ten minutes to get through the amenities. We met the other two kids—two plump little girls came in from the den—admired the African violets, and accepted refreshments. Beer for Mike and Rowdy. Iced tea for Shelly and me. We caught up on where I was from and how long Mike had been in Chicago and corresponding information on Shelly and Rowdy.

Mike didn't gossip too long. He turned to Shelly. "I'm sorry to bother you and Rowdy, but I'm trying to find out a couple of things about my dad's affairs.

And I'm sure nobody knows more about the last months of his life than you do."

Shelly picked at the hem of her shirt uneasily. "Just what do you want to know?"

"Was he working on any special project?"

"Not that he told me about. We'd gotten moved into the new Central Station about a year before, so he kept checking up on problems with that. You know, the kind of stuff that always comes up with a new building. Leaking around the skylights. Tile curled up in the men's room."

Mike nodded. "I was thinking more about problems with the department. Or maybe even personal problems."

"Not that I can say." Shelly stared into space. "Of course, the chief was under a lot of pressure."

"Pressure?"

"From the city council. That jerk Harley Duke—" She shook her head.

"Harley's always a problem."

"But he was worse then. He was bringing up something about the PD at every city council meeting. But he refused to meet with your dad to discuss his complaints. It was just one nitpicking thing after another. It got to Irish. Or I guess that's what was bothering him."

Mike didn't reply. He simply looked at her expectantly. I've used that technique myself. Hardly anyone can face silence. They'll start talking.

Shelly was no exception. She picked at a fingernail, but she talked. "I don't really know what was going on with your dad, Mike. He had always been the kindest, most cheerful, most polite man I've ever been around. But that last six or seven months, he was sort of hard to work for. One week—every night one week he stayed late and went through my personnel files. Messed them all up."

"Aren't the files computerized?" I inserted that question.

Shelly nodded. "Sure, the official records are—the forms. But there are always things that don't fit the forms. Maybe somebody writes to complain about some officer. Believe me, that letter is floating around someplace, even if no official complaint ever goes on this record. I kept those files, Irish's private personnel files."

"And he messed them up?"

"They weren't out of order. Just the papers in them were messed up. So I offered to help him. Kind of kidded him." She leaned forward. "That's the only time in the five years we worked together than Irish almost bit my head off.

"But it wasn't just me! He had a terrible fight with Chief Jameson the week before he died. Jameson was doing the preliminary budget, and he put in a tenpercent cut for training. Irish didn't like that. He even had a battle with that old friend of his."

"Old friend?"

Shelly nodded impatiently. "Yes. That security firm guy."

"Mickey O'Sullivan?" I could tell this was news to Mike.

"Uh-huh. He and Irish used to get together for lunch every couple of weeks. Mr. O'Sullivan came by the office to set something up, and they had a battle over his scheduling of off-duty policemen."

Mike shook his head. "Of course, he and Mickey

went back so far that they weren't always real tactful with each other. They got over it."

"Well, that day Mr. O'Sullivan walked out looking like fury! But you're right, because Irish called him up that very afternoon and apologized."

She picked at her hem nervously one more time. "You know how those offices are set up. I could hear anything that went on in Irish's office unless he actually closed his door."

Mike nodded, but he didn't follow up on the question. So I did. "Did he do that a lot? Make an effort to speak privately?"

Shelly turned her attention to me, but her eyes flickered back toward Mike. "Just when he held a meeting in there. Or when he talked to Mrs. Svenson. I always walked to his door to tell him she was on the line, then I closed it behind me."

Mike was still looking mystified.

Then Shelly took a deep breath, planted both feet on the floor and leaned forward with her elbows on her knees and her hands clasped pleadingly.

"Mike, you were in Chicago then. Did you know about the trouble between your parents? That they had separated?"

CHAPTER 14

There was a stunned silence, then Mike laughed.

"That's ridiculous, Shelly," he said. "Where'd you get that idea?"

Shelly looked angry. "I guess when your dad told me he'd moved out, I kind of got the drift."

"He told you that?"

Shelly nodded. "Two days before he died, Chief Svenson went out to the Northside Station to discuss a personnel problem. He'd been gone about an hour when he had a call from the city manager about a meeting that night. I paged your dad. But he didn't answer. So I figured he had his pager turned off while he and the division chief were talking. I kept trying. When he still wasn't answering at five-thirty, I called him at home. Your mom"—she looked at Mike earnestly—"your mom has always been wonderful to me, Mike. But she was a little testy that time, kind of sharp. She said he wasn't there, and I should page. So I did page again, in about twenty minutes, and that time he called in.

"Before I went home the next day, I said something about being sorry I'd had to disturb Mrs. Svenson. I guess I was mad over the way she'd snapped at me. And your dad said he'd better tell me that they'd had a few problems, and he had moved out—temporarily."

"Moved out?" Mike sounded unbelieving.

"I was—well, dismayed. Because your folks always seemed so happy. But Chief Svenson told me not to worry. He said he felt sure they would work things out."

Shelly blinked, hard, and swallowed. "Then that evening he called me at home and said he had to go out of town on personal business the next day, and he wasn't taking his pager." She produced a tissue from her sleeve and wiped her eyes. "That was the last time I talked to him."

Mike was sitting like a stone. So I spoke. "The chief didn't tell you where he was going?"

"No! He just said 'personal business.' He sounded kind of excited. A little happier than he'd been the day before." Shelly looked at me and blinked again. "To tell the truth, I hoped he and Mrs. Svenson had made up. I hoped they were going to go someplace, have some fun.

"When I heard about the wreck, Mike, my first thought was that you might have lost both your parents."

"No." Mike smiled an icy smile. "I still have my mother." He stood up. "Thanks for your time, Shelly."

He was barely civil as we said good-bye. He opened the door of the pickup and handed me in with a stiff politeness, but he had retreated behind a curtain of ice. The cab of the pickup was like a refrigerator, with the cold air provided by Mike's new mood. He drove five miles without saying a word. I couldn't think of anything to say either.

We were crossing Grantham on one of its major east-west arteries, Liberty Boulevard. Mike was driving at exactly the speed required to make the lights, so we didn't stop at all. The farther west we went, the snazzier the neighborhoods became. It was a dark night, and I wasn't familiar with the area—not much to interest a crime reporter out that way. But when Mike swung off Liberty at an intersection marked by an artistic streetlight and a pair of imposing stone pillars marked TALL TREES, I knew where I was.

"Mike! Where are you going?"

"To my mom's house."

"No!"

He was still icy cold. "I've got to talk to her."

"Okay, you've got to talk to her. But I don't. Your mom's not going to discuss her marital problems in front of me. Or did you think I'd wait in the truck while the two of you had it out?" If I sounded mad, it's because I was. "Think what you're doing."

Mike said nothing, but he turned off the street into a parking area. The truck's headlights showed a small pond and some benches, interspersed with pines and oaks. In Tall Trees, this was probably known as "the commons area." Any place else it would be a small neighborhood park.

Mike doused the truck's lights and turned off the motor. "You're right," he said. "I've got to think what I'm doing." He got out of the truck and walked away. As soon as my eyes had adjusted to the moonlight, I followed.

Mike was standing near the edge of the pond. He stooped and picked up something. Since he was under a pine tree, I assumed it was a pine cone. He hurled it into the pond, using a strong swing and a lot of follow-through. I could hear a faint splash as it hit the water. Then he picked up another pine cone and threw it.

The wooden bench was more ornamental than comfortable, but I sat on it, watching Mike throw pine cones and anger into the pond. It was a clear and balmy evening, luckily, because I wasn't wearing an outdoor jacket. The moon was almost full.

After ten minutes or so, Mike seemed to run out of pine cones. He kicked the pine needles a couple of times, then sat beside me on the bench. I was afraid to touch him, and I still didn't know what to say.

"Sorry," he said. "You're right. I wasn't thinking very clearly. It's stupid, but I feel like the props have been knocked out from under the first thirty-two years of my life."

"When you're calmer you'll see that's not true. Just because your parents were having trouble settling some problem—"

"My parents always settled things."

"Always? Mike, every human relationship has problems. No two people agree all the time."

"Oh, sure, they disagreed. They'd yell sometimes, but they settled it. My dad was a big believer in the 'never let the sun set on your anger' bit." He laughed bitterly. "When I was sixteen, I took my mom's car without permission and bashed in the radiator. They couldn't agree on what my punishment was to be. I heard them discussing my fate way after midnight— a lot of rumbles, and a roar or two—but they settled it before they went to bed. At the breakfast table I faced scrambled eggs and a united front."

"I see."

"Yeah. So if this problem was so bad they couldn't stay in the same house—"

"But, Mike, your dad told Shelly it was temporary!"

"Maybe. But, Nell, if my dad was killed—if his death wasn't an accident—Mom might know something about why it happened. She may not even realized she knows something. I've got to find out what was going on in my dad's life."

"I can see that," I said. "But if your mother didn't tell you voluntarily about the separation, she may not want to tell you at all."

"I'm sure she doesn't. I've known something was bothering her. It's going to be tricky." He stared at the moonlit scene. "Maybe I can use Mickey," he said. "And it might help if you're there."

"Huh? What are you talking about? I'm not going to your mother's house."

"If Mickey had been on the scene before my dad died—" Mike stopped talking. He seemed to be thinking deeply.

If Mickey was on the scene? Mickey had been a friend of Mike's parents for more than thirty years. What did Mike mean?

I gasped as I realized he was referring to the romance, affair, relationship, whatever they called it, between his mother and Mickey O'Sullivan. Mike was already having trouble accepting his mother's sexual attraction to a man other than his father, even now that she was a widow. If she'd been having an affair with Mickey before his dad died—well, Mike wasn't going to like it. But I hadn't heard any evidence that that was true.

I gasped again. "Mike! You have no basis in the world for such speculation!"

"They're sure seeing a lot of each other now."

"Your dad's been gone two years! Don't jump—"

But right at that moment, we both jumped. Because the beam of a spotlight hit us.

We whirled toward the street in unison, like a sit-down drill team. The light was blinding.

"Damn," Mike said, "it's the security patrol. Mickey's got the contract for this subdivision."

"Maybe it's someone you know."

"Not likely. Mickey staffs this area with full-timers," he said.

A bulky figure loomed against the light. "Sorry, folks! This is a private area, and I'm afraid you two are trespassing."

The guard asked for ID, and Mike surprised me by producing his driver's license, rather than his badge. He explained that his mother lived in the neighborhood and that we'd been on our way to her house. He laughed easily. "We just stopped to discuss a couple of things before we talked to her," he said.

The guard—I never did get a good look at him—subtly changed his attitude when he saw Mike's name. "Svenson, huh? Your dad was Grantham chief."

"Right." Mike's voice was noncommittal. "And Mr. O'Sullivan's an old family friend."

Wilda probably had no secrets from the security guards, I realized. If these guys saw their boss's car in her drive on a regular basis, they were passing the word around about how often he came over and how long he stayed. For that matter, maybe Mickey lived with her. I didn't know.

The guard didn't ask for my ID, and I appreciated his attitude, though it may have been based on sexism. I'm not a local celebrity like Irish Svenson, but sometimes people do recognize my byline.

Unfortunately, the episode left Mike and me committed to a visit to his mother. The guard was polite, but he kept standing there, obviously waiting for us to move on to the spot Mike had said we intended to visit, Wilda Svenson's house. So we got in the truck and drove around a curving street lined dotted with five-year-old oak trees and lined with town houses. Mike pulled into a well-lit drive.

Wilda's town house reflected her status as one of Grantham's top real estate operators. Two stories of buff brick with dark trim doesn't quite tell the tale. Adding a few details—wrought-iron chandelier over the arched entranceway, stained-glass insert in the front door, topiary trees in stone pots—may give a better idea of the total effect.

I got out of the truck and stared. "Wow!" I said.

The doorbell gonged like Big Ben. I "wowed" again. Then I nudged Mike. "Don't you have a key?"

"Yeah. But on Labor Day I learned it was more tactful to ring first. I hope my mom learned the same lesson yesterday."

A light went on in the hall. "Don't say anything you're going to regret," I said. "Keep cool."

Mike squeezed my hand. "I've developed cucumberitis."

Wilda smiled graciously as she opened the door. "Hello! Mike. You should have told me you were bringing Nell by."

She wore a long, coppery brown robe in a moire fabric I was willing to bet was pure silk, and she held a pair of reading glasses in her hand.

"Come on in," she said. "Mickey dropped by to watch the game."

So Mickey didn't live there. But no car had been parked in the drive. Mickey must park in the two-car garage. A smart move, if he wanted to keep his private life from being discussed by his employees. I wondered if he consulted the schedule, to make sure he didn't arrive just as an O'Sullivan car drove by.

Monday Night Football was blaring from the television set, and Mickey was putting his shoes on as we came into the den. The rumpled cushions said clearly that he'd been stretched out on the off-white couch. A circle of lamplight, a lap board, and a stack of file folders near an easy chair said just as clearly that Wilda had been looking over some papers. They'd been settled in for a companionable evening. I had the feeling Mickey might not be planning to leave after the game was over. But I also had the feeling he might fall asleep before the final play.

I was completely out of my depth. I was scared to death that Mike was going to create a scene. What if he accused his mother and Mickey of having an affair while his dad was still alive? What if he and Mickey came to blows? I could understand why Mike felt he had to talk to his mother, but I didn't want to be a witness.

Luckily, the conversation didn't depend on me. Instead, Mike and Mickey began to watch the game. Between plays, they discussed the Dallas Cowboys' Super Bowl chances and other topics of portent.

Wilda gave me the gracious hostess treatment. Where was I from? Where had I gone to college? Why did I decide to become a reporter? I had barely enough presence of mind to stumble through the answers.

This went on for the longest ten minutes of my life, then Wilda stood up. "Mickey and I were just talking about popping some corn," she said. "How does that sound?"

Mike jumped to his feet. "Great! I'll help you."

He might as well have run up a flag saying, "I want to talk to you alone."

Mickey smiled his sardonic smile, and my stomach lurched as the two of them left the room.

"What's Mike up to?" Mickey said. I shook my head. I was too scared to talk. I pretended to watch the game.

Voices rumbled down the hall, but I couldn't distinguish any words until I suddenly heard Wilda raise her voice. She sounded as if she were trying to keep her voice icy cool, but it got louder. "I don't want to go into it. It had nothing to do with you."

"Oh, thanks for assuring me of that." Mike's voice was cold, but it had an angry edge. "But you and Dad always talked things out. This must have been too serious to talk about."

"Dammit, Mike! I hope we wouldn't separate over something trivial!"

Mickey's mouth was set. Moving deliberately, he got to his feet.

Mike was speaking again. "I just want to understand what was going on in Dad's life at the time he died."

"We never understand what's going on in someone else's life, Mike. Forget it."

"I can't. He called me, you know. Said he had to talk to me about something when I came home. But I didn't come that week. Now I'll always wonder if it would have made a difference. Sometimes I blame myself—"

"Don't be stupid! It wasn't your fault." Wilda's emphasis on the word "your" was unmistakable. She was almost yelling. "How do you think it made me feel when he died, and I realized we'd never get things worked out! Never! I get to blame myself forever!"

Mickey walked purposely from the den, obviously headed for the kitchen to intervene. I followed him into a kitchen that was straight out of *Better Homes & Gardens*.

"Hey, hey," Mickey said soothingly, "Mike, maybe you'd better talk to your mom about this when you're both calmer. Wilda, you know you have nothing to blame yourself for."

Mike was glaring coldly at his mom. "There was something Dad wanted to talk to me about, something important, he said. Something he had to tell me face-to-face. But I changed my leave time, for my own convenience. By the time I came home, it was too late. For two years I've felt that I let him down. Now I find out there was a bunch of stuff going on that nobody thought was important enough to mention to me."

He shifted his glare to Mickey. "And just where do you fit in here, Mickey? Just what was going on—"

I grabbed his hand. "Mike!"

But his meaning had been all too clear. He'd come very close to accusing his mother of having an adulterous affair.

Wilda's face flamed. "My god! You're as sanctimonious as Irish was, aren't you?"

Mike gripped my hand until my mother's ring cut into my little finger. He stared at the floor tile.

Wilda drew herself up regally. "Yes, Irish was always so sure he knew exactly the right thing to do, the honest thing! He was Mr. Upright. No cheating! No stepping over the bounds of propriety! Well, he found out!"

"Wilda!" Mickey was raising his voice now. "Mike doesn't need to know all this!"

"Oh, yes, he does! He's not a little kid! He needs to understand that his father was a human being! Flawed! Just like the rest of us."

She held her regal pose, her head framed by the lit window of the microwave. Behind her, the popcorn began exploding and its sack began swelling.

"Yes, you're right, Mike. Adultery was at the heart of the problem between your father and me. But I wasn't the guilty party. Your dad had been seeing another woman. For months!"

She turned around and pounded her fist against the door of the microwave oven with a gesture that strangely echoed the motions Mike had made throwing pine cones.

"And when I found out about it," she said, "Irish said he had 'responsibilities.' His responsibilities to this bimbo apparently outweighed his responsibilities to me. He said he was going to go on seeing her! He said he had no choice!"

She whirled back to face us. The popcorn was at the rapid-fire stage now, giving the impression that Wilda's brain was shooting off machine-gun bullets. She spread her arms, resting each hand on the edge of the tiled cabinet top. She looked like an avenging goddess, standing there while the popping sound gradually grew. Steam began to fill the glass window behind her head.

"He gave me no choice! I threw him out! Damn right!"

The dramatic moment grew in intensity, and we all stood like statues. My heart was making a noise like the popcorn behind Wilda, and my stomach was jumping around the same way. I didn't dare say anything.

Then the microwave bell gave a loud *bing* and the light behind Wilda's head went off. And Mickey chuckled humorlessly. "He did it to you again, Wilda," he said. "You never learn."

Wilda's chin quivered, but she still held it high, staring at her son. "No, Mike's the one who never learns," she said. "He works around until he gets what he wants, but then it's not the thing he was really after."

Wilda had been our center of attention, but now I looked back at Mike. He hadn't moved, but his mother had analyzed his emotional situation very clearly. He looked crushed and sullen. He dropped my hand and folded his arms. His mouth almost pouted.

"You don't believe me," Wilda said quietly. "You don't believe Irish had an affair."

Mike's eyes narrowed. "I believe you believe it," he said. "But Dad would never have done something that stupid."

"Mike, he admitted it," Wilda said.

Mike shook his head. "Morals aside—and Dad's morals weren't all just talk, Mom—he really loved you. I always knew who came first around here. I was important to him, but you were everything."

"Oh, he claimed he loved me," Wilda said. "But he wouldn't tell me he'd quit seeing that woman."

Mike ignored her remark. "And Dad wasn't dumb. He loved his job. He knew his job depended on his reputation. He would never have risked a scandal."

"You're not hearing what I'm saying," Wilda said. She moved across the kitchen and took Mike by the arms, as if she were going to shake him. "None of us is perfect, Mike. We all make mistakes. Your dad was no exception. He made a mistake."

She closed her eyes, and when she spoke again, her voice was a whisper. "I was so angry. I pushed him too hard. I have to live with that—for the rest of my life."

Mike stood silently. I could almost see his brain processing data. Then he put his arms around his mother. "No, Mom. If you believed Dad was seeing another woman, your reaction was—right. It's what Dad would have expected. You have nothing to blame yourself for."

Wilda spoke into Mike's shoulder. "Irish was human. He had to find that out the hard way. We all make mistakes, and we have to pick up and go on after them. But Irish couldn't accept that. He couldn't let go of a situation he admitted was a mistake."

They hugged each other tightly, then Wilda backed away and looked up at Mike. "You didn't really think that Mickey and I—"

Mike grinned. "Aw, Mom. When I'm around you and Mickey, I can feel a lot of mutual affection and respect."

Then the two of them laughed as if this were the funniest joke of the year. Wilda pulled a paper towel from a roll next to the sink and wiped her eyes.

Mickey looked at me. "How did two normal people like us get mixed up with these crazies?" he said.

CHAPTER 15

Mike and I didn't hang around. Mickey pulled the popcorn out of the microwave, and he and Wilda walked us to the front door. Mike had only one more question for his mother.

"Did Dad tell you who this woman was?"

Wilda lifted her head firmly. "No."

"He didn't tell me either, Mike." Mickey put his arm around Wilda's shoulders. "Irish stayed with me that last week of his life, but all he told me was that he and Wilda needed a cooling-off period. I didn't know the cause of the fight until Wilda told me months later."

Mike frowned. "Apparently he went out of town the day he died, Mickey. Did he tell you where he was going?"

"No. He got only one phone call at my house. It was from Dr. Willingham."

"Dr. Willingham!" Mike sounded amazed. "He's been gone for years."

"Yeah, but he was a good counselor. I figured—I hoped—Irish was going to talk to him."

Wilda put her hand on Mike's arm. "We hadn't given up."

Mike hugged her, and she squeezed my hand. We drove away.

"Who is Dr. Willingham?" I asked.

"He was the minister of First Presbyterian back when I was a little kid. Ran my confirmation class. He left Grantham nearly fifteen years ago. Now he's at Lovers' Lane Presbyterian in Dallas. But Mickey's right about one thing. My dad always liked him. If he wanted someone to talk to—wanted counseling—Dr. Willingham could well have been the one he went to."

"Do you think your dad could have gone to see him the day of his death?"

"No, I know he didn't. Dr. Willingham came to the funeral, and I remember he told me he'd flown into Grantham from New York. He'd been there for a couple of weeks, teaching a workshop. He didn't mention talking to my dad."

"If he's a reputable counselor, he very likely wouldn't tell you or your mom anything your dad had told him, anyway."

"I know." Mike sighed. "I have no idea where my dad could have gone the day he was killed. And it could be the key."

I sat silently. I don't like scenes, and the one between Mike and his mom had disturbed me. Mike told me that one thing he liked about me was that I don't dither, but at that moment I was strongly tempted to dither like mad. My stomach was still jumping around like the popcorn in Wilda's microwave. I wasn't too happy with Mike for putting me through that, and I certainly didn't approve of his losing his temper with his mother. But he'd been upset by the news of the rift in his parents' marriage, so I tried not to judge him too harshly.

Right at that moment, Mike reached over and took

my hand. "You were great at Mom's," he said. "She's right. The news I got wasn't what I wanted to hear, but I had to know. And she'd never have told me without the little nudge from you."

"Nudge from me?"

"Yeah. That 'Mike!' like you were holding my coattails. It was perfect. That's when she lost it."

I felt as if the security guard's floodlight had hit me in the face again. I saw the scene at Wilda's house for what it was. A scene, true. But not an emotional scene. It had been a staged scene.

Mike had not really been angry. He had been pretending to be angry. He'd been goading Wilda into losing her temper, prodding her into telling him something he thought she wouldn't reveal when she was calm. And he'd used me to do it.

The whole scene had been a sham. Mike had put on a show, used a semblance of anger to egg his mother—his own mother!—into blurting out the thing that she'd refused to tell him for two years. Mickey had said as much. "He did it to you again, Wilda," he'd said.

And my obvious embarrassment, my eagerness to keep him from accusing her of having an affair, my anguished "Mike!" had convinced Wilda of his sincerity. He'd tricked his mother, and he'd made me into his confederate.

Honest Nell, the woman who never lied. I'd lied for Mike.

A lightning strike of anger surged through my entire body.

If I ever kill anyone, it will be because that particular kind of anger flashes though my being at a moment when I'm holding a lethal weapon. Mike will never know how near to death he came right at that moment. If I'd had a sword in my hand, I'd have run him through. If I'd had a club, I'd have smashed his head. If I'd had a pistol, and if I'd had any idea of how to fire it, I'd have shot him dead, dead, dead.

As my head cleared and the fury drained out my feet, I knew that this was the end of the line for Mike and me.

Reaching this stage of self-knowledge took just about as long as it takes for a flash of lightning to jump from a cloud to a mountaintop. Then the storm burst. I wasn't mad enough to kill Mike anymore, but I was mad enough to tell him what I thought.

I started with, "You mean to tell me that whole scene was a performance—" and over the next five minutes I made my opinion pretty clear.

After a couple of startled looks and a muttered, "Hey," early in the tirade, Mike didn't say anything. He simply drove, looking straight ahead, and let me talk. When we came to a shopping area, he pulled in and parked the truck. He sat silently until I at last came to the final words, which happened to be "—manipulative creep!"

"I'm surprised at your criticism of manipulation," he said. His voice was tight and cold. "You're so good at it yourself."

Before I could get beyond, "And just what does that mean?" he got out and walked away from the truck.

His last remark had really ripped it. I was good at manipulation? Me? Honest Nell? The reporter who wouldn't take information off the record because I didn't want to lie about what I knew and what I didn't know? Nell, who never lied? Nell, whose conscience had been killing her for two days because she felt obligated to tell her boss about her romance with a cop?

But Mike hadn't seemed to care about whether or not I told my boss. Now I saw why. He saw nothing wrong with sneaking around. He thought I was merely afraid of getting caught.

I hated him.

Sitting there seething, I became aware of my surroundings. The truck was in the parking lot of an ice cream and dairy products store, and Mike was inside. I could see him in the ice cream line.

Ice cream? At a time like this Mike wanted ice cream? I growled in anger. "Hell's bells!" He'd taken the keys to the truck, or I might have driven off.

The line wasn't long, but it took five or ten minutes for Mike to get whatever he had ordered. And, of course, that was about the amount of time I needed to cool down from liquid lava to semisolid basalt. When he came back out, with a covered ice cream cup in each hand, I slid across the seat and opened the door for him.

"Chocolate ice cream with marshmallow topping," he said, handing me a cup. His voice was as cold as the ice cream.

"I don't want ice cream."

"Then let it melt."

He got in the truck and turned to face me, sitting with his back against the door. He flipped the plastic dome off his own sundae and began eating with a pink plastic spoon. He didn't say anything.

I was too mad for silence. "What did you mean by that crack about my being good at manipulation?"

"I meant it as a compliment. It's why you're such a good reporter."

"What do you mean?"

"You can make people want to tell you things. Look at the way you handled Bo Jenkins."

"Bo was holding a pistol to my head! I would have told him anything he wanted to hear. Besides, even then, I didn't lie."

"Good cop, bad cop."

"What do you mean?"

"That's basically how we worked Bo, Nell. You offered him some accommodation, acted like you cared about him. I represented authority, punishment. Between the two of us, we reassured him. He let you go. You distracted him. I grabbed him. It worked."

I looked at the ice cream sundae I was holding. It really was melting. All of a sudden I was hungry. I popped the clear dome off the top gently and picked up my own pink plastic spoon. The ice cream was delicious.

"Mike, how did we change the subject from your mother to Bo Jenkins?"

"At Mom's you were the good cop, and I was the bad. It's the same thing."

"Bo was threatening me! And you! And the baby! Your mother wasn't. She didn't deserve to be tricked."

"She wasn't tricked. She knows me. She knew what was going on."

"She didn't act like it."

Mike took three bites of his sundae before he answered. "Look, Nell, you and I are in the business of gathering information. Or, at least, I was when I was a detective, and I plan to be a detective again. My job is to get people to tell me things. Most of the people I talk to are not criminals. But they may know something that helps me find out who the criminal is. Maybe it's something little—say, the day a co-worker was late to work. Now they may not want to tell the police that, because they have to work with the guy, and they want to get along with him. They probably believe he's innocent anyway—the 'ol' Joe wouldn't do a thing like that' syndrome. I have to make them believe that we've already got the information from somewhere else and I only need confirmation. Or that Joe told us himself. Or that the information doesn't matter anyway. I have to give them some excuse to tell."

He stabbed the pink plastic spoon in my direction. "And reporters do the same thing. I've watched you!"

He was right, of course. I'd done it to the Salvation Army officer, Captain Eisner, as recently as Sunday morning. I'd expressed strong admiration for the work the shelter did. I'd promised I'd write a story telling of the wonderfulness of it all. That flattery and the offer to write a story were expedient. They got Captain Eisner opened up, talking. The ploy had worked.

But I'd really meant all that. I do admire the Salvation Army. I would do a story on the shelter.

"Mike, I don't lie to people! I don't pretend to be angry when I'm not. I don't use that fake anger to make them tell things. I wouldn't do it to my own mother!"

"Yeah. Well." Mike ate more ice cream. "I guess this was one of those ends-justifying-the-means evenings, Nell. You've got to remember what your goal is. After what Shelly told us, the next step to finding out what happened to my dad was to know why he and Mom had separated. Nobody knew that but her. And she didn't want to tell me, or she would have done it a long time ago. I know her. I knew that she'd have to give herself an excuse for telling me. Now she can tell herself, 'I just got so mad that I blurted it out.' "

"Mike, couldn't you have just told her why you needed to know?"

"I didn't want to get her hopes up."

"Get her hopes up? What are you talking about?"

"My dad's death."

Mike finished off his sundae, carefully put the plastic lid back on the empty dish, and wiped his fingers with a paper napkin. I was staring, holding my plastic spoon in midair.

"Mike, you've got me completely confused," I said. "What hopes could she have about your father's death?"

"Don't you see? If my dad was murdered, he didn't kill himself."

"Kill himself!"

"Yeah. Mom and I have both spent the past two years convinced he committed suicide."

I must have stared at him like a ninny. I couldn't think of anything to say.

Suicide? Well, it made a crazy kind of sense. Both Mike and his mother had known Irish Svenson was worried about something. His mother had thought it was his marital problems. She had said, "I pushed him too hard." She was blaming herself. And Irish had told Mike he needed to talk to him, and Mike hadn't come home to Grantham on schedule. So Mike had blamed himself.

Yes, they'd probably both be glad to discover that Irish Svenson was murdered. That would be preferable to believing he'd killed himself.

Mike gathered the debris from the ice cream sundaes and put it in the parking lot's trash can. Then he drove me home. He didn't suggest going to his house, and I didn't invite him into mine. I was still mad at him, and, although he'd justified himself calmly, I could tell he was mad at me. Our affair was over.

He walked up onto the porch of my house with me, but without touching me. After I'd unlocked the door he cleared his throat. "Nell, I'm sorry I'm such a sneaky bastard," he said. "But I'm thirty-two-years old, and I'm afraid my character is pretty well set."

"I knew you'd been trained to manipulate people," I said. "You couldn't be a successful hostage negotiator without that particular skill. I shouldn't be surprised when your professional abilities overlap into your personal life. And you're right, of course. About reporters. We're professional manipulators, too."

"I could tell you I'd never trick you, never lie to you, if it would make any difference."

"No." If a guy would lie to his mother, he'd lie to his girlfriend. I left that unsaid.

Mike kicked at the door mat. "Well, we've still got to work together on figuring out the relationship between Bo's death and my dad's."

"Of course."

"I'm not sure what to do next. I'll think about it and call you tomorrow."

I went in. Rocky was watching television in the

living room. "You're home," he said. He leered just a little.

"Yes, and I'm going straight to bed."

I didn't want to talk to anybody. I wasn't going to cry or anything, but I wanted to be alone to absorb the change in my life. Upstairs, I stood in the doorway of my room and remembered how I had jumped up and down on the bed that morning, happy with the knowledge that I liked Mike and he liked me. Words like "love" and "forever" had flitted through my mind. All sorts of bright tomorrows had seemed to be opening up. Now I saw nothing but darkness ahead.

Before I got into bed, I dug out the book I call my favorite "sleeping pill." *Auntie Mame* by Patrick Dennis. I have an old beat-up hardback copy that belonged to my grandmother. She and I both thought it was one of the funniest books ever written. When things are bad, *Auntie Mame* is guaranteed to cheer me up. But I fell asleep after only a few pages.

At three o'clock in the morning I had the female equivalent of a wet dream. Mike was holding me, kissing me, caressing me, and his touch was so real that I woke up convinced he had somehow gained access to my bedroom.

But I was alone. That time it took an hour of *Auntie Mame* before I fell asleep. When the alarm went off at seven, the light was still on, and the book was lying on my chest.

I lay there, dreading the day. First, I'd have to deal with Ace-the-Ass and whatever crazy ideas he'd come up with. Then in the afternoon, I had that appointment with Lee.

Lee! I jumped out of bed. I'd forgotten about Lee.

I'd decided not to mention her call to Mike. Then, later in the evening, I'd been so busy wallowing in my own misery that I had forgotten the appointment completely.

I paced up and down the bedroom. Lee! Lee, with the young, breathy voice. Lee, who said she knew what Irish Svenson had been investigating just before his death. Who said Irish Svenson had been her friend. "The best friend I ever had."

My adrenaline kicked in. Lee! After what Mike and I had learned from his mother the night before, it was obvious who Lee might be. Probably was.

Lee could well be Irish Svenson's girlfriend.

I could hardly wait to see her. Four o'clock seemed weeks away. I raced for the shower.

I got to the office on time and read the paper, waiting for Ace to show up. I worked the crossword puzzle, waiting for Ace to show up. I made some phone calls, still waiting for Ace to show up. I called the AP office. He wasn't there, either.

J.B. was out on "my" police run, now that it was his. I could tell from the scanner that he was checking out a signal 82, an accident with injury, on the three-level overpass. The scanner was burping out routine messages, and my subconscious was tuning in to the local crime scene. I looked through some reports and waited for Ace-the-Ass to show up. And fumed. Where was the jerk?

Then the gargle from the scanner caught my ear. "—uniform," it said. "That's right. 'S' and 'A' on the collar."

The phrase reminded me of a cartoon I'd seen years before. A hatchet-faced old woman, wearing a military-style outfit with "S" on one point of the collar and "A" on the other. She was snarling at a younger man. "It stands for 'sex appeal,' of course."

The joke was that the old woman was a member of the Salvation Army. Their uniforms have an "S" on one side of the collar and an "A" on the other.

The scanner spoke again. "It was in the top of the trash can."

I leaned over the gadget and turned up the sound. A Salvation Army uniform had been found in a trash can. My heart began to thud. A discarded Salvation Army uniform. It absolutely had to be the stolen one, the one the murderer of Bo Jenkins had used to gain access to the Grantham Mental Health Center.

I kept listening, but I was dialing the photo lab's extension at the same time. This might be art for page one. The scanner began to talk again just as Bear Bennington answered. Instead of saying hello, I said, "Shhh. I'm getting an address from the scanner."

Bear waited while I wrote the numbers on a pad and reached for my city map to ID the location. Then I realized I knew that address. My yell must have blasted Bear's eardrum to bits.

"Bear, let's get going! They've found that missing Salvation Army uniform at Mike Svenson's house!"

Bear and I beat Mike to his own house. When we pulled up, the street was almost blocked by a city Solid Waste Department truck, a patrol car, and an inconspicuous beige sedan that might as well have had DETECTIVES written all over it. Jim Hammond was just getting out of the sedan.

He glared at me. "You again!"

"Why, Captain Hammond, aren't you glad to see me?"

"I thought J.B. had taken over."

"He's out on that 82 at the three-level."

"Well, stay out of our way."

"Yes, sir, Captain. Sir."

It was another lovely day in the Southern Plains' loveliest month, October. Only a few clouds hovered in the northwestern quadrant of the sky. The cops and a member of the solid waste crew were clumped around a heavy-duty plastic trash container at the foot of Mike's driveway. The three other members of the solid waste crew were sitting on the running board of the truck, smoking.

Bear started circling around outside the police sphere of action, using a long lens. I knew his pictures would look as if he'd been right in the middle of the scene.

I walked across the street, where a thin woman stood in the driveway, holding a broom. She had tightly curled gray hair and was wearing a loose red garment the ads call a "patio dress."

"You're that young lady who was over at Mike's house Sunday morning with Wilda and Mickey," she said.

Oh, golly. I'd run into the reporter's dream. The nosy neighbor. Unfortunately, she'd been nosing into my business, though she had the story slightly wrong. She'd evidently seen me leave with Mickey on Sunday morning. But if she'd realized I'd been there all night, she wasn't mentioning it. Thank goodness. I put on my best smile.

"I'm a friend of Mike's," I said. "I work for the *Gazette*. What's going on over there?"

"I don't know exactly. The garbage men looked in Mike's trash and began to have a fit. Then the police car came. I don't think it's a body or anything. Not big enough."

In Grantham the refuse cans or bags are supposed to be on the curb by eight a.m. I doubted that Mike had put the uniform in his own trash, but he'd probably put his can out before he went to work. Since he was working the day shift, he reported at seven a.m. This meant the thief who took the Salvation Army uniform—the guy we assumed killed Bo Jenkins—had had several hours to add the uniform to Mike's trash.

Right then another patrol car came around the corner, moving fast, and skidded to a stop. Mike jumped out. He started toward Hammond, but like a good cop, he scanned the area, and he saw me. He stopped walking. Then he gave me a minuscule wave and went on.

He and Hammond seemed to be quizzing the solid waste people. I stood there, chatting up Mike's neighbor. Her name, she said, was Marceline Fuqua. She'd lived there forty years, she told me.

She pointed at Mike. "Known that boy all his life," she said. "I took a casserole over when his mama brought him home from the hospital. Knitted him some booties."

I felt surprised. "Did Mike live here when he was growing up?"

"Oh, yes." She gave a kind of cackle. "The Svensons lived in that house until Wilda got rich and Irish got famous. Then they moved out west with the upper crust. But that was after Mike had left home. Wilda kept the house for rental property. Then, when Mike moved back, she gave it to him. He did the big remodeling."

That was sort of interesting.

"He used to mow my lawn," the woman said. "But he never would edge right around the flower bed. Wanted to use the Weed-Eater. It ought to be done by hand."

The solid waste truck was pulling away, going back to work and leaving the scene to the police. Mike and Hammond walked toward us. Bear stopped snapping pictures and came over.

Mike barely nodded to me. It was pretty plain that we were no longer friends. But he smiled at Mrs. Fuqua.

"Marceline, this is Captain Jim Hammond, one of Grantham's top detectives," he said. "Captain Hammond, Mrs. Fuqua usually knows what's going on around here. Marceline, did you see anybody messing with my trash this morning?"

Mrs. Fuqua leaned on her broom. "Nary a soul," she said. "Nary a soul's been over there. Except that painter."

One look at Mike was enough to tell that he wasn't having anything painted. He and Hammond muttered at each other, then Mike turned back to Mrs. Fuqua.

"You know I usually do my own painting," he said. "What did this guy look like?"

Her description, boiled down, was much the same as the description of Jesse James, the man who'd checked into the Salvation Army shelter Saturday night and had fled before dawn with a uniform. Thin, forty to fifty-ish, dark, slicked-down hair. Again, it crossed my mind that it sounded like a dozen people I knew. Including Ace-the-Ass, who never had showed up that morning.

The phony painter had been driving a white van with a ladder and some paint cans in the back. It had a magnetic sign on the door which read JOE'S PAINT AND PLASTER. Mrs. Fuqua had gone outside and looked him over, but she didn't know one make of truck from another. And she hadn't noticed the number on the license tag.

Hammond glared. "Well, I think we can rule out coincidence in this. That guy didn't pick your trash can at random, Mike. Not out of the thousands of trash cans in the city."

Mike nodded. "Yeah, he wanted to rub my nose in it."

I forgot I was a bystander and joined the conversation. "But, Mike, how'd he know how to find you?"

Hammond looked at me frowning. "What do you mean, Nell?"

Mike was looking at me, too, and he was getting a tiny smile at the corners of his mouth. A wicked sort of smile. I realized I was about to reveal more of my previous personal life than I'd wanted Hammond to know.

I fought the urge to backpedal, to try to lie my way out. That was what Mike expected me to do, I could tell. I lifted my chin and reminded myself that I'm a reporter and reporters can go anywhere and call anyone.

"Yes," I said firmly, "the other night when I wanted to reach you when you were already off duty, I couldn't find your phone number. You're not in the phone book. How did Jesse James find out where you live?" I hadn't lied.

Mike and Hammond kicked that one around. City

directory? Gas company? Lived in the neighborhood? There were lots of ways.

I got Hammond to confirm that he'd put out a notice to all solid waste crews, both city and private, asking them to watch for the uniform.

"I really thought we'd find it in some Dumpster," he said.

I had as much information as I was going to get there, and Bear was pacing, impatient to get on to his next assignment. So we left. Mike gave me another indifferent wave.

Back at the office, Ace still hadn't shown up. At that point I didn't care, even if he did owe me lunch. It was close to noon. I went down to Goldman's and ate lunch with Mitzi Johns. After lunch I wrote up the story about the stolen Salvation Army uniform being found in Mike's trash. I left it in the crime reporters' joint file for J.B. to add to his story on Bo's death.

By then it was too late for me to sit around and anticipate meeting Lee. It was time to go, if I wasn't going to be late for our appointment.

Four o'clock. Grantham Memorial Rose Gardens.

CHAPTER 16

The Memorial Rose Garden is a Grantham show-place. It was donated to the city by an early day flour mill owner in memory of his wife, whose name was Rose. One story is that Rose hated her namesake flower, and that her husband hated her and gave the rose garden to the city as a sort of perverted joke.

But, whatever his motivation, he did endow it properly, so the park is well-taken care of, year round. Its flora is not limited to roses; in October the place is ablaze with chrysanthemums in colors carefully selected to avoid clashing with the late-blooming roses. And in our climate, or so the garden page editor tells me, lots of roses bloom late as well as early. So it's lovely in October.

The garden lies south of the campus of Grantham State University. This allows the GSU administration building to look out at ten acres of flowers, centered by a fountain. That fountain spouts out of the center of a stone bowl, and at night colored lights play upon it the varying patterns of water. My grad-student friends tell me it's known as the Technicolor Teacup, or the Beautiful Bidet.

If the campus is crowded, as it is all morning and in the early afternoon, there are always people around the Teacup, particularly on sunny fall days, so Lee had picked a good spot for an inconspicuous meeting.

If it hadn't rained.

A front moved through Grantham early in the afternoon. The line of clouds I'd noticed that morning came in from the northwest, shadowing the blue skies. The temperature dropped twenty degrees, and the northwest wind picked up. By four o'clock, we had a gusty rain, the kind that blows down the neck of your raincoat. The radio guys were saying how wonderful it was, since we'd had a dry fall. Obviously, they weren't planning to meet anonymous news sources outdoors.

But I gamely went by the house, ripped my trench coat out of the cleaner's bag where it had spent the summer, and picked up my umbrella. I knew I'd never find a parking place on the Campus Corner shopping area, so I walked the half mile across the Grantham State campus to the fountain.

I went to a bench that put my back to the GSU administration building and sat there, bracing my umbrella against the wind so I wouldn't float off like Mary Poppins. At least I knew I'd be easy for Lee to find, since I was the only idiot sitting around. I left my head uncovered, since my string-straight, reddish hair is my most distinctive feature, the one Lee would probably remember from my appearance on television. Rain doesn't hurt my "do."

Since most students had gone to the campus early in the day, with no idea of walking home in the rain, the few people who passed were running or walking fast. Lots of them had no coats at all. Some had umbrellas with no raincoats, some had made ponchos out of plastic garbage bags, and some wore denim jackets and pulled their heads in like turtles. One had taken off his jacket and was using it to cover his books and papers, letting his T-shirt get soaked. A "don't-give-a-damn" type walked slowly, hair soaked and stringy, clothes sopping wet. What, me worry?

But none of them wore clear plastic raincoats and hoods, the cheap kind you can pick up at Kmart when you get caught in an unexpected rain. So I noticed the brown-haired girl the first time she came by.

The second time she passed, walking in front of me as she circled the fountain counterclockwise, she definitely stood out, but I played it cool. I didn't want to scare her off. If she was Lee.

The third time she appeared at the right-hand end of my peripheral vision I was ready to call out to her. Then she suddenly swiveled and sat down beside me.

"Nell?" It was the breathy, little-girl voice.

"Lee?"

She nodded her head. Striking eyes of a flat, light gray, their pupils rimmed in black, looked out from inside the hood. Her face was little-girl pretty, matching her voice, with a deep widow's peak and soft, fly-away hair. She ducked her head and looked up at me. "I didn't think about the weather changing like this."

"We can share this umbrella," I said. I moved it so that it blocked part of the blowing rain from her head. "Or we can go someplace dryer."

Lee turned her head inside the hood. The hood never moved. "I've got to talk fast and get back."

"Okay. What did you want to tell me about Irish Svenson?"

"He was murdered." She was turning her head the other way. I realized that she was looking around the rose garden. "He had to be."

"You said that on the phone. How do you know?"

"It was my fault." She gave me that childlike, appealing, upward look with those amazing gray eyes. Then she scanned the rose beds and chrysanthemum clumps again. We were the only people in the garden at that point.

"I was so frightened. I had to feel that I was absolutely safe, so I wouldn't tell him."

"Tell him what?"

"Everything he needed to know. If I had told him—" She was fighting back tears, but her head was still swiveling. "If I hadn't been so frightened, he wouldn't have died."

"You said it was a case of fraud. Was it against the city?"

"Not exactly. City employees." She saw something far behind me and gasped.

"What's wrong?"

"I'm not sure." She ducked down and behind me, peaking under the umbrella. "Oh, God! It's the Scamovan!"

"The Scamovan?" I started to lift the umbrella and turn, but she clutched my arm.

"Don't look! They mustn't know I spotted them!" She whirled around again, facing forward, sitting there stiffly. "What can I do?" Her voice was more wispy than ever. "I can't run. They'll catch me."

"What did you see?" I was losing patience. Was

she nuts? Should I call the guys in the white suits? Or did she actually know something? "What is it?"

"That white van."

Now I saw that a white van was turning down the street that bordered the rose garden on the left. It was moving slowly. Between the rain and its heavily tinted side windows, the inside was a blank, the driver completely anonymous. At the corner, the van turned right, passing in front of us.

Vans are extremely common in Grantham, Southwestern U.S.A., as they have become everywhere. Lots of people drive vans even if they rarely haul anything bigger than a sack of groceries. So a van wouldn't normally have caught my eye.

But this van was white, and it had an aluminum ladder on the roof. And the muddy door had a clean square on it, a square that had obviously held a magnetic sign until a few minutes earlier.

The addition of a magnetic sign that said JOE'S PAINT AND PLASTER would have made this van match the description of the one that Mike's neighbor had seen stopped in front of his house that morning. The van whose driver might have dumped the Salvation Army uniform in Mike's trash can.

I decided it was time to panic.

"Come on!" I grabbed Lee by the arm and pulled her to her feet. I forced her to wheel around, so that we were walking the opposite direction from the one the van was traveling. And right then a miracle happened. A guy wearing a Grantham State windbreaker and clutching a pile of books ran by us, going the same direction we were—away from the campus, toward the campus shopping district.

"Run!" I told Lee. "Keep up with this guy!"

The van's driver might be after us, but surely he'd hesitate to take out an innocent GSU student who was running for his car.

The guy looked around at us, and I tried to smile reassuringly. "Sure is wet!" I yelled.

The three of us pounded across the rose garden. Or rather the guy and I pounded. Lee *tap-tapped*. For the first time I realized she was wearing high heels. The wind caught the umbrella and flipped it inside out. I let it fly away, and I ran on, still clutching Lee's arm. I finally had hold of her. I wasn't letting go until she told me what she knew.

I didn't stop to watch the white van, but when we came to the street that edged the east side of the rose garden, I looked left before I pulled us out into the traffic. And I saw two things. First, our innocent escort was wheeling toward a compact car parked at the curb. Second, the white van was the second car back in the line of traffic stopped at the light at the next corner. A half block away.

"Come on!" I yelled again, and I pulled Lee into the street.

That's when she lost a shoe. She bent down, scooped it up, and we ran on. To our left the traffic was clear, which should have tipped me off that the light a half-block down was about to change. But there were cars coming from the right. We rushed across the two open lanes, but had to stop for the cars coming toward us. Lee kept looking toward the corner to our left.

She squealed. "The light changed! He's turning the corner!" she said.

I plunged ahead, oncoming traffic or no. A small red car tried to stop before it hit us, sluing sideways in the inside lane. A horn of a sporty green model in the next lane began to make a loud blasting noise. The green car stood on its nose as Lee and I dashed in front of it. We scrunched between the bumpers of two cars parallel-parked at the curb. We stepped onto the sidewalk. I could feel the curses of the northbound drivers, but I didn't look at them. I scanned the street to find the white van. It was speeding down the block, moving into the left-turn lane. It could be going around the block.

"Thank God there's never any parking at the Campus corner," I said.

"But where can we go?" Lee said. "He'll come back."

"I know a place where he won't think to look," I said.

I let Lee put her shoe on, but I kept pulling her along for half a block, until we reached an oak door flanked by stained-glass windows featuring strange blue birds. I shoved the door open.

"We can't go in here!" Lee sounded scandalized.

"Sure we can," I said. "It's the safest place in Grantham for unescorted women." I shoved her ahead of me into the Blue Flamingo.

I was truly happy to see the big, pudgy, balding guy behind the bar. Rocky was on the job, wearing his bartender's uniform of blue shirt printed with the neon-bright flamingos, getting ready for the rush hour for his gay clientele. He was alone, unless you count a flock of long-legged lawn ornaments—originally pink, but repainted electric blue—which decorate the joint.

"My stars, Nell," he said. "You look like a drowned rat."

"You look like Santa Claus," I answered. "Rocky, this is Lee. She's a confidential news source with some information for me. Somebody just chased us all across the rose garden."

Rocky came around the bar with his fists and his jaw clenched. "You just point this guy out to me," he said.

"No! I don't want you to get involved. Just let me use your phone. Then we'll hide in the ladies' room until Mike comes. If anybody comes in looking for us, you say we haven't been here."

Rocky relaxed his jaw and grinned. "I'll tell 'em our customers don't run to damsels in distress."

"You're a lifesaver."

"Let me check out the ladies' room before you go in. Some of these guys—" Rocky went to the back of the bar, looking puffed up. He loves playing protector for Martha, Brenda, and me. I quickly explained to Lee that he owned the house I lived in. I also gave her a brief account of the night he rescued Brenda from date rape in our own living room. He's considered himself our guardian angel ever since.

"Rocky's one of the good guys," I said. Lee seemed to accept this.

Rocky gave us the all clear, and Lee went back to the ladies' room while I used the phone behind the bar. It wasn't until I heard Mike's voice that I realized he and I weren't friends anymore.

Funny, but with my adrenaline pumping, he'd been the first person I thought of. Now that my brain was in gear again, I wondered if I had been smart.

But Mike and I had agreed to keep working together on the puzzle of what Bo Jenkins knew about his father's death, I reminded myself. So he should want to know what Lee had to say, even if he wasn't interested in me.

"Uh, Mike?"

"Nell?" He sounded cautious, but at least he'd recognized my voice.

"Yes." I paused. I wasn't ready to apologize, but I wasn't going to let Lee get out of there without making sure she was safe. Mike ought to want to help, if she had information about his father's death.

"Nell? You still there?"

I took a deep breath and plunged. "Mike, I need help."

"Sure." He hadn't hesitated the slightest bit before he said it. My innards gave a few of those spasms that he'd been causing.

I sketched the situation as quickly as I could. "So we're stuck in the ladies' room at the Blue Flamingo," I said. "I feel certain the guy in the white van really did intend to do something awful to Lee. I'm afraid to just walk out, and I think if I call 911, Lee will disappear, and I may never find out what she knows."

"We don't want that. I'd like to talk to her, too," Mike said. "It'll take me about ten minutes to get there. I'll pull up in the alley. Tell Rocky to open the back door."

"How did you know there's a back door?"

"I spent four months on that beat. All the businesses in that block have loading areas on the alley. Ten minutes." He hung up.

I gave a sigh of relief. The cavalry was on the way.

Rocky handed me several old cup towels from a stack behind the bar. "Here, use these to dry your hair," he said. "I put the 'out of order' sign on the door to the loo."

"Thanks." I went into the ladies' room. I assume that the city code required Rocky to provide it, whether his customers usually included ladies or not. It had one stall and a minuscule area for primping at the sink.

Lee had taken off her plastic raincoat and hung it on a hook on the back of the door. She was combing her soft, light brown hair, and her gray eyes met mine in the mirror. Even after the run through the rain, her makeup was beautifully applied. She wore a suit in a medium blue. Her blouse was cream, and she wore a pearl necklace and earrings. Her bone-colored shoes were completely soaked, but they were stylish, and her bag matched them. It was a business-like outfit, one a well-dressed office worker in our climate can wear year round.

I handed her the towels Rocky had provided. "Where do you work?" I asked.

"I have a bookkeeping job. Who did you call?"

I took off my trench coat and hung it beside hers, then perched my purse and notebook on the shelf over the sink. "Lee, I'd already been working on Irish Svenson's death. Before you called yesterday."

Her eyes widened. "Why?"

"Something Bo Jenkins said during the hostage situation. Anyway, I've been working with a guy from the Grantham PD—"

"Oh, no!"

"Lee, it's okay!"

"But I told you! People who are high up in the department are involved!"

"He's not working with anybody else in the department."

"You believe that? How do you think they knew where to look for me? He must have passed the word along."

"I didn't tell him I was meeting you!"

That stopped her.

"They must have followed you," I said. I pulled off my sodden loafers and knee socks. "Isn't that possible?"

"No. If they knew where I was living, what city I'm in, what name I'm using, I'd have been dead long ago."

I edged around her, toward the stall. "Well, all I can tell you is that we need help to make sure we get out of here safely. So I called Mike."

"Mike?"

"Yes." I went in the stall and closed the door. "I know he wasn't involved in Irish Svenson's death. He wasn't even living in Grantham when his d—when Irish was killed."

She didn't say anything. Looking under the edge of the stall, I could see her slipping her pantyhose off and her shoes back on.

"I assure you, it's okay," I said. "Let me ask you a couple of questions. You called Irish Svenson your best friend. Why?"

"Because he was the first person who ever really cared about me. He gave me the thing I care most about. He changed my life."

Oops. Maybe she really was the girlfriend. I settled

for a noncommittal question. "How did he change your life?"

Lee laughed. "He forced me to do it myself. I needed to get away, to get a new identity, or I was going to be dead. I asked him to help me. He said he would—if I'd do what he said.

"It was easy for me to say yes to that. Everybody had always bossed me around. My dad, my husband. I'd obeyed them, and I wound up in a whole heap of hurt. My husband got me into this mess—and I could yet go to prison! Irish saw that I had to learn to stand up for myself. And he saw I didn't have the gumption to do it on my own. So he ordered me to learn."

I could see her feet. She was leaning over the sink. "How could he order you to learn how to stand up for yourself?"

"Irish tucked me into a support group, and he forced me to go into counseling. My husband—he'd always scoffed at people who went for therapy. Now I can see he was afraid he'd lose control of me if I got help."

"You were abused?"

"Oh, my husband never beat me! He didn't need to. He could cut me to shreds without raising his voice. Just the way my dad could. But Irish—well, he was the first person in my life who ever built me up, who ever told me I was smart. Or brave. Who ever told me I could leave behind the mess I'd made of my life and move on—that I could be able to love somebody."

I hitched my clothes around. I could hear movement beyond the stall.

Lee spoke again. "That's why I've got to get this

settled. Legally. Personally. Finally. I can't go on living with this hanging over my head."

"What?"

"This crime I was forced into. I've got to make it right, but I can't risk jail time. I'll have to have immunity."

"The guy I called should be able to help."

"If you say so," she answered. She still sounded dubious.

"We'll have to have some help from law enforcement eventually," I said. "Reporters are limited in what we can do. As a policeman, he has access to all sorts of information that I haven't. Test results, state crime lab reports. Stuff we'll need."

I heard a soft sort of swishing noise. It might have been the door. Could the "out of order" sign have failed to keep others out?

"Lee? Did someone come in?"

There was no answer. I buttoned a button and plunged out of the stall. "Lee!"

She wasn't there.

And neither was my raincoat. I was alone in the tiny restroom, alone with Lee's plastic raincoat and hood.

I didn't stop to wash my hands, but I did grab my shoes. When I rushed out into the tiny hall, Rocky said Lee hadn't gone out the front. So I dashed out the back, into the alley.

I ran to the street, only two doors away, and looked up and down. No figure in a tan trench coat was moving among the sodden pedestrians.

I was still standing there, looking back and forth stupidly, when a black pickup pulled in the alley. The driver's side window went down smoothly.

"What are you doing out here in the rain?" Mike said.

"Hell's bells!" I said. "Mike, she ran off. She was right here, and now she's gone. She's disappeared! I had her, and I let her get away!"

CHAPTER 17

"Get in," Mike said. "We'll look for her."

We cruised the Campus Corner, looking for a woman in high heels and a trench coat. My clean trench coat.

"She may have used a cup towel for a scarf," I said. "I don't know if any were gone from the stack Rocky gave me."

"What color?"

"White. All the towels were white."

But Lee had disappeared. Melted into the air. Or maybe she had been melted by the rain and was running down the gutter. Or maybe the guy in the white van got her.

There were dozens of shops on the Campus Corner, and Lee could dodge in and out of them at will. The neighborhood was a rabbit warren of nooks, crannies, back doors, loading docks, alleys, bike paths, odd-shaped parking lots, and narrow passages between buildings. After twenty minutes, we gave up.

Mike took me back to the Blue Flamingo to pick up my socks, purse, and notebook. I took Lee's plastic raincoat, too. I might have to use it.

"Maybe she'll mail my raincoat back," I told Mike

and Rocky. "And maybe she'll put her return address on the package. Ha. Ha."

Neither of them laughed. Mike drove me home, since that's where my car was, and I directed him to Rocky's slot in back of the house. I sat there, wavering. Should I invite him in? Did I want him to come in? What if I asked, and he refused?

We'd parted on cold terms the night before. Yet the minute I needed help, I hadn't hesitated. I'd called Mike. And he'd come. Where did that leave us?

I was still in my quandary when Mike spoke. "Can I ask you a personal question?"

"Yes." What was coming? Were we going to renew our quarrel? "Ask away."

"Now that I know you're definitely a natural redhead—" He hesitated, but he didn't go into how he knew. "I've been wondering. How do you keep your eyelashes from washing off in the rain?"

The question struck me funny. "The same way I keep them from washing off in the shower," I said.

Mike cocked his head sideways and gave me the full eye contact, the look that had done me in when he gave it to me Saturday night at The Fifth Precinct. My innards twitched and quivered, just as they had that night, when I'd gone home with him and jumped in his bed. Or onto his couch.

"And just how does that eyelash preservation method work?" he said.

"Dye," I answered. "Once a month I get my hair cut and highlighted and my eyelashes and eyebrows dyed."

He leaned toward me and traced my left eyebrow with his forefinger. "Very natural." The kiss that followed seemed very natural, too. It was one of his gentle kisses. Just a hint of tongue.

I kissed him back—once, but I pulled away before he could move in for the killer kiss, the one that would completely shatter my resolve. I clapped my hands together slowly three times. "Excellently done, Mike. Just the merest reference—the natural redhead bit—to make me remember how much fun we can have if we take our clothes off. And how long did it take you to think up that move with the eyebrow?"

Mike's chin became grim. "That particular move was strictly improvised," he said. He leaned back against his door. "Did it work?"

"What was it supposed to accomplish?"

"To remind you we still like each other."

"Then I guess it worked," I said. "I'm obviously very attracted to you. Physically. You know exactly the right way to turn my hormones on. But I'm afraid you turn my brain off. It scares me."

He reached for my hand. "Listen, I'm not the guy you need to be scared of. Judging from the tale of you and this Lee running through the park, you're very likely in danger from somebody who has designs on a lot more than your hormones."

"Maybe so. But right now I'm in danger of freezing to death. I've got to get some dry clothes."

Mike opened his door. "Okay. But I hope you're asking me in. Because we need to talk about what to do next." That settled one question. He was coming in.

Rocky would be at work until midnight, of course, and Brenda doesn't leave the day-care center until six o'clock, but Martha was up in her room, tucked in under an afghan, reading. Mike waited in the liv-

ing room while I went upstairs and dried myself
from the skin out. When I came down in jeans, a
sweater, and tennis shoes, he stood up. I went past
him, into the kitchen.

"Rocky's not here to run the cappuccino machine,"
I said. "So how about some instant coffee?"

"Sure. If we can talk while the water boils."

I put the kettle on and got down the coffee and
two mugs. "Okay. And my first question is, 'Are you
in trouble over that Salvation Army uniform?'"

"Because it was found in my trash? No. Thanks to
Marceline, Jim Hammond has no reason to believe I
put it there myself. I also think he gives me credit for
being smart enough to hide incriminating evidence in
a garbage bag before I ditch it."

"Do I need to come forward to give you an alibi
for the time when Bo was killed?"

Mike grinned. "I don't know if you could. You
slept pretty good there for a while. I could have
gone out."

"I know you were there from eleven-thirty until
way after midnight, which means you didn't grow
your hair several inches longer, dye it black, and
check into the Salvation Army shelter. The guy at the
shelter said the imposter arrived around midnight."

"True. Anyway, Hammond seems satisfied with
Marceline as a witness. I don't think I'll have to drag
you into it. To be honest, he's so excited about finding out where the cyanide probably came from—"

My hair must have stood up on end, or I must
have gasped or something, because Mike stopped in
midsentence. Anyway, there was a pregnant pause
while he figured out that I hadn't known that particular bit of information—which would be of extreme

interest to the readers of the *Grantham Gazette* and which he had just blabbed.

I was deducing like mad. First, he'd confirmed that the poison which killed Bo Jenkins was definitely cyanide. The last I'd heard, Jim Hammond was calling it "probable." Second, Jim Hammond had figured out where the murderer got it.

"Hammond didn't tell you." Mike made it a statement. "And I just blew it."

"I've been out of the office for a couple of hours," I said. "He may have told J.B. But just where did the cyanide come from?"

"I think I'd better shut up."

"Aw, come on, Mike. I protect my sources."

Mike shook his head. "You know enough to figure it out. I admit I gave him a pointer. Suggested that he check a guess. Turned out I was right."

I scowled at the jar of instant coffee. Mike had given him a pointer. Something Mike knew, and I probably knew, but which Hammond hadn't known. Well, Mike and I had believed a cop might be involved. I didn't think Hammond had known that. So, where would a cop get cyanide?

"The evidence room!" I yelped it out. "There was cyanide missing from the evidence room."

"My lips are sealed," Mike said. "Let's talk about you and this Lee. Who is she?"

I let him change the subject. My sketchy knowledge of Lee, gathered in three quick conversations, didn't take long to detail. "So, you see, I have absolutely nothing to go on," I told him. The kettle shrieked, and I poured hot water into our cups. "She kept promising to tell me things, but she never did."

"She told you a few things. Have you got anything to write on? I'd like to make some notes."

Mike carried our coffee to the kitchen table while I brought a yellow legal pad and a couple of ballpoints from upstairs. Then he took my statement—went over each of the conversations I'd had with Lee, making me repeat each of them in as much detail as I could remember, and we listened to the tape of our second talk.

Then he wrote a new heading. "Deductions."

"First," Mike said. "She must have come to Grantham today from out of town."

"Why do you say that?"

"Because she said 'had the afternoon off.' But she didn't offer to meet you until four o'clock."

"So she had to drive several hours to get here."

He nodded. "We'll get a road map and draw a two-hundred-mile circle around Grantham. That would be the longest possible distance she could cover, I think."

"She could cover that if she's a fast driver, and if she left right at noon. But that radius would cover several good-sized cities. Including Oklahoma City, Tulsa, Dallas, and Fort Worth."

"Right. It's not much to go on." He sipped his coffee. "Second, Lee has obviously lived in Grantham in the past. The Memorial Rose Garden is a well-known landmark to us Granthamites, but it's not famous. And it's nowhere near the interstate highways. If I were going to meet someone in a city I'm not very familiar with—Dallas, for example—I'd suggest the first MacDonald's on I-35 south of Denton. Something simple like that. I wouldn't think of a spot that involved driving clear across town on city streets."

"Very logical. Besides, she knew the Blue Flamingo has a rather scandalous reputation. She said, 'We can't go in there!' And she referred to the Grantham Police Department as 'GPD.' "

"Well, most cities call the police department 'the PD.' But she said specifically she hadn't been a city employee?"

"Uh-huh. But she said the big case involved fraud."

"Sounds like a construction contract. Or some kind of a big purchasing deal."

Mike was getting awfully close to Ace's big exposé on his dad. Should I tell him about that? What was happening to Honest Nell, the reporter who never lied?

I sipped my coffee and agonized. How could I tell him? My boss had told me to work with Ace. I really couldn't go off on my own, without warning Jake and Ace.

Besides, I didn't yet know what Ace's tip was about. After we found that out, Ace and I would figure out if there was any evidence to back it up.

If there was any evidence. The next step, normally, would be to talk to the accused person, get his side. Since the accused person, Irish Svenson, was dead, we'd have to talk to Wilda Svenson, and to Mike, to get that side of the story.

I hoped the whole thing would peter out before that point. I pushed Ace's big exposé out of my mind and listened to Mike.

"We also know this Lee reads the *Grantham Gazette*," he was saying.

"How do we know that?"

"Because she knew who you are, Nell."

"I think she'd seen me on television during the coverage of the hostage situation."

"Yes, but she said something about your byline."

"Oh." I sipped coffee and thought along the lines Mike had suggested. "I just thought of something else. The Scamovan!"

"The what?"

"The Scamovan. When Lee saw the white van, she said, 'Oh, no, it's the Scamovan!' Or something close to that. I didn't have time to ask her to explain."

Mike shrugged. "It doesn't mean anything to me."

We both sipped coffee, then Mike put his mug down and stared into its depths as if it would tell him his future. "You saw this Lee," he said. "Do you think she could be the woman my mom believes had an affair with my dad?"

I stared into my own cup. Neither of us wanted to discuss this subject.

"That was my first thought, after I heard your mother say there had been someone," I said. "But, Mike, when I met her, she just didn't seem like the type to go out with someone else's husband. She's not a flashy, sexy type. She's kind of little girlish."

"Sounds like just the cure for a middle-aged crisis."

"Do you think that's what happened to your dad?"

"God, Nell! What does a son know about his father? Very little, I'm finding out. I always thought my dad was real puritanical. He didn't have any patience with guys who ran around on their wives. It was well-known in the department. If you were fooling around, you'd better not brag about it in the locker room, because if it got back to the chief, you were in trouble. And he said some pretty stiff things

to me when Annie and I moved in together. She had to tell him she was the one who didn't want to get married before he'd let up." He sounded more and more exasperated. "He didn't go out and booze it up with the guys. He and my mom did things together. They acted as if they liked each other!"

"He didn't want to leave her, Mike! Your mom said he didn't leave at all until she pressed him. Then he didn't move in with this woman. Remember? He'd been staying at Mickey's house. Your folks were talking, trying to work things out. I think he cared for your mother very deeply."

"Mutual affection and respect."

It was the same phrase Mike had used when he talked to his mother the night before. The two of them had laughed then, but now he said it grimly.

"What's the story on 'mutual affection and respect'?" I said. "You said that to your mother last night."

"Just a family joke." Mike's face relaxed. "When I was sixteen and fell madly in love for the first time—"

"With Shelly?"

"I don't even remember. I was a typical high school jock, full of sixteen-year-old testosterone and male chauvinism and sure that nothing bad could ever happen to the great and wonderful me. Scaring my parents into fits. Hot to lose my virginity."

"Sixteen? There wasn't a jock in my high school who would have admitted he was still a virgin at sixteen."

"Maybe not admitted it. Jocks lie a lot. Then sixteen years later, they have to apologize. Anyway, my mom gave me one of those mother-son talks, and she ended up by saying that the whole basis for relationships between men and women should be 'mutual affection and respect.' It struck me funny, since I was a smartass kid."

"The phrase does sound a little prim."

"After that, everybody I dated—well, whoever the girl was, I always told my mom we had a lot of 'mutual affection and respect.' It got to be a joke between us.

"Of course, I got a rather different lecture from my dad."

"From your puritanical dad? Let me guess. Did it involve stories about shotguns?"

"I was the one who brought up shotguns. 'Fathers today no longer own shotguns, old man.' Something like that. When you're sixteen, you know all about everything. Including birth control."

"I had some friends who thought they knew it all."

"Yeah. But they all felt bullet-proof until it was too late. And I felt that way, too, though I had more dumb luck than they did. Anyway, my dad made some reply using the word 'responsibility.' I countered with some sneering remark about being 'on the hook for eighteen years,' and my dad came real close to losing his temper. His face turned red and his eyes flashed blue, and he said, 'Eighteen years is just a beginning. If there's a kid, you're talking about the rest of your life. How would you feel if I sent your mom a few bucks every month and never paid you any other attention? How would you feel if I cut you off on your eighteenth birthday? Like it or not, you're going to be my son for the rest of your goddamn life!' And he got up and walked out."

And that's when I tried to get up and walk out.

Mike's story had caught me by surprise, stabbing me through a chink in my well-armored psyche. I had to get out of there.

Unfortunately, because of the layout of the tiny dinette, I had to climb over Mike to leave. My sudden decision to leave caught him by surprise, and I was too choked up to say anything, such as, "Excuse me." So when I jumped up and tried to go behind him, he tried to stand up. He scooted his chair back and effectively pinned me against the kitchen window. We jockeyed around, and the two of us wound up all tangled together, entwined with each other and an old-fashioned kitchen chair.

And Mike saw what I'd been trying to hide. I was crying.

"What did I say?" His voice was amazed. I couldn't answer, but it didn't seem to matter. He put his arms around me, and I bawled like a baby. The flannel shirt he was wearing got as damp as the windbreaker he had hung up by the back door.

I was crying about my own father, of course. I was crying about living the first eight years of my life with parents who quarreled all the time, with every quarrel ending with my father shouting, "You made me marry you! I didn't want to!" I was twelve before I figured that one out. I was crying about a father I never saw again after my mother died, who didn't bother to send a few bucks every month, and who wasn't around to kick me out on my eighteenth birthday. I was crying about a father who merely disappeared from my life—silently, with no explanation.

I'd been well taken care of by my grandparents, true. I'd never lacked for food or clothing, or for love.

But the love hadn't come from my father. He had never cared enough to see me.

And sometimes I'm eight years old again and remember telling my dad, "Just leave me alone!" Not knowing that he'd leave me alone for the rest of my life.

My emotional storm lasted only a minute. Then I regained control. But it lasted long enough that my nose started running. I pulled back, but Mike held me tightly.

"If you don't let me go, you're going to have a shirt pocket full of snot," I told his chest.

He laughed and eased his grip, and I pulled a paper napkin from the holder in the center of the table. "Sorry," I said. Then I blew my nose. "Sorry to be so stupid. Those of us from nonfunctional families have trouble handling functional ones. That's a nice story you told."

"It doesn't usually get that big a reaction. In fact, I don't think I ever told it to anybody before."

"It's a winner."

Mike rested his cheek on the top of my head. "Listen, Nell," he said. "When I was a sixteen-year-old smartass, I thought my parents were really dumb. Now I see that they had it right. Affection. Respect. And responsibility. I think I handle those three. As long as they're all mutual. I may be sneaky, but I don't think I'm mean."

Damn him. He was an expert at saying exactly the right thing. I guess I would have simply melted into a heap at his feet, but just as my knees were beginning to buckle, the telephone rang. I leaned against Mike, letting it ring until Martha answered upstairs, but it was no use. She hollered down the stairs. "It's for you, Nell!"

I blew my nose on another napkin, cleared my throat, and picked up the kitchen extension.

"Nell!" It was Ace.

"Yes."

"Can you get down here? I finally got hold of my source this afternoon. He was cagey, but I got the evidence out of him."

"Great, Ace," I lied. "What did he give you?"

"He's handed over the evidence that will hang Irish Svenson. And it's irrefutable. Straight from the IRS."

I'll always hope my face didn't show Mike the conflicting emotions that were racing around in my confused heart as it sank toward my tennies.

First, I couldn't believe Ace actually had what he said he had.

Second, I wanted to tell Mike about it. Share the responsibility.

Third, I knew I couldn't tell Mike about it. Yet.

Fourth, I knew that Mike's sneakiness was nothing. Nothing compared with the deal I was pulling on him. Making love with him one minute and plotting to ruin his father's memory the next.

Fifth, I knew that if Ace printed material damaging to his dad, Mike would never forgive me. I wouldn't have to worry about sorting out my feelings toward him, because he'd spit every time he heard my name for the rest of his life.

"I'll come right down," I told Ace. I hung up.

Mike frowned. "I hoped I could talk you into an early dinner," he said. "I've got someplace to go later."

"I've got to go back to work," I answered. "I may be there all evening."

He carried our mugs over to the sink. "Call me when you get through. I told the Grantham Central coach I'd speak to the C-Club tonight. The athletes. But I ought to be home by nine or so."

"Listen, Mike," I said. "Maybe we'd better let things cool for a few days. This special deal Jake's got me working on—I can't drop it."

"Big scandal?"

"I hope not."

Mike laughed. "Some reporter you are! Big scandals are supposed to be meat and drink to reporters."

"Guess I'm losing my instinct to go for the jugular." My stomach was churning again, but this time it was fright, not sexual excitement. What if Ace really did have the goods on Irish Svenson? What if Grantham's fabled honest police chief really had been up to something crooked? What if he had been as sneaky as his son—but had been mean, along with it?

I practically shoved Mike out of the house, then I headed for the office, wearing Lee's plastic raincoat. I used my electronic card to get in the back door. My feet were like lead as I went up the stairs to the newsroom.

The area was almost empty. The day crew had gone home, and the night crew was probably at dinner. Ruth Borah was alone at the city desk, holding down the phone until the rest of the editors got back. Ace was alone in the cop reporters' pod of desks, sitting at my VDT, reading my computer screen.

His face lit up when he saw me. "Hey, Nell! We got 'im!"

"Calm down, Ace. Just what do you have?"

"This!" Ace's gloated. He picked up a sheet of paper from the desktop and waved it back and forth like a flag.

I had to snatch it away from him. I saw that it was a photocopy of a federal tax form. 1099-MISC, was printed in the top left corner. The form identified "Balew Brothers Construction" as "payer." Below the "Payer's Federal identification number" and the "Recipient's identification number" was the name of the "recipient."

"Carl J. Svenson," it read.

Balew Brothers had gotten the contract for turning the old Grantham High School building into the Central Station, headquarters of the Grantham Police Department. Irish Svenson had recommended that they get the contract, despite previous problems they'd had with city projects.

The form reported a payment to "Carl J. Svenson."

The amount of money was about a tenth of the total cost of turning the Grantham Central High School building into the Grantham Police Department Headquarters and Central District Station.

It would have been enough to provide Irish Svenson with a very comfortable retirement, even if he went to another country and took a girlfriend with him.

CHAPTER 18

Ace was chortling, of course.

"You didn't believe me, did you?" He laughed. "You'd bought into the Honest Irish Svenson myth entirely."

"I never met Irish Svenson." My answer was automatic. I was reading the photocopy of the IRS form more thoroughly. It still said the same thing. "Where did you get this?"

"A usually reliable source."

"Come on, Ace! I can't believe this unless I know where you got it."

"I'm not tellin'. But it's the real item. Now we've got a story." He rubbed his hands together gleefully.

"Has Jake seen this?" I asked.

"No, he's still out at that meeting in Oklahoma City. He wasn't planning to come back to the office. But when I call him about this, he'll come in."

"No. Don't call Jake."

"Nell, he'll have a hissy fit if we print this without telling him about it first."

"Print this? What do you mean? You can't print this."

Ace puffed up like a rooster. "Not print it? Why the hell not?"

"We haven't established its authenticity. This is just a photocopy of a supposed tax form."

"A dammed incriminating tax form!"

He was right about that. If Balew Brothers had paid Irish Svenson major bucks as a "consultation fee" after the chief recommended that the company get the big construction contract, it would have been conflict of interest and illegal as all get out. But I had a naive idea that a news story ought to include both sides of a question, that someone accused in print ought to be given the chance to explain or deny— in the same issue of the paper in which his actions were questioned.

I believed it should be done that way all the time, even when the accused person wasn't the father of my boyfriend. Or ex-boyfriend. Or two-night stand. Or person who saved me from a madman with a gun. Or whatever Mike was to me.

Besides there was an element of stupidity to the form.

"Look, Ace," I said. "I never heard of anybody making an illegal payment—what amounts to a bribe—by check. Then turning in a record of it to the IRS. That's the dumbest thing they could do. If I were taking a bribe, I'd demand cash. And I'd take a cruise to the Caymans, and nobody would ever know a thing about it."

"That's part of the story. It was supposedly handled incorrectly by the accounting department at Balew Brothers. Now they're trying to cover it up. I tell you! It's the real item!"

"Well, I don't believe it," I said. "Besides, before we can print a thing, we'll have to talk to Irish Svenson's family. Find out if they know anything about this. If there was any record of it when his estate was settled.''

"Irish is dead," Ace said. "You can't libel a dead man."

"Balew Brothers isn't dead," I said. "It would be as illegal for them to pay this as it would be for Irish Svenson to accept it. And Balew Brothers has good lawyers."

Ace opened and shut his yap a couple of times, but he didn't have an answer to that.

I pressed my point. "I suggest that we wait until morning and talk to Jake before we do anything else," I said. "He'll want to keep a close eye on a story this hot. And if we talk to Mrs. Svenson before we talk to him, and she reacts by calling down here and raising hell—well, Jake needs to know what she's talking about when she calls."

Ace wasn't happy, but he had to agree I was right. He kept arguing, just to be annoying, until J.B. came in. I turned my back on him then and leaned on the top of J.B.'s VDT. Ace gave up and began writing something, using my VDT.

I was curious about the investigation into the death of Bo Jenkins, especially since Mike had let the source of the poison slip.

"Did Hammond have anything new to say about the death of Bo Jenkins this afternoon?" I asked J.B.

"What about?"

"The poison that was used."

"No. In fact, he said he still didn't have a final report from the ME."

I drummed my fingers on the top of the VDT.

"What'd you hear?" J.B. leaned toward me, giving me that boyish look that wins over his news sources.

I keep reminding myself that he's older than I am. He makes me feel as if I'm his mother. "What's Hammond up to?" he asked.

I didn't know what to tell him. If Hammond was passing information around, it was going to get out soon. But J.B. might not hear it as quickly as I would have. I'm not necessarily a better reporter than he is, but I've been around the Grantham PD a year longer, and I simply know more people. He might not know the questions to ask. And he was now officially the reporter covering the death of Bo Jenkins.

I glanced at Ace, who was tapping away at my VDT. He wasn't paying any attention to us. Then I lowered my voice. "I heard there's a chance the poison that did Bo in came from a very interesting source."

"Where?"

"I can't tell you." I glanced at Ace. He was still typing, apparently ignoring us. "But if my information is right, it would be very hot. Better keep on Hammond."

"What did you hear? Who told you?" J.B.'s voice was excited.

"I got it from a usually reliable source," I said, mocking Ace's portentous tone. "But it's strictly unconfirmed. I'm only tipping you because I know you'll keep your mouth shut. But keep after Hammond. Or Coy-the-Cop."

"Okay. Source of poison important." J.B. tapped his forehead. "Saved to active file."

"Good." J.B. would tell me if it turned out that Bo Jenkins's death was linked to the cop shop. Of course, Mike and I felt confident that was true. But our unofficial investigation had focused on his father's death, not on Bo's. Mike was being punctilious about leaving that up to Hammond and regular channels.

But if Hammond would confirm that the poison came from the evidence room, the case would break wide open, so to speak. The evidence room was not open to just anyone, even to just any cop. They had to sign in and sign out, and they had to have a reason to be in it.

Yet things like that did happen. A few years ago a law officer in another state was surprised while stealing drugs from an evidence room. He tried to shoot his way out and killed two fellow officers.

"You might give Hammond a ring," I said. "Just ask him if he's got confirmation on the type of poison used. Then just casually ask if he knows the source."

J.B. nodded.

I walked around the pod of crime reporters's desks and stared at Ace. "How come you're hanging around?"

"I'm just making a few printouts," he said. "I'm going to leave in a minute. Do you need your desk? I can do the same thing somewhere else."

"No. I'm leaving."

I didn't want to cook anything, so I walked down to Goldman's in the rain. Goldman's isn't too crowded at night, since the courthouse and downtown financial services crowd goes home at five-thirty. The deli menu doesn't offer steaks or fried chicken, but if your dinner preferences run to a bowl of chili and a hunk of cornbread, it's great. The night crew from the *Gazette* goes there a lot.

I picked up my chili, cornbread, and iced tea at the counter, carried the tray into the small dining room at the back and hid behind a low-hanging pot of ferns. I opened my notebook and put it on the table, but I tried not to read it. I just wanted something to pretend to stare at. Somebody I knew was sure to show up at Goldman's, and I didn't want to talk. I needed to think.

Because I didn't know what to do. Call Mike? Or not call Mike?

How could I fail to tip Mike off to the scandal which was likely to involve his father? But a news story had to be developed in an orderly manner. It would throw the whole thing off if Mike knew about the tax form before Ace, Jake, and I were ready. I didn't see how I could tell him.

I ate chili and kept my eyes on the notebook, staring beyond it at my quandary, until a hulking figure sat down opposite me. Hell's bells! I didn't want to see anybody.

I looked up and was relieved to see that it was only Bear Bennington, nobody I had to be nice to. Bear and I work together so much that we just growl along.

"Hi," I said. "You working tonight?"

"Yeah. I can use the overtime. You look like you're on a big story."

"Just hiding out, actually."

Bear picked up the dijon mustard and spread a massive amount on his hamburger bun. "I've been wanting to ask you a question," he said.

"Shoot."

"Who is this guy who hangs around with the cop reporters?"

"What does he look like?"

Bear looked at me in amazement. "Guy. You know

what he looks like. I've seen you talking to him. That guy that hangs around. Guy."

The light broke. "Oh! You mean his name is Guy."

"Yeah." Bear grinned. "Only guy I ever met named Guy."

"That's Guy Unitas. He's business manager for the Affiliated Police Brotherhood."

"How come he hangs around with reporters?"

"He used to be a cop reporter, twenty years ago. Got so interested in the job he sold out and joined the force. Or at least Grantham PD hired him as PIO. I don't think he was ever in uniform. Then, about the time Irish Svenson took over as chief, he left. That's when Coy-the-Cop became PIO. And Guy took the union job."

Bear nodded and gulped down a bite of his hamburger. I watched to see if the mustard sent smoke out his ears.

"He's the nosiest guy—man—I ever met," Bear said.

"Yeah. He knows everything about every cop on the force, and he tells it all. He's the biggest gossip in Grantham. A character flaw I frequently find quite useful."

"Well, you might not like it this time. He's gossiping about you. Tried to pump me about who you were dating."

I thought about that a minute. If anybody in Grantham could worm the information out that I was seeing Mike Svenson, it would be Guy Unitas. He probably knew more about our affair than I did.

I must have frowned, because Bear made reassuring noises. "Heck, Nell, I don't know anything about your social life. I couldn't tell him anything, even if I wanted to."

I decided to laugh Guy off, so I chuckled. "If he finds something out, it'll be old news. What social life I have seems to be in a continual state of upset. Don't worry about it. Guy passes gossip on to the press, so he expects to be paid off in the same coin. I make sure I give him a tidbit or two. I think we all do."

Bear swallowed another giant bite. "I guess that's why he was hanging out with Ace."

"Ace? That's a little odd. Guy usually confines his reporter acquaintances to cop reporters. Ace doesn't usually cover crime. But Ace sucks up to anybody, of course."

"Well, they were having a drink together this afternoon."

Guy and Ace had had a drink together? That afternoon? A dim light began to glow on the horizon.

"I had to shoot a grip-and-grin in the Plaza ballroom," Bear said. "Those two were in the back booth in the lobby bar."

I mentally translated Bear's statement. He'd gone to Grantham's biggest hotel, the Grantham Plaza, to take a presentation picture—called a "grip-and-grin" because of the shake-hands-and-smile pose these pictures require. And as he'd walked into the hotel, he'd seen Ace-the-Ass and Guy Unitas in the bar off the lobby.

That bar was not a Grantham hangout. Too expensive for locals like Ace and Guy. It usually drew hotel guests. The clear implication was that Guy and Ace were having a private meeting.

I laughed. I now knew the identity of Ace's "usually reliable source."

Bear looked curious. "I didn't realize it was funny for Ace and Guy to have a drink together."

"You just gave me a hot tip," I said. "Thanks! And please don't mention this to anybody else."

Bear and I ate in a companionable silence for a few minutes.

Bear's an enormous guy. Cameras look like toys in his giant hands. But he handles them gently. They're his babies.

Bear has the two physical abilities I think are vital to a good photographer. He has the eye to see the key moment, the moment that captures the action and tells the story, and he has the muscle coordination to hit the camera's shutter at exactly the right nanosecond to catch that moment.

But Bear has another physical characteristic that lifts him to the absolutely top rank news photographer. He can smile.

The smile broadens his talents beyond action shots. He can take routine shots, too. He's a master of grip-and-grin and "death-at-dawn"—also known as the "up against the wall and shoot'em." Editors and photographers hate these posed shots, but they have to use them sometimes—to publicize the Junior League's fashion show, maybe, or to honor the city's Man of the Year. Bear can line up the amateur models or the awardees neatly, and just when they look so stiff they might break, he gives his special smile. Everybody smiles back, and the shot looks pretty close to natural.

The editors and reporters love Bear, because we can count on him for a great shot in any situation.

The question is, how soon will he get an offer he can't refuse from the Associated Press or some slick magazine? Then he'll be off to parts unknown, and the *Gazette* will be back to dud photos.

Bear's big personal problem is that girls tend to consider him a brother. He thinks of them in different terms. So his romantic life is either frustrating or nil. He began to tell me about his latest disappointment, and my mind began to wander to my own romantic quandary. Mike and I had only half made up after our big fight the night before. And now this stuff came up about his father's taxes. Was our affair over anyway? Should I simply forget my personal concerns and skewer Irish Svenson's reputation?

I pondered this, giving the occasional nod of agreement to Bear, since I make it a firm rule not to give anybody else advice on their love life. Mentally, I was still deep in my own problems when Bear's portable phone rang. That brought me back to reality.

"Bear here." He listened. "Yeah. Tell J.B. I'll pick him up in front of the building in five minutes."

He closed the phone, stood up, and began putting on the windbreaker he'd hung on the back of his chair.

"Another fight at the Lone Wolf Club," he said. "Probably can't get anything, but we'll run on it. Thanks for listening to my troubles."

"Thanks to you for the tip on Ace and Guy Unitas. That's a big help to me."

"Yeah. I see you've been working on something about Guy."

I laughed. "What makes you think that? I hadn't given him a thought until you gave me that special little piece of gossip, showing that he was mixed up with Ace."

Bear shoved his arm through his jacket's sleeve, then reached out a giant hand and used a finger the size of a bratwurst to tap on my notebook, the open notebook I'd left lying on the table.

"I've been around newspapers enough to read upside down," he said. Then he waved and walked away, leaving me staring at the notebook.

I hadn't given Guy Unitas a thought in days. I hadn't spoken to him since the night of the celebration at The Fifth Precinct. He'd been at both press conferences I'd covered, but our paths hadn't crossed. He'd been a constant presence on the periphery of my work, but of no concern to me.

So why was his name the last thing written in my notebook?

I stared at the page. "Guy Unitas." That's definitely what it said. But it wasn't written in my handwriting.

Had I gotten hold of someone else's notebook? I picked the thing up and studied it. It was the kind of notebook I always use—seven-and-three-quarters-inches tall and five inches wide. Small enough to fit in a purse. Big enough to write several sentences on each page. It had a stiff cardboard cover, so I could write in it while I was standing up. It had a ring binder down the left-hand side, so that I could ruffle through it like a book. Everybody else at the *Gazette* uses an ordinary steno pad. I'm the only one who likes a notebook that opens like a book. I paged back a few pages. Yes, that was my writing, detailing the notes from Monday's press briefing.

This was definitely my notebook. But who had

written in it? And why had that person written the name of Guy Unitas? And some numbers. Above Guy's name were some numbers. And a phrase in quotes. It sounded like a resort.

The entry was on five lines. "Guy Unitas—NO!" was on the first line. "San Simeon Beach" was on the next. Then "347809021." Then "PUPID—A.P.B. president only" on the third line. The "only" was underlined. "Sorry to run out," the next line read. "I have to protect Andy."

Andy? Who the heck was Andy?

I puzzled over it some more. Ace. If Ace was getting information from Guy, could he have picked up my notebook by mistake and written in it?

No, this wasn't Ace's writing.

When had I last used the notebook? That morning I'd taken a few notes when I got a phone call. I'd put it in my purse and taken it along when I met the elusive Lee, who'd teased me with hints and then fled without telling me anything. I'd gotten it out when we ran into the Blue Flamingo, because the card with Mike's phone number was paperclipped inside the front cover. I'd had it in my hand when I went into the ladies' room. And I'd put it on the counter over the sink when I went into the stall. Then Lee had fled, Mike and I had chased her. When Mike had brought me back to the Flamingo, I'd gone in the ladies' room and picked up my knee socks, my purse, and my notebook. I'd flipped the notebook shut and stuck it in my purse. And I hadn't taken it out until I sat down to eat dinner.

So the last time the notebook had been open was in the ladies' room of the Flamingo. It had been lying open on the counter when Lee made her escape.

"Hell's bells!" I yelped it out as I understood the implications. Then I whispered under my breath. "Lee. Lee left a clue when she ran away. She wrote this."

I shoved my chair back and jumped up. I had to show the notebook to Mike right away.

CHAPTER 19

I was driving out of the *Gazette* parking garage before I remembered Mike wasn't home. He'd told me he had to go somewhere. Where? The high school. Grantham Central High School. He was speaking to a club. "The athletes," he'd said. Must be the lettermen's club.

I couldn't wait until he got home, I decided. As a former star football player for Grantham Central, he was likely to run into some old buddies among the sports crowd. They might go for coffee. I drove to the high school.

Today's Grantham Central replaced the old building which had been turned into the Central Police Headquarters. It was around twenty-five-years old. I knew Mike had graduated from Central, because people kept telling me he had quarterbacked their football team to a state championship.

Central is a sprawling structure of buff brick. The building, along with its playing fields, gymnasiums and parking lots, covers eight city blocks a half mile from the old school. The building's only unusual architectural feature is some special brickwork. Altogether undistinguished, I thought. It must have been an artistic blow to move from the old building—inconvenient, but beautifully detailed and proportioned—to Plain Jane High, isolated amid a sea of parking lots.

Those lots were semifull on a Tuesday evening, since Grantham high schools offer lots of adult-ed classes. I took a guess at where the C-Club would meet and headed for the gymnasium wing. Mike's black pickup, complete with camper shell, was in the row nearest the building. I had to park two rows back. The rain had stopped, but I leaped a few puddles. No one was in sight, so even the well-lit parking lot seemed a bit spooky as I walked toward the building. The hall inside was bright, and to my dismay, someone I knew was walking toward me.

Coy-the-Cop.

"Nell?" he said. "What are you doing here?"

"Duh," I answered, employing my usual quick wit. But associating with the sneaky Mike Svenson had changed my character; I came up with a lie. "I heard Mike Svenson was speaking. I thought that it might fit in with the feature we're looking at. On community policing." We do a feature on community policing three or four times a year, so that was probably a good enough excuse. "What are you doing here?"

"I always try to check in whenever any of our guys is speaking," Coy said. "But Mike doesn't need me. I was just leaving. See you later."

He went out, and I walked down the hall until I came to a open door. Inside, in a sort of lecture room which held seventy-five or a hundred kids, Mike was standing at a podium. He looked up when the door opened, and he saw me come in. He smiled slightly. My insides squeezed tight. Hell's bells! My hormones were rampaging around in response to a mere smile, and I was finding the sensation scary. Until Mike Svenson took over my life, I'd had everything under control.

I slid into a school desk in the back row while a tall thin girl with "basketball" written all over her asked Mike why he became a policeman.

"I always swore I wouldn't go into law enforcement," he said. "I knew my dad had found it satisfying, though there were a lot of things he didn't like about being chief. Especially the time he had to ask his best friend to resign. But I always said it didn't appeal to me. I used to claim that hassling people wasn't my style, even though I knew that wasn't a very good description of what law enforcement really is. The truth is, I was afraid I wouldn't have the nerve to be a law officer.

"Then, the summer after my freshman year in college, I got a security job. It was nothing special. Gate man at an apartment complex. I definitely was not called on to carry a gun!

"The third day I was on duty, one of the women tenants called the gate and said she had filed a protective order against her ex-boyfriend. I was to let the locksmith in to change her locks. She ended up, 'For God's sake, don't let anybody in a silver BMW in. The jerk beat me to a pulp last night, and he says he's coming back with a gun today.'

"Well, the jerk in the silver BMW showed up before the locksmith. I felt pretty sure it was him, because a pistol was lying on the floor of the front seat. I don't think he knew I could see it, but I was sitting up high, looking down into the car. I didn't know what to do, but I knew I wasn't going to let him in that gate. So I told him the gate was broken. Then I called the manager and told him to call 911. He didn't believe me. He came out to see why this stupid kid, brand-new on the job, couldn't open the gate."

That got a laugh from the teenagers.

"It turned into a Keystone Kops' deal, with the manager in a panic. But I'd been around police work a lot, so I knew that talking is usually more useful than a pistol." Mike grinned. "And I was a pretty good talker, even then. So I kept talking to the guy. The girl in the office had the sense to call the cops. They showed up, luckily without sirens. The patrol officers were able to walk up to the car without spooking the guy. And the whole thing ended peacefully."

Mike leaned on the podium. "But I found out something about myself. I might have been shaking like a leaf when they took the guy away, but I hadn't panicked while it was going on. And I had to admit that I'd enjoyed the whole episode. I enjoyed it for the same reasons I liked playing football. You practice and practice, and it's just drudgery. Then Friday night comes and you're on the field, and you're playing for keeps. And you're almost surprised to find out that all that preparation pays off. Whatever you do goes in the record book.

"You have the satisfaction of knowing that you stayed in the pocket and threw the pass, just the way the coach drew off the play, and the team made a touchdown. Or that you stopped a car that ran a red light and you walked up to it cautiously, just the way department procedure says you should, and you collared an armed robber. And because you followed the rules about searching the car and reading the guy his rights, it's a good collar. The DA gets a conviction. It goes in the record book, just the way a touchdown would. That's very satisfying.

"Anyway, that fall I changed my major to criminal justice, and I've never regretted my career choice."

Mike answered a few more questions. I sat waiting for him to finish. I clutched the notebook to my bosom. The knowledge of what Lee had written made the cardboard feel as though it were about to burst into flames, or as though the book were glowing with neon lights. I started to hide it in my purse, but I couldn't stand to put it down. I had to keep hold of it, as if it might float away if it wasn't in my hot little hand.

Finally, Mike finished with, "Thanks to Coach King for asking me to come tonight. And Ho! Ho! Go! Central!" He received a nice round of applause and a chorus of "Ho! Ho! Go!" in response, even though the Central cheerleaders did not seem to be in attendance. I admit, however, that quite a few girl athletes were present.

Then Mike had to shake hands with all the coaches, who hung around until most of the kids had left. He kept edging up the aisle toward me, but the oldest coach—a bald guy—stuck right at his heels. As they drew near, Mike was saying, "Sorry, Coach. I've got another commitment tonight." He gestured at me. "Have you met Nell Matthews, from the *Gazette*? We're working on a project, and I promised her that after this meeting we could get together to go over some things."

Mike had been right the night before, when he pointed out that we were both liars. I'd lied to Coy as I came in, and he was lying to his former high school coach as we went out. And we'd both done an excellent job of it. Made it look really casual and truthful. Was he destroying my character or making me face the truth about myself?

I shook hands with the coach, but I didn't stand up. Mike said, "Are you ready to go?"

"I wanted to show you something. Can we stay here, under the lights, for a minute?"

The coach told us we had ten or fifteen minutes before the custodian would be in to close up, and Mike squeezed into the school desk beside me.

I flipped the notebook open and showed it to him. "Mike, I didn't write this." I was surprised to hear my own voice. I was almost whispering. "I think Lee must have written it, right before she ran off."

He frowned as he read the entry. Then he whistled softly. "Guy Unitas? How could Guy fit into this?"

"I don't know. Of course, Guy knows everything about everybody in the Grantham PD. Is there something Lee wants us to ask him?"

Mike shook his head. "I wouldn't assume that, unless she told you something you haven't mentioned."

It was my turn to shake my head.

Then we both sat there and stared at the notebook. "San Simeon Beach. Guy Unitas. PUPID? What can that mean? President only. And a bunch of numbers," Mike said. "Maybe the first thing to do is get some information on Guy. Maybe I can beg, bribe or blackmail Shelly into looking at his records from back when he was a PD employee." He looked at his watch. "It's nearly nine o'clock. I can call her tomorrow at her office."

I had an inspiration. "We can get some information on him tonight. The *Gazette* files. I can pull up what's been printed about him since the *Gazette* went to this library system. That's about ten years."

We waved at the custodian, who was coming down the hall as we left, and went into the parking lot. Mike walked me to my Dodge and agreed to follow me to the *Gazette.*

"This time of night there'll be plenty of room," I said. "Just don't park next to the building. Those spots go to the circulation crew. And the pressroom parks at the back."

It was nine o'clock by the time we pulled into the first floor of the *Gazette's* parking lot. The dim lights cast their usual weird shadows.

I took Mike in the front door, so the security guard would know I'd brought him in. He didn't have to have a pass or anything, but the guard gets curious if you bring people in the back and he only gets a glimpse of them on the closed-circuit television. We took the elevator to the third floor. I waved at Ruth Borah as we headed to the back of the building, to the door with the sign reading LIBRARY.

"I thought old newspapers were filed in a morgue," Mike said.

"Not since the computer age arrived. Another bit of colorful tradition gone." I opened the door and turned on the lights. Three video display terminals and three bookshelves full of old and new phone books, encyclopedias, yearbooks, and atlases just about filled the room. I pointed to a door at the back. "Through there—that's the old morgue. That's where the bound newspapers and the microfilm and the filing cabinets full of clippings are."

Mike waved at the VDTs. "Can you work these?"

"Sure. Most of the staff can. That's why it's open

at night, even though there's no librarian on duty. Actually, we usually access it without leaving our desks." I sat down at the nearest VDT and opened the system. "Shall we start with the latest year?"

"Sure."

I told the system I wanted everything on Guy Unitas for the current year. It wasn't more than a dozen stories. "No big negotiations this year," I said. "Guy's hardly made the news."

Mike looked over my shoulder, making me uncomfortably aware of his presence, and we scanned the stories on the screen. Everything looked routine—APB Christmas drive for underprivileged kids, the APB annual fishing derby—until a long list of names appeared on the screen.

"What's that?" Mike asked.

"It seems to be the legals. Property transfers," I said. "A lot of the county records come straight to our files. You know, that stuff we run twice a week in agate—in itty, bitty type."

"I never read it."

"I don't often. But old-timers tell me you can get some great news tips that way. The land transfers tell you who's moving, and the lawsuits filed tell you who hasn't been paying their bills. But it's not my beat."

I scrolled down through the list until the highlighted name of "Guy Unitas" came up. "I see that Guy was sued by First National in August," I said. "I guess that's the last item for this year. I'll try last year."

The previous year had around twenty items with Guy's name, because the APB had renegotiated its contract that year. The elected officers actually handled the negotiations, but Guy was quoted about statistics.

Guy's name also showed up in the legals that year. He had sold a house. We went on to the previous year, the year before I moved to Grantham.

That year the stories had included the routine stuff—Christmas project and fishing derby—but another story had run on the APB's new offices. A cutline accompanied the story, but our library system doesn't display pictures.

" 'New APB offices,' " I read. " 'Guy Unitas, steward of the Grantham Amalgamated Police Brotherhood, and Merri Blakely, office manager, pose in the new APB offices at 4415 Grant Street. The APB will hold an open house at the new facilities from two p.m. until six p.m. Sunday.' "

The cutline seemed to ring a bell. "Merri Blakely," I said, "that name seems familiar."

"Coy's wife," Mike answered. "That was before they split. Guy and his wife separated around then, too. Everybody wondered if there was a connection."

"Was there?"

"Not that I ever heard. Mom might know."

We continued this process for five more years, taking an average of ten minutes a year. Guy's wife had divorced him three years earlier, the legals said. I'd already known that. But he hadn't been arrested or mixed up in a scandal or even been on the guest list for the mayor's annual whoop-de-do. He'd really stayed out of the newspapers most of the time.

"Of course, these years were after the time when Guy had worked as PIO for the Grantham PD," I said. "He left before our library went on computer. His previous life will be back there in the morgue room. The old stuff is in manila folders. Frankly, it would take us all night to look it up, and I'm not sure I'd find everything."

"It's nearly ten," Mike said. "We'd better knock it off. I'll try Shelly tomorrow."

"I'm disappointed," I said. I hit the ESCAPE key repeatedly, until the library access system closed down. "We found out very little about Guy Unitas personally. He's apparently had some financial problems—since the bank sued him. I could go to the courthouse and look up the details. And he sold his house. And he moved into a new office. Big deal."

"Let's go," Mike said. He ripped the printouts off the printer and began to fold them into a giant accordion shape.

I didn't know what we'd thought we'd find, but this was a letdown. I felt completely confused. I realized that for the past two days I'd been mixed up in three different plots—two mysteries and a romance. No wonder my head was spinning.

I shoved the romance aside and thought about the mysteries. First, Mike and I had been investigating his father's death, with its tenuous link to Bo Jenkins's murder. Second, Ace had involved me in the investigation into the alleged payoff to Irish Svenson over the renovations which turned the old Central High School building into the Grantham PD headquarters.

I gasped. "I forgot!"

"Forgot what?"

"Well, back around dinnertime, I had something I considered talking to you about. Then I found this stuff Lee must have written in my notebook, and that pushed the whole thing out of my mind."

"What was it?"

I hesitated. I hated to lay the evidence of his father's chicanery on Mike right at that moment. How would he react to the news that Irish Svenson was accused of being a crook? I wished I could forget Ace's big scoop, that Mike and I could concentrate on Lee and her apparent knowledge of his father's murder.

"It's a different topic entirely," I said.

Mike was frowning at me. I realized that he looked tired, too. "What are you talking about?" he said.

I decided the whole subject was too complex to discuss standing over a printer in the *Gazette* library. "Let's get out of here. I'll photocopy the deal I wanted you to see. We can take it with us."

I went back into the newsroom, to the desk Ace had been using, but the IRS form wasn't in any of the drawers. It wasn't on the tray on the corner of the desk, and it wasn't simply lying out on top. It wasn't there.

"Hell's bells!" I said. "I'll just have to tell you about it."

"Let's go," Mike said impatiently.

I led Mike toward the back stairs, my usual route to an exit, and we agreed that I'd follow him to his house. We were halfway down the stairs when I realized that I'd forgotten to check out with security. I turned around.

"Go ahead," I said. "I'll call security and tell them you're leaving with me. I'll be right out."

The night security guard answered on the third ring, and I wasn't more than two minutes behind Mike when I went through the back door. From the raised entry, I could look across the alley and see the entire ground level of the parking garage. During the hour we'd been in the building, a dozen campers and vans had parked in the row nearest the building. As usual, Redneck Hal's emerald green van was first in line. Beyond, the lower floor of the garage held only a few cars.

Mike had just reached the driver's side of his pickup. He was leaning down, looking closely at the door handle. I assumed he was trying to find the right slot for the key, since my car was casting a heavy shadow on the truck's door.

But whatever he was doing, he had his back to the man in black who was creeping up behind him with a club.

"Mike! Behind you!"

I hadn't known I could scream so loudly. I ran down the steps, screaming and shrieking. "Help! Murder! Call the cops!" I don't know what I was yelling. But I was loud.

I ran across the alley, straight toward Hal's van. I beat on the side and kicked the back door. "Hal! Bring your gun!" And I ran on, between the parked trucks, toward Mike, still screeching. I have a faint memory of swinging my purse around my head by its strap.

After I plunged through the line of parked trucks and vans, I had a clear view of Mike's truck, but he and the figure in black were still in the shadow of my car. Then Mike fell at my feet, and the black figure jumped out of the darkness toward me. I was knocked flat, ass over teakettle, and the attacker ran over the top of me. By the time Hal came running up, with several of the other circulation guys behind him, I was on my knees, crawling toward Mike.

"What the hell's going on?" Hal croaked.

"Where'd that guy go?" I yelled.

The roar of a motor answered me, and a white van came roaring toward us.

"There he is!" I jumped up, and this time I know for a fact I did wave my purse around my head. I know that because it caught on the side mirror of the white van and the resulting yank threw me off my feet and into the grill of Mike's pickup.

I whacked up against that grill, then I slid down it limply, like Wiley Coyote sliding down a cliff after the Roadrunner had done him in one more time. After I reached a sitting position, I fell over sideways.

I couldn't breathe.

CHAPTER 20

I lay there several minutes, trying to get my lungs reinflated. I can't say I gasped for breath. I couldn't even begin to gasp. The breath had been completely knocked out of me.

Then Mike's face was close to mine. Blood was running down the side of his head, but he was on his feet—or his knees—and I clutched his hand.

Mike yelled, "Call the paramedics!" Then he said softly, "Don't try to talk."

About that time I did get a gasp of air in. I didn't waste it trying to talk. I just tried to pump up my lungs. And with every breath I took in, my ribs hurt worse.

The ribs were the reason I wound up staying in the hospital overnight. Mike, on the other hand, got two stitches and went home. I have a confused memory that Mickey showed up at the hospital and that Wilda ran in with no makeup and her hair standing on end just as Mike was saying he was going to spend the night sitting outside my room as a guard.

The next morning, when I shook off the painkiller they had given me and woke up, I caught a glimpse of one of O'Sullivan Security's brown uniforms outside, so I concluded that Mickey had furnished the guard, rather than Mike taking the duty. I hoped they'd give me a discount.

Mickey came in with the aide who brought my breakfast and gave me the first report. Mike hadn't been seriously hurt, or so he'd told Mickey and his mom, because my yell made him duck, and the club wielded by the dark figure had struck a glancing blow.

Mickey grinned. "He's fine," he said. "He got a couple of stitches merely to save his looks."

"A scar might improve Mike's looks. He's the rugged type."

"Yeah, tough looking, like his dad." Mickey shook his finger at me. "Not so tough inside."

He told me the dark figure had gotten clean away in the white van—I was certain it was the one that had chased Lee and me, but I didn't stop to explain all that to Mickey.

"Mike said that when you rousted all those rough-looking guys out of their vans and campers," Mickey said, "the attacker lost interest in him real quick. Mike hadn't realized there were people around. I guess the guy in the white van hadn't either."

"Several of the circulation contractors usually sleep in their trucks until the presses roll," I said. "I was mighty glad they were there."

Mickey patted my hand. "If the doctors let you out, my guy will take you home," he said. "Don't try to drive today."

A few minutes after Mickey left, a knock sounded, and a burly brown-shirted guard put his head through the door. "Guy out here says he's brought you some clothes," he said.

"It's me!" Rocky was outside. He came in waggling his eyebrows. "Would that big, husky body-guard like to search me? I'd love it."

"Not funny, Rocky."

"I know, sweetie. Hey, you don't look so bad." He held a zipper bag in one hand and some clothes on a hanger in the other. "Martha picked out an outfit for you and packed up your makeup and some un-dies. She was going to send pajamas and a robe, but you don't seem to own any." He wagged his eye-brows again.

"I'm a T-shirt sleeper," I said. "And I tossed my robe in the dirty clothes. Thanks for the stuff. I hope I'll be out of here this morning."

"Well, I stopped at Ken's Gun Shop and brought you a present," Rocky said. He pulled a small paper sack from the pocket of his jacket. "Two narrow es-capes in one day is two too many. You've got to have protection."

"Rocky, I'm not interested in carrying a gun," I said. "Unless you really know how to use it, having a gun is more dangerous than not having a gun. And I don't have time to waste going to classes and keep-ing up target practice. If I had a gun, it would proba-bly be stolen, or some mugger would take it away from me and shoot me with it."

"I quite agree. Guns are dangerous. So that's not what I bought you." He reached inside the sack and pulled out a piece of cardboard with something mounted on it. "Pepper spray!"

He'd bought me a key chain with a small canister of pepper spray attached.

"And I want you to carry this in your hand every time you walk out to your car," he said firmly.

"Yes, sir," I said. I didn't know where my purse

was, but Rocky found it on a shelf in the minuscule closet. The strap was broken, but he tied a knot in it. He added the pepper spray to the car and door keys on my key chain, then insisted on reading the directions out loud while I practiced until I knew how to squirt it.

"Let us spray," he said. "Listen, kid, take care of yourself. I need all the friends I can get. Can't spare a one." He patted my cheek and left.

I was feeling fairly good. My ribs were still sore, which made deep breathing a problem, but I'd been awake long enough the night before to understand that the X rays didn't indicate that anything was broken. The nurse told me my doctor, Dr. Beatrice Deering, would be there soon, and she expected her to dismiss me. They'd kept me to watch for signs of internal injuries, but I was hoping the doctor wouldn't think I had any, since I wasn't vomiting or having abdominal pain. I was turning black and blue under the hospital gown, but I was also itching to get out of there. I washed my face and combed at my hair and put on my clean underpants. I was mentally ready for Dr. Bea to show up and tell me to leave.

But when the door opened, Mike stalked in. One look and I knew it wasn't a friendly visit.

He was holding the morning edition of *The Gazette* in his left hand. He punched at it with his right finger.

"What is this?" His voice was like ice. "How did this get in here? What are you trying to do to me?"

He handed me the newspaper. At the top of page one was a picture of the two of us. We both looked awful in the harsh flash the photographer had used in the dim garage. I glanced at the photo credit line. Bear. He must have been in the building and have run out to shoot the photo almost immediately, because it had obviously been taken before the ambulance had arrived. I was still looking limp, and Mike was kneeling beside me, supporting my shoulders. Blood was running down the side of his head. Hal was standing behind Mike with a pistol in his hand.

"What is the deal?" Mike said angrily.

"It's a lousy picture," I said, "but I guess Bear was lucky to get any kind of shot at all. I hope Hal has a concealed weapons permit for that pistol he keeps in his van."

"Not the picture! The story!"

Beside the picture there was a story about the attack on us—you can't keep something quiet when it happens in a newspaper's parking lot—but that wasn't the story Mike had tapped with his finger.

He'd pointed to the story below it. EVIDENCE ROOM EYED AS SOURCE OF POISON, the headline read.

I gasped, then grabbed at my ribs.

"How could you put that in?" He was almost raving.

I leaned back, holding my side. "I didn't. Oh, that hurts."

Mike ignored my pain. "I guess I should have known you were a reporter first and a girlfriend second. Obviously, getting a scoop is more important to you than I am. I let that stuff Hammond told me slip, and there it is in print. Do you realize I could be fired?"

I picked up the paper and read the lead. "I didn't write this," I said.

"It has your byline!"

He paced up and down, muttering, while I read the article.

After I finished, I dropped the paper on the bed. "I wrote part of it," I said. "The part about the uniform being found in your trash. But I didn't put the part in about the poison coming from the evidence room."

Mike started talking again, but I didn't listen. I was thinking furiously. How had the information about the source of the poison gotten into my article? I'd suggested that J.B. check on the source if he saw Hammond. Had he found out and added it?

No. I discarded that idea. My story had already been written and okayed by Jake before J.B. came to work. If J.B. had found anything out, he would have written it as a new story. If Jake and Ruth wanted to combine the stories, they would have done it, true, but they would have given the two of us a joint byline.

I knew Jake had read my story before he left for his meeting in Oklahoma City. Normally, he would mark it with his initials to indicate to Ruth that he'd already read it. Yet the story had been changed from the one I had written and, presumably, from the one Jake had read. Had Ruth and Jake approved this? I couldn't believe it.

Of course, anybody familiar with the *Gazette*'s editorial department computers could have gotten into the story and changed it. Since it had already been marked with Jake's initials, Ruth wouldn't have questioned it. As far as I knew, nobody had ever tampered with a story between the time the ME checked it and the time it went in the paper. But it was possible.

When reporters work together, it's impossible to keep them from knowing each other's computer access codes. In fact, all three of the *Gazette*'s police reporters do their routine work from a common file. J.B. and Chuck both could look over anything I'd written and left in the violence files. So could either of the city editors, or any of the copy editors for that matter. The editors had a master list of codes, and sometimes they needed to access the reporters' files. I once went off for a weekend and simply forgot to send a copy of an important story to the city file. Ruth realized it wasn't there, retrieved it from my file, and saved me from a heap of trouble.

Yes, at least at the *Gazette*, the police reporters all messed around in each other's files. And, since we'd been working on this Irish Svenson project, Ace-the-Ass Anderson had been admitted to the circle.

That thought made me gasp a second time, and once more I grabbed my ribs and groaned. Mike was still raving on about his stupid career, and suddenly I felt very impatient with him.

"Mike! I didn't put that stuff about the cyanide in there!"

"Then why does it have your byline? Do the *Gazette*'s standards of accuracy not extend to the identity of the reporters who wrote the stories?"

"I don't know what happened! I'll have to ask the editors."

He started to talk again, but I'd had enough. My train of thought had convinced me Ace had overheard my tip to J.B., then checked it out with one of his usually reliable sources and changed my story. But I didn't want to tell Mike that until I'd done some checking. I didn't want to talk about it at all.

"What is this?" I said. "My ribs hurt, and my professional pride is in shreds. And you're bullying me! Is this another act like the one you pulled on your mother? Are you pretending to be angry so you can manipulate me for some reason?"

Mike and I stared at each other angrily. And to my dismay, I discovered I wanted to kiss him. I understood why he was upset. I wanted to put my arms around him. I wanted to tell him everything would be all right. He wouldn't lose his job. He would find out what happened to his father.

And I wanted him to put his arms around me. I wanted him to tell me that we would find Lee and that she'd come clean and the whole mess would go away. We would discover a logical explanation for the IRS form Mike hadn't seen yet—an explanation which would show that Irish Svenson was not a crook.

But I couldn't say all those things. I was angry. I was hurt. I was afraid to trust him.

I turned over on my least painful side, and I tried to speak quietly and coldly. "Just go away and leave me alone."

He went.

I lay there trying not to shiver. I'd never been in a room that felt so cold. It was as if Mike had left his icy anger behind, emotions straight from the Arctic tundra. The heat of my own anger couldn't keep me warm, not for even a minute.

I pulled the hospital's inadequate blanket over my head, but I didn't cry. I simply curled up in the fetal position I'd always assumed when things really got to me.

It must have been the position that took me back,

back to the year I was eight. My parents' quarrels had become worse that year, and I'd spent a lot of time under my covers, curled into a ball. Finally, one night my daddy had come in. I remember that he had a suitcase with him. He put it down inside the door, and he sat down on the edge of my bed.

"Nellie," he'd said softly, "your mother and I keep fighting. We think it would be better if I moved out for a while."

I knew about divorce. I knew what was coming. I was so angry and so upset—I think my heart broke. I sat bolt upright in bed, and I yelled at him. "Go away and leave me alone!"

He got up and left without another word. So I never saw him again.

When my mother was killed a few weeks later, I thought he would come back and take me away. But he didn't. He took his suitcase that night and disappeared from my life forever. I told him to go, and he went.

Go away and leave me alone.

For twenty years I'd been telling that to the men in my life. First to my father. Then to my grandfather. He loved me, and he wanted to be a real father to me, but I pushed him away. And then he died, and I felt guilty. I told it to my college boyfriends, even Professor Tenure. I'd told them all to go, in one phrase or another. They'd all gone.

Now I'd told Mike to go. And he'd turned without a word and walked out the door, out of my life.

But no matter what I'd said, no matter how unreasonable Mike had been, no matter how manipulative and sneaky he could be, I didn't want him to go. If

I had any shred of honesty left, I had to admit that to myself.

The key moments in life take longer to tell about than they do to happen. I don't think Mike had been gone for more than a minute and a half when I pushed myself to a sitting position, grabbed my ribs and groaned, then slid off the edge of the bed. I yanked the thin hospital spread off the mattress and pulled it around me. Then, barefoot and wrapped up Indian-style, I went out into the hall and walked toward a grove of fake fig trees that masked the elevators.

Maybe I could catch up with Mike before he walked out of my life.

But when I turned the corner and saw the elevators, no one was waiting for a door to open. The down arrow wasn't lighted. The hall was empty.

I leaned my head against the wall between the elevator doors and pounded my fist against the print of a soothing winter landscape that hung there. I was too late. Mike had already left. I had missed him. Our affair was over before I figured out if it was love or lust.

"What are you doing?"

The voice came from behind me, and I whirled around.

"Mike!"

He was getting out of an easy chair in a tiny waiting area that had been hidden behind the fake foliage.

"You didn't go away!"

"Well, I went fifty or sixty feet. I thought we both needed that much cooling-off space. Are you okay?"

"I'm wonderful."

We put our arms around each other, right there in the hall. I almost dropped my bedspread, and I could hear some aides snickering. I didn't care.

We were still standing there when the elevator bell dinged and the doors gave a gentle whoosh. I heard a couple of hesitant footfalls.

Then Mike sighed deeply and spoke. "Hi, Mom."

I clutched my spread and turned around. Wilda Svenson's face was a study. Dismay. Concern. Amusement. Then she began to laugh.

I began to laugh. Mike began to laugh.

"Mrs. Svenson," I said, "I really don't spend my whole life standing around semiclothed, hugging your son."

She held up a newspaper. "So I see. Now and then you stop hugging him long enough to save his life."

"Let's not overreact," I said. "Whatever I did, I did out of pure panic. Come on down to the room."

I led the way up the hall with one end of the bedspread thrown over my shoulder like a toga and the other trailing like a bridal train. I ignored the snickers of the hospital staff. My dignified progress ended in anticlimax; I couldn't remember my room number. Mike and Wilda told me in unison. We also had to brush aside an embarrassed security guard. Apparently, when Mike went into my room, the guard had felt secure enough to go to the men's room. He seemed to think he'd be fired if Mickey found out he'd left his post for a minute.

The three of us went into the room, Mike helped me into the bed, and Wilda smiled at me. She was dressed for her office, in a dark brown wool-crepe suit, with a silk shirt, and heavy gold jewelry. A gold, brown, and ivory scarf was draped artistically around her collar.

"I just dropped by to check on how you're doing," she said. "And to thank you for keeping my son in one piece."

"That was just lucky," I said. "When I came out and looked over toward our cars, I could hardly miss the bad guy creeping up behind him. If I'd been a few seconds earlier or later—" I stopped. It was the first time I'd allowed myself to think that something had almost happened to Mike. I gulped and went on. "Which reminds me—how come I'm the one with a bodyguard? Mike, you were the one who was attacked."

"Just call me cautious," he said. "Mom, I was planning to call you about something. Why does the name 'San Simeon Beach' ring a bell with me?"

"San Simeon Beach?" Wilda looked puzzled, then her eyes widened, and she laughed. "San Simeon? Come on, Mike! What are you up to? An honest cop doesn't make enough money to need an offshore account."

"Offshore account?" Mike looked confused.

"Yes, Mike. San Simeon Beach is the place that got Jack Simons in so much trouble. He was flying down there with a load of cash and dropped his attaché case in the VIP lounge at DFW. It fell open right in front of God and Ellen Hilger." She turned toward me. "Ellen's the worst gossip at the Grantham Heights Country Club. The news that Jack was taking a trip to the Caribbean with an attache case full of cash was all over town in a flash. The IRS just loved hearing about it."

"Oh, Mike!" I said. "An offshore bank account!

That's what Lee was trying to tell me. Guy Unitas
has an offshore account in San Simeon Beach!"

Mike was grinning. "I'll bet that's it! And the
string of figures she wrote underneath must be the
account number. But what does PUPID mean?"

"That's easy," Wilda said. "If you're talking finance, it means 'Pay upon proper identification.' "

I grabbed my ribs before I gasped that time. "She
wrote 'president,' and she underlined it. That means
only the president of the APB can get the money—
not Guy!"

"Right!" Mike sounded excited.

Wilda frowned. "You're not talking about Guy Unitas having an offshore account, are you? The whole
idea's ridiculous. Guy doesn't have any money. His
ex-wife got the house in the divorce settlement—even
though she was moving away from Grantham—because he couldn't afford to pay her for her share of
the equity. I know because somebody in our office
sold the house. Guy moved into a rattrap in Central Highlands."

"Guy may not have money of his own, but he
handles a lot," Mike said.

"Union funds? Their dues income barely covers
expenses," Wilda said. "They have to finance that
office, Guy's salary, the bookkeeper, the lawyer's re-
tainer. It's a low-rent operation."

Mike frowned. "The traditional crime associated
with unions is looting the pension fund."

"I hardly see how," Wilda said. "They have to
have an outside audit. But—well, I will admit I had
quite a time getting Irish's money out of that fund. It
took nearly a year and three letters from my lawyer. I

thought it was because Irish hadn't been a member for more than fifteen years before he died."

Mike turned to me. "Listen, Nell, this has gone too far. We've got to talk to somebody with some authority to act. Do you want it to be Hammond? Or Jameson?"

"What are you talking about?" Wilda said.

Right at that moment someone rapped on the door, and the burly guard put his head in. "Man to see you, Miss. Says he's your boss."

Jake walked in. I introduced him to Mike and Wilda. I wasn't surprised to learn he and Wilda already knew each other.

Mike didn't waste time with chitchat, and neither did Jake. They began talking at the same time.

"How did that stuff about the poison get in Nell's story?" Mike said to Jake.

"Did you take that 1099 on Irish Svenson from Ace's desk?" Jake said to me.

Then they stared at each other and started over.

"Didn't you add the information about the poison?" Jake asked me.

"What 1099 is he talking about?" Mike asked me.

"Wait a minute!" I took a deep breath, then grabbed my ribs. "Both of you sit down, and let's talk about one thing at a time. No, Jake. I did not add the information about the poison to the story. I don't know how it got in. What does Ruth say about it?"

"I haven't asked her, since it's kind of early to call somebody who doesn't get off work until after one a.m. I was very surprised to see it, because it hadn't been there when I read the story early in the afternoon."

I turned to Mike. "See."

"I believed you already."

Wilda made a commanding gesture. "But what's this about some tax form of Irish's?"

Jake looked at me narrowly. "You hadn't told them?"

"No!" I probably sounded pretty self-righteous.

"Well, when they said the two of you were coming out of the *Gazette* building when you were attacked last night, I figured—" Jake sounded apologetic.

I took pity on him. "Actually, Jake, I looked in Ace's desk because I was planning to show the form to Mike. I mean, that seemed like the next logical step."

Wilda leaned between us. "What are you two talking about?"

I waved her aside. "Just a minute. Jake, the form was not in Ace's desk at eleven o'clock last night. I assumed that Ace had taken it home with him. Are you saying it's gone?"

"That's what Ace says. I never saw it."

Mike spoke again, his voice sharp. "What form?" And Wilda added to the verbal confusion. "What are you talking about? And why would one of Irish's tax forms be any of your business?"

Jake and I looked at each other. Jake shrugged. "I never saw the form," he repeated.

I sighed and turned to Mike and Wilda. "For the last two days Ace Anderson—one of the Associated Press reporters"—Mike nodded to indicate that he knew who I was talking about, and Wilda looked stony—"well, Ace has claimed that a source he trusts has been telling him that payoffs were involved in the contracts for renovating the old Central High

School building into the Central Police Station. And he's claimed your dad got one."

"Bullshit!" Mike snorted it out.

"That was pretty much my opinion," I said. "Ace never had anything to prove it. Then yesterday afternoon this unnamed source gave him a tax form which shows that Balew Brothers paid your dad a major sum as a consultant. This supposedly happened the year the construction contract was awarded."

"Absolutely not!" Wilda said.

"Why didn't you tell me about this?" Mike was pretty close to yelling.

"I didn't see the form until late yesterday afternoon!" I came close to yelling back. "Since then we've been pretty busy, between going to meetings of the C-Club, searching the back files of the *Gazette* and almost getting killed!"

We stared at each other angrily.

Jake cleared his throat. "Also, Mike, we probably should have approached your mother first." He turned to Wilda. "I assume you handled your husband's estate."

"Yes, I did," Wilda said. "And I think I can clear this up right away. What year was this supposed payment made?"

I told her.

She nodded firmly. "That was one of the years the IRS audited. I can have the forms on your desk this afternoon. Irish had no income from Balew Brothers during those years. He had no large sums of income of any kind from sources outside the Grantham PD.

"In fact, he had taken money out of his retirement

account. Money I couldn't trace. We had to pay tax
on it. When I asked him about it—''

Wilda stopped and seemed to consider her answer.
She glanced at Jake, then turned toward Mike. ''Well,
his explanation led into the problems I told you
about Monday night.''

She turned back to Jake. ''But you're obviously not
interested in money that went out, just sums coming
in. And according to the Internal Revenue Service
and our accountant, Irish didn't receive any money
from Balew Brothers or anybody else.''

''Well, a 1099 looks pretty official,'' Jake said.

''It's not.'' Wilda's voice was firm. ''As a former
bookkeeper, let me tell you. You can walk into any
government office and pick one off a stack laid out
on a table. You can type it up and put in any information you want to. It only becomes official when
it's filed with the Internal Revenue Service. And I
can't believe that I went through that hellish audit,
and the IRS missed something like that.''

''Is it possible somebody deliberately led Ace Anderson astray?'' Mike said.

I snickered, and Jake rolled his eyes. ''Leading Ace
astray wouldn't be that hard to do,'' Jake said. ''Especially now that the form's disappeared.''

''You're not going to print anything?'' Mike
sounded suspicious.

''No way!'' I must have sounded scandalized.

''Absolutely not!'' Jake said. He launched into a
short dissertation on journalistic ethics and the need
to be able to back stories up. I had the feeling he
was practicing for the lecture Ace was going to get.

My doctor, Dr. Bea, came in then. She ordered
Mike and Jake out. Wilda left, too, still promising to

have three-years worth of audited tax returns on Jake's desk that very afternoon. Jake was telling her that wouldn't be necessary.

Dr. Bea told me to go home, and the nurse with her thrust release forms at me. They left, and I started dressing. As soon as I was halfway covered, I put my head out the door, but the brown-shirted character had disappeared. I asked a passing LPN where he had gone.

"He said he was leaving," she said. "That other young man is still here. He's down by the elevators talking to a policeman."

CHAPTER 21

A policeman? Mike had said he wanted to talk to either Hammond or Jameson. But to a layman, a "policeman" probably indicated a uniformed officer. And a uniformed officer didn't sound like either of those people.

I decided to assume that Mike wouldn't leave me stranded, now that I was being dismissed from the hospital. I put on my shoes and gathered up the hospital's tissues, lotion, soap, and plastic pitcher and put them in the hospital's plastic bag. They make you pay for that stuff, so I was certainly taking it with me. I was dumping my dirty clothes in on top when I heard a rap at the door, and Mike came in. He didn't look happy.

"I understand my bodyguard is gone," I said.

"I told him I'd take the duty."

"I guess I need a ride," I said.

"You got it. But I'll have to drop you off. Jim Hammond wants me on his carpet at eleven a.m. I think he's sharpening his ass-chewing teeth."

Mike had a good reason to look serious, I realized. The goof-up which had allowed the source of the poison to get in that morning's *Gazette* could have him in a lot of trouble. And, though I suspected Ace was responsible, I had no way of proving he was the guilty party, and I had no proof of how he could have gotten hold of the information in the first place.

"Mike," I said, "I did not put that stuff about the poison coming from the evidence room in the story, and I did not tell anybody about it. I really, truly don't know how it got there."

Mike almost smiled. He put his arms around me, gently enough to leave my ribs undisturbed, and rested his cheek against the top of my head. "I believe you," he said. "You're Honest Nell."

"Don't laugh at me. I know I'm not always honest."

"You try. That's one reason I love you."

He loved me? I rested my head on his shoulder. Tears came to my eyes, and I had to blink hard to keep them from getting away from me.

Mike had just told me he loved me. We hadn't talked about the future. We hadn't declared more feeling for each other than sexual attraction. The one time he'd acted as if he might say something serious—on the first night we'd spent together—I'd cut him off in midsentence. Two days after that, I'd yelled at him and called him a manipulative creep. And here he'd just told me he loved me.

Mike might be tricky and manipulative, but I couldn't see any advantage he gained by telling me that.

I wasn't sure I loved him. And if I loved him, I wasn't sure I could get along with him, day to day. But he still dared to say he loved me. He hadn't made tentative moves to see how I'd respond. He just said it.

To a person like me—one who had always been

afraid to be serious about anybody, afraid to admit I cared—well, it's no wonder I had to fight back tears. Courage is always touching.

After I'd blinked a dozen times, I stood on tiptoe and kissed him. "Guess I'd better get out of here," I said.

When I'd signed the releases the nurse had handed me earlier, she'd said I was checked out through the business office, thanks to the *Gazette* insurance. Now, despite the objections of the floor nurse, I walked out of the hospital. The nurse kept saying an aide would be there with a wheelchair, and I kept saying I couldn't wait and walking toward the hospital's front entrance.

I did agree to wait at the door which opened onto the official passengers-pickup area while Mike went to get his truck. So I was hovering near the automatic door when I saw a thin, dark-haired guy with a skinny-lipped mouth that went all around his head. He got out of a big black car and walked toward me. My stomach had a conniption, and I looked around for a potted plant to hide behind. No potted plant was available. When I looked back, the electric eye was opening the door, and I was face to face with the new arrival. It was Guy Unitas.

"Hi, Guy," I said.

Guy gaped like a carp in a poolful of algae. "Nell! The paper made it sound as if you were badly hurt!"

"I'm too mean to hurt, Guy. What are you doing here?"

He smiled a fishy smile. "I came to see you, of course."

"Nice, but not necessary," I said. My stomach jumped around again, and a shiver crept up my spine. The words "Guy Unitas" printed in neat book-keeper's handwriting popped up on my mental computer screen, scanned from the notebook where Lee had written them. And where she had written "San Simeon Beach." And a string of numbers. Had the note Lee put in the notebook really meant that Guy Unitas had an offshore bank account?

Notebook! Where was that notebook? Had I lost it? I grabbed at my purse.

Guy was talking. "Nell, I need to talk to you. Can I take you around to the cafeteria for a cup of coffee?"

I ignored the invitation and kept looking for the notebook. It wasn't in the outside pocket of the leather satchel I call my purse. I unzipped the top and dug around inside.

"Nell?" Guy was waiting for an answer.

I breathed a sigh of relief. The notebook was there. Some good Samaritan had gathered my belongings up in the *Gazette* parking garage and had stuffed everything inside my purse. I clutched the notebook. Luckily, I calmed down before I pulled it out and waved it under Guy's nose.

Guy was squinting at me. "Coffee?" he said again.

I was relieved to see a black pickup pulling up outside.

"Sorry, Guy. I've got to leave," I said. "By the way, I'm asking them to take me off the violence beat, so you may want to talk to J.B. instead of to me. He'll be covering your office."

I moved as quickly as my sore ribs would allow. Mike opened the door of the truck for me. He waved at Guy. Casually. Then he went around to the driver's side and climbed in.

"What's Guy doing here?" he asked.

"He said he wanted to talk to me," I said. "Offered me a cup of hospital coffee. Should I go back and find out what he wants?"

"Not when there's the chance cyanide may be floating around the circles he's moving in."

As we moved off, I looked back and saw that Guy was staring after us. I couldn't read his expression, but it wasn't friendly. He began to walk back toward the car he'd gotten out of.

Car? It was no car. It was a limousine.

"Golly!" I said. "What's Guy doing traveling by limo?"

"Limo?" Mike looked into his outside mirror. "Did Guy get into that limo?"

"Yes."

"Damn! I've got to call Hammond!" He swung the pickup a direction I hadn't expected, and the seat belt caught my ribs. I gasped.

"I'll head back to the hospital," Mike said. "Aren't there pay phones right inside?"

"Yes. But why are you so excited about the limousine?"

"Airport," Mike said. His voice was urgent. "Airport pickup service. I recognize the vehicle. They pick you up at your house and deliver you to the right gate at the airport."

"Hell's bells!" Now I was the excited one. "If Guy's headed for the airport, he may be leaving the country."

As we went back down the drive, Guy's limo passed us. I couldn't see through the tinted windows that shrouded the backseat, and I tried to look away, to pretend I wasn't interested in the limo at all. Mike pulled up once more in the passenger-pickup area of the hospital. "You'd better come in with me," he said. "I'm not leaving you alone for a minute."

I moaned and groaned and clutched my ribs as I climbed out of the truck The older guy who was guarding the hospital's entrance acted as if he were going to object to Mike's truck, but Mike flashed his badge, and we went inside.

Mike dialed the extension for Jim Hammond's office, but Jim's clerk—the fabled Peaches Atkinson, a well-known character around the Grantham PD—wouldn't let him talk to her boss. I could hear her piercing voice broadcasting from his receiver.

"He's not taking calls," she said. "You're supposed to see him at eleven. That's only forty-five minutes from now."

Peaches is authority personified, either in person or over the phone. Even Mike had trouble standing up to her.

"Peaches, this is an emergency," he said.

Peaches sniffed. "Well, you can't talk to him."

"Listen, Peaches, I just found out something about the matter we were planning to discuss at eleven. And it's vital for Jim to know about it. Immediately!"

Peaches was adamant. Jim Hammond had told her to hold his calls, so the dam might be crumbling and the water might be rushing down at us, but the calls were not getting through.

"Peaches, this is a matter of life and death," Mike said finally. "Will you at least take a message to him? Now!"

Peaches ungraciously agreed.

"Tell them the person Nell and I think was behind the attack on us last night may be leaving the country. He's on his way to the airport. And so am I!" Mike slammed the phone down.

Then he began pawing through the tattered phone book that came with the phone booth.

"Who are you trying to call?" I asked.

"Mickey. O'Sullivan Security has the contract for the airport parking lots."

Mickey wasn't in his office, but his switchboard connected us to a radio in his car.

Mike told Mickey our problem. He described Guy, told them the license number of the limo he was in, and gave a brief fashion commentary on what Guy was wearing. "Blue blazer and gray pants," he said. "Kind of shapeless."

"Mike! Am I impressed!" I said. "I didn't notice what Guy was wearing."

Mike grinned and kept talking. "Just get your people to keep an eye on him," he said. "The Grantham PD is likely to want to know where he's going. But there's no warrant, I'm sure of that."

He scanned the sidewalk before we went back outside the hospital. "Now, to get you home."

"You haven't got time! We've got to get to the airport."

"I'm not taking you into a dangerous situation."

"Guy Unitas isn't dangerous. He's a wimp." I thought about that one. He might be a cornered wimp, and anything that's cornered can be dangerous. "Besides, we don't want to interfere with him. Don't we just want to make sure somebody knows what plane he's on? Where he's headed?"

Mike didn't say anything, but he headed for the airport. I think he couldn't stand not to be where the action was. Plus, there was no reason that Jim

Hammond would do anything about Mike's request to send aid to the airport. We might well be on our own, the only people who cared where Guy was going. Besides, there was no warrant out for Guy. And no one—Mike, me, or Jim Hammond—had any authority to keep him from going anywhere in the world he wanted to go.

Grantham International has only one terminal building. Mike pulled into a NO PARKING zone and waved at a woman wearing an airport security uniform. She strolled over and spoke to him. "Mike Svenson? Your man is in line at the United desk."

I got out of the truck before Mike could help me, but he didn't let me get away from him. "Wait a minute," he said. "I'm in charge this time. You go slow."

We walked into the terminal building. It was fairly crowded. The Grantham airport gets its International status by virtue of three flights a day to Mexico City. It isn't DFW, LAX, or JFK. It's simply a moderate-sized airport with around a hundred departures a day.

Guy was no longer at the United ticket counter, so we went through airport security, out to the United arm of the terminal. United has eight or ten gates, each with a small waiting area. Guy could have been in any of them, and he would be able to see us more easily that we could spot him. We spent ten minutes looking without a glimpse of him. We might never have found him, if he hadn't been paged.

"Guy Unitas, go to the red phone for an emergency call," the loudspeaker boomed. "Guy Unitas. Go to the red telephone."

Mike and I jumped behind an 1890s-style popcorn

wagon and peered over the giant heap of popped corn in its glass tank. From our hidey-hole we had a clear view of the red telephones that served the United gates. And here came Guy, answering his page. He spoke briefly on the telephone, then turned and scanned the area.

I turned my back to him and pretended to look for something in my purse. Mike ducked down as if he were working on the popcorn cart's wheel and peeked around its corner. "He's heading for the men's room," he said.

I relaxed. He couldn't leave the terminal without coming back out the door he'd gone in.

Mike and I stood there, waiting. We could see the door to the men's room clearly. It didn't seem to be getting too much business. Three businessmen in suits and a cowboy type in boots and hat went in. A man in a maroon blazer and plaid pants came out, and in a few minutes, two of the suits exited. A bushy-haired man in blue coveralls shuffled out, carrying a tool box. Guy Unitas did not come out.

I kept looking down the walkway toward the ticket desks, and after about ten minutes, I saw Jim Hammond come toward us. Mike waved, and Jim joined us. He held his portable phone in his hand.

He scowled. "Just what's going on?"

Mike began a condensed version of the tale he'd meant to tell Hammond in his office. I produced the notebook as evidence. Our story was long and complicated, and it didn't seem to convince Jim.

"Anyway, I know we can't hold him," Mike said. "No warrant. No proof at this point. But I thought I could find out where he's headed."

"Maybe he's sick," I said. "He's sure been in that

men's room long enough." More men had gone in and come out, but Guy hadn't been one of them.

"You're right," Mike said. He swung left, hard and suddenly, and almost ran across the passageway and into the men's room. Jim Hammond followed him.

Within seconds, Hammond came back out, frowning. He looked up and down the corridor.

"Wasn't Guy in there?" I said.

Hammond shook his head.

"He sure didn't come out," I said. "I've been watching."

Then Mike appeared in the door and beckoned to Hammond. They both went back in.

A minute later things began to happen. Security guards ran down the hall toward the men's room. The cowboy type and a computer nerd—plaid shirt, jeans, running shoes, and laptop case—came out and stood beside the door, with a security guard beside them. He'd obviously been told to keep them there. The computer nerd looked at his watch and talked nervously to the guard. A man in a good gray suit came out talking on a cell phone and joined the group.

Mike strode out and walked directly over to me. He looked grim.

"Guy's dead," he said. "It looks like cyanide again."

I'd had thirty seconds to expect the worst, but for a second my inner ear felt as if the United gates had taken off into the wild blue, leaving the planes on the ground. Then my ribs stabbed me with pain, objecting to a deep breath I had taken, and I grabbed them and returned to earth and to reality. Guy was dead. Cyanide.

I grabbed Mike's arm. "What happened?"

"He's in the back stall with an empty pint whiskey bottle beside him. He could have had it with him."

"You found him?"

Mike nodded. "Yeah. I saw his feet, realized their position—it wasn't right. I looked under. That's when I called Jim in." He shook his head. "After I crawled under and got close to him—I could smell the almonds on his breath. So it had just happened."

"Do you think it was suicide?"

"It's possible."

"Mike, I swear he never saw us! When he got the page, we got out of sight. There's no way he could have seen us. No way we could have spooked him."

Mike spoke slowly. "I don't think we spooked him," he said. "I think someone else did."

He sat me down in one of the plastic waiting-room armchairs and asked me to make a list of the men who had gone in and out of the rest room while we were watching. I had plenty of time to do it while I waited for Hammond to talk to us. He was standing in the hall talking on his cell phone. More technicians and detectives kept arriving.

When he came over to us, he spoke to Mike. "Looks like this solves your case," he said.

Mike frowned. "Maybe."

Jim nodded and turned to me. "You two should have come to me sooner, of course, but—I understand why Mike didn't want to do that. But if what this Lee person told you is right, Guy fits all the requirements for the bad guy she described."

I was still confused. "Are you sure?"

"Yeah! Of course, we won't have any proof until

we get an audit of the A.P.B. accounts. And find out about that offshore account."

"It's all just speculation so far," Mike said.

"Maybe so, but the theory's good. It works this way. Guy's been stealing from the union. This Lee finds out about it and tells Irish, but she's afraid, so she doesn't tell Irish everything. Then, after Irish dies, she's afraid Guy killed him, and she skedaddles. But somehow she knows, or at least suspects, that Guy called on Bo to help him—either to cause the accident to Irish's car or to cover up afterward. So, when Bo Jenkins is killed, she's convinced Guy killed both Irish and Bo. She's afraid to keep quiet any longer. But her story's kind of crazy, and she's afraid some of the cops will blow the deal to Guy. After all, we all know Guy, and lots of people in the department consider him a friend.

"So she goes to you, Nell. But Guy finds out that she's come forward."

"But how?" Mike said. "How could he find that out?"

"That I don't know," Hammond answered. "We've got a lot of unanswered questions at this point. Such as why he attacked the two of you last night. But we'll figure it out. Anyway, after his attack fails, Guy decides it's time to collect his offshore account and go on permanent vacation."

Mike was still frowning. "We have no proof of any of this, Jim."

"With Guy dead, we're not going to have to prove anything in court," Hammond said. "And we've got evidence for some of it." He held up a plastic sack, and I saw that it held a passport. "Passport for one

Gerald U. Smith," he said. "And Gerald U. Smith just happens to look a lot like Guy Unitas. Okay?"

Mike's eyes widened. "Okay!"

Hammond held up a second sack. "Letter certifying that Gerald U. Smith is president of the Grantham A.P.B. Okay?"

"Looks good!"

Hammond grinned. "But—before Guy can get out of the country, you and Nell figure out that he's leaving. You alert me through Peaches. I put it on the radio. 'Bad guy headed to airport.' Which was stupid, it turns out, because some cop who was on Guy's pipeline must have known Guy was taking a trip today, heard the traffic and called the airport to tip him off. Guy panicked and used another dose of the cyanide he'd stolen from the evidence room."

Mike frowned, but he didn't say anything.

"I know, I know!" Jim said. "We don't know how Guy could get into the evidence room. We've got a lotta gaps in there. But now that we know Guy was involved, we'll close 'em up."

Mike and I were there another hour. We had to ID the other men who'd gone in and out of the restroom. The only one who didn't turn up was the maintenance man.

"A skinny guy with long hair," Mike said. "Bushy hair."

Jim's frown deepened to a scowl after he heard that. The airport manager was on the scene by then—dealing with three television channels and Bear Bennington—and he didn't like that description either. Jim Hammond was too busy to talk to him, so the manager muttered at me.

The Grantham International Airport has a strict

dress code for its maintenance staff, the manager said stiffly. Long hair was permitted, but it had to be neat. Ponytails. Queues. Buns.

"Never bushy," the manager said. "Bushy would not be permitted. And it's the same for men and women. Long is fine. But neat."

His annoyance made me wonder. If you took away the blue coveralls and the bushy hair, which could very well be a wig, what description did we have?

A skinny nonentity. That's what Mike and I had seen. Put a Salvation Army uniform on the guy and he'd fit the description of the disguise expert who invaded the Grantham Community Mental Health Center and slipped an Almond Joy loaded with cyanide to Bo Jenkins. Put a painter's cap and coveralls on him, and he'd fit the description of the character who'd put the Salvation Army uniform in Mike's trash. If he was driving a white van, he could well be the guy who chased Lee and me through the Memorial Rose Garden, since we hadn't seen him.

Was Jim Hammond wrong when he said Guy was the baddie?

In about an hour Jim came over and told us we could leave. We were to call Peaches and set up appointments to make formal statements. We went to the truck, which was parked illegally in the loading zone in front of the United desk. But it hadn't been towed. Mike thanked the security guard before he opened the door for me.

He was frowning as he turned the ignition over. "I'd still like to know who Lee is before we write this whole thing off," he said.

We stopped at the next exit up the interstate and grabbed some lunch at a Mickey D's. I wasn't very good company. Mike had mentioned Lee. Now I kept worrying about Lee, about who she was, about why she'd run out on me in the Blue Flamingo. Where was she? Had Guy caught her?

Hammond might be happy with Guy as the killer of Bo Jenkins and maybe of Irish. But Mike was right. We needed to know who Lee was.

CHAPTER 22

I talked Mike into taking me to the *Gazette* instead of home. On the way down, I mentally reviewed what we had deduced about Lee. I had a plan of action by the time Mike stopped in front of the main entrance of the *Gazette*.

"Mike, I don't need a bodyguard," I said. "You go see if you can hang around with Hammond."

He had plainly been itching to get back to the airport, and I could use the *Gazette*'s resources to check up on Lee by myself. I didn't need Mike to slow me down.

But Mike frowned. "Will you stay put?"

"Yes," I said. "For one thing, these ribs are going to make driving uncomfortable."

Then Mike's eyes focused beyond me, and he grinned. I looked out the window on my side of the pickup, and saw one of the *Gazette*'s daytime security guards, Bill Martin, looking in at me.

"Bill!" Mike said. "You old buzzard!"

I rolled my window down, and Bill Martin reached across the truck to shake Mike's hand. They did that male bonding thing for a couple of minutes.

I shook my head at Mike. "Do you know everybody in Grantham?"

"I know all the old cops who were my dad's friends when I was growing up," Mike said. He rested his hand lightly on my shoulder. "Bill, I'm trying real hard to get this lady to be my girlfriend."

Well, that ended any pretense of keeping our romance quiet. Not that it was much of a secret at this point anyway.

Bill Martin was smiling. And Bill Martin had more teeth than any man I'd ever seen smile. I swear he has a double row all around his head.

"You got good taste," he said.

Mike grinned. "Yeah. Anyway, you know somebody tried to run her down with a car last night? I swore I was going to guard her personally, but now I've got to go someplace. Can you keep an extra close eye on her?"

Bill smiled even more broadly and shook a finger at me. "I can watch her as long as she doesn't try to jump out a window."

"I don't feel like climbing down any fire escapes," I said.

Mike seemed satisfied to leave me at the *Gazette*, since his pal Bill was on the job and I had declared my intention to stay put. I went inside with Bill and reviewed what Mike and I had deduced about Lee's identity.

First, Lee was a regular reader of the *Gazette* who lived at least one hundred and fifty miles away. That meant a mail subscriber.

Second, she had some connection with Guy Unitas. But we didn't know what that link was.

I started on the second item first. I went to the library and put in an order for all the pre-computer-era files on Guy and the Amalgamated Police Brotherhood. The librarian on duty said she'd have them ready in half an hour.

Then I went back to the first floor, where the circulation department is located, handy to the main street entrance, in case someone wanders by and wants to subscribe. That department also has a side door that opens onto the alley, as access for the guys in the vans, the people who'd saved our bacon the night before.

I'm not sure I'd ever been in the circulation offices before. The *Gazette* employees are divided into departments, which might also be known as fiefdoms. First floor, logically enough, houses circulation and classified advertising, the two departments which most often deal directly with the public. Display advertising occupies the second floor, keeping its distance from classified and from the newsroom. The news department is on the third floor, with the library in the back corner. The business offices—where the salary checks are cut and the statements are sent out and the bills are paid—occupy a sanctuary on four, looking down on the rest of us. The publisher's office is up there, which tells you something about newspaper priorities.

People sometimes get a screwy idea that a newspaper is a public service. It's not. It's a private, profit-making business. Of course, like any business, the better it serves the public, the more profitable it is likely to be.

The printing plant is in a separate building, although it's linked to the main building on each floor. The giant press extends two stories high, taking up space from the basement through the first floor, and the pressroom crew has locker rooms in the basement.

Warehouse space is in the basement and the sections of the first floor not used by the press. The computers and scanners and other gear used by the ad builders are on the second floor, adjoining the display advertising department. Our news-side page builders, who also use computers with giant screens—they can view an entire newspaper page at once—are on the same floor with the news department.

Each of the *Gazette*'s 250-odd—and some are decidedly odd—employees sticks with his or her own department. Circulation was a foreign country to me. I had no more to do with them than any other subscriber would. I had to show my employee ID before I got together with the person in charge of mail subscriptions.

Her name was Jamesetta Bay, and her elaborate cornrowed hairdo made her look like a high school kid. But she knew her equipment. Getting a printout of subscribers by area code would be the simplest thing in the world, she said.

"I have to make a printout for the auditors every month," she said. She didn't mean the *Gazette*'s accountants. She meant the ABC, the Audit Bureau of Circulation. A newspaper's circulation must be certified by the ABC. Advertising rates are based on it.

"Just what zips are you interested in?" she asked.

Luckily she had a Zip Code Directory. I read out the Oklahoma City codes, the Tulsa codes, and the Dallas–Fort Worth codes. The list of mail subscribers that came up didn't include too many names. People read the news about the town where they live and occasionally the town where they used to live and sometimes the town where they are planning to move. Few of us read newspapers from completely strange cities. Another city's news is usually pretty boring.

Jamesetta was getting interested in the project. She was the one who suggested getting maps and adding more suburbs. That brought the list to sixty names. I thanked her profusely and left. I decided that walking upstairs was going to jiggle my sore ribs, so I took the elevator to the third floor and went back to my desk with her computer printout.

The police reporters' desks were empty, including the one Ace had been using. Somehow I didn't expect Ace to show up that afternoon.

I began to study the printout of mail subscribers. The first thing I noticed was that in the entire list of fifty or sixty names, not one first name was "Lee." Or "Leigh." Or "Lea." Or "Li." Or any other variation of Lee I could imagine. There were only a dozen that had an initial "L." Which meant nothing. "Lee" could be a nickname. It could be an alias.

Obviously these subscription lists would have to be checked out by guys with badges and the authority to ask questions.

I sat, stared at the computer printout, and sulked. Was this list going to help? Was I getting anywhere at all?

I scrawled a few notes on the blank edge of the computer paper.

We had eliminated the IRS 1099 form and the possibility that Irish Svenson had been involved in a payoff as a factor. Or I had. It would still have to be checked out, but I—myself, Nell Matthews, girl reporter—was convinced that Guy Unitas had foisted a fake form on Ace Anderson.

Why did I believe that? First, because I knew how easy Ace was to fool.

Second, because Wilda Svenson said she had gone through three years of IRS audits, and everything had checked out and that Irish had had no consulting income. This wouldn't have been true if the IRS had gotten a 1099 from Balew Brothers. At least I didn't think it would. I made a note to check on this with an accountant.

In fact, Wilda had told Mike that instead of having unexplained income, Irish had lost money. Money was missing from his retirement account. Reading between the lines, I deduced that she had quizzed him about this. His explanation had led her to the conclusion that Irish had given money to another woman. Or spent it on her. I wrote "blackmail?" on my computer printout. The quarrel over the missing money had ended with Irish admitting he had had, or was having, an affair. He told Wilda he wouldn't stop seeing the other woman. And Wilda told him to move out.

In addition, Bear Bennington had seen Ace and Guy with their heads together in the back booth at the Grantham Plaza Hotel.

Yes, I was convinced that Guy Unitas had deliberately led Ace Anderson astray with the fabled form 1099. A 1099 which had conveniently disappeared almost as soon as it appeared.

But why? What had Guy had to gain from this?

I had no idea. I wrote that question out and surrounded it with big question marks. What had the episode of the 1099 actually accomplished? It had kept me from dropping the crime beat, and it had forced me to keep my affair with Mike semiquiet. It had forced me to work with Ace Anderson. It had distracted me from trying to help Mike figure out what was going on with Bo Jenkins's death and what that had to do with his father's death.

So what? How could anyone have even known that I was interested in Irish Svenson's death? What had they been doing? Tapping my phone?

I threw down my ballpoint in disgust. The whole thing was ridiculous. Tapping my phone, indeed. Who was I? The Mafia? It was silly.

But—I mulled it over. Until Lee and I had our wild rendezvous in the Memorial Rose Garden, only way we had communicated was on the telephone, and she had called me at home. She seemed pretty certain that "they"—the bad guys, whoever they were—hadn't known where she was until she got in touch with me.

Could they have tapped my phone?

It was too dumb. The thought made me feel as if I should check into the Grantham Community Mental Health Center—Paranoia Wing.

But maybe I could ask Mike, quietly and privately, if he knew how to check that sort of thing. If he'd promise not to tell a soul. Or to laugh.

A tremor of dread ran through me. If my phone was tapped, I was going to feel guilty. Lee had turned to me for help. Instead, a tapped phone would have led the crooks right to her.

But she hadn't let me help her. We'd gotten away from the van that chased us. We'd been waiting for Mike to come. But Lee hadn't trusted Mike and me. She had fled. Wearing my rain coat.

The thought of Lee put me on a new track. I picked up my ball point and scrawled some more notes on that printout. Irish had been about to break a big scandal, she'd said. Something that involved the Grantham PD. "The highest levels," she said.

Mike had talked to his dad shortly before Irish's death, and his dad had hinted at problems, but told him nothing specific. Irish apparently hadn't told Wilda either—or had he? I wrote that down with a question mark. Wilda might still be keeping something back.

But Lee had said the scandal involved high-level cops. Or did she say that? Had she said, "You'd be surprised at who's involved," or something like that? Would Guy Unitas and the APB qualify?

Despite Hammond's certainty about Guy's guilt, I wasn't sure. I couldn't picture Irish Svenson getting too bent out of shape over a scandal in the police officers' union. As chief, he'd almost been an adversary to the union. He was management, and the APB was labor. He'd have been more worried if one or more of his department heads or assistant chiefs had been linked to something scandalous.

Well, who among the powers-that-be in the Grantham Police Department had benefited from Irish's death? I scrawled some names down. Jameson, of course. He'd moved from division commander to chief. The other two division commanders and the Traffic Bureau commander had been in place before Irish died. Had he been about to fire one of them? I didn't know. I wrote their names down.

In the Detective Bureau, Hammond had hopped over two people to become a senior detective—six months after Irish died. Would he have gotten the job if Irish had still been around? The gossip was that he got along with Jameson a lot better than he had with Irish Svenson. I wrote his name down.

I really couldn't think of anybody else at the Grantham PD who might have benefited from Irish's death. So I tackled it from the other angle. Who might have had it in for him?

Well, Guy Unitas for starts. Obviously. Irish had squeezed him out of his job as public information officer and installed his own cohort, Coy, in the office. He might not have killed Irish out of pure anger, but if Irish had been threatening him, friendly feelings would not have been present to hold Guy back.

Guy hadn't seemed to be popular with the upper echelon at the Grantham PD. He kept open house at the APB office and at the Main Street Grill for union members, but supervisors are not union members. It had seemed to me that the department heads shunned Guy. At least, I could remember sitting with the breakfast crowd at the Main Street when Coy walked in, gave our table a casual wave, and took a booth at the back of the room. Guy hadn't invited him to sit down, and Coy hadn't stopped to talk.

Who could I ask about this? I needed a long-time cop who didn't mind gossiping. A guy like Bill Martin.

I picked up my phone and called the main security desk. Bill answered, and I identified myself.

"Bill, you obviously know a lot of cops," I said. "Did Mike say you're a former member of the force?"

"Yeah. I quit after fifteen."

"After fifteen? Why didn't you go for twenty? For retirement?"

"I was one of the ones who thought Mickey O'Sul-

livan got a raw deal from Chief Svenson. Mickey—
he didn't complain. The two of them even got to be
friends again. But at the time, several of us quit."

"I see."

"You'll never convince me that Mickey O'Sullivan
stole a pistol from the evidence room and planted it
on a guy." Bill's voice was forceful. "Never! I worked
under Mickey. He was a straight cop."

"He certainly seems like a nice guy."

"Nice isn't the point! A real crook can be a fun
guy to hang out with. A lot of them are characters,
real interesting to be around."

" 'Heaven for climate, hell for company,' " I
quoted.

"Right. Who said that?" He mulled over his own
question for a minute, then spoke again. "But Mickey
didn't take that pistol. And the worst of it was, Chief
Svenson didn't think he'd taken it. He knew Mickey
hadn't done it, but he couldn't prove it one way or
the other. So he asked Mickey to resign. Mickey was
supposedly his best friend, but Svenson didn't back
him up.

"I quit, and I told Chief Svenson why. Right to
his face."

I let his indignation settle a minute before I asked
a new question. "What about Guy Unitas? He left
about the same time. Did he quit for the same
reason?"

Bill laughed. "Nah. Guy never quit over somebody
else's problems. That's not the way Guy works."

"I've had the impression that Irish Svenson
bounced Guy so Coy could have his job."

"I don't think so." Bill dropped his voice slightly.
"I always thought Guy might be involved in that

gun deal somehow. He was so sharp he could cut himself, you know. I guess that's a good quality for a union exec."

"He's a former department head for the Grantham PD—"

"If you can call public relations a department."

I was a little surprised by Bill's reply. "It's a department on the organizational chart. Coy gets department manager's pay. I've seen the list."

"Yeah. What a crock. He doesn't do diddly. Shoot his mouth off when he shouldn't."

Interesting. Even though Bill was now an employee of the *Grantham Gazette*, he still had the standard cop attitude about public information. Don't tell the press—or the public—any more than you have to. Of course, it's not exclusively a cop attitude. I recalled that the director of the Grantham Community Mental Health Center had expressed a very similar opinion two days earlier.

I thanked Bill and hung up. I kept staring at my printout. Okay, I had a list of people who benefited by Irish's death. I had a list of people who might have had it in for him—whoops!

The personal side of Irish's life was omitted from that list. Lee had been convinced that someone in the department was involved, and Bo Jenkins's final words made that seem likely. Irish might have been killed by someone in the department, but for personal reasons.

Beginning with his girlfriend, the woman Wilda swore he admitted he was seeing.

Who could this alleged girlfriend have been? Irish had been pretty busy the last few years of his life. He'd been running a large police department, dealing with city councilmen, and campaigning for a new Central Station. He hadn't had a lot of time to be running around on his wife. Or even for getting out and meeting women to run around with.

Well, the classic affair was a man and his secretary. And Irish's secretary had been Shelly Marcum Smith, the former high school girlfriend of his son. An attractive woman with a jealous husband.

I thought about Shelly and Rowdy. Hmmm. That was a definite possibility. Or, at least Rowdy was. And if he was an electrician, we could assume he was reasonably mechanical. He'd probably know how to sabotage a car, how to cause a wreck. I suppose he could have called Irish, asked to meet him at the Panorama.

And, of course, the first suspect in any killing is the victim's spouse. Wilda? It didn't seem likely, but who knew?

Or how about the spouse's boyfriend? Mickey and Wilda said they hadn't been seeing each other before Irish died. I believed them—I thought. But considering that Mickey already had a grievance against Irish, possibly quite a legitimate grievance—well, it was interesting.

I looked back at the printout of subscribers, and another address made me catch my breath, an action which made me grab my ribs and groan. It was a newsstand. Some Tulsa newsstand got a half dozen copies of the *Gazette* every day. What if Lee dropped by and bought one of them? Then her name wouldn't be on the subscription list. And the Oklahoma City and Tulsa public libraries both received copies of the *Gazette*. If she read it in either of those places, we might never figure out who she was.

Hell's bells. I scanned through the list, marking places where the public would have access to *Gazettes*. When I got to the Dallas list, a name caught my eye. "Lovers Lane Newsstand." Why did that ring a bell?

I haven't hung out in Dallas all that much, but I've been there a few times, and I knew that Lovers Lane—despite its frivolous name—is a major east-west artery. And I'd heard that name recently. I was sure "Lovers Lane" had come up in conversation during the past few days. But who had mentioned it? When? What, where, why, or how? What in heaven's name—

"Church," I said out loud. "Lovers Lane Presbyterian."

Mike had said the former pastor of the Grantham First Presbyterian—a friend of his father's—was now minister of Lovers Lane Presbyterian Church in Dallas. And Mickey had told us that particular minister had called Irish the day before Irish was killed. My adrenaline began to surge.

Don't get excited, I told myself. Lovers Lane runs clear across Dallas. The church and the newsstand may be miles apart. And even if they're across the street, it doesn't mean there's any connection.

But I got up, groaning, and went back to the library for a Dallas phone book. The church and the newsstand were about five blocks apart. Bingo! This could be it.

I made a note of the phone numbers for each. Back at my desk, I called the newsstand. "Hi," I said, "I'm with the *Grantham Gazette*, and we're running a check on our mail subscribers." Another lie. Since Mike had complimented me on how well I lied, I'd been noticing how often I did it.

"I see that your business receives two copies of the *Gazette* daily."

"That's right. I usually manage to sell both of them, but I don't need any more."

I laughed lightly. "Oh, I'm not trying to increase mail subscriptions. We're simply trying to figure out what demographic group our publication appeals to. Are these papers purchased by former Grantham residents?"

"Well, one is. He's a salesman. He always stops for breakfast at the restaurant next door. Drops in here to buy a cigar. And he always asks for 'the hometown paper.' Kinda laughs."

I kinda laughed, too. "And the second purchaser?"

"I don't know much about her. Pretty young woman. Works around here someplace. I don't know why she doesn't take the paper at home. But she asked me to order her a copy, so I do. But she didn't come in this morning."

I got his name, because a reporter learns always to make a record of who she talked to. Always. Then I thanked him and hung up.

His words had excited and scared me. Lee could definitely be called a "pretty young woman." It sounded as if I'd struck pay dirt. But why hadn't she picked up her paper that morning? And what could be the connection with the minister Irish had known? Or was there one?

The phone rang, and I jumped sky high. It was the librarian, telling me the clippings from the old files were ready. I went back and picked up three file folders of material on Guy Unitas and the Amalgamated Police Brotherhood. When I went back to the newsroom, the police reporters' pod of desks was still deserted.

"Where is that guy?" I said aloud.

"Who?" Ruth Borah asked the question as she walked toward the city desk.

"J.B. or Chuck. I'm dying to know the latest on the death of Guy Unitas, and neither of them has showed up. Not even Ace the Ass is here."

"He won't be either," Ruth said. "Jake called the AP bureau chief about Ace. I don't think he'll be changing any more stories for the *Gazette* without mentioning it to the editors."

"Hurrah! Is he being transferred?"

"He may be transferred right out of the news business." Ruth gestured at the newsroom clock. "It's time for Channel Four's midafternoon update. Would you mind catching it?"

"Sure." All news media keep an eye on each other. The television stations subscribe to the *Gazette* and listen to the radio. The radio stations read our stories straight out of the paper, without changing a word. Police reporters keep one ear tuned to the radio stations. Some staff member is assigned to listen to the news on Channel Four at three-thirty, at six, and at ten p.m. We summarize their stories and give the list to the city editor. But we'd never run anything we got off the radio or television without checking it with the source.

So I walked over to the television set mounted on the wall behind the city desk and punched it on. The first item on the news was Guy Unitas's death at the Grantham International Airport. They had a sound bite from Jim Hammond, and I caught a glimpse of Mike in one long shot. J.B. was covering that.

It was the next item that really got my attention.

"Grantham Police are asking the public for help in identifying the body of a young woman who was found dead on Bridge Road around ten o'clock this morning," the daytime anchor said in his usual unctuous tones. "She was the apparent victim of a hit and run accident, but no identification has been found. Police said she had been knocked into a ditch. Her body might not have been found for weeks, but a city mowing crew happened to visit the area today for routine maintenance.

"This young woman is believed to be in her middle to late twenties, about five feet, five inches tall, with light brown hair and gray eyes," the voice went on. "She was wearing a blue suit, off-white blouse, and high-heeled pumps. Police artists will have a drawing of her later today."

I was staring at the screen and feeling my stomach sink to my toes. "Lee," I said. "Damn. Damn, damn, damn."

I turned to Ruth Borah. Her eyes were narrow and watchful.

"They got her," I said. "Oh, Ruth! She came to me for help, and somehow it led her into a trap. They've killed her."

CHAPTER 23

"I'll have to go to the police," I said. "Ruth, I'm sure this had some connection with the death of Guy Unitas. And that's going to be a big story."

"It sounds as if Guy killed this girl, then was trying to get away," Ruth said. "I hope you won't have to go to the morgue. But you'd better go on over and see if you can ID her."

"I may recognize her as Lee," I said. "But I don't know her name. Maybe this newsstand in Dallas will be a lead."

I scooped up the printout and my notebook from my desk. God, I hoped the dead woman wasn't Lee.

I automatically started on the usual route I took to walk to the Central Station. I went down the backstairs to the first-floor break room, then out the door that led to the loading dock and maintenance garage. I was opening the door to the street when the intercom boomed out, right over my head.

"Nell Matthews! Nell Matthews! Where are you going? Call the main security desk immediately!"

I nearly had a heart attack. It was as if God had found out my sins and was singling me out for retribution.

I gasped, grabbed my sore ribs, and remembered.

I'd promised Mike I wouldn't leave the building, and he'd given Bill Martin the job of keeping an eye on me.

I looked up at the security camera over my head. I'd always suspected the guards didn't ever look at the images those closed-circuit television cameras broadcast to their desk at the front entrance. Now I knew better.

I might have flouted Mike's instructions, but I wanted to get along with Bill Martin. So I went back to the break room and called him.

"Sorry, Bill," I said. "I forgot I'm not supposed to leave. But I have to go over to the PD. It's really important."

"Just a minute." Bill put me on hold, but in a minute he was back. "Nell, Holman will take the desk. I'll drive you over to the PD. Stay at the loading dock. I'll sign out a car and pick you up."

As we drove into the parking lot of the Central Station, Bill Martin repeated his instructions from Mike. "I'm not supposed to let you go wandering off."

"If there's any place in Grantham where I'll be safe, it's police headquarters," I said. "Just let me out at the side door, the one to the PD staff parking lot. I won't go any place but Hammond's office."

"Just don't go sneaking off, okay?"

I patted his arm. "I'll go straight to Hammond's office. I'll stay there. I promise."

He let me out at the side door, and I went into the detective division office. It was almost empty. No detectives interviewing suspects. No tired-looking women pleading for their men. No young toughs in handcuffs.

Nobody was there but Peaches Atkinson, the famous clerk of the detective division, who had terrorized Mike on the phone earlier. In thirty-five years with the Grantham PD, Peaches had proved she could dominate the good guys and the bad guys. Both the crooks and the detectives were terrified of her. She was six feet tall and two-hundred-pounds wide, sixty years old, and tougher than the average boot heel. Her rattrap of a face was topped off by limp white hair that always reminded me of the angel hair used to trim Christmas trees, and a phone was permanently installed between her left ear and her shoulder. She was speaking into that receiver, and the room echoed with the sound of two more phones ringing.

"Yes, I have your number," she said. "I'll have a detective call you as soon as I have one available."

She punched a disconnect button, but the noise level in the room went up, since the phone immediately began to ring again. Peaches ignored all three lines. Telephones didn't boss Peaches around any more than Jim Hammond did.

"What are you doing here?" she asked me. "I thought you'd be out at the airport with the rest of the press."

"No. I'm not on the police beat today. I'm here as a citizen. I think I know who Jane Doe is."

Peaches rolled her eyes. "That's the least of our worries now," she said. "She's not going anyplace." She punched at the phone. "Detective Division."

I waited until Peaches dispatched another caller.

"Is Hammond still out at the airport?"

She nodded.

"What about Mike Svenson?"

"With Captain Hammond," she said shortly. She tapped a phone button again. "Detective Division."

What now? I decided I'd better wait, at least until somebody came in to spell Peaches on the phone, so she could explain what was going on. Or maybe, with any luck, Jim Hammond and Mike would come back.

Anyway, I'd promised to wait there until Bill Martin parked the car and came in. I sat down near the door to the hallway and began looking at the computer printout I had grabbed as I left my desk. Whoops! Under it was a file folder from the *Gazette* library. That folder wasn't supposed to leave the building. I'd have to keep close guard on it and make sure it got back.

Waiting, I idly leafed through the folder, which contained the information on the A.P.B., the background that was too old to be in the computer files. It was mostly clippings—Guy as a union steward officer getting some award from the state Labor Department, Guy testifying on public employees' unions before the state legislature, and lots more. There was also a typed resumé dated fifteen years back.

I was still reading it when a movement outside the door caught my eye. Someone had flashed by. Had it been Coy?

Maybe he could tell me what was going on, where all the detectives were.

It took me a few seconds to make sure all the clippings were in the file folder. Then I jumped up and looked out the door. Coy was walking quickly down the hall, headed toward his own office.

"Coy!" I called.

All in one motion Coy whirled, crouched, and reached his hand under his suit coat, toward his back. This was quite a trick, because he was carrying a blue bundle over his left shoulder, almost as if it were a baby.

After his flurry of whirling, crouching, and reaching, he stood immobile, knees bent, looking at me intently. His right hand was still behind him, under his suit coat. He didn't smile or even speak.

"Good night, Coy!" I said. "I thought you were going to draw on me."

Coy straightened up and pulled his hand from behind his coat. "What are you doing here?" he said. "I thought you were in the hospital and out of my hair."

"They didn't keep me. I've come over to do my duty as a citizen, to tell the detectives what I know about that Jane Doe. If she's the same person."

Coy took a step toward me. "Just what do you know about Jane Doe?"

"Maybe nothing. But she could be an anonymous news source."

"Anonymous?"

"Yes. She called several times and I met her once, but she never told me her name."

"I see." A smile flitted over Coy's face.

I gestured toward the detective office with my thumb. "I'm trying to be a good citizen, but there's not a single detective here. Peaches says everybody's still out at the airport."

Coy laughed harshly. "Hell, Nell, I can't stop to discuss it with you. I've got to take care of a couple of things." He pivoted and started on down the hall. "Get lost!"

I stood there, gaping. Coy had just snapped at me.

Coy. The reporter's friend. Mr. Let-me-do-you-a-favor. The best pal I had in the cop shop. The person my job absolutely required that I get along with.

"Coy!" I scurried along behind him. "Hey! What's going on? What'd I do?"

He ignored me, striding along with his blue burden bouncing on his shoulder. I tried to run, to catch up with him, but my ribs hurt too badly. I gave a few ineffective bleeps—"Coy! Hey, guy!"—but he didn't stop. By the time he passed under the circular steps and turned into the main foyer, the one where Bo Jenkins had held a gun to my head, I was still twelve or fifteen feet behind. He stalked into his office, next-door to Jameson's, and slammed the door in my face. The smoked-glass window in it rattled and quivered.

I barely hesitated before I opened the door and marched in behind him. "Listen, Coy," I said, "we need to get along. If you're mad at me, tell me why."

Coy's office is one of the few in the Central Station which has a couch. The couch sits with its back to the door. I've always hated the darn thing, because you have to walk around it to get close to Coy's desk. And as seating, it's useless. It's miserably soft. Once you're down in it, you can't get out without a ladder. And it's impossible to take notes sitting on it. When Coy gives a briefing in his office, I always come early and grab a straight chair.

When I faced Coy in his office, he was standing on the other side of that couch. He had apparently put his blue bundle, the object he'd been carrying over his shoulder like a baby, down on the couch, and he was straightening up as I closed the door.

"Coy, what's going on?" I said.

He glared at me. "You honestly don't know, do you?"

"No. Tell me."

"You little shit! You ruin a plan that took four years to bring off. And you don't even know what you've done!"

"A plan? What plan? Some undercover deal? You know the *Gazette* will cooperate—"

"Cooperate!" Coy laughed harshly. He turned away and went around his desk, dropping heavily into his chair. He turned sideways and opened the bottom drawer.

"Coy, you've got me completely confused."

I rested my notebook and the file folder from the *Gazette* library on the back of the couch. "I didn't get hurt on purpose, if that's what you're referring to."

Coy laughed again, but there was no humor in the sound. He pulled a small metal lock box out of his drawer and stood up. "Get out!"

I finally decided I'd better take the hint. "Okay! Okay!" I said. "But we'll have to settle this some time."

I reached for the pile of papers balanced on the back of the couch, but I missed. The whole pile dumped onto the floor.

I dropped to my knees, groaned, and started pawing them together.

"Get out!" Coy yelled louder.

"I'm getting! But I've got to pick up these files!" I scrambled the clippings and the typed resumé back into a file folder without concern for their order. "This is from the *Gazette* library, and I'll be in permanent hot water if anything happens to them. And my ribs are killing me."

I gathered the papers together, but I could see one more bit of white, a picture which had slid under the couch. I dropped my head down, leaving my fanny waving in the air, and reached for it. The position nearly killed my ribs. But I got hold of the corner of the photograph, and I pulled it out.

No reporter can look at words written in the English language and not read them. Even as upset as I was, as bad as my ribs hurt, I read the cutline pasted on the back of that picture.

"NEW A.P.B. OFFICES," the kicker read. Then the cutline went on. "Guy Unitas, steward of the Amalgamated Police Brotherhood, and Merri Blakely, office manager, pose in the new A.P.B. offices at 4415 Grant Street. The A.P.B. will hold an open house at the new offices from two P.M. until six P.M Sunday." It was the handout photo the A.P.B. had given us when their new offices opened.

And Merri Blakely was in it. I'd turned up a picture of Coy's ex-wife. Talk about doing the least tactful thing at the least tactful time. With Coy already so mad he was spitting nails, the last thing I wanted to do was flash a picture of his ex-wife. Or current wife? I didn't know what the legal situation was.

I quickly stuffed the photo into the back of the file folder and began to climb up from the floor. I was to my knees when I saw something white fluttering down. I realized I'd missed the folder when I quickly stuffed the photograph in. It was back on the floor.

Groaning, I reached for it. But this time the photograph had landed face up. I had a clear view of Guy Unitas, standing with his arms folded. And beside him, wearing a low-cut, ruffled dress that displayed her curves, was a pretty young woman, her head covered with bleached-blond corkscrew curls.

The clothes and the hair were all wrong. But the face—I quickly made a circle of my finger and thumb and covered the hair.

Lee's flat gray eyes looked out at me, the pupils rimmed with black. My innards turned to mush, and I flipped the picture over to double-check the label on the back. It was the same caption I'd read a few minutes before.

The woman I'd known as "Lee" was identified in this picture as "Merri Blakely."

"Lee" equaled "Merri Blakely." And "Merri Blakely" equaled Coy's wife.

Lee was the woman who had left Coy so bitter he hated women. The one who had taken off, the one he couldn't even find to divorce.

And Coy was the husband Lee had described. The beast who had gotten her involved in an illegal plot.

He was the person she believed had killed Irish Svenson.

Surprise made me suck in a lot of air, and pain shot through my body. I grabbed my ribs and closed my eyes until it subsided. But when I opened my eyes, ready to reach for the photograph again, a mental pain replaced the physical agony. Because the photograph was still lying on the floor, but the toe of Coy's shoe was on top of it.

I slowly moved my gaze up Coy's pant leg, past his jacket, to his stony face. I was afraid to move, afraid to speak for a long moment. But I had to do something.

Could I convince him I hadn't identified Lee?

"Coy, I took these files out of the *Gazette* building

by mistake." I tried to keep my voice level and calm.
"I have to return them. Just let me gather them up,
and I'll go."

He shook his head. "No, Nell. You're a smart gal.
You know I can't do that."

"We can talk when we're both calmer."

He tapped his foot on the photograph. "No, Nell.
This changes everything. Now that you know who
Jane Doe is."

"But—"

And right then someone knocked on the door.

Coy and I froze. Then he reacted. He whirled to
face the door, grabbed my jaw, and held my head
against his leg with his left hand clamped over my
mouth. And with his right hand he pulled a pistol
from behind his back.

He didn't say anything, but his meaning was really
clear. If I said anything, if I moved, somebody was
going to get shot. And there was a real good chance
it would be me.

I did not move.

The raps at the door came again. And someone
spoke. "Nell? Nell!"

It was Bill Martin. He'd come looking for me. God!
I'd have given anything if I'd waited in Hammond's
office the way I'd told him I would.

I crouched against Coy's leg, hardly conscious of
the pain in my side, afraid to breathe, afraid to move,
and afraid not to. If I rolled my eyes upward, I could
see the gun in Coy's hand. If I looked at the door, I
could see Bill silhouetted outside the smoked-glass
panel. His outline moved sideways and back and
forth as he shifted from foot to foot. He called my

name again, questioningly. "Nell?" He obviously wasn't sure I was in there.

I was shooting messages at him by ESP. Go away, Bill! After the way I'd wandered off earlier, I knew Bill wasn't expecting me to be held at gunpoint. He thought I'd merely roamed away again. Despite his promise to Mike, he wasn't expecting real trouble.

Go away, Bill! We might both be in more danger if Bill persisted in trying to find me in Coy's office.

I could see movement through the smoked glass. "Nell?" Bill said again. And the door handle began to turn.

I rolled my eyes upward, and I saw Coy's hand tighten on his pistol. He was getting ready to shoot.

I couldn't let him shoot Bill.

I threw my head forward, then back. My skull cracked against Coy's pelvis.

He screamed. The gun went off. The glass in the door shattered. Bill Martin yelled and disappeared.

Coy let go of my jaw, and I dropped and rolled over. I don't know if it hurt my ribs or not. I clawed my way through the heaps of clippings, now strewn all over the floor at the end of the couch, away from Coy, away from the pistol.

Except for my ragged breath, there was no sound. Coy had screamed only once, the glass had stopped falling and Bill Martin might be dead.

Then I heard a small gasp. For a second I thought it was me, and I put a hand over my mouth. But the sound continued. It grew stronger. It developed into a loud wail.

It was a baby's cry.

A baby?

I peeked my head over the arm of the couch. The

blue bundle Coy had carried over his shoulder was moving. It raised up, and eyes looked out from under what I now saw was a blue baby blanket. The eyes were a distinctively smooth light gray. The pupils were rimmed in black. For a minute Lee was looking at me.

Then a little boy, a toddler, sat up on his knees. He wore blue overalls, and his face was all scrunched up as he cried.

The blanket fell back, and I got a good look at him.

His hair was red. Brilliantly red. And curly. It was a brighter, child's version of Mike Svenson's hair.

Behind him, Coy was clutching his crotch with his left hand.

His right held his pistol, aimed at the baby's back.

CHAPTER 24

"Pick him up," Coy ordered. "Make him stop crying."

When I didn't react quickly, he moved the pistol closer to the baby's head. "Now! Do it now! We've got to get out of here!"

I got to my feet and picked up the little boy. He pulled away from me and screamed louder.

"He doesn't know me!" I said. "The shot scared him. I don't know how to make him stop crying!"

"You'd better figure it out! Or you're both dead."

I bounced the baby up and down and patted his back. "Hey, hey, fellow. It's all right. Shhh. Shhh."

I could hear excited voices in the hall. Coy grabbed my arm and pushed me toward the door. "Okay, whether the brat's crying or not, we've got to leave. You two are going as far as the car with me. If you behave, if everybody else behaves, I'll let you go when we get there." He jabbed my sore ribs with the pistol. "Savvy?"

I groaned out loud. But I nodded. Coy pushed me ahead of him, out the door of the office, into the hall. I could see secretaries and bookkeepers popping out of doors, looking toward us timidly. They were smart enough not to approach the scene of a shooting without checking it out first.

None of them seemed to be armed, and there wasn't a uniform in sight. Here we were in the Grantham Central Police Station, and where were the cops when you need them?

Coy waved the pistol beside my head, and one of the office workers screamed.

"Everybody stand still and stay back!" Coy yelled in my ear. He pushed me ahead. That's when I gave a little scream of my own.

I had almost stumbled over Bill Martin's feet. He was lying next to the wall, beside the door. Coy didn't even look down at him. Bill wasn't moving, but I could see a pool of blood spreading. Did that mean he was still alive?

I pressed the baby's face into my shoulder and walked on.

More secretaries and clerks and a few cops were running out of offices and coming down the stairs, drawn by the sound of the shot.

"Get back!" Coy yelled. "Everybody stay back or Nell and the kid get it!"

Their faces loomed up, frozen in attitudes of horror, disbelief, and dread. Coy pushed me toward the hall we'd come down, the hall that led to the detective office and, beyond, to the door to the employees' parking lot. But when we turned the corner and could see down that hall, Jim Hammond and Mike Svenson were running toward us.

"Shit!" Coy swung me around and pushed me back into the foyer, back toward his office. But three uniformed officers had materialized there. I guess they'd come from the desk in the reception area. One already had his pistol drawn.

"Stay back!" Coy's voice was hoarse. He turned to

the stairs that led up into the rotunda. He muttered as we crossed the open space, "Move along, bitch. Women are all bitches. If it weren't for that bitch I married I wouldn't have gotten into this mess. If you two bitches hadn't put your fucking heads together, we still would have gotten away with the money."

"Gotten away with what money?"

"Shut up! It was my big chance to get even with Irish. To show the world his Mr. Righteous act was just that. An act." He pushed me up the stairs. "He was no better than the rest of us! When he got a chance to screw a good-looking woman, he took it! Then I had him. He wouldn't dare investigate. Or he'd lose his precious, lily-white reputation."

He shoved me up the curving stairs, around the first turn, then he pulled me to a stop. He shoved me against the railing, and I stood there, overlooking the foyer. He put his left arm around my neck and held me tight against him. The little redheaded boy was still crying, but his wails had turned to snivels. He rubbed his face against my shoulder, wiping snot all over my jacket. I could feel the pistol in my ribs.

Mike ran into the foyer. When he saw the little tableau on the stairway, he skidded to a stop. Jim Hammond was right behind him, but he couldn't stop as fast. The two of them banged together like cartoon characters, but there was nothing funny about the slapstick.

Coy didn't say anything. What did he need to say? He had me with a pistol against my side. I had the kid, but the position Coy held me in forced me to hold the kid over the edge of the stairway. If he shot me, I'd drop the kid. I'd drop him about twenty feet onto a terrazzo floor.

"Better get back," Coy said. His voice was cold, but he didn't shout.

"You'd better come down." Mike's voice was equally cool. They could have been having a business discussion.

"No." I could feel Coy's head shake.

"Coy, let's talk—"

"No! No talk!" Coy snarled out the words, but he still wasn't yelling. "I'm not one of your stupid, loser hostage takers. Your goddamn talk isn't going to do any good. You're just going to tell everybody to stay out of my way while I get out the back door, get in my car, and drive away!"

"Leave Nell—"

"No, she'll have to go with me. You can see why. If we get to the car smoothly, we'll leave the kid. But I ought to kill him. He caused all the trouble!"

Hammond and Mike looked at each other. Neither spoke, but I could see them communicate. Hammond was older, more experienced, and much higher in rank than Mike. But with a toss of his head and a shrug of his shoulders, he handed the situation over.

"Better do what he says," Mike said. "Clear the hall. Clear the building."

"And the parking lot," Coy said.

Hammond nodded and moved out of the foyer, out of my view. Then I heard him bellowing. "Everybody out! Clear the building. Carry this man out of here!" Did he mean Bill Martin? I hoped Bill was still alive.

"Give us five minutes to clear the building," Mike said. He leaned against the newel post at the bottom of the stairway. He looked casual, completely relaxed. For a minute I resented his easy attitude. Then

I remembered that this was his speciality: hostage negotiator. He'd done this sort of thing lots of times. I clung to that idea.

Coy swung me into a different position, and I gasped in pain. And Mike came close to losing his negotiator's cool. His fists clinched, his face screwed up, and he took one step up the stairway.

"Don't move," Coy said. "If the girlfriend gets hurt, it'll be entirely your fault."

Mike visibly controlled himself. His fist relaxed into a hand, and his face smoothed out. "I guess when Bo caved, your whole scheme caved with him," he said. He was back in the conversational mode, his speciality, the secret of his success as a law officer. Keep 'em talking—the key to hostage negotiations. "You know we found out about the offshore account."

"I've got another stash—enough to get me started," Coy said. "I've got a new ID. All I had to do was dump the little bastard."

"The kid? Where did he come from?" Mike said.

"Doesn't the hair tell you where he came from?" Coy laughed curtly. "Merri wanted a baby the whole time we were married. Of course, I'd had a vasectomy when I was married the first time, but I didn't tell her about that. The bitch was too stupid to realize she wasn't never going to get pregnant. Kept going to doctors.

"So that's one thing I have to hand your old man. She spent only one weekend with him—one little fling at a convention—and God! I practically had to threaten to kill her to get her to do it—and she turns up pregnant."

Mike's face tightened, but he didn't lose his cool.

The little boy looked up with his light gray eyes, eyes amazingly like Lee's.

"Andy," I said, "he must be Andy."

At the sound of the name, the little boy wiggled in my arms. "Andy!" he said. "Want down! I walk!"

Coy's arm tightened around my neck again. I choked, but I gripped the struggling child.

"Let Nell breathe!" Mike said. "If she passes out, she'll drop the kid."

"It'd serve him right! He should never have been born. If I'd known Merri was pregnant, he wouldn't have been. But the bitch figured that out—she was that smart at least. So she ran away."

His arm tightened, and his next words were yelled out. "And she took my money!"

"Your money? Wasn't it your fellow officers' money?"

"The hell with 'em! It's my money!"

"You were a good cop, Coy. The best undercover cop the Grantham PD ever had. My dad told me."

Coy laughed again. "Yeah, I learned a lot working undercover. Disguise. How not to look like a cop. How to keep a temporary tattoo from coming off in the Salvation Army's lousy cold shower. And where to borrow a vehicle that doesn't look like a cop would drive it. That came in real handy—just this week. I hadn't driven the Scamovan in years, but I knew where to find it.

"And Irish knew I was good. But that didn't matter to him. One slip and he sank my career. I should have been division commander, could have moved into the chief's slot. But no! he stuck me in the PIO office. Where he could breathe over my shoulder all day every day, make sure I didn't slip up again.

"Everybody thought I was Irish's pet! I was his whipping boy. He was just waiting, waiting to trip me up."

Mike was still calm. "He didn't trip you up, though. You kept the job, made yourself important to the department. You always knew everything that was going on." He smiled grimly. "It almost seems as if you could hear what was going on in the chief's office!"

Coy laughed, a laugh as grim as Mike's smile had been. "The great Irish Svenson! Honest Irish Svenson. He was no better than anybody else. I'd seen him eying Merri at the A.P.B. banquet. And she was always a sucker for an older guy who bossed her around. Oh, you'd have been proud of him, Mike! When he got a chance for a screw, he didn't waste it.

"Oh, the little cunt tried to tell me she didn't want to go to bed with Irish, but I knew she could go after anybody. And get 'em. Some women have that smell about them. Every man who sees them wants to yank his pants off."

Mike shrugged. "I guess he got the last laugh though. She left you for him."

"No! She didn't! Don't you get it? She didn't care anything about Irish. She left me for the kid! Sure, Irish helped her hide out. But the kid was the reason she left. After she found out about the kid, she took off. She traded the tapes to Irish, made him help her."

"The tapes?" Mike's voice was tight. "What tapes?"

"The videos of the two of them screwing! If I hadn't had those, I wouldn't have had anything on Irish!"

"And Merrilee took them?"

"Took everything. Took the tapes. Took the money. Took off."

He poked the gun in my ribs again. I groaned in agony. Andy kicked and wiggled. "Down! I walk!" he screamed.

Coy didn't even seem to hear my groan or Andy's scream. "The bitch! And now, Officer Michael the brave and honorable Svenson, I believe your five minutes are up. This building better be cleared, because Nell and the kid and I are getting out of here. And you're the first person we have to get by. So you lie flat on the floor."

"Wait! Wait!" Mike said. "How did you find Lee? Merrilee?"

Coy poked me again. "Little Miss Smart Ass here. She was a little careless with her keys. Bugging her phone was the easiest thing in the world. Even if she did nearly walk in on me." He laughed. "I just did it because I wanted to know if Bo Jenkins had told her anything. Finding out about Lee was an extra added attraction. And so was knowing about the two of you. And now! Hit the deck! Lie flat. And you'd better stay there."

Mike frowned. He didn't move.

Andy began to kick and struggle again. "Down! Down!" he said.

"Shut that kid up!" Coy snarled the words in my ear.

"I don't know how!"

"Try the keys! They worked with the Jenkins kid."

My key ring. I'd handed it to Bo Jenkins's son to keep him amused while we got him out of a hostage situation and to safety. Then Coy had taken the keys and apparently had used them to break into my house and bug my telephone. He'd given them back, and I'd been using them.

And that morning—that very morning in the hospital—Rocky had given me a new key chain, with a special gadget attached.

Pepper spray.

"Let me reach in my purse and find them," I said. Andy was still kicking, and I was struggling to keep from dropping him. The strap of my purse fell off my shoulder and the purse dangled from my elbow, hanging by its knotted strap. "You'll have to let me move around."

Coy moved his arm from around my neck and grabbed a handful of my hair. I could still feel the gun in my side. I managed to reach into the side pocket of my purse, to get my hand on the keys. I felt around. Did I have the pepper spray? Was I holding it right? Would it spray? How could I point it in the right direction?

What was the right direction?

God. I didn't have the nerve. If I used the spray, I might miss Coy. Even if I hit him, he might fire the pistol. If he fired the pistol, the bullet might hit Andy. It might hit Mike. It might hit me. Hitting Coy with pepper spray might be the dumbest thing I could do. Maybe I should play along, go with Coy.

Mike made some movement, and Coy swung the pistol toward him.

"I told you to get down!" he said.

"Coy, you don't stand a chance in hell of getting out of here, even with hostages," Mike said.

"Maybe not! But if I get it, I won't get it alone. Lie down!"

Suddenly I saw the whole scenario. The Central HQ and its parking lot were full of cops. Even if Coy got to the side door, he wouldn't dare go out. There would be a sharpshooter out there. Guys with nets. Stun guns.

Suppose he got to his car and drove away. He'd be followed by patrol cars, unmarked cars, helicopters. Hammond had had plenty of time to stick a remote bug on his vehicle. They could follow him anywhere.

There was no chance Coy was going to get away.

And Coy knew all about police procedure. He knew he couldn't get away.

So he was planning to take some of us with him. I could picture Mike down flat on the terrazzo floor. And as Coy passed him, he'd shoot him in the back of the head.

He'd already said he hated the baby—the child his wife had conceived with Irish Svenson. He was ready to kill the little boy.

And he was certainly ready to kill me.

I twisted my head around and tried to look at him. Coy's face was turned toward Mike, and he gestured with his pistol. His face was contorted with hate. "Get down!"

I yanked that key chain out of my purse, aimed it over my shoulder, and punched the spray button.

I hit Coy, but I got Andy and me, too. So I'm not too clear about what happened next.

I remember dropping down on my rear, trying to hold on to Andy, moving away from the edge of the stairway, feeling my way toward the wall. I remember a lot of choking and coughing from all three of us.

I remember a rush of air I later realized was Mike jumping over Andy and me.

I remember a shot and the sound of breaking glass. A high-pitched scream I realized was coming from Coy. Mike's shout of "Drop it!" The grunting sounds of two men struggling.

I managed to open my eyes just in time to see Coy and Mike, a flight above me—on the balcony under the rotunda—two stories above the foyer floor—wrestling.

As I watched Coy broke away and ran to the railing.

He dived over. Headfirst.

CHAPTER 25

I huddled against the wall, holding the screaming child, coughing and weeping. I was conscious of a form kneeling beside me, and I felt Mike's arms around me.

I clung to him and to the kid, and I tried to hang on to what sanity I had left.

"I'm going to lock you up," Mike said. "If I have to watch some creep put a gun to the head of the woman I love one more time, I'm going to—God! I don't know what I'll do. But I can't take it. Not ever again."

"I don't mean to keep getting in trouble," I said. "Can we get this baby off these stairs? I'm afraid to let go of him. If he tumbles down and hurts himself at this point, I'll be most unhappy."

Mike took the squirming, squalling, redheaded kid from me. He held him at arm's length and took a long look.

"I used to nag because I wanted a baby brother," he said.

He put the kid over his shoulder and carried him down the stairs.

Lots of cops were coming in by then, and Jim Hammond was ordering some of them out and calling for a doctor and setting up his crime scene. Mike walked Andy and me into the hall leading to the detective office, tactfully keeping his shoulders between us and the sight of what had been Coy, spread-eagled on the city seal.

Jim Hammond followed us and put his arm around me.

I groaned. "Watch the ribs!" Then I hugged him back. "Jim, I was sure glad to see you and Mike charging down that hall. How did the two of you know just when to show up?"

"Police artist," Jim said. "Merri Blakely's body was found around ten this morning. The detectives who went out there didn't take a close look at the body, because the guy from the medical examiner's office beat them to the scene. So they didn't recognize her."

"They might not have recognized her anyway," I said. "Lee had left Grantham before I moved here, but I just saw a picture of her, taken when she worked at the A.P.B. Her hair was a new color and style, her makeup was changed, and she dressed completely differently."

Jim nodded. "Yeah. Well, you'd think nearly any cop would have recognized her, but nobody did until the sketch artist got there. The artist knew her right away. She told the detectives, and they called me. They didn't want to be the ones who had to tell Coy his wife was dead. Not knowing that he knew all about it already.

"Mike had come back out to the airport to try to convince me that Guy wasn't the only bad guy in this deal. As soon as we knew who the girl in the ditch was, it became pretty obvious that Coy was involved."

I nodded. "And I saw an old picture of Lee—identified as 'Merri Blakely' and I figured it out. Unfortunately, I was with Coy when I saw the picture." I sighed and grabbed my ribs.

Jim patted my shoulder. "Mike, take this young woman out of here, okay? I can get statements tomorrow." He shook his head. "There's no hurry, since we've got the whole thing on videotape. Again."

He patted the little boy on the head. "But where did this kid come from?"

I realized that our standoff in the rotunda might have been televised on the police department's security cameras, but the sound hadn't been recorded. Jim Hammond had no way of knowing what Coy had told us about Andy's birth. Or his conception.

"Merrilee Blakely was this little boy's mother," I said. I glanced at Mike, leaving any further explanations to him. He didn't offer any.

"I guess when she found out she was pregant," I said, "well, Coy didn't want her to have the baby. That must have been one reason she left him."

Hammond looked bland. "Colorful hair. One of the cars outside can take him to the children's shelter until we sort out where he belongs."

"Lee—his mother was one of my news sources," I said. "I'd like to look after him."

Hammond looked dubious.

Andy was still wiggling. "Down!" he said. "I want down."

Mike stood him on the floor, and he took a few steps, but the bustling scene seemed to intimidate him, and he didn't go far. His nose was a mess. I dug in my purse for a tissue and knelt beside him. He fought me, but I got his nose wiped.

"How did Coy get hold of him?" I asked. "He didn't want him."

"When we looked in Coy's car, out here in the lot," Hammond said, "we found a note on the front seat. A sort of a receipt. From a place called 'Big Mama's.' It may sound like a bar, but one of the women officers said it's a child-care place. One of these places some woman runs in her home."

"Oh, I guess Lee left him there when she came to meet me yesterday," I said.

Hammond nodded. "Apparently. Of course, when his mother didn't show up to pick him up last night, I'm willing to bet this 'Big Mama' was afraid she was stuck with an abandoned kid. Coy must have found the receipt in Merrilee's purse after he and Guy snatched her at the Campus Corner. There was nothing on the receipt to indicate it was for child care."

"So Coy didn't know about the kid until he picked him up?" Mike said.

Hammond nodded. "Probably not, though we won't ever know what Merrilee told him and Guy before they killed her. She obviously told them about the offshore account, because Guy was on his way to San Simeon Beach, via Dallas, with the false ID he'd need to get the money.

"But when Coy showed up at Big Mama's this afternoon and said he was from the Grantham PD, Big Mama apparently palmed the kid off on him. Coy probably found it easier to take him than to argue."

"He said he intended to leave him here," I said. "He said he was going to pick up his extra passport at his office and leave the little—leave Andy. Oh! What about Bill Martin? The *Gazette* security guard. Is he alive?"

Hammond gestured over his shoulder with his thumb. "He was cussing a blue streak as they loaded him in the ambulance. He might still be outside. Beat it, you two." He reached down and patted Andy's red head. "I'll square it with child welfare."

We sidetracked into Coy's office so I could collect the folder for the *Gazette* library. As we got in Mike's truck, somebody handed me a diaper bag. I was relieved to find that it contained a change of clothes for Andy. We drove to Mike's house, and I learned that he did own a bathtub. It was in a second, smaller bathroom at the back of his house. I ran water, and Mike lifted Andy into it.

Mike found a couple of plastic glasses to use as tub toys, and we were sitting on the bathroom floor, watching Andy happily splashing water around, when I heard Wilda's voice.

"Mike!" She'd come in the back door.

This was going to be sticky. Wilda was not likely to be happy to learn that her husband not only had had an affair, but also fathered a child.

"We're back here, Mom." I saw Mike frown, and he got to his feet. "Might as well get it over," he said. But he stood in the bathroom door, blocking it, as Wilda came back.

His mother pushed him aside and came right in.

"Mickey heard that a kid was involved," she said. "He heard that he had red hair. That you and Nell took him home."

"We're not exactly sure where his home is yet,"

Mike said. "But his parents are both dead. We know that."

Wilda sat down on the lid of the commode and stared at Andy. "Who was his mother?"

"Apparently his mother was Coy Blakely's estranged wife," I said. "She went by Merri when she worked for the A.P.B. I met her once. She told me her name was Lee."

Tears welled in Wilda's eyes. "Coy pushed her at Irish. Irish wouldn't tell me, but I knew she was the one he'd been seeing."

Andy crowed and threw water high in the air. Then he got to his feet. I grabbed at him, since Mike's bathtub was not equipped with a rubber tub mat. But Andy didn't slip. He leaned on the edge of the tub and looked up at Wilda. His gray eyes were clear and unafraid. The freckles that covered his nose, the red hair, the round pink bottom—they all added up to completely adorable.

"Oh, Mike!" Wilda said. "His hair's exactly the color your's was at that age. And he's got freckles like Irish!"

"Up!" Andy said firmly. "I frew with bath."

I reached for a towel, but Wilda took it away from me. She wrapped it around Andy and lifted him out of the tub. She cuddled him into her lap and put her arms around him. When she looked up at Mike, there were more tears in her eyes.

"Irish would have loved him," she said. "We wanted another child so much! But after Alicia died—we were afraid to try. I had my tubes tied.

"But why didn't Irish tell me Merrilee was going to have a baby? He told me the affair he'd had was over, but he still had to see this woman. He wouldn't tell me why. But he couldn't abandon her if she was pregnant. I'd have understood that."

"He probably thought it would hurt you even worse," Mike said.

Wilda squeezed Andy tightly, but Andy wasn't having any. He kicked and pulled away. His bare feet popped out of the end of the towel.

"Piggies!" he yelled. "Do piggies!"

Wilda leaned back. She couldn't seem to talk, and Mike had leaned against the door frame, with his arm covering his eyes. I longed to get up and put my arms around him.

Instead, I reached for the plump bare toes. "This little piggy went to market," I said. "This little piggy stayed home."

By five-thirty the hostage situation at the Grantham Police Headquarters was on the national television news. Two hostage situations at the same place in the same week—heck, we were probably going to make *Time* magazine.

At five-forty-five Mike got a call from Dr. Willingham, the minister of Dallas's Lovers Lane Presbyterian church.

"Yes, we have him here," Mike told him. "He seems to be fine."

They talked a few more minutes. "Okay, then. We'll see you tomorrow," Mike said.

He hung up and turned to Wilda. "Dr. Willingham says he'll come tomorrow and tell us the whole story."

The whole story made me wish I'd known Irish Svenson. He must have been a heck of a guy.

When he had been minister of the Grantham First Presbyterian Church, Dr. Willingham said, he and

Irish had been acquaintances, rather than close friends. So he'd been surprised when Irish had called about two and a half years earlier and asked for a counseling appointment.

Once there, Irish had confessed to having an affair. "I've done the stupidest thing a middle-aged man who loves his wife can do," he'd said.

"People always think ministers are going to be shocked by their peccadilloes," Dr. Willingham said. "But believe me, after the first couple of years in the ministry, you've heard it all before."

But when Dr. Willingham launched into his usual advice to the repentant adulterer, Irish cut him off. "I think I've learned my lesson," he'd said. "The problem is this girl. First, she's about as stable as a bass boat on a choppy lake. Second, she's mixed up in something crooked that involves my department, and she swears the other people involved are dangerous. Third, she's pregnant. And fourth, she's determined to have the baby and keep it."

Dr. Willingham had admitted this combination of events went beyond the scope of his usual counseling session.

"So," Irish had said, "all I have to do is to hide her from the bad guys in my department—whoever they are. And she's in a job where she knows every cop in the Grantham P.D., so that's not easy to figure out. Then I have to make sure she sees a doctor and has money to live on and can get a job after the baby is born. Get her into counseling, so that there's a chance she'll be sensible enough to raise a kid. Then— after the baby is born she says—she'll tell me what's going on in my department. And I want to do all this without hurting Wilda."

"It was a tall order," Dr. Willingham said. "But I did my best to help." He'd helped Irish find an apartment for Lee. One near the church. He got her into a support group which the church sponsored for single parents, and into treatment with a psychologist whom he respected. Lee hadn't been enthusiastic about the support group and the psychologist, but Irish had pushed her until she cooperated.

Dr. Willingham had deduced from hints Lee and the psychologist threw out that she'd been an abused child—probably sexually abused—and certainly she'd been emotionally abused by every important person in her life. She'd told me things that backed that up.

"The psychologist thought she was making real progress. Becoming less of a victim," Dr. Willingham said.

Dr. Willingham also found Lee a sort of godmother: an older lady in the church. "Recently widowed. No kids. Frankly, she needed to worry about somebody besides herself."

The godmother had checked with Lee every few days and had made sure she went to the doctor. Irish had paid a year's lease on Lee's apartment and bought her a car, as well as helping with other finances. The church had hired her as a bookkeeper and helped her get health insurance.

"She was a good bookkeeper, too," Dr. Willingham said. "She was a computer whiz. Got our financial records set up in much better shape than we'd been."

When Lee went into labor, the godmother had been her coach in the delivery room. Andy had weighed more than eight pounds, Dr. Willingham said, beaming.

He turned to Wilda apologetically. "By then we'd all sort of adopted Lee. She was trying so hard to turn her life around. And, believe me, if Irish hadn't helped her—hadn't forced her into it, really—she would never have been able to."

Wilda nodded. "If he thought you ought to do something, he'd bully or he'd cajole or he'd threaten until it was done."

Dr. Willingham smiled. "That was Irish. Anyway, I was in New York when Andy was born, but Lee's coach called me. And I called Irish out at Mickey's house." He opened a file folder he'd been holding in his lap. "Andrew Svenson Foster. That's the name on Andy's birth certificate. Irish drove down to Dallas and went to the hospital to see Lee and the baby the day after he was born."

He opened a file folder he'd brought along and produced a photo. It was definitely Irish Svenson. Red hair, broad, freckled face, and blue eyes. His hands looked like hams holding the tiny baby. He was grinning.

"I didn't see Irish that day," Dr. Willingham said. "He talked to Lee a long time."

"She must have told him the details she'd been withholding, the skinny on what Coy and Guy were up to," Mike said.

Dr. Willingham nodded. "He left a message at the church to say thanks for the help I'd given Lee. But he said he had to go straight back to Grantham. He said he had an appointment."

"With Coy," Mike said grimly.

"It must have been," I said. "But why? Why would he meet Coy at all? And why would he meet him at the Hotel Panorama?"

"That's easy," Mike said. "He wanted to smooth things over without a scandal."

"Without a scandal!"

"Right. I told you, that was Dad's big character flaw. He was proud of his reputation, of his department's reputation." Mike turned to his mother. "Right?"

Wilda frowned. "I'm afraid you are. If he could have gotten Coy and Guy to give the money back—"

"And to resign," Mike said. "Maybe admit guilt. Leave town. He would have gone a long way to avoid a scandal."

"But why meet at the Panorama?"

"Coy had bugged Dad's office," Mike said. "The tech crew found the bugs this morning, still in place. Lee probably told him everything that happened in that office was recorded. Dad wouldn't have wanted any recording going on while he laid the law down to Coy. And maybe Coy suggested they meet at the Panorama."

That made sense. I thought about it.

Then Dr. Willingham spoke to Mike. "Your dad didn't tell you anything about all this?"

"No. The last time I talked to him, he said he had some important business matters he wanted to go over with me. He said something like, 'There's a blowup coming in the department, Mike. I want to get this taken care of. I may have to resign.' But he wouldn't tell me any details."

He grinned ruefully. "I've spent the past two years waiting for the blowup in the department. And that was why I never pushed on finding out more about his accident. I was afraid he'd committed suicide."

"But he didn't give you a hint that he was in any danger?" I said.

"He wouldn't have been afraid of either Coy or Guy," Wilda said. "He always thought Coy was a bully, but basically a lightweight. And he despised Guy."

Dr. Willingham leaned forward. "What do you think happened, Mike?"

"I think Coy probably distracted my dad while Guy either cut or loosened his brake line," Mike said. "That would be the simplest way to disable a car. The driver wouldn't notice anything until he hit the brakes, and there weren't any. And it could be made to look like an accident—almost."

"Almost?" I was puzzled.

Mike nodded. "You'd have to disable the emergency brake system, too, if you wanted to make sure it worked. And having both systems go out at once would look suspicious."

"I guess that's where Bo came in," I said.

"Right," Mike said. "I imagine Coy and Guy followed the car to the city-county police garage. They'd want to replace at least one of the brake lines—hide the sabotage—before the state crime lab began to examine the car. They might have needed Bo to help them, but it's more likely that he caught them at it. Either way, they convinced Bo to help them—out of fear, maybe, or even loyalty to them."

"Or maybe even loyalty to your dad," I said. "One of the crazy things Bo said was, 'I wanted to protect him!' It could be they convinced him that Irish had been killed because of some guilty reason and that he'd be helping keep Irish's reputation stainless if he covered the crime up."

Mike shook his head. "Could be. Of course, a year later, when Bo went off the deep end, Guy and Coy had to get rid of him. He probably lived six months longer than they wanted him to because he left town and hid out. But once he was in the Grantham Mental Health Center, and once Nell had said she'd still be willing to interview him, they had to act fast. Coy fell back on his skills as an undercover cop, greased his hair down, and put temporary tattoos on his arm. He stole the Salvation Army uniform. Then it was cyanide and an Almond Joy for Bo.

"But even dead, Bo blew up their scheme. His death scared Lee so much that she made a move toward getting them arrested—instead of simply continuing to hide out."

"I guess I'm still thinking like a bookkeeper," Wilda said, "but I don't understand why the auditors didn't catch the problem with the pension fund."

"The union president is probably asking that very question," Mike said. "I don't think they could have hidden the shortage much longer. Coy mentioned his 'stash.' I think they were ready to run for it, even if they didn't find Lee and the money."

"Anyway, Lee called me," I said, "and trapped herself with the tap Coy had put on my phone. And I'm not sure just why he did that."

"It may have been standard practice for him," Mike said. "He'd apparently tapped any phone he felt like tapping. But Coy and Guy were able to intercept Lee after she met you, and they kidnapped her from the Campus Corner. She was desperate to hide Andy's existence, so she told them what she'd done with the money. But they killed her anyway. One of them ran over her, hoping it would look like a hit and run. But Guy was still nervous, and he found out that we were at the *Gazette*."

"Maybe Coy told him," I said. "I ran into Coy out at the high school when I went there looking for you. Maybe Coy followed us."

Mike nodded. "Anyway, one of them saw that both our cars were in the *Gazette* parking garage. They knew we had our heads together. Of course, whoever it was didn't know that the line of cars nearest the building was full of tough circulation guys. When he decided to take us out, Nell and those guys ruined his plan."

I brought up one point that had been worrying me. "Why did Guy come by the hospital to see me?"

Mike shrugged. "Probably he wanted to know whether or not you suspected him, Nell. Or maybe he really was going to drop cyanide in that coffee he offered you. We'll never know."

I shuddered. "I'm just glad we spotted that airport limo—"

"And got Guy killed."

"You don't think it was suicide?"

Mike shook his head. "No, I think Jim Hammond figured that one right. Coy heard Jim send a car to the airport, and he tumbled to the fact that Guy was about to be—well, questioned. Maybe stopped. Guy must have been in a very nervous state. Coy knew he'd break. So Coy dressed up in blue coveralls and a wig, got into the men's room while you and I were looking for Guy in all the United waiting areas. Then he called the airport on his cell phone and had Guy paged. He called Guy into the restroom and gave him a pint of whisky—probably told him it would steady his nerves or something."

"Then Coy walked out," I said. "I watched him go. And I had no idea it was him."

"We knew Coy was an expert at disguise, thanks to his undercover days. The wig hid his face, and if he changed his walk—"

I nodded.

"But luck continued to run against Coy," Mike said. "He and Guy had left Lee's body in the high grass along Bridge Road, where the road deadends at the old bridge, thinking she might not be found for weeks. But the mowers moved in to get ready for the repair crews, and they found her within hours. Simply a fluke.

"And that left Coy in a really hard spot. Lots of cops knew Merrilee Blakely. Somebody was going to recognize her, even though she'd changed her hair and her way of dressing. So he got ready to make a run for it. He made a quick stop to check out the receipt he'd found in Lee's purse—"

"And he got stuck with the kid," I said.

Mike nodded. "He went to his office to dump the kid and to get his fake ID from his desk drawer. And he ran into Nell."

We all were quiet for a few seconds.

"It's a sad ending," Dr. Willingham said. "Lee had worked so hard to change—and now she's dead."

"If only she would have trusted me the day we met," I said. "If she would have waited for Mike at the Blue Flamingo, if she would have told me more—if she would have told Irish the whole story earlier."

"It's easy to see why Lee distrusted people," Dr. Willingham said. "But that distrust doomed her."

He might have been talking about me, I realized. The men in my life had offered me love—my grandfather, now Mike, even stuffy old Professor Tenure. Was I always going to be afraid to accept it, afraid to trust anyone?

Dr. Willingham turned to Mike. "Irish told me he was going to make some financial arrangements about Andy," he said. "Mike, I think he was going to explain all that to you. He wanted you to understand that you weren't being partially disinherited arbitrarily. And I think he wanted you to have the authority to carry out his instructions if he didn't— well, if he didn't live to see Andy grow up."

"Yes," Mike said. "With Lee gone that's going to be more of a responsibility."

Dr. Willingham shook his head. "I don't think Irish expected you to take care of Andy personally. Of course, none of us thought about Lee being killed." He leaned forward earnestly. "Mike, finding a home for Andy is not going to be any problem at all. I can think of four couples in my church who are trying to adopt. Any of them would love and care for the little guy."

Mike looked inscrutable.

Dr. Willingham juggled his file folder nervously. "One couple would be Margaret and her husband."

"Margaret!" Mike sounded surprised.

Dr. Willingham turned to me. "Margaret is my daughter. She and Mike were in Sunday school together. She directs the preschool at Lover's Lane Presbyterian, so she's been around Andy since he was a baby. But she's no smarter than her mother— married a Presbyterian minister. Rick has a church in north Dallas."

"Margaret was the best-tempered person I grew

up with," Mike said. "And she had the best sense of humor. Did Lee have a will?"

Dr. Willingham coughed gently. "I'm her executor. And Andy's guardian."

"Then the question is really up to you."

"My primary responsibility would be Andy's welfare. But Lee had no family, so you're apparently Andy's only blood relation, Mike. I wouldn't want to do anything without your input. But we don't want to wait too long."

Mike smiled solemnly. "I know. It's easy to get attached."

Andy had been playing happily with a set of cars which Wilda had brought him that morning. Now he got to his feet and brought Mike a blue one. "Uhnnn," he said, growling out the sound effect which traditionally means a racing motor.

"Thank you," Mike said. He got down on his knees and ran the car back and forth on the floor. "Uhnnn, uhnnn."

Andy smiled approvingly. He took a red truck to Dr. Willingham. "Uhnnn," he said seriously.

"Uhnnn," Dr. Willingham growled. He slid off his chair and sat on the floor, running the truck back and forth. "Uhnnn. Uhnnn."

I laughed, and Andy rewarded me with a sporty green car. I joined the racers on the floor, and Mike took my hand. He squeezed it. I squeezed back.

"Uhnnn! Uhnnn!" I said.

FEAR IS ONLY THE BEGINNING